Earl Tiffels
28 JUNE 2007

EARL GRIFFIN

THE ESCADARA

Earl Griffin

Copyright © 2007 by Earl Griffin

ISBN 0-7414-3556-X

Published by:

INFIꝈITY
PUBLISHING.COM

1094 New DeHaven Street, Suite 100
West Conshohocken, PA 19428-2713
Info@buybooksontheweb.com
www.buybooksontheweb.com
Toll-free (877) BUY BOOK
Local Phone (610) 941-9999
Fax (610) 941-9959

Printed in the United States of America

Printed on Recycled Paper

Published January 2007

To Judy for lovin' the gunfighter; and
To Priscilla for lettin' the gunfighter love her.

PROLOGUE

Great Gran Katty paused, as if trying to remember something she had never really quite known. She looked down at me and said. "I can't say I remember the old trader or the post. What I know of it I learned from my father much later."

We found the old comanchero, Jose Pieda' Tafoya's, trading post at the Quitaques. Father left me outside with the equipment. He carried his big Sharps rifle into the dark one room lean-to that was Tafoya's trading post.

The trader eyed him curiously. Father told him that he intended to start a ranch on the high plain above the Quitaques. Old Tafoya told Father that was the land of the Comanche and Kiowa, brutally cold in the winter, unbearably hot in the summer, with no place to hide from the Comanche or the Kiowa or the cold or the heat. And any of them could and would kill you. Father told him he had heard of a man who had found a canyon in the plain and who was beginning a herd there. He asked the trader if such a man existed.

"Si, senor. Pero es muy malo hombre."

Father never forgot those words. "How will I know him?" Father asked.

"On his left hip there will be a black pistola. You cannot mistake it, senor. Muy negra. Muy negra. And if you see it out of its holster you are a moment from eternity."

Father bought a leather pouch filled with shells for the black pistol and a large bolt of white linen cloth. We left Tafoya's immediately. Father rode a large buckskin gelding and led the mule I was on along with the nanny goat for my milk. We traveled for ten more days. Father worried. He thought once that he saw some buffalo, but wasn't certain. There was nothing, just grass and grass and grass, no houses, no trees, no life, just nothing, but tall blowing grass. It was madness, our water was low. The goat was giving barely

1

enough milk to feed me twice a day. We were alone, on a grass sea that rolled and pitched before us each morning from horizon to horizon, looking for one man, who may or may not have existed, somewhere amidst thousands of acres of empty uncharted plains. Each night Father would use his instrument to check our direction of travel and our progress. Even so on April 2nd we traveled all day and ended up a quarter of a mile from where we had started that morning. We just traveled in a great loop through the grass. We were lost. Only God knew where Father and I were.

THE PLAINS AND THE GUNFIGHTER
APRIL 3, 1868

"There is a God, Katharane." Reid Stuart called back to his infant daughter. "For unless I am very mistaken that is the man Jose Tafoya vowed we'd never find." Reid Stuart sat on his horse. He had not forgotten the trader's warning. Somehow he had to find a way to get into the camp he could see within the semi-circle of flattened grass a half of a mile in front of him on the prairie. "Katharane. You're going to ride us into that camp." He drew the mule up to him by its lead and lifted his daughter from her carriage and set her on the saddle in front of him. Then he clucked to the big buckskin, and he and Katharane rode slowly into the sunset and the camp.

He watched the silhouette of the man he could see against the dark background of tall grass. "Katharane. Wave your arms for daddy."

The gunman cocked his pistol. Every instinct told him to shoot. This could be a renegade riding into his camp. He hesitated. He studied the rider's tall cavalry officer's boots. They were unmistakable with his pants stuffed into their tops. During the war the gunman had watched boots like these flash past him in a gallop. Then the gunman saw the baby. Tough experience on the mirage riddled plains had taught him to be skeptical of the first impression of a thing that his eyes carried to his brain. He tried to focus through the mirage on the front of the saddle. He could not.

Reid Stuart and Katharane rode into the camp.

"'do somethun for ya'?" The gunman asked.

"You can uncock that pistol." Reid Stuart said and leaned his elbow onto the saddle horn.

"'might as well. If I was gonna' use it you'd already be dead." The gunman eased the hammer of his pistol back against the brass shell casing. The pistol had not left its holster.

3

Reid Stuart lifted his baby daughter off of the saddle and handed her to the man. The gunfighter took the baby. He held her out in front of him and studied her. He lifted her up and down, twice, as if weighing her. He turned her. He rolled her onto her back. He looked up at Reid Stuart and asked again. "What can I do for you?"

"Smoke?" Reid Stuart offered a hand rolled smoke down to the man with the black hat. He noticed the man's hat was different than most. The rim circled a short crown. It had a hand woven draw string with two black onyx stones knitted into it.

"Don't smoke. Whiskey?"

"I don't drink." Reid Stuart replied. He stepped down from his horse.

The gunman studied the lean man in front of him. The man stood several inches taller than he did, but weighed ten pounds less than he did. The man did not cast much of a shadow even in the setting sun's almost horizontal rays. And he was not wearing a sidearm. "This ain't no place to be unarmed."

"Is that coffee I smell?" Reid Stuart asked. He squatted next to the gunman's fire.

"Yes." The gunman said and nodded at the tin cup on the lip of the shallow fire pit. "Help yourself."

Reid Stuart picked up the cup, pulled one of the long deer-skin gloves from his belt and used it to lift the round tin can from its perch on a flat rock in the center of the fire. He poured the tin cup full of coffee.

"Why are you here?" The gunman demanded.

"This is good coffee." Reid Stuart replied while blowing on the hot coffee. "I want to raise cattle."

The gunman nodded. "'not much else to do out here." He paused, and then he added. "besides die."

Reid Stuart looked at the gunman and his daughter and said. "I didn't bring her out here to die."

"Maybe not. But unless you know a helluva' lot more about this country than you seem to, there's a fair chance she will." The

4

gunman looked at the baby and added. "And much too soon."

The baby twisted in the gunman's hands and blew bubbles at him on her lips. He smiled at her and asked Reid Stuart. "What's she doin?"

"She's just being happy."

"Happy?" The gunman frowned, swallowed, and then he clamped his front teeth down on his bottom lip. He knelt on his left knee. He held the baby in his left arm, picked up a forked stick, caught the edge of the can in the fork of the stick, wedged it there with the thumb of his right hand, lifted the can and filled the tin cup Reid Stuart held in his right hand. "Comanch' and Kiowa steal the cattle, slaughter 'em, eat 'em. Slaughter you, too, if they get a chance."

"I'll raise cattle faster than they can steal them."

The gunman eyed Reid Stuart and said. "You ain't even wearin' a gun."

Reid Stuart set the coffee cup on the ground, stood up and walked to his buckskin horse. He pulled the heavy Sharps from his saddle scabbard and wrapped two bandoleers of ammunition around his arm. Then he threw the flap of his saddle bag back and pulled out the leather pouch filled with cartridges. He walked back to the fire, squatted down, laid the pouch on the ground, propped the Sharps against his left shoulder and picked up the tin cup.

The gunman opened the pouch and studied the shells he found inside. "That's what I shoot." He looked at Reid Stuart curiously.

"So I was told."

"Tafoya?"

Reid Stuart nodded.

"Two bandoleers of fresh cartridges, a buffalo gun and a baby." The gunman pushed his black round rimmed hat back on his head. Several locks of curly blonde hair fell across his furrowed forehead. "I doubt any man could know more'n me how crazy this is. How brutal these plains are. How many ways they can kill ya' and will, if you make a mistake. And how little chance you got ah' makin' a go of this." He sighed, a deep ragged

5

sigh, spawned by an old and familiar grief, breathed out past his lips in a strange mournful whisper. He studied the baby. "But I can't leave this one out here to die." He eyed Reid Stuart to be certain that Reid Stuart had heard him.

Reid Stuart grinned. "No. You can't do that." He had already guessed that his daughter was his passport to this land that only the gunman and the Indians seemed to know.

"What's her name?" The gunfighter asked.

"Katharane Diane Stuart."

"Katharane." The gunman spoke the name slowly. "So it's a little Katty girl I have here." He bounced the baby on his knee and his face took on an expression that was his alone. His lips never opened. His teeth never showed. But his gray eyes brightened and the skin across his cheekbones tightened and a faint soft glow seemed to pass across the burnished features, the heavy falling eyebrows and the small hawkish nose. The gunfighter closed his eyes. He had come to this great empty land after the war to be alone. He had survived here all alone for two or more years. Now he was faced by a man with a baby. Neither had a chance to survive without his help. He wanted to escape, to go out again to the dark lonely plains, alone. But he could feel the warmth of the baby in his hands. And it felt good to know the warmth of another body against his again.

Reid Stuart waited. It could still go either way, he figured. Either way. He edged his thumb over the hammer of the Sharps rifle.

The gunfighter opened his eyes, lifted Katharane to where he could look into her eyes and said. "No. I can't let the Comanch' have you."

Reid Stuart leaned his rifle against the gunfighter's saddle, stood up, walked to the mule, opened the top of one of the three boxes harnessed to the mule and removed a small wooden bucket. Then he walked to the goat and milked her. Reid Stuart carried the wooden bucket with the goat's milk in it back to the camp.

The gunman had two prairie hens skewered on a long stick, roasting them over the fire. He handed one to Reid Stuart and tore a piece of the white meat off of the breast of the other

6

prairie hen. He chewed on it for a long time. Then he took it out of his mouth, pinched off a small bite and put it in the baby's mouth. She swallowed it, and cried for more. The gunman sat for an hour chewing up small bites of his supper and feeding them to the baby.

Reid Stuart slowly ate the other prairie hen and wondered if the small quiet man feeding his infant daughter could be as dangerous and unpredictable as Tafoya had warned. When he finished his supper Reid Stuart caught his buckskin and the mule and led them away from the camp. He hobbled their front feet and left them to graze. As he returned to the camp he looked for the gunfighter's horse. In the darkness he could not see it. In the dark camp Katharane lay asleep on a pallet made of his and the gunfighter's saddle blankets, a buffalo hide and directly underneath the baby a soft, almost white, tanned doe skin. His saddle was on one side of and at the head of the baby's makeshift crib and the gunfighter's was in a like position on the other side. The gunfighter was not to be seen. Reid Stuart knelt down, picked up a stick and poked at the ashes of the dead fire.

"Leave that fire be. 'Lest you want to invite the Kiowa nation here tonight." The gunfighter said as he walked to his saddle and lay down alongside of the pallet with his head just below the saddle.

"Cold camp tonight?" Reid Stuart asked. He stretched out on the other side of the pallet.

"Cold camp always on the plains." The gunfighter said. He closed his eyes and added. "If you wanna' stay alive."

"I want to stay alive." Reid Stuart said.

Reid Stuart opened his eyes. It was dark, but the blackness was gone. Stars shone everywhere in the sky above him. Stars so bright they had to be close enough to touch. Katharane? Reid Stuart felt for his daughter. He touched her leg, moved his hand up her back until he felt something cold and wet and hard on her back. He heard the hammer on the gun cock. Then he felt the hair on the back of the hand which held the gun and realized that the gunfighter had slept with his pistol in his hand resting on Katharane's back. "It's me. Stuart." Reid Stuart said quietly.

The hammer on the gun clicked as it was set back against the shell casing.

THE CANYON

APRIL 4, 1868

Reid Stuart sat up. He tried to stretch the soreness from his lower back. Stars still shone in the night sky. "Damn! It's not even twilight, yet."

"'gotta be off these plains before the sun starts up." The gunman said. He tied his bedroll to the back of his saddle. "Death can come up with the sun. 'ride in on ya' out of a blindin' plains sunrise and you can't even see it comin' till it's too late."

Reid Stuart rolled Katharane onto her back and undressed her. He reached in his saddle bag and pulled out a large square of the white cloth which he had cut from the bolt packed on the mule. He spread the cloth on the buffalo hide, laid the still sleeping baby on the cloth and offered the doe skin back to the gunman.

"Keep it." The gunman said. "And the hide."

Reid Stuart removed the soiled cloth from his daughter. He handed the dirty cloth to the gunfighter. "I'd advise catching it by the edges."

"Christ! What's that smell?" The gunfighter grasped the edges of the cloth. He bent down and picked up his short handled shovel.

"What are you doing?" Reid Stuart asked.

"'fixin' to bury this damn thing."

Reid Stuart chuckled and said. "You'll be doing a lot of digging."

"You mean she does this a lot?"

"Fairly regularly."

The gunfighter shook his head and sighed. "Can't be helped. 'gotta bury it. 'can't afford to leave sign for those Kiowa. 'less they know about us the better we are for it." He walked away.

When the gunfighter returned Reid Stuart was trying to clean Katharane. He tried not to waste any water. The dry cloth chafed Katharane's tender skin and she cried. "Daddy's sorry Katharane. But we're short on water."

The gunman handed his canteen to Reid Stuart. "Use all you want. 'by noon I'll have us to more water than you can say grace over."

That first morning when they broke camp before sunrise Reid Stuart was surprised to find that the gunman rode a black filly. Fillies were seldom used as mounts. And he was even more surprised to find that the gunman had a string of three mustangs.

The gunman rode southeast through the grass. Like a sailor at sea he seemed always to know his bearing. He navigated across the flat endless ocean of grass with only the slightest adjustments to their course. Reid Stuart felt like a child. He was totally dependent upon the man whose buckskin clad back he followed. It was the first of many days during which he had to trust the gunman's judgment on faith alone, because he could find no landmark, no hill, no valley, and no change in the tall grass by which to set his compass, just more grass. He did not yet know that on the plains the sky was bluer where it and the canyon form the horizon than it was where it met only the plains. He did not know that the gunfighter sailed them at that blue sky.

By ten o'clock that first morning Katharane was weary and complained loudly about not having been changed or fed. Reid Stuart had watched the sun tear itself away from the flat eternal meridian of the plains. He realized that the gunfighter was right. A man was totally blind to anything riding out of that sun for the first half hour or more of its rise into the sky. He was reluctant to question any action of the gunman. But Katharane was a baby, not yet twenty months old. She needed his attention. He had to stop. He trotted his buckskin up to the gunman's black filly. "I need to stop and tend to Katharane." He said slowly. "When you think its safe enough to do so."

"Safe as it's gonna' get for awhile. I reckon'." The gunfighter said and reined in his horse.

Reid Stuart unfolded the doe skin, laid Katharane on it and

removed the soiled cloth. He handed it to the gunfighter who already held the short shovel in his left hand. The gunman walked away. In a few minutes he returned.

Reid Stuart handed Katharane to the gunman. "Where are we going?" He asked the gunman.

"The canyon." The gunman answered. He carried the baby back to his filly and set her on the saddle. He balanced her on the saddle with his left hand, put his left foot in the stirrup, stepped up and swung into the saddle behind her. He shortened the mustangs' lead rope and rode away.

Reid Stuart shoved the doeskin into his saddle bag, climbed onto the buckskin and trotted after the gunfighter and his child. Reid Stuart thought he heard the sound of waves breaking against a great reef. The sound of the breakers grew louder and louder. And then the grass beneath him was gone. There was grass to his left and to his right. There was grass behind him. And the sky was still above him. But Katharane, the gunfighter, the three Mustangs and the grass beneath him had disappeared.

"What the hell?" He exclaimed for the plains were gone. And after having ridden for days across what seemed like a never ending glacier of grass Reid Stuart thought he was flying for the first ten feet of his descent into the canyon.

The buckskin had stepped off of the side of the canyon wall without breaking stride. He, too, had become overly accustomed to the never varying turf of the plains. He had managed to gather himself and land on his feet on the small ledge next to the gunfighter's black filly and the mustangs.

The mule stumbled against the buckskin, but stayed on its feet. The goat was not as fortunate. She rolled underneath the mule, which promptly stepped on her and then kicked her as she scrambled to her feet.

The gunfighter looked at Reid Stuart and asked. "Flatland goat?"

Reid Stuart rubbed the back of his head and said. "I suppose she is." Reid Stuart looked up. The wall above was a sheer sandstone face. He would not have ridden off it had not the buckskin followed the mustangs. They sat at the top of what the gunfighter called the Indian trail. The trail slid at an angle down the canyon wall to the floor of a large canyon. The canyon floor was far below them. Little black cedar trees appeared to dot the canyon floor. But they were not trees; they were buffalo, hundreds and hundreds of buffalo. A narrow stream came out of the large canyon and turned beneath the Indian trial. Its water looked dark and deep. But that was because they were so high above it. As they got closer Reid Stuart saw it was red and murky and shallow. Where the main canyon turned he could see the other rim. It was fifty miles to that rim. The breakers he had heard were the sound of the wind as it fell off of the plains and wailed down into the canyon. Reid Stuart surveyed the steep narrow trail that fell into the canyon. "We're going to ride down that?"

"Katty and I are." The gunfighter said. "And 'less you can fly you will, too."

"I can't fly."

"That's good to know." The gunfighter said. He eased the black filly off of the ledge and onto the trail. They moved as easily down the trail as they had across the flat prairie. The flatland goat soon found her high country feet and stepped effortlessly down the trail. But the buckskin and the mule stumbled stiff legged down the steep meandering trail.

For an hour and more the horses, the mule and the goat stepped over folded scrub cedars, around scattered flint rock boulders and across sandstone slides until they reached the floor of the canyon.

Another canyon branched off to the east. A great open chasm lay to the north. Another canyon, a mile and more across the large canyon's floor from them, ran to the west. The gunfighter led them north into the great chasm.

Reid Stuart studied the stream that flowed along the bottom of the large canyon. It came from the canyon to the west. "What about water?"

"Right." The gunfighter said. He untied his canteen and lifted the two empty water bags from the cantle of his saddle.

"Long walk from here." Reid Stuart said.

"What?" The gunfighter asked. "Oh. No. 'stream's too

gyppy tasting. There's a fresh water spring flowing out of the canyon wall about twenty feet above us." He nodded his head at the red sandstone cliff. "Better water. Not as good as up the canyon." He said and gestured with his shoulder to the canyon that ran to the west. "But better than that in the stream."

The water was cool and sweet and tasted good to Reid Stuart. And he was relieved to have his canteens and the water bags filled with it before they rode further north into the main canyon.

The gunfighter was trailing something or someone. He had not told Reid Stuart who or what, but Reid Stuart could cut sign well enough to know they were following the freshly made tracks of half dozen horses or so, and one cow.

MUSTANGERS IN THE PALO DURO
APRIL 4, 1868

"Do you know them?" Reid Stuart asked.

"No."

"What are they doing here?"

"They're Mustangers." The gunfighter said. He stepped down from his black filly. "They're catching Spanish Mustangs."

"Did you know they would be here?"

"No."

"Then why have we been trailing them since the junction of the canyons?"

"You noticed."

"I noticed." Reid Stuart said. He counted the men gathered in the clearing. "I count four."

"There's five horses carryin' saddles." The gunfighter said. He untied the front Mustang's lead rope from the filly's saddle and retied it to the mule's harness. "They've got a lookout. Probably on that high ridge." He nodded towards a sandstone rise across from and below the flint rock ledge he, Reid Stuart and Katharane were on. He untied the lead for the last Mustang and tied it to his saddle.

"Why have we been following them?" Reid Stuart asked again.

"They've got something we need."

"What?"

"'figgered you'd've seen that Jersey milker by now." The gunfighter said. He remounted.

"Only her track. But what has that to do with us?" Reid Stuart asked.

The gunman chewed on the inside of his left cheek. "I aim to trade this Mustang for that Jersey milk cow. That's what it has to do with us."

"For Katharane?"

The gunman nodded. "Damn sure ain't for you." He studied the camp. "You may like goat's milk for all I know. But Katty girl's gonna' have cow's milk."

Reid Stuart smiled. Then he frowned. "Do you think they will trade for just one Mustang?"

"'dunno." The gunfighter shrugged. "'might. They don't know we got more than one Mustang." He dropped the leather loop off of the hammer of the black revolver. "And all they use the milk for is the colts."

"Colts?"

"Sometimes the mares don't heal. They cripple up and have to be put down or left. They use the cow to raise those mares' colts."

Reid Stuart still did not understand. "What cripples them?" He asked.

The gunfighter stacked his hands on his saddle horn the right one down first, then the left one on top of the right one. "Mustangs run in a band of from twenty to maybe forty head. 'got one stud that's fought away all the other stallions and leads the band of mares. 'stangers walk their horses toward the band. Stud comes out to make a fight. 'stangers drive him off. So he stampedes the band. He'll kick or bite the mares until he gets 'em all runnin'. Then he'll take the lead and carry 'em a few miles and stop. 'stangers just keep walkin' after 'em. Band won't leave its range 'cause stud won't cross into another stud's range, 'cept maybe in a bad drought, cause it means a fight to the death for the stud. So they run in a circle. 'stangers picket the circle and keep walkin' 'em. Never lettin' 'em stop. Three, four, maybe five days and nights, whippin' 'em with their riatas 'till they bleed if necessary to keep 'em walkin'. They walk 'em down to the ground. Once down they pick the mares they want and slit the ligaments in their forelegs."

"Why?"

14

"'makes their forelegs stiffen. That way one 'stanger can tend fifteen to twenty head while the others catch more. In a couple of weeks the ligaments either heal or cripple up. They keep the ones that heal and drive them back to New Mexico for trade."

"And the ones they cripple?"

"'cripple hasn't a prayer on these plains. Dependin' on the 'stanger they either slit their gullets or just leave 'em to starve or to be taken by wolves. Then they take their colts and raise 'em on the cow's milk."

Reid Stuart looked at the gunfighter's mustangs. "You didn't clip their forelegs, did you?"

The gunfighter stared at Reid Stuart. "Only because I have a better way of catchin' 'em. But if I needed to, I would." He watched Reid Stuart.

Reid Stuart sighed and said aloud. "I don't see how they can possibly give their cow. They would be out of business." He paused. "But possibly if you told them that you wanted it for Katharane, for a baby...."

"'none of their damn concern why I want that milker." The gunman cut him off.

"Well. Just thought." Reid Stuart shrugged. "I guess it's worth a try to make the trade. The worst they can do is refuse, and you will come back with your mustang."

"Stuart." The gunfighter said. "When I come back I'll be bringin' that cow with me."

"But how can you know they will trade."

"They'll trade that milker to me or I'll kill them and take it."

Reid Stuart stared at the gunfighter.

"Learn this now, Stuart. On these high plains if we're gonna' keep her alive." The gunfighter pointed at the baby's carriage. "And ourselves, we have to take what we need every chance we get. And we have to take it any way we can. Most of the time that means with this." He patted the revolver.

"But to kill four men for a milk cow? Even for my child?"

"You don't have to kill four men. Just one." The gunfighter said as he picked up the filly's reins. "When I ride in the lookout will most likely move across behind me. Right in front of you. If the shootin' starts he'll stand up to get a clear shot at me. When he does, you get him."

"And if I don't?" Reid Stuart asked. "I'm not much on shooting a man in the back." He added.

The gunfighter smiled. "Then I'll have to kill him on my way out with the cow." He spurred the filly and trotted away.

Reid Stuart stepped down from the buckskin, walked to the mule and pulled a short forked metal rod out of the mule's pack. He returned to the front of the buckskin where he knelt and drove the rod into the ground. He laid the long barrel of the Sharps in the fork of the rod and stretched out prone on the ground behind the gun. He felt weak and old and weary. He was bone tired of killing. He had not come here to fight. He was fought out. He resented the gunfighter's care less attitude about the thought of killing four men for a milk cow. And yet he sensed in the gunfighter knowledge, an awareness of this land and what the land itself demanded of them if they were to survive. He pulled the butt of the heavy rifle against his right shoulder and cleared his eyes and watched the gunfighter ride into the camp.

The trade was made without incident. The gunfighter rode out of the camp leading the milk cow. They trailed back down the canyon before the gunfighter stopped and let Reid Stuart milk the cow and feed the baby.

Katharane clung to the tough leather teat. She enjoyed the cow's milk. And after Reid Stuart had changed her and the gunfighter had buried her leavings she fell to sleep in the carriage. They pressed on. The gunfighter was anxious to keep riding. Another hour passed and they wound their way steadily back through the canyon. Reid Stuart drew the mule up to the buckskin and looked into the carriage. The baby, her belly still full of the cow's milk, slept quietly. He let the mule drop back on lead. The spring afternoon was beautiful. They rode back through the canyon toward the Indian trail.

16

The gunman led them out amidst a herd of several hundred buffalo. The buffalo drifted along in front of them. They trampled the thick gramma grass that covered the canyon's floor. Where the buffalo had not walked the grass was belly high to the horses. The buffalo kicked up a small cloud of dust. Above the dust the sky was ablaze with sunshine that cut into the top of the canyon's walls, then painted itself out as it descended down the walls and disappeared into the shadows. It was warm, but the air was still fresh and cool from the winter's cold that had only recently left the canyon. It was a walled world unto itself, created by nature and limitless years, safe from the howling wind of the plains, filled with buffalo and deer and wild turkey and water. It seemed so safe. But even then the gunfighter was guiding them passed danger.

The dust from the buffalo made Katharane sneeze and she complained.

"Are we staying in this buffalo herd for a reason?" Reid Stuart asked.

The gunfighter looked over his shoulder and nodded. Then he looked ahead and continued to ride. After a while he turned to the right and led Reid Stuart across a shallow draw and up a small rise to a plateau that paralleled the bottom of the canyon. He stopped and waited for Reid Stuart to ride up to him. The gunfighter pointed at the tracks along the plateau. "Kiowa. They started following us out here on this flank shortly after we got water."

"Did you warn those Mustangers?"

"If they ain't got sense enough to know when there's Kiowa about, then warnin' 'em wouldn't't've helped them."

Reid Stuart looked back the direction they had come from. "Are they still following us?"

"No." The gunfighter said. "They're waitin' on those Mustangers. They want their rifles and horses. But I don't aim to leave them an easy trail in case they change their minds after they finish with those Mustangers."

Reid Stuart grabbed the black filly's bit. "You didn't warn them on purpose. You want them to ride into the Kiowa."

The gunfighter nodded. "You got it."

"Jesus Christ, man! That's like murdering them!" Reid Stuart cried.

"It's buyin' us time to get where we're goin'. That's what it's like, Stuart." The gunfighter snapped. He jerked the filly's head free from Reid Stuart's grip and rode back into the buffalo herd.

"Where are you taking us?" Reid Stuart asked after he caught up with the gunfighter, again.

"Passed the Keheahquehono. Headwaters of that stream you saw from the Indian trail." The gunfighter answered. "To the lodges of the Kwerhar-rehnuh Comanches."

"We're riding in the middle of a buffalo herd to hide our tracks from one band of Indians and we're going to knowingly ride into the camp of another band of Indians?" Reid Stuart shook his head.

"The Kwerhar-rehnuh have a half-white chief, Kwanhah. I've dealt with him before." The gunfighter explained.

"But why should we go to any Comanche camp?"

"To trade."

"Christ! Wouldn't it be safer to trade with Tafoya?"

"Tafoya doesn't have what we need."

THE SQUAW WOMAN
APRIL 5, 1868

The gunfighter's world was new to Reid Stuart. But its savage and brutal nature was not. He had seen it before in a cornfield at Antietam. After that and after he had recovered from his wounds he had vowed to find a place free of the terror only the creativity of men could create. He sighed. His old haunting search for peace was still with him. But he had come too far to go back. There was no back for him to go to. Not with Katharane.

The gunfighter, Reid Stuart and Katharane passed the Indian trail and passed the mouth of the smaller canyon and into another canyon. The walls of this canyon were so steep and high that as the sun began to sink into the plains the canyon's wall covered them with shadow. The gunfighter stopped only to let Reid Stuart feed or change Katharane. And when Reid Stuart did so, the gunfighter backtracked watching for signs that the Kiowa were following them. They rode into the night, until the gunfighter decided they were safe from the Kiowa. They camped on a ledge along the wall of the canyon.

"What'cha doin'?" The gunfighter asked Reid Stuart. The gunfighter sat on the heels of his boots on the edge of the ledge and blew on the cold coffee in the tin cup.

"That coffee would taste better hot." Reid Stuart said.

"Yep." The gunfighter agreed. He continued to blow on his coffee as if it were hot and had to be cooled to drink.

Reid Stuart chuckled. "I'm putting down the date in my journal." He handed the leather journal to the gunfighter.

The gunfighter read aloud the words that Reid Stuart had written. "Five April of the year Eighteen Hundred and Sixty-Eight." He looked at Reid Stuart and his eyes were sad and anxious. "You know, Stuart. I can't remember the last time I knew what the date was. A man should never be without the date.

Without that how's he to know when he lived or when he's to die?"

Katharane interrupted them with a loud squall. The doe skin teat the gunfighter had fashioned for her was dry. Reid Stuart tended to her. Then he placed her in her carriage on the mule. The gunfighter packed their gear. They rode in silence through the morning. The canyon narrowed. A rock outcropping ran down the center of the canyon floor. A thousand years of water had cut a thin deep slit in the rock.

Reid Stuart studied the deep slits in the rock. They grew wider a foot or so down. The rock was only a thin layer of shale. The chasm beneath the shale fell away to blackness, its bottom hidden from any light. The chasm widened. The gunfighter led them along the edge of the open rip in the rock floor of the canyon.

"Does this place have a name?" Reid Stuart asked.

"Indians call it the Tule." The gunfighter answered.

Silence settled back in around them. The gunfighter was alert, his eyes and his mind seemed to be always ahead of where they rode, around the next cluster of scrub cedar which now began to dot the canyon floor, across the five foot wide gap in the canyon floor or up along the steep canyon walls.

"Not much of a talker. Is he, Katharane?" Reid Stuart spoke to his daughter who was now awake in her carriage. Her hands appeared above the sides of the carriage and she worked her small fingers open and closed, acknowledging her father's voice. "No. He's not much of a talker. This silent partner of our's. This Mr...." Reid Stuart stopped. "My Lord, Katharane. We don't know his name."

The baby made a sound like the soft rush of wind through the cedars. "Ooohooo-ooh."

The gunfighter whirled around on his saddle. "Was that Katty?" He asked.

"Yes. That's her happy sound." Reid Stuart watched the look he had noticed at their first camp pass across the gunfighter's face, again. Then the gunfighter turned back to his riding. "Do you have a name?" He asked the gunfighter.

"Your Papa is sure big on puttin' names to things, Katty." The gunfighter said, addressing his remarks to the child the way Reid Stuart had, speaking to Reid Stuart in the third person.

"Think he is going to tell us his name, Katharane?" Reid Stuart, realizing that the gunfighter was more comfortable with the child than with him, continued the third person conversation. At least, the gunfighter was talking, a little. "No. I don't think he is. But we have to have something to address him by. We can't just be calling him 'you' all the time. Can we, Katharane?" Reid Stuart paused. The gunfighter did not answer. Reid Stuart continued. "No. We can't do that. Let's see. What shall we call our mysterious friend? Moses, maybe."

"Shit!" The gunfighter snorted. "Don't tell him, Katty. Let him figure it out for himself."

"No. He's no Moses. Even if he is leading us out of the wilderness. Or into it." Reid Stuart was anxious to keep the gunfighter talking. "Tafoya said he was the only man he knew who knew the country north of the Canadian. Maybe we should just call him Canada."

The baby burst forth loudly with several "Oooohooohoohs." She clapped her hands. She was enjoying the two men talking to her even though she could not see them.

"Yes. You approve. Do you, Katharane? Very well. Canada he shall be until or unless he chooses to confide in us with his Christian name."

"Canada's Christian enough for me, Katty." The gunfighter said.

"Now that we know your name, Mr. Canada, I want to formally introduce you to Katharane Diane Stuart and her father, Reid Stuart." Reid Stuart said.

"Pleasure to make your formal acquaintance, Miss Katty." The gunfighter said to the baby, then he spoke to Reid Stuart. "As for you, Reid Stuart. Haul your skinny ass up here. I need to show you something."

Reid Stuart trotted his buckskin up to the black filly. The chasm opened to twenty feet in width where it collided with the canyon wall and disappeared into and underneath the sandstone face of the wall. Ten feet above the chasm and along the side of the wall a narrow ledge ran the width of the chasm.

"See that ledge?" The gunfighter asked.

"I see it." Reid Stuart answered.

"Mark it well. Know where it is. If anything goes wrong from here on, grab Katty and make for that ledge. The Comanch' don't know it exists. They cross where the buffalo do at the other wall where the gorge is only a few inches wide. They won't be so quick to follow you across that ledge."

"I'm not certain I will be so quick to cross it myself." Reid Stuart said.

"Cross it you will. Or we'll leave you behind." The gunfighter said. He eased his black filly backwards to the mule, reached into the carriage and lifted Katharane out and set her on the saddle in front of him. "I'll carry Katty across with me. 'be sure she makes it." He stood up in his stirrups and shifted his weight, testing his cinch. It was tight. "Let me get across with her and the mustangs. Then you follow with the mule, the cow and that sure footed goat of yours." The gunfighter looked at Reid Stuart. "If you get in a bind, drop lead on that mule. That buckskin your ridin' seems steady enough to make it across. 'most likely."

"Thanks."

"Good luck, Stuart." The gunfighter said and he spurred the filly up the steep wall of the canyon and onto the narrow ledge. The mustangs surged up the wall behind her. More of the black filly's belly hung out over the chasm than balanced above the narrow ledge, but she moved swiftly along the ledge. The gunfighter kept his right hand on Katharane's stomach and held her firmly against him. Katharane bounced up and down on the saddle and waved her arms.

"Be still child." Reid Stuart prayed softly.

Katharane cried out. "Bye bye! Bye bye!"

A few seconds later the black filly and the two mustangs clambered down from the ledge on the other side of the chasm. "Your turn." The gunfighter called across to Reid Stuart.

The buckskin, the mule, the cow and the goat ascended the

wall of the canyon to the ledge easily enough. But once on the ledge the cow lost all confidence in her footing. She balked. The buckskin stopped. Reid Stuart looked back at the cow. The gunfighter had risked his life to get her for Katharane. Reid Stuart did not want to lose her. "Come on, boy." He clucked to the buckskin. But the cow would not move. The caravan was in danger, any sudden move could cause the entire group to tumble into the chasm.

"Cut her loose, Stuart. And bring the mule." The gunfighter shouted.

Reid Stuart hesitated. He looked at the gunfighter and thought, 'If he was here instead of me, he'd find a way to get Katharane's cow across.' Then he remembered that the goat was behind the cow. He had taught the goat to come to him when he whistled, partly to entertain Katharane, but mostly to make the goat easier to catch to milk. He whistled.

The goat hit the milk cow between her back legs and pushed furiously. The whistle meant her heavy udder would soon be emptied and she would receive a lump of sugar. She had no fear of the ledge. The cow kicked at the goat, missed and swayed dangerously close to the edge.

"Cut 'em loose! They'll take you in." The gunfighter cried.

Reid Stuart touched the buckskin with his spurs. "Step on." He called to the horse. The buckskin started forward. The goat was between the cow's hind legs. The mule took up the slack and pulled against the cow. Finally, the cow stumbled forward and the caravan was moving again. They made it across without further incident. Reid Stuart stopped his horse next to the black filly.

"Damn stubborn fool, you are, Stuart." The gunfighter said.

"Canada, my friend. You are not the one responsible for that child's well-being." Reid Stuart said.

"Maybe not. But I'm damn sure the one most capable of carin' for her here."

A stream flowed into the crevice where the gorge in the

canyon floor met the canyon wall. The floor of the canyon alongside the stream was covered with short grass and the footing was even and sure. So Reid Stuart laid his reins across the buckskin's neck and let the horse follow the black filly deeper into the canyon. He looked up. The top of the canyon appeared wide, but the depth of the canyon distorted his perception. The canyon was steadily becoming more narrow. Now one wall of the canyon was completely dark, sunless, the other alive with sunlight.

Ahead the canyon walls seemed to always continue. The shallow plateaus which had shelved them earlier were gone. In there place giant fingers of shale and sandstone grew straight up and disappeared into the prairie sky. The walls had become vertical facings of red clay and pink wind blasted shale and sandstone. And the canyon had become very narrow.

As the canyon had narrowed Reid Stuart had felt the breeze die away. A strange stillness settled in around him, the gunman and the baby. The shallow ocean of sunlight they had waded through earlier now was only a narrow stream of white light against the dark gray green grass, and it shone only on the center of the canyon floor. Reid Stuart drew his Sharps rifle from its scabbard. They were in a narrow gorge, edged on both sides by hundreds of feet of vertical rock, with a path not more than ten yards wide through it. The stream, almost hidden beneath the thick grass, was now flowing with them instead of against them. They were descending ever so slightly. He stood in his stirrups and stared over the gunfighter's right shoulder. Before them the gorge opened into a wide canyon. There was a blue haze at the far end of the canyon. As they neared the haze the floor of the canyon was sprinkled with silver dollar patches of rock and giant flat sided boulders. The stream reappeared from the grass and flowed swiftly across a bed of white slick rock. Suddenly the canyon floor was gone. It fell a hundred feet or more into another canyon. The stream cascaded down into the far canyon below.

This far canyon was immense. It opened from the neck of the canyon which Reid Stuart, the gunfighter and Katharane were in like the ocean opens from the throat of a bay, vanishing in every direction, limitless, forever, inaccessible. Reid Stuart surveyed the scene. Above him and where the canyon's lip turned away from its fall into the far canyon and joined with the wall of yet another canyon there was a rock platform. On the platform a mammoth boulder stretched fifty feet above them. The flint rock platform extended twenty feet out over the far canyon and ran from his sight around the boulder in the other direction.

The gunfighter led the two mustangs up a gentle slope until they were a foot or so below the platform. Reid Stuart followed. The gunfighter turned the filly to face the platform and spurred her hard. She jumped onto the platform. The mustangs leaped after her. Reid Stuart faced the buckskin to the platform and hit him hard with his spurs. The buckskin, the mule, and the goat made the jump easily. But Katharane's cow only managed to get her front feet onto the platform. Reid Stuart dismounted, caught her by the tail and rolled her onto the platform. Then he remounted.

The gunman pointed at a clearing in the new canyon separated from the platform by a stand of short stubby cedar trees. A dozen tepees sat scattered across the canyon floor. Women and children moved among the tepees. Beyond the tepees a large herd of horses grazed.

"We gotta' get into that camp." The gunfighter whispered.

"Are you certain we have to ride into that camp?" Reid Stuart asked quietly.

"I'm certain. 'But not how to go about it." The gunfighter hesitated.

Katharane ended his hesitation. She squealed. The camp suddenly swarmed with armed warriors. The gunfighter eased the filly and the two mustangs off the ledge and toward the Indian camp. Reid Stuart followed him.

A dozen mounted bucks met them as they emerged from the scrub cedar stand. Reid Stuart cocked his Sharps.

"Easy, Stuart. Don't spook 'em." The gunfighter called a name out to the bucks. "Kwanhah. Kwanhah." He repeated the name over and over.

Finally, one of the bucks pushed his horse against the gunfighter's horse. The baby wrinkled her nose at his pungent odor and snorted. The other bucks, who had also stopped their horses but who had kept the strangers encircled, hooted with laughter.

"Kwanhah." The gunfighter called the name again.

The buck nodded and turned his horse and rode toward the camp. The gunfighter, the baby, and Reid Stuart followed, with the other bucks forming their escort on each side. The buck in the lead stopped outside of one of the three poled buffalo skin lodges. A stout young buck with braided hair stepped out of the lodge.

"Kwanhah." The gunfighter addressed him. "Chief of the Kwerhar-rehunuh."

The buck raised his hand in greeting and walked to the gunfighter's horse. As he approached the other bucks backed away. The gunfighter reached down and clasped the Indian's forearm. Then he stepped down from the filly and lifted the baby off of the saddle. "Get down, Stuart." The gunman said.

Reid Stuart followed the gunfighter, his daughter and the chief into a lodge. Three squaws sat against the buffalo hide walls of the lodge. The chief sat in the middle of the dirt floor. The gunfighter sat across from him. The interior of the lodge was dark. Only a dingy gray light penetrated the buffalo hides and a few rays of bright sunlight shone through the small opening at the top of the lodge where the three poles came together. Reid Stuart waited for his eyes to adjust to the strange light.

"Sit here, Stuart." The gunfighter pointed to the dirt floor to his right.

Reid Stuart sat next to the gunfighter who held the baby on his lap. A squaw brought a square chunk of half-cooked, half-burnt, mostly raw fatty meat to the chief. The baby reached her right hand out to the smoking meat.

The brown eyed, smooth skinned young chief pinched a small piece of the smoking fat from the chunk of meat, held it to his lips and blew on it. Then he put his finger with the cooled fat on it against the baby's lips. Katharane opened her mouth and bit down firmly upon the fat and the chief's finger. The chief grunted and tried to pull his finger free. But Katharane held her bite and stared into his eyes. He smiled brightly and said something to the squaws. They giggled. He laid the hunk of meat he now held in his left hand on the bare skin of his left thigh, reached over and squeezed the baby's nose closed with his left thumb and forefinger.

Katharane shut her eyes and tried to hold on. Her face reddened, then she opened her mouth to breath and the chief withdrew his finger. He said something to one of the squaws and she came forward and reached for Katharane. The gunfighter handed the baby to the squaw.

"What's this?" Reid Stuart asked.

"It's all-right. Kwanhah told her to feed the child." The gunfighter explained.

Kwanhah spoke to the squaw in their dialect. She and the gunman laughed. Reid Stuart looked at the gunman. "What did he say?"

"He told her to watch her fingers. Katty had the bite of a wolf pup." The gunfighter translated for Reid Stuart.

"Kat-tie." Kwanhah said the name slowly.

"Katty." The gunfighter repeated the name for the chief.

Kwanhah turned to the squaws, pointed at the baby and said. "Katty." They nodded. One was regurgitating small bits of the dark buffalo meat and feeding it to the baby, who devoured each bite as soon as it was placed in her mouth. Another was inspecting the makeshift diaper Reid Stuart had fashioned from the bolt of cloth. Then the half-white Comanche chief Kwanhah Parker turned and stared into Reid Stuart's blue eyes. Neither man yielded. Each held the other's gaze.

"Katty Stuart." The gunfighter pointed at the baby. Then he put his hand on Reid Stuart's shoulder and said. "Reid Stuart."

Once again Reid Stuart felt the disquieting sensation that his well being rested with the effect his infant daughter had upon a stranger, a savage fierce stranger.

Kwanhah nodded and extended his right hand to Reid Stuart.

"Take hold of his wrist." The gunfighter instructed Reid Stuart.

Reid Stuart did so, and held it tightly. But his grip seemed weak compared to the vice like clamp of the warrior's.

The gunfighter began a discussion with Kwanhah in the

chief's dialect. They gestured often, and their voices rose and fell with their emotions. Reid Stuart could not understand the strange tongue. But he deduced from their gestures that the conversation involved Katharane, and that Kwanhah and the gunfighter were not yet in agreement.

Finally, Kwanhah grunted and stood up. The squaws stood up immediately. One of them held Katharane. Reid Stuart rose as the gunfighter rose. He followed Kwanhah and the gunfighter out of the lodge. The squaws, with Katharane, followed.

Katharane rubbed her eyes with the backs of her hands, trying to block out the bright sunlight. The buck that had first confronted the gunfighter and the baby made the face the child had made at him. Katharane promptly responded with the same face. The buck howled with laughter. And Kwanhah smiled. The Comanche were fascinated by the child. They touched her bronze skin, her dark hair. They looked into her blue eyes as they milled around the squaw who held her.

Kwanhah spoke loudly in his tongue and held up his bitten finger. The bucks roared with laughter and delight and struggled amongst themselves to get even closer to the baby. Kwanhah walked to the two mustangs still tied on lead behind the gunfighter's filly. He ran his hands across the mustangs' backs and down their flanks. He nodded with approval.

Reid Stuart noticed some of the Comanche's ponies. Compared to them the mustangs appeared to be thoroughbreds.

Kwanhah barked a command to one of the squaws. She left, but soon returned with a short squatty squaw, who appeared to be in her late teens. She was ugly. Many of the other squaws openly jeered at her, until Kwanhah silenced them with a command. Kwanhah looked at the gunfighter.

The gunfighter nodded slowly and said. "She'll do."

Kwanhah and the gunfighter gripped wrists again. Then Kwanhah said something to the ugly squaw. She cried with anguish and fell on her knees and began to jabber. Kwanhah stepped to her and kicked her solidly in the ribs, knocking her onto her side in the dust where the Comanches and their ponies had worn the grass from the canyon's floor.

Two of the squaws which had been in Kwanhah's tent jerked the ugly squaw to her feet. Kwanhah took the baby from the other squaw, who mildly protested giving up her prize. He handed the child to the ugly squaw and barked another command at her. She took the child in her hands and clutched her to her breast and disappeared into Kwanhah's tent.

Slowly Reid Stuart realized a trade had been consummated. But he was still uncertain as to the exact nature of the trade. "What have we just traded two good mustangs for?" He asked the gunfighter.

"One damn ugly squaw." The gunfighter replied.

"Why in God's name have we done that?"

"Because we have to have someone to take care of Katty, dammit." The gunfighter retorted. "That squaw's barren. Comanch' have no use for a squaw that can't bear children. Only reason she ain't enslaved by 'em is that she's Kwanhah's niece."

They spent the night in Kwanhah's camp. Katharane slept with the ugly squaw in Kwanhah's teepee. The next morning as Reid Stuart and the gunfighter prepared to leave the ugly squaw cried and pleaded to be left with her people. But the gunfighter tied her hands together and tied the mustang's lead rope through this and around his saddle horn.

The squaws jeered at the wailing ugly squaw tied on lead behind the gunfighter's horse. Only her sister showed her any compassion. She stood next to the ugly squaw, her face buried in her girl child's neck and moaned.

Reid Stuart rode his horse in front of the gunfighter and his daughter. "Dammit man! We can't do this! I've just come from fighting in a war against slavery." Reid Stuart said to the gunfighter.

"Shut up, Stuart. I can't change it now even if I wanted to. Which I do not!" The gunfighter whispered. "I cut her loose and Kwanhah will take it as an insult, an affront. We insult him and this damn squaw will still be taking care of Katty. Only difference will be is she'll be doin' it here. And mine and your scalps will be swingin' from that lodgepole with those others." The gunfighter nodded at the pole beside Kwanhah's lodge on which half a dozen tufts of dried matted hair hung.

"Those are human scalps?" Reid Stuart winced.

"What the hell did you think they were! Skunk hides!" The gunfighter hissed.

Kwanhah walked to the gunfighter's horse. He looked up at the child. Katharane reached done and grabbed the braid of hair which hung against the front of Kwanhah's left shoulder and pulled on it. The chief smiled and many of the bucks laughed. Kwanhah reached up and hung a buffalo hide necklace with three green colored stones attached to it around the child's neck. The Comanche seemed to catch their breaths. Many began a soft chant. Kwanhah looked up at the gunfighter and said in English. "My mother's." Then he turned and walked away.

THE MARKING OF THE DEAD
APRIL 6, 1868

Reid Stuart, the gunfighter, Katharane, the mule, the cow and the goat retraced their steps back through the canyon. They brought Katharane's new mama with them. This time they crossed the gorge at the Comanche crossing instead of the ledge. It was almost dark when again they approached the big canyon.

"What's the matter with her now?" Reid Stuart asked.

The squaw jerked at the mule's mane. The gunman had finally relented under Reid Stuart's constant protest about the inhumanity of making the woman walk on lead behind them and had allowed Reid Stuart to help the squaw onto the mule in front of Katharane's carriage. She had ridden there silently till now. Now she uttered frightened bursts of guttural noises, and gritted her teeth so viciously that they grated audibly.

"Kiowa." The gunfighter said.

"Where?" Reid Stuart asked. He surveyed the canyon.

"'don't know."

"Then how..."

"She smells 'em." The gunfighter cut him off. "If they were Comanch' she wouldn't be so upset. Besides, I've been thinkin' Kiowa, too."

"Can you smell them, also?" Reid Stuart asked.

"No. But I can feel 'em." The gunfighter said. "And I feel Kiowa." He stopped his black filly. "'gonna' camp in one of those crevices tonight." The gunman pointed at a dark shadow in the sandstone face of the canyon wall above them.

"You think they're that close?" Reid Stuart asked.

The gunfighter nodded at the squaw. She flared her nostrils. Then she moved her head slowly side to side and her eyes wallowed wildly in there sockets. She was a frightened rabbit, ready to bolt at the slightest movement.

"What about our animals?" Reid Stuart asked.

"After I milk that cow you hobble 'em in that stand of cedar we passed 'bout a quarter of a mile back." The gunfighter answered.

Reid Stuart draped his arms over the heavy Sharps which he carried across his shoulders like a yoke. A leather pouch filled with cartridges hung from his belt against his left buttock. The slender skinner's knife rode in a sheath against his right hip. He passed beneath the crevice where the others waited, realized this and backtracked to where they had dismounted. He scanned the cliffs above him, but in the late canyon light he could only see the vague reddish outlines of the crevices. A pebble landed at his boot. He swung the rifle down from his shoulders and cocked its large hammer.

"Stuart."

Reid Stuart searched the crevices trying to find the source of the hushed voice.

"Stuart." It whispered louder. "Up here."

Reid Stuart saw a shadow move to his right and twenty feet up the canyon wall. He climbed slowly up the steep face of the wall toward the movement. He reached a large crevice that folded back into the wall itself as if wrapped around some invisible pillar.

"Get in here, Stuart." The gunman whispered.

Reid Stuart stepped into the crevice. The squaw crouched at the back of the crevice, a dozen feet from its opening. Katharane lay on her back, her head one the squaw's knees, her legs dangling off each one of the squaw's heavy thighs and her round soft belly rising and falling in cadence with her quiet sleep. The gunman sat in the mouth of the crevice, listening. Reid Stuart listened, also. "Horses." He whispered to the gunman.

The gunman held up his right hand. Slowly he pointed at the band of Indians that rode through a clearing beyond their hobbled livestock. "'bout a dozen Kiowa. Young bucks. They're goin' round toward my canyon." He whispered.

Reid Stuart began to ask the gunfighter what he meant by 'his canyon' when he noticed the gunfighter's mustang being ridden by a buck, and strapped to its flanks, their hands bound together across its rump, were the old mustanger the gunfighter had traded with for Katharane's cow and a teenage boy. They had to hop in a sideways manner to keep their bare bloody feet from being trampled. Each few steps the mustang pitched and kicked at either the old man or the boy. The Kiowa laughed and hooted at the buck riding the mustang.

"Is there any chance for them?" Reid Stuart whispered into the gunfighter's right ear.

"No." The gunfighter shook his head. He and Reid Stuart watched the Kiowa until they passed beyond the clearing. Then they squatted on their boot heels. The gunfighter handed Reid Stuart a thin strip of hard dark cold meat. "Supper." The gunman said. He flipped a strip of the meat at the squaw who caught it with both hands and immediately began to gnaw at it.

"You mean dinner." Reid Stuart said.

"I mean supper, Stuart." The gunman snorted.

"With two rifles we may have had a chance of helping those poor bastards." Reid Stuart said. He chewed on a bite of the meat.

"I don't aim to take chances." The gunman said. He bit down on his strip of jerky.

The two men chewed the dark meat quietly for several minutes until Reid Stuart again took up the conversation. "Why don't you use a rifle?"

"'cause I like to smell a man when I kill him." The gunman answered.

Reid Stuart studied the gunman's almost invisible dark eyes. He found no trace of humor, no twinkle of satire nor wink to acknowledge the statement to be a ploy to provoke him. The gunman was serious. He meant what he had said. "Any chance of them finding us tonight?" He asked.

"None." The gunman answered. "Kiowa ain't much for

fightin' after dark. Besides, they'll be busy with their party."

Reid Stuart wondered what the gunman meant by party. But he was tired and much of what the gunman told him was disquieting, so he stretched out on the floor of the crevice, put his hat over his face, rested his head on his hands and went to sleep. At first he thought the screams were only part of some terrible dream, that the clear light high plains air's amplification was imaginary and the canyon's high walls' trebling echo was just the wind. Yes, the wind, but no, the anguished screeching was not caused by the ceaseless plains' wind. And he knew it when he heard the squaw's soft frightened moaning chant and the gunfighter's snarled command. "Shut the fuck up, squaw. Do not wake Katty." Reid Stuart sat up quickly.

The canyon came alive with screams and pleas and yelps and howls and laughter; hard, unmerciful, bitter laughter.

Reid Stuart eased next to the gunman, who sat cross legged in the mouth of the crevice. "What's happening?" He asked.

"'party's startin'." The gunfighter answered.

"What party?" Reid Stuart asked. But before the gunman could answer three short rapid screams shot through the night and rose above the canyon's walls and away on the wind.

"The party." Reid Stuart mumbled. "You knew this would happen."

"I knew."

"But why..."

"Ain't no why to it, Stuart." The gunman cut him off. "It's their way. The dirty stinkin' lot of 'em are Kiowa dogs."

'It's our way too, now.' Reid Stuart thought to himself. 'Our way, too.'

"No! No! No!" The cries reverberated through the canyon.

"Good God." Reid Stuart dropped his head and mumbled. "What are they doing to them?"

"Since that was the boy squallin', I expect they're cuttin' off their ears first. The old 'stranger ain't talkin' to the pain yet.

But he will when they start with the coals on his eyelids and his testicles. He will." The gunfighter mused. "If that don't get him to singin' they'll put fired coals up his butt. That old 'stanger's tough, but he'll sing their pain for 'em before he dies. Stinkin' Kiowa'll see to that."

Reid Stuart gagged. "Christ! I need a smoke."

"You light a fire and I'll put it out in your ass." The gunman threatened. "It's pitch dark out there, Stuart. They ain't a light for a hundred miles in any direction. You strike a spark to light a smoke and it'd throw a shadow up that canyon for a hundred feet." He nodded at the wall behind them. "Be me and you a screamin' our guts out to those Kiowa come tomorrow night. Me and you and them two." The gunman stared at the sleeping baby which the big eyed squaw held against her soft greasy stomach.

Reid Stuart looked at his daughter and the Indian woman. "Look at the Squaw Woman's eyes." He whispered to the gunfighter.

The squaw's eyes were like two separate but attached fire dancers trapped in a bone facade, jumping and jerking and leaping, as if struggling to free themselves from their sockets, their captors and dart away into the night.

"Those are a Comanch' squaw's Kiowa eyes, Stuart. She knows what those Kiowa devils are up to." The gunman said. "Don't you ever forget them. You're one of a handful of white men whose seen 'em."

"Who could forget them? They are not human." Reid Stuart replied.

An angry human howl joined with the boy's wails to form a chorus that filled the canyon with an unholy hymn that pitched off of its walls and wallowed across the scrub cedars and grass that covered the canyon's floor. The agonized symphony now shrieked by both the boy and the old mustanger did not appear to bother the gunman. He squatted comfortably on the loose dirt of the crevice's floor. But it etched long lines across Reid Stuart's forehead, and tightened his stomach and brought to his mind memories of the hurt surprised cries of his young soldiers at their first wounds and the dull knowing broken moans of his old regulars who stained the field at Antietam blue with fabric and the blue fabric red with their blood. He was many many miles from that warm and bloody September seventeenth day of 1862. But not so far as to let him forget. Not that far. He had listened to the sound of frightened men dying enough for a lifetime. Even talking to the nonchalant gunfighter would be better than listening to this symphony.

"Did you have a home before you came to these canyons?" Reid Stuart asked.

For a long while the gunman was silent, then he asked coldly. "That child's ma dead, Stuart?"

Reid Stuart's stunned anger drowned out the torturers' music. He heard now only the fury beating in his mind. 'Okay! You son-of-a-bitch. Maybe you like to listen to men die. I do not. But...'

The gunman's voice, softer now, almost gentle, broke through Reid Stuart's angry thoughts. "...things a man doesn't ask of me. No reason for it maybe. Other than I won't allow it. I know you are just trying to make conversation. It's been almost three years since I sat down and talked to a white man. You get accustomed to the emptiness, the quiet, the absence of any cause to say a word. Hell! I imagine a man could forget how to speak if he lived alone, really alone like these plains can make you, long enough. Maybe I've been alone too long. I don't know. But I do know there are things you and I can't ask of the other. If they get told, they get told. But they just have to be left be. Heard, taken in, then left be." The gunman put his left hand on Reid Stuart's right shoulder. "Tomorrow morning we're going up that canyon, Stuart. And we're gonna' see and do things you don't know, and still won't believe even tomorrow night, that men can do to men. And, unless you say for me to take you and her outta' this canyon now." The gunman glanced at the baby. "Come tomorrow night you can't be shed of, you can't ride away from and you can't pray off your soul."

Reid Stuart stared at the gunman.

"You say the word now, Stuart, and I'll take you and your Katty back to Tafoya's tomorrow and you won't be any worse for it. But come tomorrow night I can't and I won't. Come tomorrow night, and if we're still alive, you're cursed with me and that Katty girl's as much mine as your's."

'Katharane will never be any part your's.' Reid Stuart thought silently, angrily. His anger was fed by his memories of that bloody Maryland field of torn bodies. He had vowed never again. Never again would duty or circumstance force him to do what he had done that day. Now, tomorrow, this arrogant cold gunman would try, unless he abandoned these plains where he hoped his long search had ended, and where he and Katharane could begin, again. Tomorrow he would abandon Katharane, surrender her back to her mother's world, or ride again through the smell of the tortured dead into battle. He looked at his infant daughter asleep against the squaw.

"What about the Squaw Woman?" Reid Stuart asked. The name he had used for her earlier fit. She was his and the gunman's and Katharane's Squaw Woman.

"I'll have to keep her, I guess." The gunman muttered. "'don't have a lot of choice."

Reid Stuart was silent.

"Well?" The gunman asked.

"You will know in the morning." Reid Stuart said. "Before then you have no need to know." Reid Stuart lay on his back again and closed his eyes. But he did not sleep. He thought and waited for morning.

"'sun'll be up soon, Stuart." The gunman said to the long slender shape lying on its back on the dirt.

"I know." Reid Stuart said.

"Well?"

Reid Stuart rolled onto his side and stood up. Two bandoleers of the long fifty caliber cartridges crisscrossed his chest. "I hobbled our horses below." Reid Stuart said.

"I wasn't asleep long." The gunman frowned.

"Long enough." Reid Stuart replied.   Then he asked. "What do we do now?"

"Now we make sure Katty will be safe." The gunman answered. He drew his heavy Bowie knife from its sheath and stepped to the squaw and began cutting her right earlobe free from

37

her jaw.

The squaw awoke, startled. She grabbed for her ear, but she did not cry out. She feared the Kiowa more than the gunman. The gunman caught her wrist and held the knife, a small trace of blood running down its broad blade, against the squaw's nose. She clutched the stirring baby to her belly. The gunman spoke very slowly. His Comanche dialect was forced and irregular, but intelligible enough that the squaw understood. At least Reid Stuart thought she did because her eyes grew wide and took on some of the glazed look they had the night before when the Kiowa were torturing the old man and the boy.

"Let's go." The gunman said to Reid Stuart as he turned away from the squaw. He shoved his knife back into its sheath and strode out of the crevice and slid down the steep canyon wall on the heels of his boots with the palms of his hands acting as rudders behind him.

Reid Stuart followed him. He moved slower because he carried his Sharps rifle. The gunman laced the hobble he had freed his filly from around his saddle horn. Reid Stuart squatted and balanced the heavy rifle across his lap while he untied the buckskin's hobble. He looked up at the gunman who had mounted the filly. "Was that necessary?"

"'long as that squaw is more afraid of me than anything else, Katty's safe with her." The gunman answered.

"And what did you tell her to make her that afraid of you?" Reid Stuart asked.

"I told her if anything ever happened to Katty I'd slit both her nostrils open and sew them to her cheeks." The gunman replied. He slapped his reins against the filly's neck and she stepped forward into a walk.

Reid Stuart lifted himself up into the tall buckskin's saddle and trotted alongside the gunfighter. "And she's so afraid of that, Katty is safe with her?" Reid Stuart asked.

"'split nostrils on a Comanch' squaw is the sign she's been unfaithful. 'mark of disgrace." The gunman explained without taking his eyes away from the dimly lit trail which he followed through the grass. "Two nostrils." He held up the first and second fingers on his right hand. "Means she's been unfaithful more than once. By sewing them to her cheeks they never heal, never be hidden. One thing that squaw fears more than those Kiowa is bein' disgraced among her own kind."

"Her own kind gave her to you and I." Reid Stuart reminded him.

The gunman shrugged. "So. She's still Comanch' and she still thinks like a Comanch'. 'disgrace is the most disgusting state a Comanch' can imagine in life."

"You've actually seen this done among the Comanche?"

"I've seen it done." The gunman answered. His gaze never left the track made by the Kiowa.

The two men rode silently for some time. Until Reid Stuart asked. "Would you really do that to the Squaw Woman?"

"If Katty's not fat and sassy when we get back, you will know it."

Reid Stuart let his right hand slide down his rifle until he found its hammer. He eased the buckskin behind the black filly and fell back one length, two. 'If I kill him now, I will have to fight those Kiowa alone. And they'll be ready.' Reid Stuart thought.

"Stuart." The gunman's hiss broke through Reid Stuart's thoughts. "'see the outline of those tall cottonwoods." He whispered and pointed at the faint silhouettes of a cluster of tall ragged trees, outlined by the faint predawn light across a wide grassy flat from him and the gunfighter.

Reid Stuart eased his buckskin beside the gunman's filly.

"That's where I make their camp to be."

"We'll be totally exposed crossing that meadow." Reid Stuart said.

"Meadow?" The gunman shook his head. "The things you say, Stuart. We ain't crossin' that meadow, as you call it. Those cottonwoods grow off the side of a stream and close to the canyon wall where there's plenty of water and protection from the wind and cold. We're gonna' skirt your meadow and find you a place on that wall where you can use that artillery piece you carry. Then I'm goin' down and pay my respects to 'em. Come on." The gunman led Reid Stuart through the scrub cedars and around the grassy flat, across a small narrow stream and to the canyon wall. "Hobble that buckskin." The gunman said as he stepped down from his filly. "I'm gonna' see if them Kiowa are still bedded down. Sun'll be up anytime now." He led the filly to the canyon wall and dropped her reins. He walked slowly along the wall for a short distance, then very quickly he scampered up the wall to a small knoll twenty feet above the canyon.

Reid Stuart hobbled his horse, pulled a short metal rod with a forked end from beneath the buckskin's saddle, picked up his Sharps and followed the gunman. The gunman lay on his belly in the thick short grass of the knoll and stared down into the small grove of cottonwoods. He felt the grass move as Reid Stuart slid the long Sharps rifle in front of him as he crawled through the grass to the gunman. He laid the rod next to the gun. "I brought my crutch with me." He whispered to the gunman.

"Good. 'can't afford to miss." The gunman whispered back.

"I won't." Reid Stuart laid his hat out to his right and down in the grass. The gunman's was slid down his back, held there by the choke string.

"They're there." The gunman whispered. "And still bedded in. We owe that old 'stanger and his boy some thanks for that."

In the still twilight darkness Reid Stuart could discern the figures of two men hanging from their wrists which were apparently tied to the cottonwoods from which they dangled. "Dead?" Reid Stuart asked.

"They ain't screamin', are they?"

"No."

"Then they're dead." The gunman pointed at the edge of the grove nearest to the corpses. "I'm gonna' bring judgment on them Kiowa from there first. You see?" He asked Reid Stuart.

"Yes."

"When I cut loose, pick a target and shoot. Take your time. No need to panic. One thing about Kiowa, they'd murder their own Mama just to hear her scream. But they're real easy to kill." The gunman whispered encouragingly.

"That's good to know." Reid Stuart whispered back.

"One other thing, Stuart. After the first volley, I'm gonna' have to be movin' pretty quick down there. Please, try not to shoot me with that cannon."

"If I do there is one thing you should know."

"What's that?"

"It will not be by mistake."

The gunman chuckled softly and crawled away. Reid Stuart picked up the metal rod and drove it into the soft but shallow sod two and a half feet in front of him. He picked up the heavy Sharps and slid its barrel into the fork of the rod. He unlaced one of the bandoleers of cartridges and laid it to his right. Then he pulled five of the long cartridges out of the bandoleer and laid them on top of it. "I will be lucky if I get off three shots. But having a couple to spare cannot hurt." He whispered to himself. He was ready. He watched the gunman ride slowly up to the body of the boy and the old mustanger. He rode nonchalantly, as if he was completely relaxed and sure of his way. He rode between the mutilated bodies and the Kiowa camp, keeping the camp to his left. Then suddenly, violently he drew his pistol and fired and fired.

Reid Stuart saw the body of the first Kiowa to die jerk in its sleep from the gunman's bullet, dead, never to awaken. Then his first shot lifted a kneeling buck, who had rolled onto his knees awakened by the gunman's shots, off his knees and blew a hole the size of the end of the Sharps' barrel through his stomach. Methodically, mechanically, mercilessly Reid Stuart's right hand breached the Sharps and slid another long cartridge into place, closed the breach, cocked the hammer, found the trigger as he found his second target and squeezed. It was remarkable how quickly and efficiently he could work the big gun, how he could kill three men with it in less than a minute and a half.

In that same time the gunman had killed four, spurred his

filly across the shallow creek and spooked the Kiowa's ponies. The early sun's first rays slid down into the canyon and projected the shadow of a crouching buck out onto the loose sand of the creek bed. Reid Stuart could hear the gunman's pistol, a shot then the sound of the filly's flying hooves and another shot. The gunman had the Kiowa as he wanted them, on foot. Mounted, he rode them down and shot them. The shadow moved. Reid Stuart sighted the Sharps on the tall cottonwood from which the shadow began to emerge. It moved again. Now Reid Stuart saw that the shadow came from a boy who was hugging the trunk of the cottonwood tree. He could also hear the sound of the gunman's filly returning to the clearing. The boy peeped around the tree.

'Be still boy.' Reid Stuart thought.

The boy knelt down and when he stood up he held a long lance in his right hand. He still clutched the trunk of the tree with his left. The filly was at the edge of the clearing. The boy slid his face across the rough cottonwood bark, trying to see the horse without being seen by its rider. He walked his fingers up the lance's crooked shaft and drew it back behind his head.

Reid Stuart aimed the Sharps at the boy's right temple and the face of another boy, a young boy in gray, wearing a cap, leaning against a tree, his eyes frozen open and a line of blood flowing down his soft cheek, flashed into his mind's eye. He forced the memory from his mind, aimed and squeezed the trigger. The Sharps roared through the now silent morning, its echo booming off into the distance. The Kiowa boy's face exploded, throwing a lustrous red mist against the motley white of the cottonwood's bark. The filly reared. The gunman steadied her. He stood up in his stirrups and yelled. "Nice shot, Stuart!" Reid Stuart did not answer. He dried the tears from his eyes, picked up his rifle, pulled the rod free and stumbled down the canyon wall to his horse.

The gunman kneeled over the young boy. He stood up as Reid Stuart approached. He held his Bowie knife in his left hand. "We got 'em all, Stuart." He beamed, happily. "Every last murderin' one of 'em." He was very pleased.

Reid Stuart dismounted. He walked to the gunman. And then he stopped. He did not breathe. He did not blink. He stared at the Kiowa boy's forehead. "What in the name of God are you doing, man!" He cried.

In the center of the boy's forehead the gunman had carved a mark. It was an E. But not a true E. Its bottom member was broken. It drooped at an angle down toward the boy's left eyebrow.

"'markin' 'em. Put the fear in the rest of 'em 'bout comin' into my canyon." The gunman answered. He walked to the next cadaver. It lay face down in the washed sand of the creek beneath the cottonwoods. He pushed it with the toe of his boot. Then he kicked it in the ribs. "'case he's possumin'." The gunfighter explained. He kneeled and rolled the Indian onto his back. Then he began to carve the mark into the dead Kiowa's forehead.

Reid Stuart grabbed his wrist.

The gunman looked up at him. "I told you last night, Stuart that you were gonna' see things you wouldn't understand or believe. I know you think I'm doin' this for my own jollies, but I'm not. If we're gonna' take this land from 'em and hold it, and that's what I understand we, you and I, intend to do. Then we have to be more frightenin' to them than they are to us. They outnumber us hundreds to two. They are gonna' outgun us by at least ten to two every time we engage them. We gotta' out think, out ride, out fight and out savage then by at least that." He jerked his arm free and bent back to his task. "A good fifty percent of makin' it on these plains is just in your mind and in the mind of those who would drive you off of them. So go cut the Mustanger and his boy down. Maybe that'll make you feel better about this." He carefully carved the mark in the center of the corpse's forehead.

Reid Stuart walked away.

The gunman worked silently for almost an hour. Until he had marked the last Kiowa. Then he walked to the trees where the old Mustanger and the boy had been hung and tortured. Now they lay on their faces in the loose sand. Reid Stuart sat on a hollowed out fallen cottonwood. "I didn't have anything to cover them with." He said.

"Bad?" The gunman asked.

"Bad." Reid Stuart answered. He sighed and said. "Real bad."

"They only had three revolvers among 'em and a handful of old muskets. 'revolvers made sense, the muskets don't. 'not enough fire power. That old 'stanger should've known better." The gunman said. He carried the three pistols stuck in his gun belt. "Let's get back to Katty. We'll bring the mule and gather up those old guns so the others can't use 'em. We can bury these two then."

"What about them?" Reid Stuart nodded at the defiled Kiowa corpses.

"'wouldn't be no point to my markin' 'em if we were to bury 'em." The gunman answered. He walked to his black filly and mounted, and waited while Reid Stuart mounted the buckskin. Then they rode away.

Reid Stuart stared into the dark crevice. For a moment standing in the bright sunlight and looking into the shadows of the crevice blinded him.

"Is Katty there?" The gunfighter asked impatiently from below.

Reid Stuart shaded his eyes. At the back of the crevice the Squaw Woman sat on her knees. The baby turned her face from the squaw's breast and smiled. Then she turned back to the squaw's black nipple. Reid Stuart stepped into the crevice.

"Well?" The gunman called from below.

Reid Stuart led the answer from the crevice. He helped the squaw, who carried the baby, down the canyon wall. The gunman reached down from his horse and snatched the baby from the squaw. The squaw groaned in protest. The gunman kicked at her in response to her protest. He set the baby on his saddle in front of him. She squealed gleefully. "Like I said, Stuart. Fat and sassy." He picked up the filly's reins. "'let's catch up our stock and get goin'."

"Where to?" Reid Stuart asked suspiciously.

"Home." The gunfighter answered.

HOME

THE ESCADARA

SPRING, 1868 – SPRING, 1869

Reid Stuart followed the gunfighter into a small canyon. It grew narrower, and the scrub cedar stands grew in size and multiplied in number, and the large open flats of grass shrunk until they became little gray windows between the thick dark stands of cedars. Reid Stuart worked the buckskin through one of these stands of cedar. He emerged onto a large meadow. At the meadow's far side the point of a pie's wedge was formed by the steep walls of the small canyon as they intersected. The meadow was filled with lush gramma grass, some winter wheat still green in the early spring shade, and it was dotted with deer, several wild turkey and cattle. The deer bolted away. The turkey slid through the tall grass and disappeared. The Longhorn cattle stood with their calves, their heads raised, watching the riders. Some of the calves were babies. One calf was newly born within the hour. Others were tall lanky yearlings. Two bulls stood with their heads down, eyeing each other.

"Cattle." Reid Stuart said. "Cattle, Katharane." He laughed. He looked at the gunfighter and repeated. "Cattle."

The gunman nodded. He handed Reid Stuart the mustang's lead rope. Then he backed the filly to the mule and lifted Katharane out of her carriage. The Squaw Woman eyed him cautiously and moaned and reached for the child. The gunman ignored her. He rode back to Reid Stuart and reclaimed the mustangs' lead rope. "Tell him we know what cattle are, Katty." The gunfighter said to the child that sat on the front of his saddle.

Reid Stuart smiled happily. He counted the Longhorns. "Fifty head of grown stock." He grinned at the gunfighter and pointed at Katharane and said. "We have our cattle herd, Katharane."

"We got the beginnin' of a herd, Katty. And we." The

gunfighter emphasized 'we'. "'got 'em only as long as we can keep the Kiowa, the Comanch', the drought this summer and the blizzards next winter from killin' 'em. Them and about three times again their number."

"Another hundred and fifty head?" Reid Stuart asked.

"And more. 'best as I can figure." The gunman answered. "Strung out down this canyon." He looked over his shoulder. "A few have even managed to survive out in the big canyon." He slid the filly and the mustang in front of the buckskin. "Come on. I left those ponies against the far wall. They're tired. They'll graze. Then come to water. We can pen 'em then." He reined the filly close to the canyon wall and let her walk slowly on.

Reid Stuart followed them up a steep path carved out of the side of the canyon wall. Near the top of the wall he stood in his stirrups. He could see the edge of the vast flat prairie. A crude gate, made of three long cedar poles piniomed between two heavy cedar posts which had been sunk into the trail and against the canyon wall and extended across the trail to another pair of posts at the edge of the trail, blocked their path.

The gunfighter slid the long cedar poles between the pair of posts at the edge of the trail. He led his filly and the mustang through the open gate. Reid Stuart followed on his buckskin with the mule, the cow and the goat. The trail opened onto a flat shelf which had been eroded out of the canyon wall. In the middle of the shelf was a large pool of water. At its top, nearest the prairie, a spring bubbled out of the canyon wall and flowed into the pool. At its other end the pool emptied over the lip of the shelf and disappeared down into the bottom of the canyon.

The horses, mule, cow and goat drank from the pool. The gunfighter carried Katharane to the spring. He caught some of the water that bubbled out of the canyon wall in the palm of his hand. He held the water to the baby's lips. She tasted it with her tongue, then pulled at his hand splashing the water into her mouth, down her chin and onto her stomach. Reid Stuart helped the Squaw Woman down from the mule. She waddled along the pool toward the gunfighter and the baby. The goat spied a green gourd vine which grew out of the side of the canyon and near the spring. She ambled over to it. Reid Stuart walked to the far edge of the pool. Below him four mustangs grazed, trapped in a large oblong corral formed by the convergence of the canyon's walls, and a deep wide chasm in the canyon floor which ran from the beginning of the canyon out and across it to the far side of the canyon, and some twenty yards of cut cedar posts which had been laced together side by side to form a barrier across the only opening between the canyon wall and the chasm.

"Your horse corral?" Reid Stuart asked.

"That's right." The gunman answered. He handed the baby to her father. "Here. Give her to the squaw."

'Why don't you?' Reid Stuart thought. But he took his child and handed her to the Squaw Woman who immediately sat down with her and gave Katharane her teat.

The gunman nodded at the open gate. "Those Kiowa ponies will smell fresh water. They'll make their way up the trail 'bout sundown. We'll slip behind 'em and close the gate. Then when they've watered we'll drive 'em off the ledge and down into the pen. 'let 'em mix with my mustangs for awhile. Maybe we can trade 'em for supplies later." He said thoughtfully. "Come on. Somethin' else I wanna' show you."

Reid Stuart followed him. The goat chewed on a piece of the gourd vine. The gunfighter kicked at her and missed. "Damn stinkin' gourd eatin' goat." He cursed.

"You don't want her eating the gourd vine?" Reid Stuart asked.

"Not if you're gonna' milk her for Katty." The gunman said. "You ever tasted milk from a gourded up cow. It's rank."

Reid Stuart kicked at the goat. She dodged his kick, also, and continued to chew on the gourd vine unperturbed.

"Here it is." The gunfighter said. He pointed at a short narrow opening in the prairie floor in front of him.

"Here is what?" Reid Stuart asked.

"Home. The Escadara." The gunfighter said and disappeared down into the opening.

Reid Stuart hesitated, then he followed the gunfighter down into the dark dugout. Both of its ends were covered with cedar logs. The center, where he had followed the gunfighter into it, had been left uncovered. When his eyes had adjusted to the faint light of the dugout, Reid Stuart stepped off its dimensions, a habit from surveying. The dugout was twenty steps in width and eight in depth. Because he had to bend over to avoid its sod roof at its mouth, he guessed it to be about five feet in height there and, having been dug into a swale in the prairie that rose away from the edge of the canyon, which allowed greater height at its rear while maintaining the same thickness of sod roof overhead, it was slightly greater than six feet in height in the rear. Its packed dirt floor had a two and one-half inch cant to the front. And its mouth was two and a half steps deep. Its sod ceiling was some thirty inches thick. A crude rock hearth with a three inch dirt flue leading up through the sod roof had been constructed at one end of the dugout. The soot and smoke, which appeared to have blown back down the flue as frequently as they went up it, had discolored the grass roots which penetrated the dirt walls. A rough wooden table stood near the fireplace on four short T framed wooden legs. A heavy cedar stump was the only chair. At the other end of the dugout a small cot slid into a slot in the wall and a cedar tripod supported the end of the cot nearest Reid Stuart. Several buffalo hides lay on the cot.

"Are the four of us supposed to live in this?" Reid Stuart asked.

"Yep." The gunfighter smiled. "'course we'll have to do some expansion this summer."

"Can it be expanded?" Reid Stuart asked doubtfully.

"Sure." The gunfighter answered. "You just keep diggin'."

The Squaw Woman led Katharane into the dugout. The Squaw Woman shuffled about the dark dugout. She scratched at the hard dirt floor with her bare toes. She pressed her face against the walls and sniffed odors Reid Stuart could not smell. Katharane toddled behind her, holding to the ragged hemless end of the sacklike doeskin dress the squaw always wore. The child giggled when she bumped into the heavy legs of the squat squaw.

The gunman rolled up the confiscated rifles and pistols in an old worn buffalo hide and shoved the buffalo hide under the cot. Reid Stuart unpacked, checked, repacked and stored his surveying equipment in the back of the dugout.

"Surveyor?" The gunman asked.

"Was." Reid Stuart answered.

"Where'd you learn to do that?"

"At the academy."

The gunman frowned.

"West Point." Reid Stuart explained.

"I know what the Academy is." The gunfighter retorted.

Reid Stuart listened to the black filly pick her way down the trail. He sighed. The gunman's moods were unpredictable, he feared. He picked up the old quill, the precious jar of ink, his journal and carried them to the rough table. He opened his journal and carefully numbered several entries. He worked at his journal until the afternoon sun no longer gave enough light for him to see. He closed the journal and left it on the table. He recorked the ink jar and replaced it and the quill in the wooden crate with his sextant and Bible. As he did, he heard the gunman riding back up the trail. He stepped out of the dugout and greeted him. "Did you have a nice ride?"

"'been pennin' those Kiowa ponies." The gunfighter answered.

"I thought perhaps you went to visit someone."

The gunman eyed Reid Stuart curiously and said. "There ain't another white man or woman within two hundred and fifty miles in any direction you choose to ride. And, at any given moment, the closest Kiowa or Comanch' can be more'n a hundred miles."

"You mean we are alone?" Reid Stuart surveyed the darkening prairie. Like a sailor a long time at sea he looked for any light that might give him hope that somewhere in the darkness another soul waited. But there was no light, only grass and grass and grass and darkness.

"You see that moon?" The gunman pointed at the immense orange moon that sat just above the vague outline of the rim of the far canyon. "You and I are the only two white men who will see that moon on this prairie tonight."

The Squaw Woman and Katharane slept together on the two legged cot. The journal lay on the table. The gunfighter picked it up. "What'cha write in there today?" The gunfighter asked.

"You're welcome to see for yourself." Reid Stuart answered.

The gunman opened the journal. He frowned as he struggled to read Reid Stuart's tense, jerky script. "'can't make much of this out." He grumbled.

"Here." Reid Stuart reached for his journal. "I'll read it to you." He laid the leather journal on the table and read: "Seven, April, Eighteen Sixty-Eight. Arrived in small canyon, after morning encounter with Kiowa. He is a hard man. Hard like this land. I am yet uncertain as to his intentions." He glanced at the gunman, but he received no response. "But now am comfortable that Katharane is safe. Safe as she can be here. Canyon filled with game, deer, turkey, quail, even antelope and buffalo. But more important, cattle. He has cattle with which a herd can be built. There are many things to do. The dugout in which he-we-live is crude and cramped and unstable." Again Reid Stuart paused, but the gunman sat quietly. Reid Stuart continued. "I can shore up the walls with rock. But I am doubtful as to the strength of the sod ceiling. Next we must mark our range. This is most important and must be done with all dispatch. Then we must increase the water pools capacity as much as possible. Then mark our-the-stock. All these things we must do if we are to build a ranch."

The gunman interrupted him. "Only one thing we gotta' do, and that's to keep her alive." He pointed at Katharane as she slept on the squaw's stomach.

"Since you seem to think you're so good at doing that, we'll put you in charge of keeping us all alive." Reid Stuart said quietly.

The gunman frowned as he continued to stare at the baby. "'reckon that's how it has to be." He said. He looked at Reid Stuart. His eyes were sad.

Reid Stuart thought that for an instant, one beat of time, he saw what might be fear in the gunman's eyes.

"Well, I'm done in, Stuart. I'm gonna' turn in." The gun-fighter said. "Grab you a buffalo hide. Shake it out good." He grinned. "Get out as many of the varmints out as you can. Then pick you a spot on the floor." The gunfighter drug an old buffalo hide from a stack of three and spread it on the floor between where Katharane and the Squaw Woman slept and the opening from the dugout. "Goodnight to you, Reid Stuart." He said as he rolled himself up in the buffalo hide.

"Goodnight, Canada." Reid Stuart answered.

The Squaw Woman shuffled passed Reid Stuart. He sat up, stretched and looked about the dugout. "Where's Katharane?"

The squaw stared at him. He stood up and walked out of the dugout. He heard the gunfighter's voice coming from the corral. "That's it. Stay in the middle of 'em. You got 'em. Stay with 'em, Katty. Think the middle of his back. No matter what he does, you're always in the middle of his back." The voice was soft and soothing and coaxing. Instead of its usual abruptness, it was a patient drawl, and it floated gently and kindly in the early morning air.

"Damn!" Reid Stuart exclaimed.

Katharane bounced up and down in the middle of a small paint pony's bare back. She clutched it's mane with both hands. Her eyes were open wide, but not afraid, expectant. The pony trotted around the gunman in a wide circle, held on lead by a long braided hair rope.

"Mornin', Stuart." The gunman greeted him. "Just givin' Katty a little ridin' lesson. She's a born horseman."

"Don't you think she's a little young to put on a horse alone?"

"No."

"Well, I do." Reid Stuart said.

"Well, you think wrong, Stuart." The gunman said. "Ridin', and doin' it better than anyone, may be what keeps her alive here. Sooner she learns, sooner she's able to have a chance on her own."

"I don't intend for my infant daughter to be alone."

"I don't either. But it might come to that, no matter what you and I intend." The gunman growled. He clucked to the paint pony to increase its pace. The baby bounced even higher. Suddenly the gunfighter dropped the braided rope and leaped at the pony. The pony jumped. Katharane sailed off its back and up into the air. The gunman snatched her from her fall and set her back on the pony. He talked to her calmly. She giggled and rubbed the pony's back with her hands.

"How did you know he was going to jump?" Reid Stuart asked. He held the braided rope and rubbed the pony's neck.

"I didn't." The gunman answered.

"Then...." Anger swept across Reid Stuart's face. "You son-of-a-bitch! You made this pony jump on purpose."

"She has to learn what to expect, Stuart. And there's only one way for her to learn. She has to be taught. Her first time on a horse alone and that horse threw her. She will never forget that. And they'll never be another horse throw her. You can bet on that." The gunman explained. He lifted Katharane off the pony and handed her to Reid Stuart.

The Squaw Woman squatted outside of the dugout. She reached for the baby. Reid Stuart handed Katharane to the squaw, who retreated into the dugout with her. He and the squaw ate cold buffalo jerky. Katharane sucked the cow's sweet milk through the soft doe skin teat. The gunfighter did not return to the dugout for the noon meal.

After Katharane was asleep, Reid Stuart walked to the spring. He knelt and reached down into the pool's lukewarm water. The water was eight inches deep. The pool's bottom was covered with three to four inches of silt near the sides. Reid Stuart reasoned that the silt would be at least twice that depth or more near the center of the pool. 'The silt can be dug out easy enough. And by laying rock along the lower sides that drop to the next shelf, and mortaring the rock with prairie sod and sand it can be made to hold at least twice the volume it holds now.' Reid Stuart thought. He paced around the perimeter of the second pool. 'Not half the area of the first one.' He thought. 'And only half as deep. But the lower lip can be built up, and it will hold a goodly amount of water, too.' He stepped off of the second shelf and walked around the large muddy wallow. Nowhere did water flow out of it, nor were there any signs that it ever had, no washes, no smooth rocks, no narrow carpet of thick switch grass, like where the first pool flowed down into the second pool. He sat down and pulled his boots off. He rolled his pants legs up and waded into the shallow pool. He tested its bottom with his feet, and dug at its heavy sod bottom with his toes. He discovered that as he approached the canyon side of the pool the bottom remained muddy, but as he walked to the front of the pool, where the water from the second pool drained into this pool, the water became much cooler and the bottom changed from the slimy mud to a smooth hard rock surface. Five feet from the bank he felt his toes being lifted by cold water. He slid his foot forward and it was lifted upward by a steady flow of cold water. 'Artesian flow. I'll be damned. A second spring, buried in the bottom of this pool. But why doesn't this one fill up?' He walked slowly forward, until he felt his toes being sucked into a narrow slit in the rock floor. "So that's it." He said aloud. "The spring's flow is drained out the bottom. It must come out in the canyon below. We can dig out the far end of the pool, drain the artesian flow towards it." He reasoned out loud. "We will have an artesian fed reservoir."

Reid Stuart straightened from his digging, stretched his tired back and watched the filly come up the trail. The gunman let the horse drink from the pool. He looked at Reid Stuart. "You bathin'?"

Reid Stuart smiled. "No. I've surveyed this pool. We can make it hold at least twice as much as it does now." He wet his lips and continued. "We can enlarge the dugout, as well. But the next thing we need to do is to mark our stock." He hesitated, then added. "If you're interested."

The gunman frowned. "'not particularly thrilled. But we're partners. Good or bad, we're partners." He bit his lip and looked away, and said. "And before we're done you may well believe it's more bad than good."

"I've known bad. I can deal with it." Reid Stuart replied. Then he said. "I haven't told you what my number one item is."

"I know what it is." The gunfighter said. "I looked at that journal again this morning." He shook his head. "'damn fool thing. 'wantin' to mark off the range. We can have all the range we want, as long as we can hold on to it."

"Marking it may be the only way we can hold on to it." Reid Stuart said. "We're not always going to be the only ones wanting it. Others will come. They always do."

"They ain't as long as they're Kiowa and Comanch' waitin' to kill 'em for their trouble."

"The Kiowa and the Comanche cannot stop them forever." Reid Stuart argued.

"We'll see." The gunfighter snorted.

Reid Stuart sighed. "Yes. We will. But first we will dig out the reservoir and mark the stock." He looked at the gunman. "And then mark our range."

The gunfighter shrugged and said. "We'll see."

From daylight until ten o'clock each morning they searched the canyon for the Longhorn cattle. By ten the heat drove the cattle to brush and shade and Reid Stuart and the gunfighter from their saddles. Then they worked in the first pool, scooping the heavy wet mud across the rolled lips of the buckets, lifting the buckets free of the water, carrying it to the edge and shaking it out of the buckets. Days became weeks and the summer days grew long and heavy with the heat.

July third, eighteen hundred and sixty-eight, Reid Stuart sat on the buckskin and stared at the scorched prairie that seemed to flow to the canyon from every direction. "The buffalo live on the plains. Why not the cattle? We haven't scouted them to be certain."

The gunman shook his head and said. "Not enough sure water this time of year for cattle to stay out on the plains. Buffalo can go longer, travel further and find water better than cattle."

Reid Stuart pushed his hat back. "God. What a waste of country."

"How so?" The gunman asked.

"If cattle can't live on it, what good is it?"

"Good in itself, I reckon." The gunman answered. He swung the filly toward the trail leading down into the canyon.

"They are like a woman these plains, Stuart. The miles and miles of grass drew the buffalo here. The buffalo drew the Kiowa and the Comanch`. But it is the canyon that allows us to be here. The canyon is the prairie's mystery and our life. Without it these plains would be nothing but a brutal and barren bitch."

The pistol barked through the early morning. "Damn." Reid Stuart cursed. He stood knee deep in the pool. Already the rough rawhide of the bucket's handle cut into his tired hands. The pistol cracked again. Then Katharane's faint giggle drifted down to Reid Stuart. He waded out of the pool, sat down, pulled his boots on and walked up the trail to the dugout.

Pop. The hollow, dried gourd danced off of the ground. Katharane giggled. Pop. Again, the gourd took flight. Katharane stood between the gunfighter's legs, pointed both of her index fingers at the gourd and yelled. "Pop! Pop!" Quickly, the black gun barked twice. The first shot bounced the gourd into the air. The second shot exploded it. Reid Stuart stood at the edge of the dugout and watched.

"Ooohooh!" Katharane laughed. She looked up at the gunfighter and said. "Pop, pop, pop."

The gunfighter bent down and pulled a green gourd from the vine. He rolled it out onto the flat packed hard pan of the dugout's yard. Pop. The heavy green gourd hopped only half as high as the dried gourd. But the black pistol spoke again, even quicker, and the gourd flew sideways, and again, even quicker than the second shot had followed the first, the third shot followed the second and slammed the ruptured gourd into the ground.

"Damn." Reid Stuart muttered.

Katharane squealed with delight, clutched the back of the gunfighter's buckskins behind his knees and pulled and pushed as hard as she could.

"You liked that, did you Katty girl?" The gunfighter asked as he reloaded the pistol.

"Do again, Pop." The child leaned against her grip on the gunfighter's buckskins and beamed up at him. "Do again."

He smiled and finished reloading his pistol. "All-right."

"That is an awful waste of good ammunition, Pop." Reid Stuart called from the top of the dugout. "And of the precious little time we have to clean those pools before it becomes so unbearably hot."

"'man ain't never wastin' time when he's sharpenin' skills that keep him alive, Stuart." The gunman replied. "But you are right about the ammunition." He cocked the pistol. "Last time for today, little Katty."

Reid Stuart tried to count the canyon's report of the pistol shots. He could not. They followed one upon the other too quickly for Reid Stuart to differentiate between them. "How many?" He asked.

"How many gourds' you see bounce?"

"Three."

"Three shots."

"Impressive. But what do you do if they're out of that pistol's range?"

The gunman picked the child up, set her on his shoulders and set his round rim black hat on her head. The hat almost covered her eyes and she pushed the front up until the head band rested against her forehead. "I get within range." The gunman answered.

July brought unyielding heat. The plains sky was a sun that seared through deerskin shirts, turned unprotected skin to brittle layers of scabs and sucked the life out of land, riders and horses. But Reid Stuart and the gunfighter, for now the gunman had indeed become a knowable if not entirely known person to Reid Stuart, rode everyday. They searched their canyon and out into the big canyon for the wild Longhorns. Some days they found none they had not marked, but more often they roped and branded a half-dozen or more.

Katharane waddled down the trail. She held both arms up, her small hands half closed, and smacked her lips and called. "Pop. Pop." The Squaw Woman followed her, chiding the child for being on the steep trail alone. Katharane ignored her and continued down the trail. The gunman spurred his horse and, as the horse surged up the trail and passed the child, he leaned out and down and swept her into his arms and up onto his saddle. Katharane bounced on the saddle and waived her arms and growled at the horse and laughed. The Squaw Woman turned around and followed the horse, calling to the child even louder, protesting the gunman's daring pick up with loud grunts and groans. He cursed her.

Night, after weary night, Reid Stuart and the gunfighter slept, almost without knowing or understanding they had eaten and almost without caring, and always without conversation. Katharane played about their bedrolls as they slept, until she tired and allowed the Squaw Woman to lay her next to her on the cot.

August came, almost without distinction, just with more heat and more work.

"Today's Katharane's birthday."

The gunman spun around and stared at Reid Stuart. "What?" He asked.

"Today's Katty's second birthday." Reid Stuart replied.

"Shit! What are we doin' here then?" The gunfighter swore. He kicked the old Longhorn cow that struggled against the braided rope that held her by her horns to his saddle and the rope by which Reid Stuart and his buckskin held her heels.

"Why are you kicking her?" It troubled Reid Stuart that the gunman spared no opportunity to inflict abuse upon the cattle. He could see no reason for it.

"'cause you ain't close enough to kick." He cursed at the cow. "Damned old kicking bitch! Have a dose of this." He rolled the hot running iron down her hip to begin the drooped E brand. "This is it for today. Soon as she's finished we're headin' in."

"It's not two hours passed mid-day." Reid Stuart protested.

"It's two hours passed mid-day on Katty's birthday. And by God! I'm done." The gunfighter replied. He pressed the hot iron harder than necessary against the tough hide and left a long deep angry red mark for the drooped part of the E.

"Suit yourself." Reid Stuart said. "I think I'll scout along the mouth of our canyon before I come in." He sought solitude, even from the usually quiet gunman. Today he struggled with thoughts and memories that were his and his alone. He welcomed the chance for a long quiet ride.

"Well I'll be damned." The gunman glared at him. "'guess it's up to me to help little Katty have a birthday."

Reid Stuart did not answer.

The gunman tossed the running iron on the ground and picked up his filly's reins. "You can snuff the fire and pick up the irons, then." He said as he stepped up into the saddle. "Stay out of that big canyon by yourself." He warned. "See you at the place." He spurred the filly and loped away.

Reid Stuart let the buckskin pick its way slowly up the trail leading to the dugout. Whoever and whatever the man he called Canada had been or was, Reid Stuart felt no uneasiness in entrusting Katharane's care to him. He sensed that something deep within the gunman, something strong and real, tied him to Katharane, something that maybe not even the gunman understood for certain. Thoughts of Katharane's mother troubled him, and he was quiet and sullen and weary until he heard Katharane's laughter. "Katharane." He murmured. He spurred the buckskin.

The child's laughter rolled off of the edge of the ledge above him. The laughter came to him strong and filled with the gurgling of a baby's fun and excitement, then faded, came again higher pitched at first, then lower, deeper from her throat. With each rise of Katharane's laughter Reid Stuart's spirits rose and he urged the buckskin to quicken its steps up the canyon wall. The buckskin pitched up onto the ledge beneath the lip of the canyon in front of the dugout, where Reid Stuart reined him in and laughed aloud. "You are one hell of a sight." He called to the gunman.

"It's her birthday, ain't it?" The gunman retorted without taking his eyes away from the child.

"Yes, today is August the thirteenth, eighteen sixty-eight, Katharane's second birthday." Reid Stuart said. "But what possessed you to take her swimming?"

The gunman stood in the middle of the large pool. The water rose above his bare white knees. His buckskin shirt's ragged tail hung halfway down his hairy thighs which had not been exposed to the sun in years. He held his straight rimmed black hat by its crown and tried to shade the child's naked pink flesh from the setting August sun as she floated on her back in the cool water. He turned slowly, following the small round belly of the child as she floated around him. "Her and the Squaw Woman were about to smother in the dugout. Kept slippin' out here to the pool to get cool. So I decided to teach her to swim." The gunman explained.

The Squaw Woman adjusted her feet where she squatted in the edge of the water. Her deerskin chamois dress floated up about her waist. And a ripple crossed the pool and raised child's buttocks and the gunman lowered his hat as if to hide the baby's nakedness. "Be still, Squaw." The gunman barked at the Squaw Woman. "And don't you be pissin' in this water. You hear?"

The Squaw Woman grunted.

"Stinkin' Comanche bitch." The gunman cursed her.

"You traded for her." Reid Stuart reminded him. "Besides, what do you think Katharane's doing in the water?"

"Okay for Katty to, but that squaw's got no need to." The gunman argued.

"Well, Canada. There are a few things even you can't control." Reid Stuart laughed.

"Huh! I can always shoot her." The gunman retorted.

Reid Stuart looked at the bloody black grip of the revolver which was buried in the black leather of its holster. Even in the pool the gunman wore the holster about his waist and strapped against his bare leg. "You are certainly a sight, pants off, that damn pistol strapped around your shirt. God knows what's floppin' around under that shirt. Bent over trying to shade a bare butted baby from the sun. No Kiowa or Comanche could sneak up on you, they'd be laughing too hard."

"By God! I'm ready if they do." The gunman answered. He rubbed the butt of his left hand against the grip of the black revolver. "Taught Katty to float in twenty minutes. Smart child, must get it from her mother."

"Must have." Reid Stuart winced. He had thought of Katharane's mother often this day. What thoughts must she have on her daughter's birthday? "I counted another twenty-two head of Longhorns near the mouth of the canyon." He pulled the bridle over the horse's ears and took the bit from its mouth. He hung the bridle across his saddle. The horse lowered its head and sucked water from the pool.

"'half won't make it to next spring, after the winter and the Kiowa get through with 'em." The gunman said.

"So you have told me." Reid Stuart sighed.

"Told you right, too."

"Well, bring Katharane to the dugout. It's late and I want to celebrate my daughter's birthday with her before she goes to sleep."

"Didn't earlier today."

"Maybe not, but I do now."

Katharane squealed. The sound reverberated through the stifling dugout. Despite the heat and Reid Stuart's and the gunman's entreaties for her not to do so, the squaw burned a fire each night. Reid Stuart glanced at the dirt ceiling. "I hope it holds." He murmured.

"It will." The gunman said. "You worry too much, Stuart."

The child hugged the small wooden doll to her chest and squealed again, and laughed, and held the toy out to the Squaw Woman. The woven strands of the filly's tail gave the doll two black pigtails, made to look even blacker by their contrast to the white doe skin shift the gunman had stitched to the doll with the thin strands of buffalo hide he had carefully sliced from one of the old hides with the sharpened tip of his Bowie knife.

"So that is what you have been whittling while we were riding?" Reid Stuart chuckled. "My precious Katharane. I am afraid Daddy has no gift for you on your birthday." He said, morosely.

"Sure he does, Katty." The gunfighter said. It had become his and Reid Stuart's custom to speak to each other through the child, a conversation in third person. He handed a small bundle wrapped in buckskin to Reid Stuart.

"What..."

"Your gift to Katty on her birthday, Stuart. I was plannin' on givin' these to her for Christmas, but now'll do."

"But..."

"I told you we were partners." The gunman cut him off. "Now. Give Katty her birthday present."

Reid Stuart held the package on his lap. "Come Katharane." He held his hands out to his daughter. Katharane ignored him. She stared at the doll on her lap. Her mother had named her Katharane in respect to his mother, and Reid Stuart insisted on calling his child Katharane in respect to her mother, refusing to see her as Katty or to call her by the gunman's nickname for her, even though this was the only name he heard her called. Now, this one time, he relented. "Katty." He said softly. The child raised her head and smiled at her father. Then she stood up from the dirt floor where she sat, held her doll in her left hand and walked to him. Reid Stuart lifted her onto his lap. He untied the buckskin cord which held the wrapping around the gift. A small white doeskin dress, stitched along its sides with a black rawhide cord, lay on the brown buckskin. On top of the dress rested a pair of moccasins made from the same white doeskin. The soles of the moccasins were made from three layers of buffalo hide, and each one had a single draw string of black rawhide.

"Ooh!" Katharane giggled.

"Katty's pretty." Reid Stuart said gently to his daughter. He slid the moccasins onto her dirty bare feet. She laughed. He pulled the stained doeskin shift over her head, exposing her nakedness, and slid the armless white doeskin dress down across her sun pinked shoulders. Katharane stood up on his lap and clapped her hands. Reid Stuart and the gunman laughed. The gunman rose from where he squatted on the heels of his boots and stepped out of the dugout. Reid Stuart set Katharane on the dugout's floor and followed him out of the dugout.

The August sunset was a massive orange mirage above the dark high plains. Its oppressive heat only slightly faded by the darkness.

"Thank you."

"For what?" The gunman asked.

Reid Stuart rolled his smoke and lit it. "For Katharane's gift."

"No need." The gunman said.

Reid Stuart turned his head so the smoke he exhaled would not drift into the gunman's face.

"That smoke'll kill you someday." The gunman said.

Reid Stuart ignored him. "Why did you do that?" He asked.

"Do what?" The gunman tried to ignore Reid Stuart.

"The dress. The moccasins."

"'child needed 'em. She has precious little to wear."

"Yes. She did need them." Reid Stuart agreed. "But why did you have me give them to her? Why did you do that for me?"

"Did I do that for you?" The gunman shifted uneasily.

"Yes." Reid Stuart answered. "I believe you did." He inhaled his smoke, then exhaled it and watched as it rose and floated away into the prairie night.

The gunfighter sighed. "We're partners, aren't we?"

"Yes. We're partners." Reid Stuart said. He put his right hand on the gunman's left shoulder and said. "And friends." The gunman trembled beneath his touch. Katharane's shrill voice cut through the moment and the dusk. The two men turned and looked down into the dugout.

The child pointed her finger at the Squaw Woman and screamed furiously at her, and reached for the doll the squaw held just above her reach. A string of guttural sounds and exclamations flowed out of the child's mouth. She gripped the Squaw Woman's dress with her left hand and reached for the doll with her right hand. Slowly the two men realized that the child was arguing with the squaw in the broken dialect of the squaw's Kwerhar-rehunuh tongue. "My God! Stuart. That stinkin' damn squaw has taught Katty to talk Comanch'."

"We should have known this would happen. We leave

62

Katharane with her everyday. And when we are here we seldom speak to her. All she hears is the Comanche the Squaw Woman speaks to her. What else could she learn to speak?"

"By God! She'll not speak only Comanch'. I'll cut that squaw's tongue out first."

"That is not a rational solution."

The two men stared at the child and the squaw. Suddenly the gunman stepped to the box in which Reid Stuart kept his sextant. He pulled the lid off.

"Take it easy with that!" Reid Stuart protested. "That instrument cannot be replaced this side of the Mississippi." He picked up the lid the gunman had tossed onto the floor and asked him. "What are you looking for anyway?"

"That book I saw in here the other day."

"My Bible."

"Yes. I'm gonna' read from it to Katty every night. So she can learn to speak English." The gunman found the Bible, lifted it out and carried it to the table. He opened the cover. Printed on the inside of the cover was an inscription which read: "May, West Point Academy, 1858. Reid Stuart, My son. Their officer. Wage not war for war's sake. But neither shirk your duty." KRS

"That had to come to be a pretty hard standard for you to live by." The gunman said. "Who's KRS?"

"Katharane Rachel Stuart. My mother." Reid Stuart said quietly.

"'beautiful name."

"She was a beautiful person." Reid Stuart mumbled.

"'know where some of your beauty came from now, my Little Katty girl." The gunman said to the child as he picked her up and set her on his lap. He opened the Bible to Book One, Genesis and began to read in a soft rhythmic tenor. "In the beginning God created heaven and the earth."

The Squaw Woman edged closer. She was fascinated by the sight of a man speaking sounds from a leather pouch.

"Git away. You damn stinkin' heathen squaw." The gun-fighter cursed her.

She stopped. But she did not retreat. She had learned that the gunman yelled at her much more often than he hit her.

"Let her listen. She might learn to speak English, too." Reid Stuart interceded on the squaw's behalf.

"Who the hell wants to talk to her?"

"Katharane does." Reid Stuart said. "So desperately that she is learning to speak her language."

"Shit!" The gunman cursed. But he relented and let the squaw squat on the floor near them. He read verse to verse to verse. Neither Katharane nor the Squaw Woman understood the words, but both sat transfixed by the slow soft music of the gunman's voice. He read until the dying fire quit and darkness made him stop.

The late summer days came and went. Reid Stuart and the gunman spent these days hunting, finding, roping and burning the Escadara drooped E into the wild Longhorns tough hide. The gunman braided one end of each of two ropes together and attached iron rings, which he took from his saddle endangering the strength of its cinch, to form a Honda on each end of the long rope, whereby he could form a loop at either end, dally the middle of the dangerously long rope around his saddlehorn and rope two of the Longhorns on one pass.

One early morning Reid Stuart heard the filly crashing through the brush along a dry draw that emptied from their canyon into the big canyon. He loped his buckskin to the sound. In the draw the gunman had an old Longhorn cow on one end of the long rope and her second summer yearling on the other end, and with the lariat he kept tied to his saddle he had roped this summer's calf of the old cow. Reid Stuart quickly heeled the old cow before she could commit to a charge which would have put the gunman and his black horse in great jeopardy. He smiled at the gunfighter. Three generations of cattle, this meant that the Longhorns were indeed surviving the winters, the Kiowa and the summer heat, surviving and multiplying.

It was hot, endless, bone tiring work. Work that left little energy or time for anything else. Yet each day the weary men rode into the dugout's yard before dark, and they sat on their tired horses, watching the open restless prairie beyond the dugout, and allowed Katharane to run and play above the dugout, where she and the Squaw Woman were sequestered each day. And every night in the fading light of the squaw's cooking fire the gunman would read from Reid Stuart's Bible to the child and the squaw.

Katharane grew. She learned the alphabet from the gun-man and her father. And by the time the late September rains brought their more or less seasonal drenching to the high prairie, she was toilet trained. The gunman's constant surveillance of her at night and his morning cursing of the Squaw Woman, during which he threatened the squaw with countless acts of personal violence if he returned and found the child soiled, had somehow enhanced Katharane's disposition toward tending to her own hygiene. The child rarely forgot to remove herself from the dugout before she relieved herself. And Katharane set an internal clock keyed to her father's and the gunman's daily return. As they approached the trail to the dugout they would hear her chanting the alphabet as she marched down the trail to meet them with the Squaw Woman clucking along behind her. "Pop. Pop. Pop." and "Stuart. Stuart." Katharane would call when she spotted them.

The gunfighter would bend low from his filly, sweep Katharane into his arms and set her on his saddle in front of him. The squaw would protest this daring, and what she perceived to be, dangerous move with grunts and groans, for which the gunman would loudly curse her. And Reid Stuart would follow the strange procession to the dugout, his heart heavy with concern. 'Was his daughter even aware he was her father?' He wondered. He spoke with the gunfighter about his concern that Katharane knew him only as Reid Stuart, not as her father. "I'll be damned if I'm gonna' call you daddy, Stuart." The gunfighter had scoffed. But after that Reid Stuart noticed that each night when the gunfighter lifted Katharane onto his lap to read from the Bible to her he would point at Reid Stuart and say to the child. "Katty's daddy." And one morning Reid Stuart heard the gunman berating the Squaw Woman. "Katty's daddy. Daddy. Father. Do you understand father you damn heathen Comanche bitch? Christ! 'even tryun' to reason with this stinkin' squaw for you Katty. You'll be the death of me."

The rains put an end to the branding. Reid Stuart tallied his entries in his journal that enumerated each branding by date, location, count, sex, age and work done. "We have two hundred and sixty head marked." Reid Stuart said proudly. He smiled and almost forgot the leaking sod roof above them. A stream which began to run down the rear wall of the dugout reminded him how precarious their housing really was.

The next day he began the engineering feat of hauling rock and cedar timbers up out of the canyon to reinforce the dugout's walls and roof. He expertly stacked the flat rocks edge on edge, using a mixture of prairie sod, grass and sand to mortar the rocks together. He rocked the walls of the dugout. Then he built a fireplace and fashioned a rock flue through the sod roof. Katharane and the Squaw Woman watched as hour upon hour he stacked rock upon rock.

The gunfighter seldom helped Reid Stuart with the rock, more often he either dug the mud and moss from the second pool or hunted. And as October stole hours from each day of Reid Stuart's earnest efforts to add permanence to the dugout the gunman returned with more and more deer carcasses for the squaw to skin and butcher, which she did happily.

Just as daylight crept into the cool predawn of the canyon the black filly would fly from a dark stand of cedar into and among the several does grazing in a grassy slough, and the black gun would leave its holster and fire and fire even before lightening quick hooves could carry the does beyond its modest range, and the gunman never missed. Each time at least two does would die. Does' skins dried, draped across the cedar poles which covered each end of the dugout, and the squaw cured strip upon strip of venison.

He stood outside the dugout on the last morning in October and demanded. "Stuart. 'bring that cannon of yours and come with us."

"Well certainly. I'm not doing anything more important than trying to keep the roof above our head from burying us alive." Reid Stuart retorted, as he emerged from the back of the dugout where he was laying rock.

"'ain't gotta' worry about that. It's gonna' be frozen solid.

And sooner than you think. Now come with us." The gunman handed the buckskin's reins to Reid Stuart. He had saddled Reid Stuart's horse for him. The Squaw Woman sat on the mule. Katharane sat on the front of the gunman's saddle.

"May I ask where you are taking us?" Reid Stuart asked, surly.

"Huntin'."

"And you need all of us for that." Reid Stuart said disgustedly.

"Right." The gunman said and spurred the filly down the canyon trail, the mule following and Reid Stuart's buckskin loping behind after Reid Stuart had grabbed the Sharps and a bandoleer of cartridges and swung quickly into the saddle to pursue the gunman.

Two hundred buffalo grazed quietly, their heavy full bellies bending the tall grass as they moved along the edge of the stream in the big canyon.

"How many do you want me to bring down?" Reid Stuart asked the gunman.

"Four. If you can." The gunman whispered.

"Four!"

"Sshsh! Dammitt!"

"What can we possibly do with four buffalo? Two will be more than the mule can pack out for us." Reid Stuart whispered.

"Where there's buffalo this time of year, there's Comanch'." The gunfighter answered softly. "Two for us. Two for trade. 'case we need 'em."

The Sharps boomed. The young cow bowed on her front knees, then she rolled onto her side and lay still. Reid Stuart opened the Sharps' breach, pulled the long hot cartridge out of the chamber, slid in another and closed the breach. A second cow dropped onto her side, dead. Again Reid Stuart reloaded. All four legs collapsed from beneath the third cow he killed.

"Kill a bull this time, Stuart."

Reid Stuart looked up at the gunfighter. "Why? His meat will be tainted by his rut."

"Comanch' like their hides, prestige to have a bull buffalo's hide in your hutch, like that old one." The gunfighter pointed at a massive bull, his coat tarnished almost gray by years in the hot prairie sun and toughened by many months of exposure to the winter's snow and ice.

Reid Stuart aimed four inches behind and a foot beneath the right front shoulder of the great bison. He squeezed the trigger and the belligerent Sharps bucked and kicked against his shoulder. For a moment the old bull seemed perplexed. He swung his great head as if looking for his unseen assailant. Then he snorted, bloody clots blew from his wide nostrils, and he slowly toppled over like a large tree slowly surrendering to the last blow of an axe.

The Squaw Woman led the mule to the first dead buffalo. Katharane waddled beside her.

"What is she doing, taking Katharane that close to those buffalo?" Reid Stuart asked.

"Squaws do the skinnin', guttin' to." The gunman explained. "She knows to get to it."

"There is still several hundred buffalo out there. She shouldn't take Katharane amongst them." Reid Stuart continued his protest.

"'buffalo won't bother 'em. 'just drift off a ways to graze." The gunfighter said. He handed the buckskin's reins to Reid Stuart. "Come on." The gunfighter said. "I ain't anxious for any Comanch' to find us. Bad as I hate to, you and I'll have to skin one of those buffalo for that damn squaw."

Reid Stuart and the gunfighter walked to the old bull. "Well. Let's get to it." The gunfighter said. He knelt on his left knee, jerked his knife from its sheath, stabbed it hilt deep into the tough old bull just below where the bottom of his ribcage came together and shoved it down along his belly. "Christ! I hate that smell." The gunfighter swore. Thick gray layers of bowels and intestines oozed out of the bull's open belly.

Reid Stuart took his knife and raked them out onto the

ground. "Canada?"

"Yes."

"How long do you think it will take us to get the ranch started? Producing?"

"Dunno'." The gunman muttered.

"You don't know or you don't care?" Reid Stuart asked.

"Both." The gunman stared across the open canyon. "If it happens, it happens. If it don't, it don't. That's all."

"That's all!" Reid Stuart snorted. He reached into the open belly of the buffalo and drug more of its innards out. "Don't you ever think about the future? Don't you ever wonder about your life?"

"Life and death are not somethin' to be thought about, Stuart." The gunman said. "Life and death are here and now. Right here and right now." The gunman dropped the loop from the black revolver's hammer.

Reid Stuart stood up and followed the gunman's eyes. The Indians approached in a semi-circle, a dozen of them, the leader in the center, shielded on each side by the forward ends of the half circle formation. They rode slowly. Behind this mounted advance the squaws followed and led the ponies which drug the travois loaded with hides, poles, pottery, every item of their day to day lives. The children ran amongst the squaws and ponies, laughing and playing.

"Kiowa?" Reid Stuart asked, nervously.

"Comanch'." The gunman answered.

"They're riding for Katharane and the Squaw Woman." Reid Stuart said. He picked up his Sharps. The gunman stepped in front of him and ambled slowly forward, which slowed Reid Stuart's quick pace.

The Squaw Woman bent over the dead buffalo and struggled to cut through the thick cartilage below the ribs. She sought the dead cow's heart. Katharane stood beside her. The blood from the first cow's heart had dried on the child's face, streaking it white and pink and brown. She had licked the blood from her fingers before it could dry. She ran her tongue around her lips and watched the Squaw Woman dig into the buffalo with the knife. The riders' shadows crossed the buffalo's corpse, the Squaw Woman and Katharane.

Katharane raised her head and looked up into the Comanche chief's face. She smiled, recognizing Kwanhah, the young Kwerhar-rehunuh chief. She spoke to him in his language and held the necklace away from her chest for him to see. Kwanhah smiled. Katharane poked the Squaw Woman and said. "Mama." The squaw grunted and continued to work with the knife intent on freeing the bloody organ from its sinewy home. Katharane poked harder and said much louder. "Mama." But she received no response. So she screamed at the squaw in the dialect of the Kwerhar-rehunuh. The bucks laughed. The squaw backed away from the buffalo on her elbows and knees, her large butt swaying from side to side. She sat up on her knees. She held the buffalo's heart in her hands. She stared at the bucks, fearful of what they intended for her and the child. Katharane saw the heart and clapped her hands. The bucks crowded around Kwanhah, the squaw and Katharane. The Squaw Woman handed the heart to Katharane and told her to give it to Kwanhah.

Katharane carried the large bloody heart cupped in the palms of her hands. She walked around the rump of the buffalo, beneath the heads of several of the bucks' horses and to Kwanhah's horse. She stood there, holding the hot heavy heart in her hands and stared up at the chief.

The half-white Comanche looked down at the child. She wore a doe skin smock that hung from her shoulders to her knees. The necklace was tied around her neck. Blood dripped from the heart, staining her smock and her moccasins. Kwanhah shifted his heavy war lance from his right hand to his left hand. He bent down to Katharane, put his hand beneath her butt, gripped the back of her right thigh and lifted her onto his horse. He took the buffalo heart from Katharane, bit a chunk from it, then he handed the heart to the brave nearest to him.

The brave tore a piece from the heart and passed the tattered organ to the next brave. And so the heart was shared among the Comanche. The blood from the large chunk Kwanhah held in his mouth filled Kwanhah's mouth. He swallowed it. He bit through the tough muscle. He took the smaller piece from his mouth and held it in front of Katharine. She opened her mouth and pushed her face toward it. For a moment Katharane waited, then he dropped the piece into her mouth. Katharane chewed it quietly.

The gunfighter approached Kwanhah's horse slowly. He raised his right hand to the chief. Kwanhah gripped the gunman's wrist. The gunfighter's left hand never left the butt of the black revolver. Kwanhah slid his left hand up the shaft of his lance. The gunfighter pointed at the cow beside the Squaw Woman and then the old bull. "Katty. Tell Kwanhah, chief of the Kwerhar-rehunuh, they are his." The gunfighter said.

Katharane bent her head back until she could look up into Kwanhah's face and said in his dialect. "They are yours."

Kwanhah nodded and motioned for the squaws to begin the butchering. They rushed to the fallen buffaloes. Excited yelps drew the group's attention away from the butchering. Three younger bucks had separated a cow from the herd. Two of the Comanche hazed the cow farther and farther from the herd. The third Comanche, who rode a lank hairy pony and carried a long lance without feathers, moved in upon the tiring cow. Kwanhah trotted his horse toward the chase. The third Comanche urged his pony alongside of and against the cow. The cow yielded to this pressure and swerved toward the hazers. Balanced by the lumbering cow's weight the third buck's inexperienced pony stumbled as the buffalo separated itself from its attacker. The buck, lance raised to strike down into the cow, in turn lost his balance and his seat on the running horse. In a desperate effort to save himself from the embarrassment and shock of falling from his horse, the buck dropped his lance, clutched at his pony's mane, missed and sailed across the stumbling horse's shoulder, throwing up dust as he burrowed face first through the thick grass and into the hard sod beneath it. He stood up. He was not seriously injured, but he was savagely shamed by losing his lance and his mount.

The other Comanche laughed and shouted derision at the fallen buck. To Reid Stuart's and the gunfighter's stunned surprise, and the Squaw Woman's dismay for she wailed and worked her bloody hands as if trying to reach out across the prairie and pluck Katharane from where she now rode before the enraged Comanche chief, who shamed by his warrior's shortcomings, forced his charging war horse to close with the wearied cow.

Kwanhah's single braid of dark hair streamed behind his head. Katharane leaned forward and rode the running horse with her hands, gripping its mane the way the gunman had taught her. Her auburn hair, streaked and highlighted by the sun, flew about her face. Kwanhah's horse's lithe body stretched to its fullest length as it gathered the prairie beneath it and gained swiftly on the buffalo. Kwanhah rode upright. He held the braided hair hackamore in his left hand, his long feathered war lance in his right. Katharane leaned forward and clung to the horse's mane. Kwanhah moved his horse up to the buffalo's right flank. He dropped the hackamore across the horse's neck. He pressed his right knee against the horse's ribs and eased him against the running buffalo. The cow's hot sweaty rough hide chafed against Kwanhah's naked left leg. The Comanche ignored the pain, raised his lance and gripped it with both hands. Against the waves of brown autumn buffalo grass and the marbled white streaked Indian summer sky the powerful burnt tawny skin of the great Comanche chief shimmered above the glistening sweat splattered black back of his horse. He raised his lance high above Katharane's bent form like a great angry scythe. Reid Stuart's stomach swam with fear. The gunfighter nervously gripped and released the black revolver. The Squaw Woman wailed louder. Kwanhah drove the lance between the buffalo's third and fourth ribs. Blue black blood shot up the lance's shaft. Kwanhah urged his warhorse against the buffalo's shoulder, raised his left foot and slammed it against the staggering beast's shoulder as he jerked his lance free of its ruptured rib cage. The exhausted cow stumbled and collapsed.

To his warriors it appeared that their young chief had kicked the fatally wounded buffalo off of its feet. They screamed with wild delight. Some even wept with pride. They lashed their ponies and rode to the fallen cow ahead of the squaws, children, Reid Stuart, the gunfighter and the Squaw Woman who also ran towards Kwanhah, his fallen prize and Katharane.

The younger squaw's gutted Kwanhah's buffalo. Two of the older squaw's carefully skinned it. After this was done, each organ of the buffalo was removed. The butchering continued until only its skeleton remained. In turn the old bull and the cow which the gunfighter had given to Kwanhah were also gutted, skinned and butchered.

Katharane played with the younger Comanche children. She was a prize for them as she had ridden with Kwanhah during the killing of the buffalo. They marveled at her deep bronze skin, and to see it they would dart in upon her from behind and lift her smock high above her waist. Katharane would giggle and laugh and chase them.

The gunfighter warned Reid Stuart that he should not assist the squaws in butchering the buffalo as the bucks would not approve and it could provoke a confrontation with them. The bucks built a large bonfire from cedar, dried buffalo chips and a dead cottonwood they found along the stream. As night came a celebration began and continued long into the night. An old gray haired toothless woman told a story of Kwanhah's great kill in rich animated tones. For her story she was rewarded with regurgitated buffalo meat given her, at Kwanhah's insistence, by two of the younger squaws. The bucks danced or squatted and ate the buffalo meat. When Kwanhah finally left the fire two of the youngest squaws followed him.

Reid Stuart looked about for his daughter. "Where's Katharane?" He asked the gunman. "She was with the Squaw Woman when I saw her last."

"'squaw and her sister have her." The gunfighter answered. He pointed at a small teepee at the edge of the encampment. "'let's you and I throw our saddles on the other side of it. We can sleep there."

Reid Stuart dropped his saddle next to the gunfighter's. He sat down on the heels of his boots and pulled a long stem of grass from a clump that had not been trampled and chewed on it. "The grass along that stream was waist high. Did you notice that?" He asked the gunman. "Does the grass always grow like that in this canyon?"

"'best as I can tell, it does." The gunman answered. "'buffalo can't even eat it all. And they come by the thousands."

"But do they come every year? And do they graze the same range each year?"

The gunfighter shrugged his shoulders and said. "'dunno'."

"And the buffalo, they don't stay year round, do they?"

"Nope. They come in the fall and leave in the spring after the big winter blows have left the plains. You can bet the worst of the winter storms are done when you see the buffalo leavin' the canyon and movin' back out to the plains."

"That's what worries me. How will this land hold up to year round grazing by large herds of cattle?"

"Shit, Stuart. You oughta' be worryin' if we're gonna' ride out of here alive in the mornin' instead of how many cattle this canyon can graze. We got a hell of a long ways to go before we have enough cattle to worry 'bout what they got to eat." The gunfighter laughed.

"I guess you're right." Reid Stuart said. He inhaled smoke from his smoke, which he had rolled while they talked. "But I have a need to believe that the canyon and the plains that we claim as the Escadara can support grazing stock for many many years. I need to believe that, Canada."

"Why?"

"To give me a sense of purpose to my life." Reid Stuart said. He nursed the cigarette he held between his lips. "And to Katharane's."

"Katty has a purpose in just bein' Katty." The gunfighter said. "That's purpose enough."

"Is it?"

"Yes. It is."

Reid Stuart smoked his cigarette and watched the gunman stretch out against his saddle. "Canada?"

"Yes."

"I brought Katharane here to make a life that would be our's, mine and her's."

The gunman looked up at Reid Stuart. "How so?" He asked.

"I came here. I brought Katharane here." Reid Stuart sighed, and struggled to explain. "To a place where I could build something that would be her's, Katharane's. Something no one could take away from her."

"'reckon it'll be yours to leave to Katty since they ain't no one else here, and damn few willin' to do what it'd take to take it away from ya'." The gunfighter said. "But that's about all you've got."

"That is a lot." Reid Stuart said. "A very lot." He took the smoke from his lips. "Katharane's mother." He looked into the gunman's gray eyes. "I loved her so much. I thought I could gain acceptance for her. I thought if I loved her enough. But that night, that night when she said she was leaving me, taking Katharane and leaving me because I could not gain that acceptance for her, make her more than..." Reid Stuart swallowed. "I thought she loved me, I wanted her to love me enough to..." He wet his blistered lips. "But I saw it in her eyes...I saw. Hell! I don't know what I'm trying to say. What does it matter? I'm here. And I've brought Katharane here. What difference does that one moment make?" He crushed the fire from his smoke.

"It matters everything." The gunman said. Reid Stuart looked down at him again. The gray eyes were deep, bottomless, as the gunman spoke to the empty dark sky above Reid Stuart. "Because in that moment you were faceless to her. And you knew it. At that one moment. That one damnable moment. You suddenly knew she no longer saw herself in your eyes. And you could no longer see your face in her eyes. You didn't exist there anymore. So you did not exist. That is why you came here."

Reid Stuart secured the soggy graying buffalo rumps to the mule's pack. He tied a heavy still bloody buffalo hide across the wet meat. The gunman, the Squaw Woman and Katharane stood in front of the black filly and the buckskin. Kwanhah and four braves stood across from them. The silence was intense. Reid Stuart felt the skin on his forearms crawl. He stepped next to the gunman and softly asked. "What is happening?"

"Kwanhah's decidin' if he let's us leave with Katty or not." The gunman answered and dropped the leather guard from the hammer of his black revolver.

The Comanche's chief eyes danced across Katharane's upturned face. "Sister." He said in English. "Child of the canyon."

He said in his Kwerhar-rehunuh dialect. He raised his head and his eyes dueled with the dead gray eyes of the gunfighter. Slowly he extended his right arm.

The gunfighter gripped it as he had that April day in the far canyon. Then he bent down and picked Katharane up. "Get that damn squaw on that mule and get mounted, Stuart. We gotta' go, now!"

Reid Stuart boosted the Squaw Woman onto the mule. He swung up onto his buckskin. The gunfighter led them out of the Comanche camp. Kwanhah watched them as they disappeared into the tall grass.

"Is there a reason we're riding away from home?" Reid Stuart asked.

"Yes." The gunfighter answered. "'case Kwanhah changes his mind, we don't wanta' leave 'em too easy a trail back to the dugout."

"Does it ever get any easier?" Reid Stuart asked, almost to himself.

"'fact is, Stuart." The gunman answered. "It's fixin' to get harder. A lot harder."

Two weeks later winter came to the high plains, immediate and intense. An arctic wind wailed across the dugout and turned the drying buffalo hides which were stretched across the cedar poles into a permafrost ceiling.

The high plains winter drug on. The cold numbed the mind and tired the soul. Days meant nothing. Time was counted in the number of cedar stumps burnt and after the last of the stumps were consumed the number of buffalo chips which remained. And it seemed an endless procession of northern winds whipped down upon the dugout from the frozen plains.

Finally, on another of the changeless gloomy cold mornings, Reid Stuart asked. "How long can it last?"

"If we're lucky we'll catch a break in March." The gunman answered.

"When is March?" Reid Stuart asked. The months had escaped him.

"'day's February 20, 1869. My birthday." The gunfighter replied. "March is the next month to come, even on these plains."

"How have you kept track of the date?" Reid Stuart asked.

"'been markin' the days in your Bible. 'read to Katty every day. 'mark that day."

Reid Stuart sighed. "I had forgotten to do that in my journal."

"I know. 'plains' winter can work on a man if you ain't used to it." The gunfighter said. "And you ain't." He added.

"It can work on anything." Reid Stuart said. "I wonder if they'll be any cattle left come spring."

"Some. There'll be some, Stuart." The gunfighter assured him. "Them Longhorns are holed up on the canyons, ridin' out these blows.' come Spring they'll be back out grazin'. You can bet on it." He noticed the tired worn glaze in Reid Stuart's eyes. "And it's a good bet, too." He smiled and encouraged his partner. "We'll win this one."

Reid Stuart's cracked lips parted in a smile. He put his hand on the gunfighter's shoulder and said. "Good. Happy birthday, Canada. How hold are you?"

The gunman frowned. He thought for several minutes, then he said. "'born in '40. That'd make me twenty-nine. Twenty-nine years old today."

The high plains winter broke near the middle of March. A wet norther blew in and dumped four inches of snow on the dugout. When the sun appeared two days later and melted the snow, it was back to reclaim the plains for seven months.

As the gunman shoved a box of the cartridges he had reloaded during the winter into his bedroll, Reid Stuart laid strips of the venison jerky on a buffalo hide. "How much of this jerky do you want me to pack?" He asked the gunman.

"Enough to last the four of us a week." The gunman answered.

"Where are we going?"

"River of the Tongues."

"And we can get our supplies there?"

"Yep."

"Without getting ourselves killed?"

"'more'n likely." The gunman stood up. "Comancheros will be meetin' there with the three tribes before the spring break out onto the plains. 'truce is enforced during the meetin'. There will be everything we need there."

"Are you certain they will trade with us?" Reid Stuart asked. He lifted the heavy pack from the floor.

"'Comancheros will trade with anybody."

"And the Indians will let us trade with them?"

"They'll let us." The gunman patted his black pistol.

Farther and farther down the shallow narrow river they rode, until their canyon fell from Reid Stuart's sight as he glanced back over his shoulder. He had noticed that everything on the plains, no matter how large or small, seemed to either rise up to him if he was approaching it or settle back into the plains if he was moving away. Their canyon settled back into the plains and was lost to him.

The gunfighter forced the milk cow into the stream, the five Longhorn yearlings followed her, and the gunfighter, leading his string of Mustangs, fell back along the small herd's right flank. "'drift out into the stream." He called back to Katharane, and smiled, as the child, only past her second birthday and already riding alone, reined her paint pony to the stream and scolded it for its delay in responding to her. "You too, Stuart." The gunfighter called back to Reid Stuart. "We're gettin' close to the prairie dogs. 'break a horse's leg if you drift into one of their towns."

Reid Stuart led the mule with the Squaw Woman and three of the Kiowa ponies into the stream. "Does this stream have a name?" He asked the gunfighter.

"Comanch' call it the Prairie Dog Town River." The gunfighter answered. "And there's why." He pointed ahead at the river's right bank. Sunlight bounced off the top knots of a thousand small furry heads that flashed in and out of as many burrows. "Prairie dogs, Stuart."

"There must be hundreds of them." Reid Stuart exclaimed.

"Thousands, Stuart, thousands. Prairie dogs are the only creature on the plains that outnumber the buffalo. Some of these towns go on for miles. Below the River of Tongues." The gunfighter pointed ahead of them to the south southwest. "They say there is one town that covers an area ten miles wide and twenty miles long."

"That's impossible." Reid Stuart said. But the prairie dog town to his right extended along the shallow stream which the gunfighter called a river until distance made it disappear from sight.

"Not the way they say." The gunman argued.

They rode on. They watched the prairie dogs dart into their holes, their tails more numerous than the stars above the plains at night, and then pop their heads out and chatter at the riders as they passed. Katharane giggled when they chattered and waved her hand at them. At the movement of her hand most withdrew into their holes, a few sat up on their hind legs and clattered loudly.

The gunfighter dropped back alongside Katharane. "Want me to sing you a song, Pretty Katty?" He asked.

"Me do, Pop. Me do." Katharane said.

"Frog went a-courtin', he did ride. A sword and pistol by his side." The gunman's voice was soft and smooth, and he managed to carry a ragged tune. "Kemo, kimo, there oh where oh. Me come a ho, come a ho. Come a rummy diddle, pully widdle nip cat catch a bug. Sing song Polly catch a kimeo."

Katharane laughed and clapped her hands.

"He rode till he came to the mouse's door.Said he, "Miss Mouse, are you within?" Kemo, kimo, there oh where oh. Me come a ho come a ho. Come a rummy diddle, pully widdle nip cat catch a bug. Sing song Polly catch a kimeo."

Katharane mouthed the words and mimicked the gun-man's tune.

"He took the mouse upon his knee. Says he, "My dear, will you marry me?" Kemo, kimo, there oh where oh. Me come a ho come a ho. Come a rummy diddle, pully widdle nip cat catch a bug. Sing song Polly catch a kimeo. "I must first ask Mr. Rat's consent. Or else I could not live content." Kemo, kimo, there oh where oh. Me come a ho come a ho. Come a rummy diddle, pully widdle nip cat catch a bug. Sing song Polly catch a kimeo. Old Mr. Rat laughed and shook his fat sides. To think Miss Mouse would be a bride."

Katharane drowned out the chorus with her laughter. "Mr. Rat!" She cried.

"Oh, where will the wedding supper be? Down in the meadow by a white oak tree."

"Meadow." Katharane sang.

"Oh, what will the weddin' supper be? Two black beans and a bumblebee."

"Black bean and bumblebee." Katharane sang.

"Old Mr. Rat began to sing. The old cat and kitttens came a tumblin' in."

The gunfighter began to hum another tune. Slowly, Reid Stuart realized it was the same tune he had heard his Confederate prisoners sing. He rode on silently.

The sun rose over their third campsite since leaving the dugout. Reid Stuart and the gunfighter sat on their horses on a long rolling rise and watched hundreds of buffalo march across the undulating grasslands. Like a great army going to battle some unseen foe, they marched slowly, but surely, driven on by officers and wills unseen and unknown.

"'buffalo are movin'." The gunfighter said. "Winter's done for sure."

"Where do they go?" Reid Stuart asked.

"North. Back up across the Canadian. The ones that don't bog in its quicksand. From there on, just on. 'followin' the melt. I guess." The gunfighter answered.

"All of them?"

"No. 'good number stay. But the big herds move out."

That afternoon the gunman and Reid Stuart again sat on their horses on a ridge ahead of Katharane, the Squaw Woman and their small caravan of animals. The gunman pointed at a large clearing shaded by tall cottonwood trees which grew from the sandy bank of a muddy red stream and the thirty odd tepees which occupied it. Across the stream from the tepees and the cottonwoods were three large heavy wagons. Some forty mules grazed on an island formed by the stream and one of its vagrant channels which circled the plot of land where the mules were hobbled. A half dozen men, wearing broad straw hats, sandals, burlap pants and rough hide shirts, moved about the wagons. Around the tepees children played amidst scrawny half-starved dogs. Women worked over open fires or squatted on the shady side of a tepee and talked excitedly to each other. A large group of bucks squatted under a group of cottonwoods.

"Kiowa." Reid Stuart almost whispered the word.

"Kiowa." The gunman repeated. He pointed at tepees further north and west of the first group. "And Comanch'." He said and pointed at the wagons. "Comancheros, Mexican traders. And Tafoya is with them." He pointed at a man nearest one of the wagons. Reid Stuart could not recognize the trader, but he trusted the gunman that it was him. The gunman looked at him and smiled. "This is the River of the Tongues. 'Indians make good sense with the names they give to a place. And with the way they do business. Let's go and do some tradin', Stuart."

"Are you insane? If those Kiowas know what we did to that group at the mouth of our canyon, they will not be happy to see us." Reid Stuart said.

"Damn right they know. And they'd sweat blood for a chance to lift our scalps. But that's sanctuary down there. Sanctuary." The gunman repeated. "Ain't no killin' tolerated durin' the meetin' at the place of the Tongues." The gunman looked up and down the stream. "Let's swing around to the north and come in from down river. That'll take us into Kwanhah's camp. 'what you say, Stuart?"

"I say this is insane." Reid Stuart argued. But he followed the gunman back to Katharane and the Squaw Woman.

The gunfighter slid the necklace which Kwanhah had

given Katharane over her head. "Precious one." He said to Katharane and bent down from his filly to where his face was close to her's. "You wear this and don't take it off until I tell you to. Okay?"

"Okay, Pop." Katharane said and returned his smile.

The gunfighter lead his group into the Comanche camp. The Comanche children recognized Katharane. They ran to her paint pony, unafraid of the two men who drove the Longhorns and lead horses into their camp. Kwanhah watched the gunman and Reid Stuart drive the Longhorns into the small pen the Comancheros had constructed on the brush island. The Mexican Comancheros roped the Longhorns, strung them out and staked them down.

"Are they going to butcher them here?" Reid Stuart asked.

"No." The gunfighter answered. "They'll leave 'em tied down for a day or two to take the fight out of them. Then they'll loose hobble 'em to make 'em easier to trail with their caravan." He handed the lead rope of the Kiowa ponies and his Mustangs to Reid Stuart, and said. "'hobble these horses at those cottonwoods that stood at the edge of the Comanch' camp. We'll camp with Kwanhah. 'do the barterin' with those theivin' damn Comancheros in the mornin'."

The Squaw Woman took Katharane and found the squaw's sister's tepee. Reid Stuart joined the gunfighter at the edge of the Comanche camp. He heard raised voices coming from the Comanche camp. "What is happening?" He asked the gunman.

"Kiowa." The gunfighter said. He nodded at the four men standing in front of Kwanhah and his two warriors. "Arguin' with Kwanhah that those ponies we brought in are their's."

"What should we do?"

"We make camp."

Reid Stuart frowned.

"Kwanhah'd come nearer given those Kiowas' the lance than he would giving them horses. He hates Kiowa." The gunfighter explained.

"Does he like us?" Reid Stuart asked.

The gunfighter shrugged. "'dunno'. Maybe." He answered. "But he worships Katty. We're safe with these Comanch' as long as Katty's with us."

Reid Stuart sighed. Again, his well being rested upon his young daughter's hold upon another wild and savage man.

The next morning the gunfighter and Reid Stuart sought out Tafoya.

"Well, senor. I see that you found him and that you are still alive. I congratulate you." Tafoya said to Reid Stuart. "And the child? The baby?" The old trader eased a step closer to Reid Stuart and away from the cold hard stare of the gunman.

Reid Stuart pointed at Katharane who stood next to the Squaw Woman and the squaw's sister.

"You have traded her to Kwanhah?" He asked, astonished.

The black loop fell away, the first click of the black gun's hammer being cocked made Tafoya audibly catch his breath. "'not to that heathen, nor any other. And that's the last time you speak of her and live." He snarled at the old Mexican.

"Si', Si'. My friend." Tafoya stammered. "I mean no disrespect when I inquire of the child."

"'know damn well what you mean. You damn child swappin' thief." The gunman cursed Tafoya, and moved very close. "And make no mistake. River of Tongues, meetin', sanctuary makes not a damn to me. You so much as cast an eye to Katty and I will blow your right eye out the back of your head."

"Si', Si'. Forgive an old fool, my friend." Tafoya pleaded with the gunman. He believed the gunman intended to kill him on the spot. "There is no need to waste your bullet on such an old usurper. I will die soon enough. Please, my friend." He held his hands out, palms up to the gunman.

"'can't be soon enough for me." The gunman warned. "And I ain't your damn friend." But he eased the hammer back to safe and dropped the black loop across it.

"Your needs?" Tafoya turned to Reid Stuart, grateful to be released from the gunman's cold stare.

"Cartridges. Salt. Tools." The gunman said.

Tafoya raised his eyes at 'tools', but said nothing.

"Coffee. Tobacco. And that young roan mule." Reid Stuart said, and pointed at a young red colored mule that stood next to one of the wagons.

"One of my mules?" Tafoya said with the feigned anguish of an experienced trader.

"That mule." The gunman said, and pointed at the same mule.

Tafoya watched the gunman's hand massage the butt of the black pistol and weighed that his chance of gain by further negotiation was nil. "As you wish." He said. "And in return?" He asked.

"You get to keep suckin' air." The gunman growled. "'steers, horses. Your gettin' the best of it. Ain't ya'?" He moved his thumb against the black loop.

"Si', Si'." Tafoya immediately relented. "Miguel will portion your goods." He said and smiled at the gunman. "I trust you will be reasonable in the portions?"

The gunman stared silently at him as Tafoya's Miguel helped Reid Stuart carry the barter back to his and the gunman's camp. A teenage Mexican boy led the roan mule to the camp. Reid Stuart returned to Tafoya's wagons where the gunman waited.

"You understand you cannot leave until tomorrow." Tafoya said, placing his hand on Reid Stuart's shoulder.

"Why not? We have finished our business here." Reid Stuart said. He was anxious to have the gunman away from Tafoya. The cold, cold anger still boiled in his eyes.

"The meeting. It is not over until tomorrow. Everyone is safe. Here. During the meeting. But once you leave?" Tafoya squeezed Reid Stuart's shoulder. "The Kiowa. They say you stole those ponies from them." He crossed himself. "And marked their dead."

"We understand." The gunfighter muttered. "And maybe while we're ridin' clear, those Kiowa will be waitin' for you and their ponies."

"May be." Tafoya said. "But it is the markings that anger them the most. They can steal more horses." He smiled and walked away.

Reid Stuart turned to the gunman. "What provoked that?" He demanded.

"What?"

"That confrontation with Tafoya." Reid Stuart demanded. "He asks about Katharane, and you are ready to kill him."

The gunfighter stared into Reid Stuart's eyes, the anger still hot in the gunman's eyes. "That." He snarled, and gestured at one of Tafoya's other wagons. In it three young girls sat, their hands bound to each other's hands, their eyes dull and lifeless.

"Oh God!" Reid Stuart cried. "They are white children."

"They are that." The gunman agreed. "And they are barter for that damn stinkin' Mescan. 'barter from them Kiowa dogs." He gritted his teeth in his fury, his hatred of the Kiowa and Tafoya.

"But he can't..."

"He can. And he does." The gunfighter cut Reid Stuart off. "And if you ask him, he will smile and tell you, 'Yes, senor. I have traded for them to spare them the life of a Kiowa slave. Would you have me leave them to their captors?' Tell you that he is takin' 'em to the canon de rescate to return them to their families. And if he is, its to sell them back. 'most likely he's figurin' his gain when he gets them to Santa Fe to trade to the white slavers." The gunfighter spit.

"We have to stop this!" Reid Stuart said.

"We can't."

Reid Stuart stared at the gunman. His anguish and his disbelief rising with his voice. "You were ready to break the truce, kill Tafoya for just looking at Katharane. But you will let him take these children?" He looked at the pitiful captives.

"They're not my concern. Katty is." The gunman said. He looked deep into Reid Stuart's eyes and said. "God does not exist along the River of Tongues, Stuart. I exist. And this." He patted the black revolver. "And with it I can and I will decide who else exists here. I decide you and I and Katty." He said firmly. Then he turned and walked away.

When Reid Stuart returned to their camp the gunman held the Sharps. "'good bet Kwanhah would back us if I killed Tafoya for Katty. He won't if we go gunnin' for those captives."

"Because he trades white captives, also?" Reid Stuart asked.

"'never known Kwanhah to deal in 'em." The gunfighter answered. "'maybe because his mother was white. 'maybe because Comanch' are better than those skull suckin' Kiowa and Tafoya. I don't know. But I do know I can't let you go after those girls. You'll get yourself and them killed. It is a hard thing. But we must leave it be."

Reid Stuart studied the gunman. "There are some things a man cannot live with?"

"Only one thing out here." The gunman retorted. He nodded at Katharane.

Katharane and the Comanche children played in the dry river bed above the Comanche camp and beneath the Kiowa camp. Some of the Kiowa children joined them. They pointed at Katharane's necklace. The story of her necklace had made its way to the Kiowa camp and there was much interest in the dark skinned little girl that wore a necklace given to her by the Comanche, Kwanhah Parker.

Among the Kiowa ponies there was a small white mustang. Katharane spotted the unusual little horse. She moved close to the spirited little horse. The mustang shook its head. Katharane calmly reached up to its nose. The mustang dropped its nose down to her. She rubbed the top of its nose.

The Kiowa's knee jarred against the mustang's long jaw and the horse jerked its head away from the child's hand. Katharane backed away from the Kiowa. Three other braves joined him. Katharane backed out into the dry river bed. The Kiowa braves followed her. The first brave led the white mustang by a short braided rope which he held clamped around the horse's neck.

The Comanche children ran for their camp. The smaller children were crying. Comanche women quickly appeared to quiet the children. Kwanhah and two bucks walked toward the Kiowa camp. Reid Stuart and the gunfighter rose from where they were tying their bartered items onto the mule's pack. "What is happening?" Reid Stuart asked.

"'dunno'." The gunfighter answered. Then he cursed. "Shit." He began to walk quickly through the Comanche camp.

"What is it?" Reid Stuart asked, again, as he followed the gunman.

The Comanche women and children moved slowly in the direction of their chief. The other braves, the gunfighter and Reid Stuart pushed passed them.

"Katty." The gunfighter finally answered Reid Stuart's questions. He pointed at the Squaw Woman whose heavy hips twisted back and forth as she trotted ahead calling the child's Christian name in her haggard English. "Kath-ran. Kath-ran. Come." She ignored her sister's entreaties to stop and not to go closer to the men or the Kiowa. The gunfighter and Reid Stuart caught up with the Squaw Woman as she reached Kwanhah and his two braves.

Katharane gazed at the white mustang. The horse pointed its ears. She laughed. The Kiowa shook the braided hair rope by which he held the mustang and pointed at the rawhide necklace which Katharane wore. She frowned. The buck reached for the necklace with his left hand and with his right he offered the rope by which he held the white mustang.

"No. Mine." Katharane said.

Again the buck offered the white mustang in trade for the necklace. "No." Katharane whimpered. "Mine." She clutched her necklace with her right hand and said again. "No. Mine." She stared at her moccasins.

The buck stroked the white mustang's neck and spoke to the horse. The mustang lifted its ears again and Katharane giggled again. The buck offered the hair rope to her. She reached for it with her left hand, still clutching her necklace against her chest with her right hand. The buck drew the rope away and pointed at the necklace. "No." Katharane shook her head. "Mine."

"Stinkin' dog eatin' Kiowa. Teasin' her like that." The gunfighter swore.

The Kiowa braves formed behind the buck with the white mustang. The Comanche moved up behind Katharane. A shadow passed above her. She looked up into the face of Kwanhah, the young war chief of the Kwerhar-rehunuh Comanche. "No. Mine." She repeated to him. She sagged against his heavy thigh and put her left arm around it and rubbed her forehead against the rough skin and repeated again. "Mine. Mine." Then she stepped in between Kwanhah's powerful legs, pointed her left forefinger at the Kiowa buck and screamed. "No! No! Mine!"

The Kiowa buck was furious. Not only had the child rejected a prize trade, she had screamed an abuse at him as best as he could know from her tone and the sight of her tiny finger wiggling threateningly at him from beneath the heavy thighs of the Comanche chief. He screamed a curse at Katharane. She screamed back.

The gunman dropped the loop from the black revolver's hammer. Reid Stuart cocked the Sharps. Kwanhah looked down at the child. "Mine." She continued to argue, looking up into the Comanche's eyes. He smiled brightly at her. Then he raised his eyes and there was no smile nor even the hope that any had ever existed on the dark and angry features of the warrior. He gestured to one of his braves and barked an order. The brave vanished and returned with two of Kwanhah's own war ponies and carrying Kwanhah's shield and lance. He brought these to his chief. Kwanhah pointed at the white mustang then at his two war horses. The Kiowa hesitated. Kwanhah pointed again at the white mustang and his two ponies. And then he pointed at his shield and lance. The women grabbed the children and fled. The Comanche bucks pressed closer upon Kwanhah and Katharane, careful not to touch nor disturb either one.

Reid Stuart glanced at the ashen faced gunfighter. "What?" He asked.

"Trade or fight. We gotta' get Katty outta' there." The gunman said.

"How?"

88

"I don't know."

Slowly the fight passed from the Kiowa buck's eyes. The mischief of taunting a child was now the reality of impending combat with a superior foe. He would be embarrassed but not shamed by the trade. Two of Kwanhah's own war ponies for one small white mustang under any other circumstances would be considered a major coup. Now it would be seen as a dignified escape from death. He handed the braid rope to Kwanhah, took the rawhide lead from the Comanche buck and skulked away with the two ponies.

The roan mule which Reid Stuart had traded for resisted the pack. Reid Stuart balanced the heavy pack on the mule with his left hand and drew the cinch tight underneath the mule's belly with his right. He lead the roan mule to the mule on which the Squaw Woman sat and tied its lead to the Squaw Woman's mule. He walked to the buckskin and mounted and took up the Squaw Woman's mule's lead and moved up to the gunfighter and his black filly. "The Kiowas left early?" Reid Stuart asked.

"Yep. The murderin' theiven' devils moved out ahead of us so they could waylay us." The gunfighter answered.

"That is what I was afraid of." Reid Stuart said. "Where is Katharane?"

"Up there." The gunfighter nodded. "'ridin' next to our escort outta' here."

Katharane sat on the small white mustang next to Kwanhah.

"We'll fall in with Kwanhah. They're headin' back to the big canyon. 'be quite a surprise for them Kiowa dogs, won't it?" The gunfighter smiled.

Reid Stuart chuckled. "I wonder how many times a Kiowa raiding party has been foiled by a two year old?"

MARKING THE ESCADARA RANGE
SPRING, 1869-SUMMER, 1873

Reid Stuart bent over, wrapped his long fingers around the bottom of the heavy stone pillar and slid it toward the spring. He repeated the maneuver four more times, straightened up and put his hands on his hips. The pillar was five inches by five inches and almost forty inches long. He had rough hewn it and five others from the exposed rock at the mouth of their canyon. With the mules he had drug the pillars up their canyon, then using ropes, both mules and his and the gunman's strength had hoisted them up to the pools, and the mules had drug them to the mouth of the dugout, where, during the evenings while the gunfighter read to Katharane and the Squaw Woman, he had smoothed and shaped them.

"'gonna' break your back doin' that." The gunfighter said. He sat on his black filly.

"Are you offering to help?" Reid Stuart asked from where he bent over the marker.

"'no sense in both of us gettin' the sore back just because one of us has some damn crazy idea of stickin' up markers ever' damn place."

Reid Stuart straightened up and said. "These markers are the most important thing we are doing right now to establish this ranch."

"Sure, Stu'. 'keep tellin' yourself that and maybe your back won't hurt quite so much tonight." The gunfighter said, as he watched Katharane climb from the dugout and skip to her father and him. "Meanwhile I'm gonna' do some reconnoitering' down the canyon a ways. 'see if anything or anybody is tryun' to visit us."

"Me go, Pop. Me go." Katharane begged. She danced around the filly and held her hands up to the gunman.

The gunfighter looked at Reid Stuart.

"Tell your moth..." Reid Stuart stopped." Tell the Squaw Woman you are going with Canada."

Katharane ran to the dugout calling to the Squaw Woman. "Mama. Mama."

"I am surprised you bothered to ask." Reid Stuart said.

"'don't remember hearin' my voice. Do you?" The gunman retorted.

"Me go with Pop." Katharane's voice echoed in the dark dugout. The Squaw Woman grunted an unintelligible response. "Uh-huh." Katharane replied. She ran from the dugout to the black filly. The gunman bent down and lifted her onto his saddle.

"We're not goin' long or far." He said to Reid Stuart and rode away.

The black filly soft footed its way down the trail from the pools. Katharane rode on the slick worn leather of the saddle in front of the gunman. Her eyes took each step the filly took. She saw a doe with her first fawn and grunted as they stepped into the scrub cedar and vanished. She laughed and clapped at a young Tom turkey in strut. The canyon was filled with life. Green grass grew through the tawny folded layers of last year's residue. The cedar was fragrant and in bud. The gunman slapped the filly for reaching for one of the tempting cedar buds. "'git the swollen belly doin' that." He warned.

"No." Katharane scolded the horse, too.

The gunfighter smiled. The child mimicked him. She imitated his actions with a strained precision of movement and voice. Katharane pointed at a gray streak of hair that flashed along the canyon wall. The gunfighter drew his pistol. But the wolf was gone. He reined the filly to the spot where the wolf had been. A newborn calf lay with its head on its forelegs. The afterbirth still clung to its hips. The calf raised its head and blinked. "Damn lucky we rode up on you, little one." The gunman said.

"Damn lucky." Katharane repeated.

"Sorry, Katty." The gunfighter said. "'bad choice of words on my part." He looked in the direction the wolf had disappeared.

"Funny that calf's mama ain't about."

"Mama." Katharane repeated loudly.

Then the gunman heard her coming through the cedar. She was hot and angry and blowing through her nose. "We rode up on the killer. 'baiter had its mama busy." The gunman thought aloud. Without waiting to see the embattled Longhorn cow, he spurred the black filly and she charged away. He guided her in and out of the scrub cedar until the angry mother gave up the chase and returned to her newborn calf.

Katharane giggled and bounced her legs off of the saddle. She enjoyed the darting twisting ride through the cedars. The gunfighter eased the filly into a walk. Katharane kicked the sides of the saddle and said." Go."

The gunfighter laughed and said. "We're done goin' for a while, Katty." She acquiesced.

Down the canyon they rode. The child moving with each fluid step of the filly, her legs sticking out passed the cantle of the saddle, her hands holding tightly to the saddle horn and her head constantly turning to see what she could see. She saw a canyon filled with cool spring air, the increasing early season flow of artesian springs, grass seldom if ever touched by hoofed grazers and wild creatures.

The gunman rode upright and straight behind Katharane. And on this morning the canyon seemed very pleasant to him, more than just a place to be alone. Slowly the warmth of the child made him realize he was not alone. It was not another morning of him and the canyon. It was a morning of him and Katharane and the canyon. He stopped the filly on a point that overlooked the distant mouth of the big canyon.

Katharane pointed at the canyon and said. "Mine."

The gunman placed his left hand against the child's stomach and said. "'canyon ain't no man's, Katty."

"No!" Katharane said boldly. "No, Pop. Mine."

Her warmth penetrated the soft doe skin dress. The gunfighter could feel it underneath each finger of his left hand. He pressed his fingers against her stomach. She giggled. And out of that part of his mind that had struggled with Herculean effort to forget, it came, the real and living memory of the touch of another person. A memory that was deep and strong, and followed by the agonizing remembrance of its loss, of that hurt, that pain and those long empty hours that had tortured his mind until relieved by the numbing poultice of time and indifference. For more mornings now than he had present recollection that strong poultice had kept soothed and sedated his need for that contact, and for those mornings' nights let him sleep without longing to awaken, indifferent to the light and whether it came or not. Suddenly fear choked the gunman.

The black filly sensed the fear and became alert and skittish.

'Not now. Not here.' The gunman thought. Here he had gone on without those feelings, had replaced them with the vast open prairie and the deep canyon. 'Damn you for bringing this to me, Reid Stuart.' The gunfighter cursed silently. 'Damn you for bringing my Katty to me.' His sides heaved. He cried. His tears were wet and full. They blistered his face and washed the salt of his perspiration into the corners of his mouth. He cried and cried until he heard the child's voice.

"Pop. Pop."

He looked down into Katharane's brown eyes, eyes so brown they appeared green in the light, and he gave up his soul to those eyes.

With the toe of his boot Reid Stuart pressed the dirt around the base of the pillar that now stood above the first pool. He balanced himself by holding to the top of the monument.

"Got it set, have you." The gunman said. He let the filly drink from the pool as he lowered Katharane from his saddle.

"I have." Reid Stuart said. "Hello, Katharane." He greeted his daughter.

"Me Katty, Daddy."

He shook his head. "No. You are Katharane. He calls you Katty." He nodded at the gunfighter. "But you are Katharane Diane Stuart. And it is 'I am Katty.' Not 'Me Katty.'"

The child ignored him and trotted to the dugout from where the Squaw Woman called to her.

"You carved the brand into each side." The gunman said.

"Yes. Each side of this one faces Escadara range. The others, the ones that will mark the boundaries, the brand will only be carved on the side away from our range."

"'guess we'd best set the ones we're gonna' place on the plains now. While it's still cool enough. 'summer'r be too hot to stand that kind of work." The gunman mused.

"We?" Reid Stuart asked. "I didn't think you were involving yourself in this useless endeavor."

"'hate to." The gunman retorted. "But I can't let you kill your damn fool self doin' it alone."

"And that is your only reason?" Reid Stuart asked.

"Only one I can think of." The gunman lied.

"Did you find any cattle?"

"'saw one. With a newborn calf."

"That is a good sign." Reid Stuart said. "And so is this." He stepped back from the stone. The drooped E blemished the smooth face of each of its sides.

The gunfighter grumbled. He wanted to leave. Before he had not cared when they left. He had been content to let Reid Stuart fuss with setting the first of the plains markers just so for as long as he wanted. Especially on a late April afternoon when the air was still alive from the winter cold and the grasses were just beginning to bloom, and the plains seemed so soft and gentle. This afternoon was one of those rare afternoons. But far out across the open plains something troubled the gunfighter and he picked at Reid Stuart to finish placing the marker so they could leave. "You finished?"

"No. I am not. And since I am doing all the work I do not care to be rushed."

"Well hurry your ass up anyway. There's a storm buildin'." The gunfighter said. He laid his left hand against the side of Katharane's face and stared at the distant cloud with her.

She had begged and cried her way into accompanying her father and the gunfighter. The Squaw Woman had protested to the point of confrontation with the gunfighter, from whom she had received a loud cursing for her concern. Katharane had ridden away with them on her white mustang, the squaw groaning her displeasure from the dugout. The storm grew into the south southwestern sky. It was a massive thunder head. The flat crest across its top was a soft and beguiling white white, and it boiled ever higher into the late afternoon high plains sky. Its belly was dark and blue. It appeared to be cold and still and quiet. But it was in reality pregnant with upward whirling ice. And its black underside was alive with wind and rain.

Katharane listened intently. She stood next to the gunfighter with her hand on the back of his leg.

"'not thundering." She said.

"It's thunderin'. See the flashes." The gunfighter pointed at the base of the blue belly of the distant cloud. "That's lightnin', and when it's lightnin' it's thunderin'. It's just too far away for us to hear it."

"Is it coming our way?" Reid Stuart asked. He struggled to twist the heavy stone marker which was set down into a deep hole.

"I can't tell it's goin' anywhere right now. Except up and up and up. But when it moves, and it will, it'll come roarin' north northeast right at us." The gunfighter answered.

Reid Stuart glanced at the storm. Katharane and the gunfighter were silhouetted before him against the quickly darkening sky, the sunset partially obscured by the rising storm. Cast against the awesome storm cloud the gunfighter and the child looked like minuets staked to the flat plains. "You could help me get this thing righted." Reid Stuart said.

"Huh!" The gunfighter snorted. "You're worse than an old woman about these damn rocks, Stuart." He was anxious to start back to the dugout. It would be dark before they reached the dugout if they started now. He did not like riding after dark with Katharane with them, especially with storms about. But he walked over and took hold of the stone pillar and held it upright as Reid Stuart packed dirt down into the hole and around the stone.

At regular intervals Reid Stuart walked to his instrument and checked the position of the stone. Each time he did this he made notes in his journal. Finally he packed the remaining pieces of the displaced prairie sod around the marker, walked to the instrument, made a last computation and wrote this in the journal.

"You and that damn journal." The gunfighter grumbled. "What are you writing in there anyway?"

"Measurements." Reid Stuart replied. He lifted the instrument off of the tripod and carefully placed it back in its wooden case.

"Measurements of what?" The gunfighter asked. "Katty. Don't get too far."

Katharane pointed at the storm, as if the storm by remaining stationary had forced her to move closer to it. But in obedience to the gunfighter's warning she retreated two steps. She continued to watch the storm.

"Measurements of the Escadara." Reid Stuart said.

"Hell! The Escadara's all the plains and canyon we want it to be."

"For now. But not forever. The day will come when the Escadara's no more than the measurements in this book and the accuracy of these markers we are placing." Reid Stuart said. He tied the tripod to the pack on the mule.

"Hmmm." The gunfighter was not impressed. "Katty. I told you not to wander off." He scolded the child in his soft pleading way with her.

"Me didn't, Pop. Me didn't move." She argued.

The gunfighter looked at the storm. Katharane had not moved. The storm had. It pitched and rolled in the darkening sky. Its top seemed to reach out above them. He walked to Katharane, knelt on his left knee, folded his right arm around her butt and stood up with her. "'git mounted, Stuart. We gotta' ride." He demanded.

Reid Stuart picked up the mule's lead rope. The gunfighter walked quickly passed him and set Katharane on her white mustang. He pulled his knife from his belt, bent down and cut the hobble.

"Those things can be untied, you know." Reid Stuart protested.

"No time. 'storm's gonna' catch us if we don't put some hard ridin' in." Distant thunder rumbled softly across them, accenting the gunfighter's warning. He led, riding at a quick walk, moving south-southeast.

With more time on the plains Reid Stuart had become more aware of direction and location. "The dugout is more to the south, isn't it?" He asked the gunfighter.

"'tryun' to right angle away from that storm. If we stay in its track we can't outrun it. But we may can ride across it before it hits us."

Reid Stuart looked over his shoulder at the storm. It was a real and angry presence now.

"It's turnin' on us." The gunfighter called back to Reid Stuart.

"Which way?"

"'can't tell for sure, yet. Maybe it'll drift more to the north." The gunfighter answered.

Then the advance guard from the storm answered Reid Stuart's question. A cold damp wind began to whip against their backs.

"Dammit!" The gunman swore. "It's driftin' south." He spurred the filly into an easy lope. Katharane's mustang followed. Reid Stuart urged the buckskin to keep up. But the mule drug heavily upon its lead. It struggled to keep the pace. But it was tiring quickly. The wind increased. Thunder cracked down around them from white fingered lightning bolts that stabbed into the plains behind them. The gunfighter spurred the filly. She ran. Katharane's mustang took up the pursuit. The mule could not do so.

"The mule can't hold this pace. You and Katharane go on!" Reid Stuart yelled ahead to the gunman.

The gunfighter slowed the filly until Reid Stuart passed

him and he was alongside the mule. There he took the slack of his left rein and began to whip the mule across its rump with the slack. He lashed the mule and yelled. "Run! You mule. Run!"

The storm was closing in on them.

"Pop! My pony's tired." Katharane called to the gunfighter, seeking his permission to slow the horse.

Instead the gunfighter came up behind Katharane's small horse. His leather rein cracked across the small horse's rump and, as he had demanded of the mule, he demanded of the little horse. "Run! You mustang. Run!" He yelled.

"No! Pop! You no whip my pony!" Katharane shrieked.

The gunfighter ignored her and whipped the horse mercilessly and yelled. "Run! You mustang. Run!"

Katharane wailed. Her little horse raced on. But the mule stumbled and went down on its front knees. Reid Stuart reined the buckskin in. "The mule is down!" He yelled to the gunfighter.

Katharane used the distraction to rein her tired mustang to a stop. The gunfighter snapped the filly to a halt. "Leave him go, Stu'! Leave him go. We gotta' ride! Dammit! We gotta' ride!"

The heart of the storm was passing just to their north. A continuous series of bright powerful lightning flashes lit up the sky, followed by a fusillade of thunder. Then the air went empty.

"My ears! Pop. My ears!" Katharane cried.

"Look! To the north." Reid Stuart shouted and pointed. Grayish sand swirled upward from the plains into the late day sky as a whirling funnel left the heavy wall of clouds and snake tongued down toward the plains. "What is that sound? Is it wind?" Reid Stuart called loudly to the gunfighter. The dull solid roar seemed to rumble up from the ground like the pounding noise of many buffalo running, not down from the clouds like the swish of the approaching rain.

"Damn!" The gunfighter cursed. An immense bolt of lightning lit up the sky, and thunder, the sound of a heavy mortar, followed it. The gunfighter looked ahead. He spotted a depression in the plains and spurred his filly passed Katharane's mustang. He reached out and yanked Katharane's reins from her and rode for the depression. When he reached it he jerked his filly to a stop and jumped from the horse. Reid Stuart reined up beside the filly and mustang, and dismounted.

"'loose hobble the horses!" The gunfighter yelled to be heard above the roar of the approaching storm. "'give 'em enough length to move, but not so much we can't run 'em to ground if we have to." He jerked his saddle and blanket off of the filly. Then he tied his reins up on her neck using her mane. He threw the saddle against the slope of the rise on the southwest side of the depression and tossed his blanket on it. The wind turned. From the northeast the long grass flowed at them, breaking underneath and passed the horses, laying out flat to the southwest above the depression. "'wind's changed. Hurry up, Stuart!" The gunfighter cried. He drug the Indian harness from the back of Katharane's white mustang, doubled the hackamore's lead which the little horse wore and tied a knot around it. He lifted the harness with his left hand and with his right hand he picked up Reid Stuart's saddle.

The buckskin moved steadily west in a short gaited walk. Katharane's white mustang stumbled after him, not yet used to the leather hobbles Reid Stuart had tied around its front feet. Reid Stuart knelt beside the filly's left foreleg. He tied the long strip of leather around her right ankle. Then he reached for her left foreleg.

"'no time!" The gunfighter yelled. He slapped the black filly on her butt and commanded her. "Kai! Kai! Go on. Git outta' here." The black filly trotted away after Katharane's mustang and Reid Stuart's buckskin. The gunfighter dropped Katharane's harness above his saddle and threw Reid Stuart's saddle next to his. "'lie down between the saddles, Katty." He ordered the child. Katharane lay down in the tall grass. The gunman dropped his saddle blanket over her. "Come on, Stuart." He called. "'crawl underneath your saddle, loop your arm through the stirrup and lay on the blanket and against Katharane. Pull your legs up under as best you can."

Reid Stuart did so. The gunman crawled underneath his saddle and laced his right arm through the stirrup. He rolled over onto the blanket and pulled Reid Stuart's saddle against his. "'stay with it and hold to that saddle, Stuart. I don't give a damn how rough it gets." The gunman commanded. "Katty..." A rumbling swallowed up the gunfighter's voice. Hailstones hissed through the grass and ricocheted off of the saddles, more and more and more, larger and larger and larger, until sheets of rocks of ice washed the grass from the prairie and deafened Reid Stuart and the gunman.

Katharane whimpered from beneath the blanket and underneath Reid Stuart and the gunfighter and the saddles. "It's allright, Little Katty. 'won't be long now." The gunfighter soothed her. But the pounding continued. The wind tried to lift the saddles and expose the men that huddled beneath them. "'hang on to 'em! Hang on, Stuart!" The gunfighter yelled.

Two large hailstones bit into Reid Stuart's hand as he clung to the saddle. He winced, wanted to cry out, to withdraw his hand to safety beneath his chest. But he did not. He held to the saddle. The storm broke into a crescendo above them. Then, as quickly as it had come upon them, it passed away from them. It was over, stopped, silent, no wind, no rain, just empty air.

From beneath the heavy soaked blanket Katharane cried and coughed. The gunfighter threw the saddle off of his back and stood up. Reid Stuart pushed his saddle to his side and sat on his knees next to the blanket. The gunfighter pulled the blanket away and lifted Katharane into his arms. She was wet, dirty, crying but unhurt. He held her against him, turned and looked out across the darkening prairie in the direction the horses had taken.

"Here mule! Here mule!" Katharane called from across the gunfighter's shoulder, as she had heard her father do.

The gunfighter and Reid Stuart looked with her at the mule. It lay on its side fifty yards away from them. Reid Stuart picked up his heavy Sharps and followed Katharane and the gunfighter towards the mule. Before he reached the mule the gunfighter stopped. "'take Katty." He said to Reid Stuart.

Reid Stuart looked at the gunman.

"It may be bad, Stuart." The gunman said. "'take Katty. And I'll see to the mule."

"No. It's my mule. I'll see to it." Reid Stuart answered.

"Get up mule! Get up." Katharane called. She coughed, laid her head back on the gunman's shoulder and shivered.

The mule's left ear twitched. The two men stared at each other. "She didn't see it." The gunfighter said to Reid Stuart. "I'll head off in the direction the horses took. 'give me a few minutes to get her out of range. Then do what you have to do."

"What about the horses?" Reid Stuart asked and swallowed.

"'depends on how far they got before the storm hit 'em."

"But..."

"'storm was driftin' away from them when it hit us. 'horses may have found the right angle and gotten out of the worst of it." The gunfighter tried to sound convinced. He was not. And Reid Stuart knew he was not. The gunfighter walked away, carrying Katharane.

Reid Stuart walked to the back of the prone mule. Then he stepped around its head. As if stripped by the fragments of a heavy mortar's round all the skin on the left side of the mule's face was gone, only ligaments, sinew and bone remained. Much of the mule's tough hide from its neck to its hip had been peeled away, melted free of the tissue which held it to the bone. Reid Stuart cocked the hammer on the Sharps as he lifted it against his shoulder. He did not look to see how far away the gunfighter and Katharane were. He fired when he felt the gun's butt against his shoulder. The report boomed out across the prairie.

The gunfighter pulled Katharane's head back against his shoulder and continued walking. Reid Stuart walked after them. When he overtook them he put his Sharps across his shoulders and draped his arms across the rifle. "Should I have unloaded the mule?" He asked.

"'no hurry. 'mule ain't goin' nowhere." The gunman said.

"I know that. Dammit!" Reid Stuart cried in frustration with the gunman's seeming sarcasm.

"'sides, let's try to find the horses first." The gunman said in a quieter tone.

"Can we?"

"Can we what?" The gunman asked.

"Can we find the horses?" Reid Stuart asked.

"'dunno. Maybe." The gunman answered. He raised his head from studying the battered prairie and was met by Reid Stuart's angry glare. "What?" The gunman demanded.

"'dunno. Maybe. That's what you always say." Reid Stuart complained.

"It's the truth. I don't know that we can find those horses. So git your nose to pointin' at the dirt between your boots and see if you can find any sign. We got maybe half an hour of daylight. Then we're stuck on these godless plains afoot in the dark. That ain't somethin' that's good for your health." The gunman said as he set Katharane on his shoulders. He began walking in a long arcing loop. Reid Stuart walked the other direction in a sweeping maneuver which emulated the gunman, always watching the ground before him. They met at a point a hundred yards from where they had begun. "Nothun'. 'not a damn sign one." The gunman cursed. He put his hands on Katharane's knees. She whistled and sang a shrill piercing Comanche chant.

"Katharane child! What are you doing?" Reid Stuart asked.

Katharane pointed. From far out on the prairie, almost lost in the failing late day light her white mustang walked toward them. Katharane called again. The mustang tried to trot, stumbled against its leather hobbles and settled back to a short gaited walk. The black filly and the buckskin appeared, trailing behind the mustang.

"He come to me. Mama taught me how to make him." Katharane said.

"You done good, Katty. You done real good." The gunman said. He patted her knees.

"The Squaw Woman did good, too, teaching Katharane this." Reid Stuart said.

"'bout time that damn squaw did somethin' worthwhile." The gunman snorted.

"She's cared for Katharane each day since we took her from her people. That is something. Isn't it?" Reid Stuart demanded.

"She ain't got no choice but to do that." The gunfighter retorted. He caught the mustang and bridled it. He set Katharane on the horse. "'swing around and bring up that filly and your Dad's buckskin, Katty." He told the child.

Katharane bounced up and down on the mustang's bare back as it loped around the black filly and the buckskin. Reid Stuart caught the buckskin as it walked before Katharane and her mustang. The black filly, not hobbled, edged away from the gunfighter. Katharane rode to the filly and rubbed its neck. The filly stood still. The gunman grabbed the filly's left ear and jerked his braided bridle around the horse's nose. The gunfighter and Reid Stuart led their horses to the saddles. Katharane rode behind. The gunfighter lifted Katharane off the mustang. He handed the black filly's and the mustang's reins to her. "'guess we'd best put your saddle on Katty's mustang." He said to Reid Stuart. "And see if we can load the mule's pack on your buckskin. He's the strongest."

"All-right." Reid Stuart agreed. He picked up his saddle blanket and laid it across the mustang's back, swung his saddle on top of the blanket and drew the cinch up tight against the mustang's stomach.

The gunfighter saddled his filly and set Katharane in the saddle. She still held the mustang's reins. "Katty. You stay here." The gunfighter told the child. "Come on, Stuart. Let's get the mule's pack on that buckskin, and head for home." He carried Katharane's Comanche harness to the mule.

Reid Stuart patted Katharane on the leg, then led the buckskin to the mule.

"'mule sleeping, Pop?" Katharane called.

"You stay put, Katty." The gunfighter called back.

"O-Kay!" Katharane replied.

For an hour the gunfighter and Reid Stuart worked in the dark unpacking the mule's corpse and fitting the pack and its contents onto the buckskin. The gunman tied Katharane's harness on top of the pack. He and Reid Stuart led the burdened buckskin back to Katharane, the black filly and the mustang. Reid Stuart mounted the mustang. The little horse snorted, unaccustomed to the weight.

"Daddy ride my horse?" Katharane asked.

"That's right." The gunman answered her as he swung into the saddle behind her.

She stood up on the saddle, turned around and draped her legs across the gunfighter's. She put her face against his chest and settled towards sleep. "Mule go, Pop? Mule go?" She asked sleepily.

"'mule's gonna' rest some more. Then he'll be along." The gunman answered.

They rode slowly into the night and for home, for the Escadara.

The buckskin lengthened its stride beneath Reid Stuart to stay up with the gunman and the black filly.

"Are you in a hurry?" Reid Stuart asked the stone faced gunfighter.

The gunfighter had been silent and brooding most of the three days he and Reid Stuart had been out on the plains placing the third of the seven markers Reid Stuart planned to set along the perimeter of the arc he was surveying as the northern and western boundaries of the ranch. Now the gunfighter pushed his little horse hard and steady through the thick grass of the late spring plains straight on line for the dugout. He did not answer Reid Stuart. The sound of Katharane's cries rang in his ears and he longed to be at the dugout to read to her from Reid Stuart's Bible and to have her laughter dislodge from his memory her screams of protest at his and her father's refusal to allow her to accompany them. Screams that had pierced his ears and his heart until he and Reid Stuart had ridden so far out onto the plains that they could no longer see her or the Squaw Woman who held her clamped to her skirt, but could only catch the faint remnants of her cries on an occasional breath of wind, until the wind had come up and washed all sound of her away. But, "Me go, Pop! Me go, Pop!" screamed with all the child's fury Katharane possessed tugged at the gunfighter's mind. He spurred the filly and rode on.

Reid Stuart pushed the buckskin to stretch its gait and

keep pace. The blue of the sky mirrored against the horizon told him they were nearing the canyon; that, and the gunfighter's constantly increasing pace. Slowly the low outline of the dugout, discernible to Reid Stuart only because he knew what to look for, rose from the prairie. The black filly loped away. The tired mule blew through its nose. Reid Stuart settled the buckskin into a comfortable walk and let the gunman ride away. Their last mule was too precious to risk injuring it or breaking its wind just to sprint with the gunfighter's black filly to the dugout. And Reid Stuart knew he would have to wait until the gunfighter had made his peace with Katharane before he would receive her attention anyway. This was easier to accept by arriving several minutes after the gunfighter. Reid Stuart heard shouts. He urged his tired horse into a trot. The shouts grew in volume and anger as he approached the dugout.

The gunfighter cursed, "Damn Comanch' squaw! I'll slit your nostrils for sure this time." "No, Pop, no!" Katharane screamed in return. From somewhere inside of the dark dugout the Squaw Woman pleaded a Kwerhar-rehnuh woman's entreaty to a demanding buck. This angered the gunman more. "I ain't one of your ruttin' damn bucks, Squaw!" He roared.

Reid Stuart halted the buckskin and the mule above the dugout. Katharane stood between the gunman and the dugout, trying desperately to block his entrance into the dugout. Her long sun streaked auburn hair was plastered against her head. Green strings hung like braided ringlets in her matted hair. Her face was dirty and red from screaming and crying. "What is that in Katharane's hair?" Reid Stuart asked the gunman.

"Buffalo dung!" The gunfighter yelled. "That damn heathen Comanch' squaw! 'done rubbed buffalo dung all in her's and Katty's hair. I'll cut her damn fingers off." He swore, stepped around Katharane and jumped down into the dugout. The Squaw Woman came clambering out the other end on her hands and knees. She wailed as she tried to get to her feet. The gunman's boot caught her on the butt and sent her face down into the hard pan of the dugout's yard. Her nose bled and she continued to wail.

Katharane screamed at the gunman. "No hurt my mama! No hurt my mama!" She ran to the gunman and rammed her face into the inside of his buckskin clad right leg and bit. The gunman continued his pursuit of the Squaw Woman who scrambled on her hands and knees, trying to flee from him. Katharane wrapped her arms and legs around the gunman's leg and bit with all of her strength. Her teeth finally cut through the worn buckskin.

"Hey!" The gunman cried. "You're bitin' me, Katty."

The child struggled to hold her grip with her teeth, her arms and her legs as the gunman lifted her away from his leg. Reid Stuart laughed.

"What's so damn funny?" The gunman asked.

"You." Reid Stuart replied. "Now give Katharane to me and I will wash her hair. And leave the Squaw Woman be. She was only doing what she knew to do."

"She ain't sleepin' in that dugout smellin' like hot buffalo shit." The gunman argued. But he handed Katharane to Reid Stuart.

"Well then, my friend. I would suggest you find a way to convince her to wash her hair." Reid Stuart said, then he added. "A way short of doing her bodily harm, unless you want me to turn Katharane loose on you again." He carried Katharane to the first pool, cleaned the snot and tears and dust from her face and began to wash her hair. Then he heard the Squaw Woman scream and he turned to see the gunman on his filly, rope dallied about the saddle horn, dragging the Squaw Woman on her large butt toward the pool.

Katharane twisted free of Reid Stuart's grasp, ran to the Squaw Woman and sat down in her lap. The Squaw Woman folded her arms around the child. Together they cried an angry, frightened Comanche incantation. The gunman drug them both into the second pool. The squaw tried to stand up. The gunman jerked the rope and she splashed back down into the pool. Reid Stuart laughed. And Katharane laughed in response to her father's laughter. She stood up in the Squaw Woman's lap, put her hands underneath the squaw's chin and pushed. The frightened squaw went over onto her back. She stood up, spitting water, clutching Katharane to her chest. Katharane coughed and rubbed the water from her eyes. The gunman jerked the squaw off of her feet again. Then he stepped down from the black filly and waded into the pool. He grabbed the Squaw Woman by her hair and shoved her underneath the water. She went under still clutching Katharane in her arms. The gunman brought them both up together. The Squaw Woman cried. Katharane gasped for breath. Green water and buffalo dung streamed from their hair and across their shoulders. "Hold your nose, Katty girl." The gunman said and shoved the squaw and the child under again. Finally he was satisfied that most of the dung had been rinsed from their hair. He pulled Katharane free of the squaw's grasp and waded from the pool with her. The Squaw Woman waddled out of the pool and fled to the dugout.

Reid Stuart wrapped the buckskin's reins around its neck and left it and the mule to drink from the pool. He walked beside the gunman and squeezed water from Katharane's hair. "Why would the Squaw Woman put buffalo dung in their hair?" Reid Stuart asked.

"Comanch' do it." The gunman answered. "'think it protects 'em from the sun, I s'pose."

"Chief Kwanhah told Mama to." Katharane said.

They stopped. Reid Stuart and the gunman stared at each other. Then the gunman looked at Katharane and asked her. "Kwanhah of the Kwerhar-rehnuh was here?"

Katharane nodded.

"While we were gone?" The gunman questioned the child.

Katharane nodded again.

"What does it mean?" Reid Stuart asked.

"'means we can't leave Katty no more. That stinkin' half-breed might decide to claim her." The gunman answered. Then he swore. "Damn that squaw!"

"Kwanhah say Katty go. Mama say no."

The gunman stared hard into the child's eyes.

"Mama say no." Katharane repeated.

"It would appear we owe Katharane's being here to the Squaw Woman." Reid Stuart said.

"Damn stinkin' squaw." The gunman muttered as he continued on with Katharane to the dugout.

"This will be the last one we set on the plains this year." Reid Stuart said as he eased the buckskin back alongside of the mule and checked the straps by which he had tied the stone marker to the mule.

"Damn right it will." The gunman retorted. "It can get hotter than hell in June on these plains. And we're passed two weeks into June, Stuart."

Katharane trotted her white mustang ahead of Reid Stuart and the gunfighter. She was happy to be with them. "There it is!" She cried and pointed at the marker her father and the gunman had placed three weeks earlier, which grew out of the prairie like a lonely white bear grass pod. From this marker Reid Stuart would continue his survey.

"Good thing we got you with us, Katty girl." The gunman called to her. "This damn Yankee surveyor would'a had us to the Mexican border without finding it."

Katharane beamed and Reid Stuart could not suppress a smile. From the marker Reid Stuart led them across the grass. The June heat came up shortly passed mid-day and climbed until four o'clock when it began to fade. At half passed six Reid Stuart stopped along a shallow rise. Beyond the rise the grass was gone, torn beneath the buffalos' hooves that had marched across it the day before and flattened beneath their heavy bodies as they had wallowed against the prairie that morning before rising to graze throughout the day. The herd spread across the open prairie beyond the wallows like the cedars of the canyon, four and six clustered here, one or two over there, another half dozen farther on and on and on across the plains. Against the flat true canvas of the high plain's western horizon the sun began to paint colors pure of tone, vivid of hue, surreal in composition and blend. Reid Stuart, the gunfighter and Katharane sat on their horses and watched. Katharane pointed across the prairie and above the thousand grazing buffalo at the sunset and asked. "Pop, is that where God lives?"

"Well, Katty girl. That's probably as close to a look at heaven as any of us will ever find on this earth, I reckon." The gunman answered.

Reid Stuart nodded and said. "We'll camp here and set the

marker on this rise tomorrow."

Katharane slept on a buffalo hide spread between her father and the gunman and atop a mattress made from bending the tall big blue stem grass beneath the hide. The gunman lay on his back with his head resting against the seat of his saddle. Reid Stuart leant on his left elbow and against his saddle and asked. "How many cattle survived the winter?" He blew smoke through his nose.

"Don't drop no fire from that smoke into this grass." The gunman warned.

Reid Stuart squashed the fire from his smoke between his thumb and forefinger. "Do you think we have more cattle this year than we did last year?" He persisted.

"'dunno'. Maybe." The gunman answered. "We'll know soon enough. 'gotta' start ridin' 'em down and markin' 'em again soon as we get back. That'll tell us for certain."

Reid Stuart rolled over onto his back and said. "Yes. It will." He listened to Katharane breathing slowly and deeply. He looked above him at a black darkness alive with fire white stars. "The stars seem so much larger here on the plains. They are brighter than I can recall them ever being." He said softly.

"That's a star touchin' sky, Stuart." The gunfighter said.

"A star touching sky. Are you a poet, my friend?" Reid Stuart asked.

"No. 'can't lay claim to the phrase. 'comes from a Comanch' legend."

Katharane rolled onto her stomach without waking.

"What is the legend?" Reid Stuart asked.

"'seems a great Comanch' war chief rode onto the plains one night in late spring before the beginnin' of a planned raid far south into the Tejano's country below the Double Mountain fork in the river." The gunman paused, then continued. "The chief was troubled because clouds had hidden the moon from them on a raid the year before and they had lost many of the horses they had stolen. If the clouds hid the moon again he feared they would not return from the raid. So he rode out at night onto these plains to seek counsel from the spirits that dwell beyond the canyons. And the spirits came to him. They told him to ride his pony as fast as he could across the plains and when he was beneath the brightest star he could find to reach his hands up. He did. And when he reached up his hands he caught that bright star. And the Comanch' carried it with them to light their way back from their raid. And it was one of the most successful raids in their history. So the Comanch' call this the star touchin' sky, the land where a brave warrior can reach up and grab a star."

"Is this a commonly known legend?" Reid Stuart asked.

"Common among the Comanch'." The gunman answered.

Reid Stuart chuckled and said. "I meant was it commonly known among the Texans."

"Texans know it as the time of the Comanche moons. The time when their stock is stolen, their women raped and butchered and their children taken. That's how the Texans know it."

"Oh." Reid Stuart said.

"Remember Stuart." The gunman said without looking at Reid Stuart. "Sooner or later we got a fight to make with the Indians. Whether we want it or not."

The gunman watched Katharane ride down the rise and across the buffalo wallows and dismount by lying across the deerskin covered Comanche harness on her stomach and sliding down the side of the mustang. She wrapped the mustang's reins around a handful of the tall grass and left her little horse to graze. Then she disappeared into the tall switch grass on the other side of the three wallows.

"What is Katharane doing?" Reid Stuart asked. He twisted the marker, then rested his left hand on top of the marker and wiped the sweat from his face with his shirt sleeve. The mid-afternoon June sun had grown angry and hot and dry.

"'goin' to shade." The gunman answered. He walked to his black filly.

"Are you going to shade, too?" Reid Stuart asked.

"'gonna' do a little scoutin' after I check on Katty." The gunman answered as he swung his leg across his saddle. The gunman squinted against the glare caused by the reflection from the flat unvarying prairie as he picked up the filly's reins.

"Is something wrong?" Reid Stuart asked.

"All the buffalo are driftin' away from the wallows." The gunman answered. He nodded at the buffalo.

"So?"

"So." The gunman answered. "This time of day they should be movin' back towards the wallows for beddin' down. They did last night. You hear 'em layin' down in the wallows last night?"

"I heard them."

"Well. Our bein' here didn't stop them from comin' back last night. What's changed?" The gunman rode away before Reid Stuart could answer or ask another question.

Katharane smiled up at the gunman from where she lay on her back shielded from the hot sun by the long thick interlaced blades of grass which folded over her. He winked at her as he turned the filly and rode across the wallows and down the buffalo track for a quarter of a mile. He stopped the filly and searched the waves upon waves of grass. He sat in his saddle, uneasy, and tried to make his eyes see through the grass, see what he sensed was there. Slowly he discerned the slight undulation in the never ending blanket of grass. "Shit! 'a damn gully." He cursed. "They're movin' up a damn gully." He turned the filly and started back to the buffalo wallows and Katharane. Then he sensed the movement through the grass. He stood in his stirrups and strained to see through the grass. He saw only grass. But he heard Katharane crying. And he heard the sound of bodies moving through the grass. He reined the filly right and ran her up the low rise where the grass was shorter.

Katharane saw the filly make the rise. Immediately she ran from the cover of the tall grass out onto the hard baked clay where the buffalo had trampled the ground clean. She ran for the filly, screaming with fear. A Kiowa buck rose from his crouch in the high grass and charged after the crying child.

The gunman lashed the filly with his reins. The little horse jumped forward and ran toward Katharane and the Indian chasing

111

her. "Run! Katty! Run!" The gunman yelled. He saw the buck raise his lance. He pulled the black pistol from its holster. But he was too far from them to use it. "Get down, Katty! Get down!" He cried.

"Shoot him, Pop. Please! Shoot him!" Katharane screamed, her arms flashing at her sides, her short little legs flying across the flat packed buffalo walk.

The gunman could not shoot. He was still too far. The buck was going to reach Katharane before he could get close enough to shoot. "Stuart!" The gunman's voice was shrill and crackling and angry and filled with dread, but driven loudly through the late dry heat by the hope and faith and trust he had come to hold in this one name which raged from his throat.

The Sharps roared from the rise behind the gunman. The buck seemed to straighten in mid-stride, stop and stand upright. His head jerked to one side, his eyes rolled back and he swallowed his tongue. Then his knees buckled and he fell forward onto the ground, his face splashing the dust up on all sides of it.

The gunman raced on to Katharane and swept her up into his arms. She lay her head against his shoulder and sobbed as he loped the filly back to the rise where Reid Stuart waited on his buckskin. He had the mule tied on lead behind him. The gunman handed Katharane to Reid Stuart. Then he turned the filly back toward the buffalo wallows.

"Where are you going?" Reid Stuart asked.

"To get Katty's mustang." The gunman answered.

"There is more than just one Kiowa." Reid Stuart warned him.

"There won't be when I'm done." The gunman called over his shoulder. He reined the filly to her right and rode down the far side of the rise and disappeared into the grass.

Reid Stuart watched the mustang. He saw one buck reach up from the grass and grasp the mustang's hackamore. Another buck crouched beside the mustang's back legs. He spotted two more bucks hiding in the grass between the mustang and the buffalo wallows. He dismounted and stood Katharane behind him. She gripped his buckskin pants behind his knees and pushed her forehead against his legs and whimpered. "I want Pop."

He laid his Sharps across the buckskin's saddle and sighted on the nearest of the two bucks crouching in the grass before the wallows. In the periphery of his vision he saw the black filly racing through the grass, he squeezed the trigger and the Sharps roared. The buck bounced off of his butt and dropped backwards into the grass.

Katharane's mustang jerked free of the buck holding its hackamore and trotted out into the wallows. The gunman killed the buck that had held Katharane's mustang and the one that had crouched at its hind legs. The other buck that had squatted in the grass at the edge of the wallows was slowly crawling on his belly back into the tall grass. The gunfighter could not see him. Reid Stuart knew he could not shoot him because the trajectory from where he stood on the rise with Katharane to where the Kiowa crawled toward the tall grass and escape was too flat. He would miss and he knew it. The gunman looked to the rise. How to tell the gunman where the buck was, Reid Stuart thought. He sighted the big Sharps at a point in the buffalo wallows on a line between the buckskin and the buck but twenty yards short of the buck and fired. Clouds of dirt leaped out of the packed wallows. Katharane's mustang trotted farther up the rise. A puff of dirt drifted up from where the bullet had struck the wallows. Reid Stuart reloaded, sighted at a point on the same line but twenty yards passed the buck and fired. The bullet whistled into the tall grass and thudded into the heavy sod. A few seconds later a slender smoky column of dust rose above the grass.

The Kiowa lay still and flat after the first shot, trusting to the never varying landscape to conceal him. A third bullet struck the ground on line with the buck but ten yards short of him, a fourth struck on the same line ten yards passed the Kiowa, who still lay motionless in the grass. The gunman smiled, cocked his pistol, rode the filly out onto the wallows and on the line of Reid Stuart's fire. He walked the little horse passed the first shot, then the third. Then his spurs sent the horse leaping forward and a bullet through the back of the Kiowa buck's skull ended his silent and still wait for escape. The gunman turned in his saddle, waved his pistol to Reid Stuart, put it back into the black holster and dismounted. He pulled his knife from its sheath.

Reid Stuart looked down to his daughter. He knew what the gunman was doing. He felt no need nor desire to watch. He picked Katharane up and set her on his saddle and stepped up and into the saddle behind her. He rode the buckskin slowly up to the mustang that now stood on the rise a dozen yards from him.

The gunman tightened the cinch against the black filly's belly, checked that his bedroll was tied securely across the back of his saddle and led the filly away from the dugout and to the first pool. Reid Stuart followed him.

"Me go with you, Pops!" Katharane pleaded from the dugout where the Squaw Woman restrained her.

"'you make those drawin's of Katty's hands?" The gunman asked Reid Stuart.

"Yes." Reid Stuart answered. He unfolded the page he had torn from his journal. "I traced her right hand on the front of the page and her left hand on the back."

The gunman took the page from Reid Stuart, refolded it and slid it between the tongue of his gun belt and the inlay where the belt was laced together below the middle of his stomach.

"What are you going to do with the drawing?" Reid Stuart asked.

The gunman did not answer. Instead he said. "'be back in three to five days, Stuart." He patted the filly's neck as she drank from the pool. "You stay off those plains while I'm gone. You hear?"

"I hear." Reid Stuart answered. He rubbed his thumb across a five dollar gold piece. He offered it to the gunman. "Bring me some tobacco and Katharane something sweet if Tafoya has it."

The gunman climbed into the saddle. He did not take the gold piece. "I'll see to your tobacco, Stuart. And to Katty's needs." He said.

Reid Stuart reached the gold coin up to the mounted gunfighter, offering it to him again.

"Put your money away. I've got no need of it." The gunman said. He lifted the filly's reins off of her neck.

114

Reid Stuart still offered the gold piece as he said. "I also want you to bring something pretty for the Squaw Woman."

"'hell with that damn squaw." The gunman said. "Take care of Katty." He rode away.

Reid Stuart watched him disappear down into the canyon. He rubbed the coin with his thumb one more time, then he carried it back to the dugout.

"Pop? Pop?" Each morning for three days since the gunman had left Katharane had walked along the front of the dugout and called for him. Each morning the squaw had trailed her, coaxing, pleading, offering chewed buffalo meat, trying to entice the child into her lap and to eat. And each morning Katharane had refused, until by noon hunger overcame her resolve and she ate.

The fourth morning Reid Stuart rose early, saddled the buckskin, put the Comanche harness on the mustang and loaded the pack and one of the two remaining stone pillars onto the mule.

Katharane's eyes danced. "Me go." She said.

"Yes. You shall go with me." Reid Stuart assured her. He picked her up and started out of the dugout.

"No plains." The Squaw Woman mumbled timidly, and in English.

Reid Stuart stopped, looked at her, uncertain if he had heard what he had heard.

"No plains." The squaw murmured again, again in English. She gnashed her teeth and twisted her hands together and reached for Katharane.

Reid Stuart did not surrender his child to her. But he did acknowledge her warning. "No. No plains. We are only going to the mouth of our canyon." He paused, trying to determine if the squaw understood his words. "To where the big canyon crosses." He explained.

"No plains." The Squaw Woman said louder and with more clarity. She disappeared into the corner of the dugout, rummaged in her bedding, found something and carried it to them. She reached up and hung the necklace Kwanhah had given the child around Katharane's neck. "No plains." She said again and then she retreated into the darkness of the dugout.

"Katharane. Please don't get too far ahead?" Reid Stuart called. He urged the buckskin to lengthen its stride, but the mule hung back, refusing to vary its hip swaying walk, and preventing the horse from increasing its pace. The mustang disappeared around a stand of short cedars. 'Damn. I wish Canada was here.' Reid Stuart thought. He jerked hard on the lead rope, forcing the mule to trot, and goosed his buckskin, who obligingly trotted around the cedars. Katharane sat on her white mustang fifty yards farther down the canyon. She looked back at her father and pointed at the blue wide opening into the big canyon. Reid Stuart trotted the buckskin to her. "Do not ride out of my sight again." He commanded her.

"Me found it." Katharane said.

"I. I found it." He corrected her, and added. "Yes. You found it." He sat on the buckskin and surveyed the wide opening out into the big canyon. "I wonder if it is safe to take you there, child?"

"Me go." Katharane said.

"I. I go." Reid Stuart patiently corrected Katharane's grammar and restrained her. "Not yet." He tried to see what he thought the gunfighter would see. Were the buffalo grazing in a peculiar pattern? Or were they drifting into groups and gathering together for protection? And was it protection from wolves or from Indians? "He would know, Katharane. Canada would know." Reid Stuart said. "And I don't." He shifted the heavy Sharps from where he rode with it across his saddle and set its butt against his right thigh. "I don't." He repeated. Had he come to rely so much upon the gunman's judgment? "Yes. Yes, I have." He said aloud. But he was not an invalid without it. He could still find his own way. He had before. He heeled into the buckskin and followed Katharane toward the big canyon.

"Here." Katharane said. She sat on her mustang atop a small promontory that rose from the flat floor of the big canyon above the shallow Prairie Dog Town stream a mile from the point where their canyon intersected the big canyon.

Reid Stuart led the mule up onto the promontory. Below, the narrow shallow gypsum tainted stream twisted through a turn and flowed away from him and Katharane, an ever shrinking string tied to the flat floor of the big canyon that went on and on until lost to their sight. Behind them their canyon invisibly cut into the rolling grass of the big canyon, unable to be located except by chance or by those with knowledge that it was there. Reid Stuart stepped down from the buckskin, unleashed the heavy stone pillar from the mule and let it drop into the grass. He untied the pick and shovel from the mule and carried them to Katharane. He dropped the tools in the grass and reached to help Katharane dismount. The child shook her head. She turned the mustang, rode to the far side of the promontory and sat there on her horse on guard, as she had seen the gunfighter do. Reid Stuart picked up the shovel and stomped it through the thick matted grass and down into the never before turned sod. He worked steadily for almost an hour. Then he rested.

He studied the empty canyon between him and the mouth of their canyon. Someday it would be filled with cattle, Escadara cattle. Within the boundaries marked by his stone pillars twenty thousand buffalo grazed at times and never seemed to even disturb the grass. Surely that many cattle could graze here. Twenty thousand head, a fortune in hides and beef. He looked at the empty canyon and smiled, a fortune...The empty canyon! The buffalo had left. He stepped from the shovel and started for the buckskin and his Sharps. Two mounted bucks cut him off. 'Damn!' He thought. 'This may be it. Katharane. Katharane. Oh God! Katharane.' "Canada." The whisper died in his dry parched throat. He whirled and ran for his child. The two bucks pursued him.

Katharane sat on her white mustang, next to Kwanhah on his horse. A half dozen Comanche bucks sat on their ponies behind Katharane and Kwanhah. He held her mustang's hackamore. His eyes were dark and cold and unforgiving. But, at that moment, Reid Stuart could not think of anything for which he had cause to ask the Comanche's forgiveness. He heard the two bucks' horses closing on him as he sprinted for Katharane. He looked at her. She was a beautiful child and would someday, he prayed, be a lovely woman. His heart hurt with pride and fear and hope and dread for her. A loud piercing cry broke the still air.

Katharane's eyes opened wide and filled with fear. "Daddy! My Daddy!" She screamed. She held both of her hands out to her father and worked them, open and then closed.

Reid Stuart glanced over his shoulder. One of the buck's had given up his pursuit, but the other buck's pony broke through the tall grass that flew back up from underneath Reid Stuart's crotch as he ran. The angry buck, a club gripped and held above his head, kicked the pony at the end of every stride.The buck's eyes glittered, bold, defiant and unafraid. Reid Stuart felt his heart leap. He stopped running and turned to face his attacker.

Kwanhah dropped the hackamore and drove his heels into his pony. The horse sprang forward, cutting off the charging buck. The buck jerked his pony to a halt. He sat face to face with his chief. Silently, without emotion or resentment, without question or complaint, he lowered his club and joined the other braves.

Katharane rode to her father. Reid Stuart gripped Katharane's hackamore near the mustang's jaw. She smiled at him. "Daddy." She said, quietly. He winked at her. She giggled.

Kwanhah rode to the promontory. Reid Stuart led Katharane's mustang and followed him. The bucks followed behind Reid Stuart and Katharane.

Katharane sat beneath the mustang, using its body to shade her from the mid day sun. Kwanhah and his braves sat cross legged before their ponies or squatted on their heels beside their mounts. They all watched Reid Stuart fight the unyielding canyon floor with his pick. Reid Stuart rolled the heavy pillar to the hole. He placed the butt of the pillar on the lip of the hole. Then he lifted the top of the marker until its bottom slid into the hole and the pillar dropped down against the rocky bottom. He turned the marker until the carved letter faced the big canyon and away from his and Katharane's and the gunman's canyon. With his right boot he pushed the thick sod against the marker. He turned the pick upside down and used the top of the handle to tamp the sod down into the hole around the pillar. When he had mashed the last bits of sod into place around the pillar he looked at Kwanhah.

Katharane lay asleep on the grass with her head against Kwanhah's leg. The Comanche chief lifted Katharane into his arms, stood up and carried her to Reid Stuart. He handed the child to her father. Katharane awoke. She rubbed her eyes and rested her cheek against her father's bony shoulder. Kwanhah pointed at the marker, then at the necklace around Katharane's neck. He spoke in the hard guttural sounds of the Kwerhar-rehnuh Comanche. Reid

Stuart looked at Katharane. She answered Kwanhah in bits and bursts of his tongue.

"What did he say?" Reid Stuart asked Katharane. But she did not understand how to translate Kwanhah's language into Reid Stuart's. She spoke both and she understood both, that was all.

Kwanhah pointed at the sun, then to the east and across the sky to the west.

'Movement of the sun,' Reid Stuart thought. "Time." He said and nodded to Kwanhah that he understood.

Kwanhah spoke in his tongue and a brave came to him. Reid Stuart shook his head that he did not understand. Kwanhah spoke again. Another buck came to him.

"He came to you." Reid Stuart said. "Time comes to you."

Kwanhah pointed at Reid Stuart.

"Time comes to me." Reid Stuart said. "The time will come to me." He looked at the chief and waited for him to give this meaning.

Kwanhah lifted his lance and placed the tip of it against Reid Stuart's chest and pushed. Katharane put her hand in her mouth. Reid Stuart swallowed and said. "The time will come to me when you will kill me." Kwanhah pulled his lance away. "Why?" Reid Stuart asked. Kwanhah mounted and barked a command to his braves. They all mounted and began to ride away.

Reid Stuart raised his chin and said boldly. "Or I may kill you." He carried Katharane to her mustang and set her on the harness. Then he pulled his Sharps from his saddle scabbard and cocked its heavy hammer. Kwanhah turned, lifted his lance, pointed it at the sun and shook his head. Reid Stuart set the hammer of the Sharps to half cocked. "It's not time." Reid Stuart said, paused, and added. "Yet." Kwanhah turned and rode away.

Katharane held up her right index finger and turned her head and listened. Reid Stuart stopped reading from his Bible. "Pop." She said confidently. She climbed out of the dugout and ran towards the spring.

"Katharane, wait!" Reid Stuart barked. He grabbed his Sharps and followed after her. But he, too, believed that the horse he could hear approaching was the gunman's black filly. Something in the peculiar cadence of the hooves' reports as they struck the hard rock of the canyon trail sounded so familiar.

"Pop! Pop!" Katharane sang and danced next to the spring. The black filly leaped onto the ground above the first pool. The gunman swung low and to his left and swept the child up onto the saddle in front of him. She laughed and giggled and bent her head back to look up at his face. He winked at her. Reid Stuart waited near the dugout. The gunman and Katharane rode to him.

"Welcome home." Reid Stuart said. He reached up to the gunfighter. The gunman gripped his wrist.

"'good to be home, Stuart." The gunman said and squeezed Reid Stuart's wrist. "I missed Katty."

Reid Stuart smiled. "And she's missed you. She's looked for you each morning."

The gunman smiled. He looked at the child and asked. "Is that right, Katty girl? Did you miss this worn out old gunfighter?"

"Yes. I did, Pop. Me miss you." Katharane answered, matching in part her grammar to her father's.

The gunman's gray eyes danced. He looked at Reid Stuart. "'forgotten how good it feels to be missed. Ain't much to be missin' ya' when it's just you and these plains." He said wistfully.

"I thought once, while you were gone, it was to be just you and these plains again, my friend." Reid Stuart said.

"Trouble?" The gunman asked.

"I will tell you about it later." Reid Stuart said. "Come on. Get down. Come in. Tell us about your trip. Was it successful? Did you remember my tobacco?"

The gunman stepped out of the saddle. He carried Katharane on his right arm. He set her on the ground, reached into his saddle bag and pulled a dark pouch from it. He tossed the pouch to Reid Stuart. "'best Tafoya had. And all he had at that. 'hope it'll do."

Reid Stuart untied the leather tie which held the pouch closed, sniffed its contents and said. "It will do just fine. Just fine."

The gunman reached back into the saddle bag and withdrew a thick roll of brown paper. He unrolled one fold of the brown paper and lifted a short stick of hard sugar candy off of the paper. He handed the candy to Katharane.

She held the stick of candy in the palm of her hand and looked at it. "What's it?" She asked.

"Candy." The gunman answered. He bent to her, closed her hand around one end of the stick and stuck the other end in her mouth.

The child slowly worked her lips against the stick. The candy began to melt in her mouth. She giggled. "Pop bring me candy." She said to her father.

"He brought you candy." Reid Stuart corrected her. Then he asked. "It is good, isn't it?"

Katharane nodded her head without giving up her grip on the candy. She wandered into the dugout to find the Squaw Woman and show her the prize.

The gunman reached into his saddle bags one more time. When he turned back to Reid Stuart he held three strands of beads, one red, one yellow, one blue. He handed them to Reid Stuart. "For that damn squaw." The gunman said.

"No!" Katharane screamed. She came scurrying out of the dugout. The squaw followed her, smacking her lips. "No Mama. No take my candy!" Katharane clutched the stick of candy with both hands and ran for the gunman. She stumbled and put out her hands to break her fall. The half eaten stick of candy dropped into the dust. The child stared at her candy and began to cry.

"Damn that squaw! I'll skin her." The gunman cursed.

Reid Stuart stepped between the gunman and the Squaw Woman with his back to the gunman. He offered the strings of beads to the Squaw Woman. She took the beads and returned happily to the dugout.

The gunman picked Katharane up and tried to soothe her. "Don't cry little Katty. Pop's got more candy for you." He offered her another stick of candy from the brown paper.

She shook her head. "Me want that one." She sniffed and

pointed at the dirt covered stick that lay on the ground.

The gunman returned the other stick to the brown paper roll and put the roll back into his saddle bags. He knelt, picked up the half eaten stick from the ground and carried it and Katharane to the spring. He sat on the backs of his boots and washed the stick of candy in the spring. The stick dissolved to half again its original size. But most of the dirt had been washed away. The gunman handed the stick of candy to the child.

"My candy, Pop. Katty's candy." She said and shoved the remainder of the candy into her mouth and sucked at it.

The gunman walked with Katharane holding his hand and nursing the candy back to Reid Stuart and the black filly.

"Was your trip a success?" Reid Stuart asked.

"Pretty much." The gunman answered. He reached across the filly and pulled a silver colored repeating rifle from the saddle scabbard and handed it to Reid Stuart.

"All right! You bought yourself some long range fire power." Reid Stuart said approvingly. He took the rifle from the gunman and admired it. He used the lever and opened the breach. A live cartridge flipped out the top of the breach.

"It's a repeating rifle." The gunman said.

"I know. We had them by the end of the war." Reid Stuart said. He bent and picked up the cartridge.

"We didn't." The gunman said.

Reid Stuart flinched, regretted saying what he had said, but did not try retreat from it. Instead he continued as if he had anticipated or not heard the gunman's statement. "Have you fired it?" He asked.

"Once." The gunman frowned.

Reid Stuart waited for him to continue.

"I shot at a big boulder in the canyon." The gunman said. He stopped and frowned again.

"And?"

"I missed."

Reid Stuart and the gunman looked at each other. "First time I've missed something I've shot at since the war." The gunman sighed, shook his head and said. "'can't be missin' and keep Katty alive."

Reid Stuart smiled. Katharane was never far from his partner's thoughts. "Don't worry about it." He said. "I can have you hitting everything you shoot at in no time."

"Good." The gunman said.

"Did you get anything else?"

"Just ammunition for the repeatin' rifle, some coffee and a bottle of whiskey." The gunman answered. He shoved the brown paper bag of stick candy back into the saddle bags. He untied the saddle bags and handed them to Reid Stuart. "'carry these and the repeatin' rifle into the dugout for me, and I'll drop my saddle and blanket. Katty and I will turn the filly loose below the bottom pond."

Reid Stuart took the saddle bags and the repeating rifle from the gunman and said. "I will have the Squaw Woman help cook something for us to eat."

The dugout was hot from the frying buffalo fat that sizzled around the large steak that popped and bubbled in the bottom of the large black skillet. Reid Stuart shook the long wooden handle that was attached to the hot skillet which sat on three iron rungs that protruded from one side of the rock fireplace. The Squaw Woman dipped both of her hands in a wooden water bucket and brought them out cupped and filled with wild grapes, dripping with cool spring water. She dropped the grapes into a wooden bowl which the gunman had carved from a piece of cottonwood he had found drifted against a ledge below the mouth of their canyon.

"Quite a feed, Stuart." The gunman said as he stepped down into the dugout.

Reid Stuart lifted the hot skillet off of the iron rungs and set it on the rock hearth. "Cold jerky can carry a man only so far." He cut the hot juicy buffalo meat into three equal pieces. He laid the pieces of meat on three small tin plates that were set around the wooden table. The gunman sat at the table on a large cedar stump. Katharane sat to his right on a smaller cedar stump. And

Reid Stuart sat on a large gnarled cottonwood stump at the end of the table nearest the fireplace. He cut the piece of meat on Katharane's plate into thirds. He lifted one of the pieces of meat with the blade of his knife and offered it to the Squaw Woman, who took the hot meat in her hands and retreated to the dark corner of the dugout behind the fireplace. "You would think she would eat at the table with us by now." Reid Stuart complained.

"Who wants her to?" The gunman asked. He cut one of the pieces of meat left on Katharane's plate into small bites.

"Berries." Katharane said. She watched the wooden bowl expectantly.

"Berries what?" Reid Stuart prodded her.

"Berries please." She said.

The gunman picked up the bowl and raked wild grapes onto her plate.

"Thank you." Katharane said and picked up one of the grapes with her fingers and ate it.

"You are most welcome, Miss Katty." The gunman chuckled. He raked a large pile of the grapes onto his plate and handed the wooden bowl to Reid Stuart. ""wild grapes are sure pretty this year."

Reid Stuart poured half of what remained onto his plate and then he carried the bowl to the Squaw Woman. "Yes. They are." He said as he returned to the table.

When their meal was finished, Reid Stuart cleared the tin dishes and the wooden bowl from the table. He stacked them on the stone hearth, picked up a wooden bucket and stepped out of the dugout. "You could do these dishes, once." He complained to the gunman as he carried the bucket to the spring.

"Teach that damn squaw of your's to do 'em." The gunman retorted.

"I have tried." Reid Stuart sighed. "She buries them."

"Watch her. When you catch her bury'n 'em, slap the shit out of her a couple of times and throw her and the dishes in the reservoir. Maybe she'll get the idea." The gunman suggested.

"I believe I would rather wash them myself, instead of resorting to your domestic tendencies, Canada."

"Then wash 'em and stop grittin' at me about doin' 'em. I ain't interested." The gunman opened the wooden crate. "'gonna' read to Katty." He said. He lifted Reid Stuart's Bible out of the crate. Katharane clapped her hands.

"I will join you when I am finished washing our dishes." Reid Stuart muttered. He carried the dishes to the reservoir. When he returned with them to the dugout Katharane lay asleep on the gunman's lap. The squaw snored on the cot. The gunman carried Katharane to the cot and laid her next to the squaw. Katharane took her feet and pushed against the squaw's large butt. The squaw wiggled over. The child had her place to sleep. The gunman picked up the repeating rifle. He carried it to the box which held the sextant and sat on the box. Reid Stuart stretched a buffalo hide on the dugout's dirt floor. He sat down on the hide and pulled his boots off. He lay on his back, folded his arms behind his head, and listened to the quiet of the high plains' night. "Katharane and I set the marker in the canyon."

"I saw it."

"Kwanhah and several of his braves found us there." Reid Stuart said quietly.

"And?" The gunman asked. He held the repeating rifle on his lap.

"And he told me that someday he would kill me, but not this day."

"And you told him?"

"That I would kill him first."

"You're learnin', Stuart."

"He could have killed me at his whim and taken Katharane. But he did not." Reid Stuart looked at the gunman. "Do you know why?"

The gunman shrugged. "He had a half-white sister, born of Nocona, his father, and a white girl, a Parker girl, taken from down around Weatherford near the Brazos. Kwanhah's mother. Rangers caught 'em in camp along the Lower Tongues. 'took his mama and that baby sister. Maybe he sees Katty as that sister." He breached the rifle. "And maybe he just wasn't in the mood to kill ya'. 'hard to say."

"If he had killed me and taken Katharane, would you have gone after her?"

The gunman sat silent.

"Would you?" Reid Stuart demanded.

The gunman stood up and laid the repeating rifle on top of the box. His gray eyes flickered in the firelight. He looked down at Reid Stuart.

"Would you?" Reid Stuart asked again. This time almost prayerfully.

"Why?"

"I need to believe you would have done that for me."

The gunman thought for several moments. Then he said. "I'd a gone." He looked at the cot where Katharane and the Squaw Woman slept. He looked back down at Reid Stuart and said. "But not for you."

"You love her. And it's killing you." Reid Stuart said. Their eyes met, and that moment was as close as Reid Stuart had come to understanding the hard quick handed lonely man he called Canada.

The gunfighter blinked and said. "I told ya', I'd a gone after her. What else would you ask of me, Stuart?"

"Nothing. Thank you." Reid Stuart said and rolled over onto his buffalo hide blanket to sleep.

The high plains' summer sky opened up in July and August and scorched the plains, the men and the horses. But Reid Stuart and the gunman rode relentlessly. Day after searing day they found, roped, marked and logged the Longhorn cattle. And the Longhorns were there. The tough, resistant, adaptable Texas Longhorn had conquered even the brutality of the plains' winters and the stifling heat of her summers. They were flourishing in the canyons, multiplying there. They had gone forth into a wilderness and adapted themselves to that wilderness. They grazed the buffalo range defiant of the wolves, the weather, the range itself.

Katharane was confined to the dugout most days because of the tortuous sun. She complained loudly each morning as her father and the gunman rode away. The gunman wore out horses and Reid Stuart's patience getting back to the dugout before night fell so Katharane could play above the dugout and in the spring.

"Dammit man!" Reid Stuart swore. "These horses are almost winded. We will ride them to death at this pace."

"I'll ride 'em down, then you, if I have to, Stuart." The gunman retorted. "I promised Katty I'd be back before dark, and that's what I aim to do." He spurred the hot thin wind drawn Indian pony.

Katharane met her father and the gunfighter where the trail from the canyon broke out onto the flat plateau which held the first reservoir. "Swim. Swim." She begged and pointed at the pool.

In a moment the gunfighter stood in the middle of the pool, wearing his hat, his shirt and his pistol. Katharane swam from the spring to him. She held onto his knees and bobbed up and down in the cool thigh deep water. The squaw circled the pool, moaning and pleading with Katharane to come out. The child ignored her. The gunman cursed her.

Reid Stuart left his partner and his daughter to their swim, the Squaw Woman to her vigil, and walked to the dugout to prepare their evening meal. As darkness came Katharane, the gunfighter and the Squaw Woman came to the dugout. With Reid Stuart they ate fried buffalo meat and venison. The early summer wild grapes were gone, withered by the heat. Now they lived off of fresh fried red meat three meals each day. After the meal the gunman took Reid Stuart's Bible from the wooden crate. He lifted Katharane onto his lap and opened the Bible. Reid Stuart stirred the fire until the remnant of an old twisted stump flamed again. The gunfighter read in the wandering light of the fire. "Psalm twenty-three, Katty."

"Psalm twenny-tree, Pop." Katharane tried to repeat the words.

"The Lord is my Shepard. I shall not want. He maketh me

to lie down in green pastures." The Squaw Woman crept close to the two men and the child and listened. "He leadeth me beside the still waters. He restoreth my soul. He leadeth me in the paths of righteousness for his name's sake." Katharane began to doze. The back of her head found the gunman's chest. "Yes, though I walk through the valley of the shadow of death, I will fear no evil for thou art with me, thy rod and thy staff they comfort me. Thou preparest a table before me in the presence of mine enemies." Katharane turned her face against the gunman's chest and settled to sleep. "Thou anointest my head with oil. My cup runneth over." Katharane slept. The gunman looked down at her. He began to close the Bible.

Reid Stuart put his hand on the gunman's wrist and said. "Finish it."

The gunman kissed the top of the child's head and read. "Surely goodness and mercy shall follow her all the days of her life. And she shall dwell in the house of the Lord forever." He closed the Bible. As he laid it on the wooden crate, Reid Stuart said. "Amen."

Winter caught them unprepared. Without warning or benefit of the usual September rains the first frost came the second week of October, followed by a blowing snowfall that drifted deep and impassable in the swales of the prairie and the gullies in the canyons.

The second day after the snowfall the gunman led the filly and the mule to the dugout. Reid Stuart led the buckskin from the corral below the pools. He mounted his horse. The gunfighter helped the squaw onto the mule and then set Katharane on his saddle.

"I do not believe my eyes." Reid Stuart said.

"What?" The gunfighter asked.

"You, helping the squaw onto the mule."

"Time's precious. 'ain't no buffalo in the canyon, I checked. 'snow will be drivin' them across the Canadian. It came in on us from the south. 'buffalo tend to move away from the snow, not with it. We gotta' catch 'em on the plains before they make a crossin' on the Canadian or we're goin' into an early winter without meat. And this snow and the drifts are gonna' make for some tricky slow ridin." His concern showed on the gunman's face.

"We will catch them." Reid Stuart assured him.

"We'd better." The gunman said, and swung up behind Katharane. "Katty'll ride with me, safer and warmer for her that way. Even if it is slows us a little."

"When you find their track I will go ahead and do the shooting. You can bring Katharane, the Squaw Woman and the mule at a slower pace. We will not loose any time that way." Reid Stuart said.

"'could be Kiowa close to 'em." The gunman warned. "They like to drift out from the Canadian and wander down to the canyons this time of year. And if they hadn't already, this snow will have blown 'em out of the Canadian's breaks for sure."

"I will watch myself." Reid Stuart answered.

The gunman led the small caravan out onto the snowy sun dancing prairie.

"How many?" Reid Stuart asked.

"'can't tell." The gunman answered. "'must be a lot. 'snow's packed flat twenty yards wide for miles."

Reid Stuart stared at the wide packed ruts which cut through the deep snow and carried away from him for miles. "It will not be difficult for me to find them." He said. He pulled the long Sharps from its sheath and rested it across his saddle.

"'don't get between them and the river." The gunman cautioned him. "And keep that buckskin staked near their path. 'case you need to get out quick. 'bein' on this packed snow will let you outdistance any Kiowa ponies easy enough." The gunman swung back up into his saddle behind Katharane. "'three quick shots in succession means trouble. I'll drop the squaw and Katty and come in a hurry." The gunman picked up his reins. "'follow it with two more and I'll take Katty and the squaw and high tail it for home." He looked at Reid Stuart. "And you'll be on your own."

Reid Stuart smiled. "Don't worry. This will go well." He said to the gunman. He moved his buckskin out onto the road the buffalo had plowed through the snow, and began his pursuit of them. The snow alongside of the buffalo plowed road grew deeper and deeper as Reid Stuart kept the buckskin loping steadily after the unseen buffalo. He topped a rise and before him a black sea of smoking movement rolled away from him across the prairie and off of the wall of the Canadian River's gorge. He rode to within a few yards of the stragglers which trailed the bunched main herd. He turned the buckskin off the road and into the belly deep snow and spurred the horse. The buckskin pitched through the deep snow until Reid Stuart could see the trail by which the buffalo seemed to swim off of the white prairie and down into the Canadian River's bottom.

Reid Stuart sat on his horse, steam pouring out of the buckskin's nose, and watched in disbelief as wave after wave of buffalo plunged into the river. Some swam through, some walked across their drowned and drowning kin. "My God!" Reid Stuart said aloud. "They are fording the river across their own dead. They are drowning themselves by the hundreds." He shook himself from his stunned spectating and stepped out of the saddle. He sank down into the deep snow. He laid the Sharps across his saddle. Then he remembered the gunfighter's warning. He remounted and spurred the buckskin back through the snow to the buffalo track. There he hobbled his horse, and then he trudged back along the narrow slot the buckskin had cut through the snow.

He stood waist deep in the snow, aimed at a young cow and fired. The Sharps jarred him. He rocked in his unsteady stance in the snow. The cow dropped to her knees. Reid Stuart knelt, pushed his right knee into the snow. From this position he killed two more cows as they approached the edge of the descent to the Canadian. But this did not deter the great herd. They bent around their fallen members and continued their surging descent to and into the river. Reid Stuart retraced his steps back to the buckskin. He untied the hobbles, remounted, picked up the buckskin's reins and followed the remnants of the great herd as they too rumbled off the flat plains and down into the river. At the dead cow which was nearest to the rim of the Canadian's gorge he dismounted and ground hitched his horse. He pulled his long knife from its sheath and bent over the cow. Then he heard Katharane's voice.

"Daddy. Daddy." She rode on the front of the gunman's saddle. The black filly with Katharane and the gunfighter, and the mule with the Squaw Woman, trotted up the buffalo trail.

"Good job, Stuart." The gunman said. "You caught 'em before they made the Canadian."

"They didn't make the Canadian, not all of them anyway." Reid Stuart said.

The gunman looked at the river. Buffalo corpses, rolled up like boulders, lay caught in eddies and shallows or against the cut banks on each side. Shiny black hooves stuck up out of the water. Where the main herd had forded the river a carpet of corpses dammed the water back and made it rush around each end of the hairy mangled bodies.

"'buffalo are strange creatures. They know bein' caught out on the plains in winter means certain death. So when the early snow hit 'em they formed up and headed away from it. Plowed right through drifts and ever' thing, even pitched into that river while others of 'em where drownin' by the droves. But they got the hell off these plains, and that's what we gotta' do." The gunman said. He handed Katharane down to Reid Stuart and dismounted. "We gotta' get these cows skinned and butchered and on that mule and outta' here before night falls. 'weather ain't right. I'm afraid another blow may be movin' in on us. That's why those buffalo didn't stop or bed down this side of the Canadian. They're headin' for the upper breaks and cover. We're gonna' have to make cover to." He pulled his large knife from its sheath which hung on the saddle. But before he could begin the squaw reached for his knife. She worked her fingers pleadingly and moaned. He handed the knife to her.

The Squaw Woman sat on her knees before the dead buffalo, gripped the knife with both hands and began to open the body cavity. Katharane struggled to be released. Reid Stuart set her down and she climbed onto the neck of the dead buffalo which lay on its side and sat there, talking with the squaw in the Kwerharrehnuh dialect.

"Stuart. That damn Comanch' squaw is teachin' our Katty how to butcher buffalo."

The squaw worked swiftly. The knife never seemed to stop. It moved in and about the carcass, making neat precise incisions, severing ligaments, rolling back cartilage until the heavy

131

innards of the buffalo dropped out onto the muddy packed snow, and all the while the squaw talked to Katharane in the dialect of her people, and the child answered in that same dialect.

Reid Stuart and the gunman watched for several minutes. Then the gunman said. "Well. Let's you and I skin those other two while she's guttin' that one." The two men skinned the other two cows. They drug the heavy wet hides out onto the deep snow and stretched them out to dry in the sun. The Squaw Woman was gutting the second cow. So Reid Stuart and the gunman skinned the first one and laid its hide on the snow to begin drying. The sun and the snow's reflection and their work made them sweat. The gunman dropped the old bull buffalo hide he wore as a heavy slicker onto the snow, also. Reid Stuart slid the hide he wore over his head and laid it on the snow. Then he untied the ties which held his buckskin coat closed and laid it on the hide. They worked hard throughout the remainder of the morning and into the afternoon. Yet, with only a third of the last cow butchered, the gunman stood up, wiped his hands and proclaimed. "Let's pack it up and make for home, Stuart."

"I hate to waste this animal." Reid Stuart said, remorsefully.

"'can't be helped." The gunman said. "Night ain't no time to be caught in a blizzard out here."

Reid Stuart looked across the unbroken whiteness upon which they seemed misplaced and so very small and appreciated the gunman's concern about riding across it in the dark. He grasped the wet hide the gunman was struggling to drag out onto the trail and together they tugged it free of the snow and onto the trail. They packed the bloody hunks of buffalo meat onto the hides, wrapped the hides around the meat and tied the hides at each end. Then they tied the meat laden hides onto the mule, one hide on each side of the mule and one across its rump, leaving its back free to carry the Squaw Woman.

"Do you think the Squaw Woman should ride with me? It may be too much for the mule." Reid Stuart asked.

"Have you smelled that bitch?" The gunman snorted and nodded at the squaw. The blood stained and smeared squaw squatted next to the partially butchered cow and fed small bites of its heart to herself and to Katharane. "'bad as she smells, I'd leave her before I'd let her ride close to me." Then he added. "'side's, mule won't mind. I don't think he can smell."

Reid Stuart chuckled and said. "His back may object more than his nose." But he led the mule to the squaw and Katharane and helped the squaw onto the mule. Immediately they departed. Reid Stuart led the mule which carried the buffalo meat and the Squaw Woman. He followed the gunfighter and his daughter.

Since they had left the easily followed trace of the buffalo herd the gunman had been silent. Reid Stuart had watched him slide Katharane underneath his buffalo robe. Then darkness, and with it a hard cold, had come upon them. He had heard Katharane complain of being cold, and he had seen the gunman reach underneath the buffalo robe with his left hand and after a few minutes she was quiet again, apparently warmed by what he had done. Now they rode through a cold starless darkness. The still night cast shadows of the animals and there riders against the flat snowy plains.

The gunman rode straight and stiff. He tried to see beyond the darkness, tried desperately to see a landmark, a star or just some difference in the pitch black sky above them by which to navigate. He could not. He was lost, lost and riding across the endless plains, the wind rising from the north, carrying on its breath cold and snow and cold and blizzard and freezing rain and ...He trembled. Katharane lay against his naked skin beneath his buckskin shirt, warm and content and asleep. But the temperature was falling and soon she too would feel the first bite of the cold. The first bite and the second and so on until...., unless through some innate sense he could find the canyon. He spread his nostrils. Maybe he could smell something, a whiff of cedar or cottonwood that would tell him they approached the life giving safety of their canyon. He smelled only the warmth thrown up from the soft friction of Katharane's face against his bare chest. 'Not this way. Dear God! Do not take her from me this way.' He urged the filly on through the snow.

"We're here! We're home!" Reid Stuart shouted. "You found it!"

The gunfighter reined the filly to a halt. He stared back across his shoulder at the dugout he had ridden passed without seeing.

"How did you find it?" Reid Stuart asked as he took his sleeping daughter from the gunfighter.

"I don't know." The weary gunfighter said as he stepped down from the black filly. "I knew I had to. So I did." Softer he said. "Stuart."

"Yes."

Very softly, almost imperceptibly, the gunman said. "I think I prayed to find it."

The harsh winter penned them in the dugout. During the long hours the gunman read from Reid Stuart's Bible to Katharane or drew letters in the dugout's dirt floor. Katharane spent hours on her hands and knees on the dirt floor. First, she traced the letters the gunman had drawn in the dust. Then she made her own likeness of the letters. Reid Stuart worked at the large piece of granite which he had badgered the gunman into helping him haul to the dugout. He chiseled at the granite, shaping more markers.

Winter seemed to leave as it had come, early. Late January brought bright, sunny days, days in which Reid Stuart and the gunman could ride without wearing the heavy buffalo capes which lay tied across the backs of their saddles. But in February, on the gunman's birthday, the plains winter showed its treacherous nature.

"Will we reach the dugout before it hits us?" Reid Stuart asked as he stared at the blue cold which rose relentlessly into the northern plains sky. He and the gunman long trotted their horses up their canyon.

"I think so." The gunman answered.

Reid Stuart and the gunman stepped onto the yard above the spring and in front of the dugout as the norther hit. They tucked their heads against their shoulder and side stepped against the wind, carrying their saddles on their hips. They stepped down into the dugout and stood their saddles on there fronts at the end farthest from the fireplace. Reid Stuart moved toward the fireplace.

"No." Katharane said. She blocked his way.

"I am going to warm myself at the fire, child." Reid Stuart said.

"Me make something for Pop." Katharane said. She pointed at the floor of the dugout.

The gunman stepped around Reid Stuart, squatted on his boots' heels and examined the dirt floor. In the loose dirt he read: HAPPY B DAY POP KATTY. He took the child into his arms. "'best gift this worn out old gunfighter ever got." He told her, and he kissed her forehead.

"There will not be many more such springs as this, amigo." Tafoya said. "Soon the soldiers will come even to these breaks." He waved his hand at the rugged Quitaque country. "And they will come to drive the Comanche and the Kiowa and myself from its lair." The Comanchero sighed. "They may come to drive you also from your canyon, mi' amigo."

"I've fought Yankee soldiers before." The gunman said. He jerked the cinch against the black filly's belly.

"Yes. And you lost." Tafoya murmured.

"Yes. But this time I got a Yankee on my side." The gunman said. He pulled his stirrup back down from where it rested against the seat of his saddle.

Tafoya looked across the dry ravine to where Reid Stuart, Katharane and the Squaw Woman were saying farewell to Kwanhah and the Kwerhar-rehnuh. "And you have the child." Tafoya put his hand on the gunfighter's shoulder. "You are burdened again, my friend, burdened by her. Be careful. You have come far and striven hard to be done with such burdens. Be careful she does not destroy you."

"I'm not worried 'bout her destroyin' me, 'bout Yankee soldiers destroyin' me. The only thing I'm worried about right now is why some lunatic Mescan left my package at a tradin' post twenty miles out of my way when he knew damn well I would be here." The gunman said. "And why a wise old thief, such as you, would send back an entire Spring's trade with the likes of them." The gunman nodded at the Comancheros who were forming the horses, cattle and wagons into a caravan to begin their long journey back to the New Mexico territory. "'just so he can ride with me to a post that he's abandonin' any ways. That's what worries me, amigo." The gunman swung up into his saddle.

Tafoya looked up at him. "Maybe I long for your company." He smiled. "And maybe I wish to know this child woman that can stir a heart as hardened as your's, my compadre."

"'swing up on that mule of your's, Mescan. And watch what you say to me about Katty. It would bother me for a mile or two if I should find need to shoot you for it."

Tafoya mounted his mule. "I will not give you need to shoot me, amigo."

Two horses were tied outside of Tafoya's lean-to. The gunman looked at Tafoya.

The Comanchero smiled. "Guests. They have been here almost a month, waiting for me to return from the Spring trades." He explained. He stepped down from his mule. "Come, compadre. What you seek. It is inside."

The gunman stepped down from his filly. Katharane slid off of the white mustang and ran to the gunman. "More candy, Pop." She reminded the gunfighter of his promise of earlier in the day, when he had mentioned they were going where he had gotten her candy from before. Reid Stuart dismounted. He looked at the squaw who sat on the mule and wrinkled her nose at some unfamiliar smell. He pulled the long Sharps from its sheath. "I'll wait here with the Squaw Woman." Reid Stuart said to the gunman. Tafoya led the gunman and Katharane into the dark lean-to.

"Well. Here's the bartender. He's back." A red faced cowboy who sat behind the three plank wooden table across from the single plank bar of Tafoya's said loudly. "Parley with them Indians, did you, Mexican?"

"Looky!" A short cowboy who sat next to the red faced one said. "He's brought us a little girly to play with." He pointed at Katharane.

"He'd best brought us more than that." The red faced cowboy growled.

Tafoya heard the loop slide off the hammer of the black

136

revolver. He smiled and walked around the end of the crude bar. "They are here, mi' amigo." He said to the gunman. He bent and lifted a wooden box from beneath the bar.

The two cowboys watched curiously as Tafoya opened the box and the gunman reached in and lifted two small black revolvers out of the box. They were slick with oil, black, with no bead or groove, and they had black walnut grips.

"And, the smith, he sent you this." Tafoya said. He pulled a small holster with twin scabbards from the wooden box and a leather pouch filled with cartridges.

The gunman took the holster and kneeled beside Katharane. She smiled at him. He turned her to him and slid the holster around her middle. He hooked the tongue of the holster through the slot between the lips of the other tongue. Then he pulled the soft string of black leather through the top slit in the tongue overlap and back through the bottom slit and tied the string behind the top tongue lip.

The second cowboy laughed, again. "Looky. A little girl with pop guns."

The gunman reached with his right hand and picked up one of the small pistols. He slid it into the right scabbard of Katharane's holster.

"Do you think she might be that gunfighter the Mexican spoke of?" The red faced cowboy chortled. The other cowboy laughed.

The gunman put the other pistol in Katharane's left scabbard. Then he stood up.

"Hey! Girly!." The cowboys called. "Come show us your guns." They laughed and poured more whiskey from the bottle on their table.

The gunman turned and faced the cowboys. Their laughter quieted. But it was too late. Tafoya moved to the other end of the bar. He smiled happily now.

"Take the pistol from your right scabbard, Katty." The gunman said quietly.

Katharane pulled the gun from the scabbard and held it

with both hands. "This one, Pop?"

"Pop!" The red faced cowboy snickered. Then he sobered.

"Yes." The gunman said. "Hold it with both hands." She gripped the pistol with both of her small hands. The cowboys shuffled their feet, nervous now. "Put both of your thumbs on the hammer." The gunman told the child.

She did. But sought reassurance from the gunfighter. "Like this, Pop?"

"Like that." The gunman coached her. "Now pull the hammer back as far as you can." Katharane cocked the pistol.

"Hey. What the hell you doin'?" The red faced cowboy whined. "She might let that thing go off." He raised his hands from the table.

The gunman turned and let his left hand rest against the black holster. The cowboy dropped his hands back to the table. "Now point it at the bottle on the table." The gunman instructed the child.

"Just point it at the bottle, Pop?" Katharane asked. She held the pistol in front of her with both hands.

"Just point it at the bottle and squeeze your fingers." The gunman said. His hand hung beside his black revolver.

"Dammit, man! We were just playin' with her, for Christ's sake!" The red faced cowboy cried. But he did not move.

"Now Katty, squeeze the trigger." The gunman said softly. She did. The bottle exploded. Glass shards ripped into the second cowboy's face.

"Shit!" The cowboy cursed and tried to clutch his face. But the gunman's black revolver spit smoke and fire and sent him reeling backwards against the wall, fatally wounded, before his hands reached his torn face.

"Christ!" The red faced cowboy cursed. "He was only reaching for his face, you murdering bastard."

The black revolver sat quietly in its holster, but the gunfighter's gray eyes challenged the red faced cowboy.

"No man. For God's sake! You can't just shoot me. You can't!" He pleaded.

"I'm not going to." The gunman said almost gently. "I'm gonna' let Katty do it."

"You're crazy!" The red faced cowboy screamed.

"Use both of your thumbs, Katty, and cock the hammer again." The gunfighter coaxed.

Katharane stared at the pistol she held in her hands. Reid Stuart reached down and took the pistol from her. The red faced cowboy dropped his face against the slatted boards of the table and wept.

"Bring Katharane." Reid Stuart said to the gunman. He walked out of Tafoya's before the gunman could argue with him.

The gunman picked the child up and carried her out of the lean-to. The red faced cowboy staggered out after them. He climbed onto his horse. He reached for the other cowboy's horse.

"Leave it." The gunman commanded.

He did. He rode away.

The gunman looked at Tafoya who now leaned against the opening into the lean-to. "I oughta' kill you, Mescan."

"Why, amigo?"

"This is what you brought me here for. To do your gun work."

"Why does that trouble you, mi' amigo? Always before you have had no worry about such things as this."

Katharane turned her face so she could see Tafoya. "It is her." Tafoya said. He smiled at Katharane. "She has taken your freedom in such things from you. I wonder, my friend, how much more you will allow her to take from you?"

The gunman let his hand move to his gun. Tafoya's eyes widened. The gunman lifted the black loop and placed it around the hammer of the black pistol. "You can have the horse. I'm takin' the saddle." The gunman said. "With a little work I can fit it to Katty."

"As you wish, mi' amigo."

"What about that dead man in there?" Reid Stuart asked.

"I will put some dirt and rock over him, mi' amigo's friend." Tafoya said. "And after that." The trader shrugged.

Reid Stuart looked at the gunman. For several moments he waited as if he struggled with a decision. Then he said. "Let's go home."

"Home?" Tafoya smiled. "Well, my friend." He said to the gunman. "You have given up much more than I supposed." And to Reid Stuart, he said. "Take care of your child, Yankee. Take care of her against everyone." He looked back to the gunman. Then he turned and went back into the lean-to.

HIDE HUNTERS, INDIANS AND SOLDIERS

Blood matted the tall thick prairie grass, and stripped, naked, rotting carcasses pot marked it.

"They're turnin' the plains to blood. Stupid bastards." The gunman cursed. "We'll all pay for this, and in blood, too."

"What do you mean?" Reid Stuart asked.

Katharane rode her mustang in and out of the mutilated corpses as if she was playing some morbid mounted game of hop scotch.

"'killin' buffalo like this is the same as if they were killin' the Indians themselves. And Kwanhah knows this, even if the others don't. They'll be raids everywhere this year. You can bet on it."

"Against us?"

"Against all whites." The gunman said. "Damn bloody butcherin' hide hunters. Damn their sorry hides for bringin' this on us." He rode to Katharane. Reid Stuart followed him. Katharane pointed at the two deep ruts in the sod.

"Where are they going?" Reid Stuart asked.

"To find more buffalo to kill." The gunman answered.

"Not my buffalo!" Katharane cried. "You must not let them kill my buffalo, Pop."

"Katharane." Reid Stuart tried to warn his daughter against provoking the gunfighter. But the gunfighter was already following the two ruts. Reid Stuart hoped the hide hunters did not cross onto the Escadara range. The gunman's mood was dark and dangerous. But along a shallow rise the ruts swung and began a route if followed long enough would take them not only onto the Escadara range but to the dugout. The gunman put his filly into a quick trot.

Suddenly, Katharane realized that the hide hunters course

led to the dugout. "Mama's there." She cried, and she pushed her white mustang into a steady lope.

Reid Stuart and the gunman let her lead. Reid Stuart watched for any scouts the hunters might have out looking for buffalo. The gunman studied the sign. They were closing quickly upon the wagon.

"Ease up, Katty." The gunman called to the child. He and Reid Stuart rode up to her. "Listen." He said.

Distant muted claps of thunder drifted to them across the prairie. "Sharps." Reid Stuart said.

"Bastards have found another stand." The gunman said. He studied the prairie before them. "You ride a semi-circle out to the right, Stuart. Try to find a rise to shoot that cannon of your's from and cover us. Katty and I'll go in on 'em."

"You're taking Katharane with you?" Reid Stuart frowned.

"She'll be safest with me." The gunman answered.

Reid Stuart did not argue. But he was not certain that he agreed. He reined his buckskin and moved forward to ride the point for the trio. The gunman put Katharane to his right and a half of a horse length behind his black filly. They moved forward to encounter the hide hunters.

The hide boss paled. He rose from where he lay in the prairie grass beside one of his shooters and turned to face the source of the Comanche cry that had broken the stand and sent the remnants of the two hundred and fifty or more buffalo stampeding across the prairie.

The shooter jumped to his feet. "Who was the stupid son-of-a-bitch that spooked 'em!" He cursed loudly.

The hide boss stared at Katharane as she confronted him on her white mustang. The gunfighter sat beside her on his black filly. "She did." The hide boss said and nodded at the child.

A teenage boy, one of the hide skinners, raced his horse up to the hide boss. "What the hell happened?" The young skinner demanded. "Why'd you bust 'em?"

"We didn't." The hide boss said.

Two more shooters joined the hide boss, the foul mouthed shooter and the young skinner. A fat skinner, a Mexican and the cook stood up from the back of the wagon to stare at Katharane.

"Did you not see the marker you passed?" Katharane asked the hide boss.

"We saw it." He replied.

"Then do you not know you are trespassing upon the Escadara?" She asked.

"Reid Stuart's high range?" The hide boss rubbed his chin. "I'd heard tell of him. But I didn't really believe he existed."

"He does. And it is our range, my father's, mama's, mine and Pop's." Katharane watched the group's eyes move to the gunfighter and back to her. She raised her chin and said. "And you are trespassing upon it."

"Ain't nobody's range, girly." The young skinner leered at her. "And maybe you'd best learn that now. Or someone might decide to skin you just to see if you are white." Before he could move, if he intended to move, so quickly its echo was fading off into the distant prairie before anyone could catch their breath the black revolver's blast knocked the young skinner from his saddle.

"You murderin' son-of-a-bitch! That was my baby brother!" The foul mouthed shooter screamed. His scream died, consumed by the volume and noise of Reid Stuart's Sharps as it roared out across the prairie. The fat skinner flipped backwards off of the wagon and landed face down among some of the bloody hides that stained the grass around the wagon.

"Be still! Damn you! Be still!" The hide boss yelled. "Be still or die!" The skinners, the shooters, the cook and the Mexican stood very still.

"You bastard! He only had a knife! He couldn't done you no harm." The foul mouthed shooter screamed at the gunman again.

"Shut your yap, Moody. Beaner's dead 'cause'n he made a move toward that girl. You so much as wiggle your nose at her and that black gun's gonna' get you, too." The hide boss warned him.

Reid Stuart reloaded. He was too far from them to know what was being said. He shot because the gunman shot. If the gunman shot again, so would he.

"We ain't lettin' 'em get away with murderin' my brother. Are we?" The foul mouthed one cried.

"If any of us get outta' here alive, we're gonna' be damn lucky." The hide boss replied. The butt of the black revolver gleamed in its holster. The gunman's hand lay quietly against the holster. His eyes stared straight at the hide boss.

"There's only him, the girl and one shooter, dammit! Mooar." The foul mouthed one argued.

"And that might be more'n enough to do us. But just in case it ain't, take a look." The hide boss nodded at Kwanhah and the five Comanche braves which had ridden onto the edge of the circle where the stand had begun, and sat on their ponies just behind Katharane and the gunman.

"Six stinkin' dog suckin' Kiowa ain't good enough to make me belly crawl, neither." The foul mouthed one cursed.

"Them ain't Kiowa, boy. Them is Comanche. And they ain't just six, neither." Mooar said.

Five more Comanche braves eased their ponies into the circle next to Kwanhah and his group of braves, and a half dozen others appeared to the left of Katharane and the gunman.

"Go." Katharane ordered them. Her voice shook. She felt sick to her stomach. "Go." She ordered again. "No one but my mama's people can kill buffalo upon the Escadara."

"What the fuck is the Escadara, you stinkin' little breed bitch?" The foul mouthed one screamed at her. The lance split his sternum, glanced upward and exited through the back of his neck. He swayed in his saddle, like some macabre scarecrow almost freed from its wooden perch but still impaled upon it at the base of its skull, then he fell sideways. The hide boss caught him and eased him to the ground. The gunman set the black revolver's hammer back against the brass shell casing and slid the gun back into its holster. One of the braves dismounted, walked between the gunman's and Katharane's horses and to the dead skinner, pulled the skinner's sharp hooked bill harpoon knife from its sheath, walked to the dead shooter and scalped the corpse.

"Oh no. No." The hide boss whimpered.

"Dear God." The cook groaned.

The Comanche, all but Kwanhah, yelped their delight as the buck held the bloody greasy scalp in his hands and bit into it. He ground his teeth into the tough skin until he cut a narrow slit in it. He tore a thin strip of buffalo hide from the inside seam of his ragged hairy black trousers. He worked the strip through the slit in the scalp. He put his left foot across the bridge of the foul mouthed one's nose and stood with his right foot on his stomach and jerked Kwanhah's lance free. He tied the scalp to the lance just beneath the feathers which were bound to its shaft at the top of the shaft just beneath its stone spearhead. Then he held Kwanhah's lance above his head, the blood glittering along the sharpened edges of its flint rock head, the two eagle's feathers twisting in the strong prairie breeze and the scalp hanging bloody and dead along the shaft. The Comanche screamed their approval as the buck handed the lance to Katharane, who took it reluctantly with her right hand.

"Go." Katharane's voice was barely a whisper. "Go." She said again, louder. She looked at the hide boss.

The hide boss lead Moody's horse to the wagon, mounted it there and signaled the cook, who clucked up the mules and swung the wagon around. The other skinners and the remaining shooters followed the wagon.

The gunman cut them off, forcing the cook to rein the mules in hard. "Leave the hides." He demanded.

The hide boss studied the gunman for a few seconds. Then he told the cook and the Mexican. "Throw 'em out. Throw 'em all out. 'don't want it said that Wright Mooar carried anything back to civilization from Reid Stuart's Escadara. 'don't want that curse on me."

The cook and the Mexican tossed the heavy hides over the sides of the wagon. "What about Moody and Beaner?" The cook asked.

The hide boss looked to the gunman for an answer. The

gunman stepped down from his black filly and walked to the skinner's body. The gunman pulled his knife from his belt and with four quick strokes he carved the drooped E into its forehead. "Now you can take 'em." The gunman said. He walked back to his filly and remounted. Kwanhah nodded at him.

The cook and the Mexican lifted the two bodies into the wagon, and the hide hunters once again resumed their retreat.

Kwanhah reached forward and took his war lance from Katharane. The gunman swept her off of her white mustang and held her against his chest. She trembled.

"You did real good, little one. You did real good." The gunman whispered to her. He held her close to him and stroked her hair. She stopped trembling. He looked down at her. The child was asleep.

"20 June 1874." Reid Stuart pressed the quill against the paper and the period at the end of the date spread in all directions, making a large circle on the white paper. He laid the quill beside the ink jar, picked up the paper and read aloud what he had written as his journal entry for June 20, 1874. "Spring came to the plains late this year. So Canada tells us. It has been both a wonderful and an awful spring. Wonderful weather. We have had rain without the barrage of violent storms of prior years. The canyon and the plains are abloom with grass. Glorious grass! And from our beginning count, a good calf crop. Our herd is growing...Awful in that we have killed men for trespassing upon the Escadara range. And we may yet face the same fate, death for trespassing upon the Comancheria. I worry for Katty-Katharane. Reid Stuart 20 June 1874." Reid Stuart laid the piece of paper in the leather journal and packed it, the quill and the ink back into the wooden crate. He sat down on his cot. The dugout had grown. He had added rock to reinforce the walls, a cot for himself, one for the Squaw Woman and a small one for Katharane. He looked. Katharane's cot was empty. She lay curled against the gunman's right side. The gunman slept on his back. His right arm draped around her, his left arm at his side, the black revolver beneath his hand. With warmer evenings the fat squaw's abundant body heat was not as welcome nor as comforting to the child as it was during the cold winter nights and Katharane, almost eight now, was becoming more and more aware of the Squaw Woman's heavy odor. Katharane had fled from the squaw's foul heat to the more pleasant security of the gunman's cot.

Reid Stuart stripped to his buckskin pants and stretched out on his cot. The cool plain's darkness carried him to sleep.

The Squaw Woman raised her chin. She flared her nostrils. She took one step backward, another and another, then she turned and ran to Katharane. She grabbed the child and disappeared into the dugout.

Reid Stuart stared at the empty prairie. "What is it?" He asked the gunman. He could see nothing but the hot baked grass of the prairie. Then he saw the gunman's hand draw the black pistol. He squinted, trying to see something other than the brown grass. Nothing, then he saw the flash from the black pistol's muzzle and he heard its report and almost with the report he heard the scream. Then he saw riders, dust and horses, arrows bouncing off of the hard packed yard. He ran for the dugout with the gunman. They landed on the dugout floor together.

"How many?" Reid Stuart asked, as he picked up his Sharps and moved to one of the three rock gun ports he had fashioned in the joint of the back wall and the ceiling of the dugout.

"'dunno'." The gunman answered.

A dozen horses thundered across the top of the dugout. Katharane cowered against the Squaw Woman. And the deadly black pistol took two of them down before the rest passed out of sight beneath the first pool. "They're flankin' us, Stuart!" The gunman cried. As he began to reload the pistol the Squaw Woman bolted from the dugout.

"Mama!" Katharane screamed.

"'desertin' Comanche Squaw dog." The gunman cursed her.

A Kiowa buck charged after the squaw from below the horse pool. Reid Stuart blasted him from his horse with the buffalo gun.

"The squaw made the horse corral." The gunman said. They heard a horse gallop away from the corral.

"Mama left me." Katharane murmured.

"'can't blame her, Katty. She's just a Comanch' and she knows what those Kiowa bucks would do to her." The gunman stopped speaking. He glanced at Katharane before he looked at Reid Stuart.

Reid Stuart saw the blind fear in his eyes. Slowly its meaning came to him. "She's just a child. Surely they'd just take her as a captive." He almost pleaded with the look in the gunman's eyes.

"She's nigh eight years. 'be a close call whether they'd take her as a slave or a woman." The gunman said as he finished reloading the revolver. "Besides. Do you know what it means to be a Kiowa slave."

"It means she would be alive." Reid Stuart argued. Then he asked. "How much water do we have?"

"'nough for three days, maybe four. But they got enough for all summer."

"Mama's gone." Katharane mumbled softly.

"Put her to bed on the floor, Stuart. I'll take the first watch. Then I'll load shells while you take the second. It's almost dark. I figure they won't come at us 'till dawn."

"Mama! Mama!" Katharane cried in her sleep on the floor. "Mama."

"Damn squaw. I'll slit her nostrils for leavin' Katty." The gunman cursed.

"Do you honestly believe you are going to get an opportunity to do that?" Reid Stuart asked.

The gunman did not answer. He kneeled beside Katharane and rubbed her back. "Poor little thing. She's lost two mamas in her short life."

Reid Stuart felt his stomach burn. He tried to fight back the angry words which flew to his lips, but he could not. "You mean she's had two mothers taken from her. Don't you!" He said bitterly.

"No." The gunfighter said slowly. "Far as I can see neither

mother had cause for abandonin' her." He said and continued to rub the child's back. "Not that damn squaw to the Kiowa." He raised his head and stared through the growing darkness at Reid Stuart. "Nor your Yankee wife to you, Stuart."

Reid Stuart stood up and started to the gunman. A shadow flickered in the corner of his eye. He spun, raised the Sharps with its hammer already cocked and fired at the moonlit silhouette that bent over the spring to drink. The Kiowa howled with hurt and surprise and rolled down the canyon wall to the second pool and out of sight of the dugout. Katharane cried out.

"Sshsh. Little Katty. Pop's here." The gunman quieted her. "Ya' hit him. But I don't know if ya' killed him." He said to Reid Stuart.

"The bastards may drink. But they will do it from the second pool and not from Katharane's spring." Reid Stuart swore.

The gunman smiled. "'sound's like something I'd say, Stuart."

Reid Stuart sat back down upon the floor. His anger with the gunman was gone. "It does. Doesn't it?" He said.

The Kiowa made one feint at the dugout the next day. But they did not carry through with their charge. Katharane drank as she pleased from the bucket. Reid Stuart stood at one of the center gun portals in the back of the dugout and watched his daughter curl up on the buffalo hide the gunman had stretched on the floor for her as the sun began to set. "Is there any way out?" Reid Stuart asked.

"'man. 'movin' after dark. 'might slip through 'em and make it down the canyon." The gunman answered.

"Could you do it?"

"I might. But I doubt it." The gunman counted the cartridges for the repeating rifle. "But I'd be afoot and two hundred miles from the nearest white man. I'd just be savin' myself. 'nothun' more." The gunman stood up and walked to the portal through which Reid Stuart stared at the empty prairie. "There ain't no help to be had, Stuart, even if I made it through. We're alone. 'watchin' those Godless plains ain't gonna' change that."

"I know." Reid Stuart said. "But I either watch these plains or pray. And I haven't prayed for so long it seems all too convenient to do so now." He looked at the gunman. "Even if it is for my child." Reid Stuart turned and stared back through the gun port at the empty prairie.

"'you believe in God, Stuart?"

"Yes. I do."

The gunman put his hand on Reid Stuart's shoulder and said, "Then pray. Pray for Katty. I am. And I don't even know if I believe in a greater power or not." He squeezed Reid Stuart's shoulder and stared at the prairie with him.

The Kiowa sang and chanted and waited. The sun rose and the sun set, and the water in the bucket slipped slowly away. The two men stopped sipping from it a day before the child finished the last few drops. And then the following day she felt the first true thirst she had known in her young life. She frowned and watched the bucket as if she expected somehow it would fill with water. It did not.

"You may go, if you wish." Reid Stuart spoke to the empty prairie. "You have done more for Katharane and I than we have had right to ask of you."

The Kiowa chanted and croaked incessantly in the coming night below the pools.

"'wasn't goin' nowhere when you came. 'stayed 'cause of this Katty girl." The gunman answered. He rubbed Katharane's back as she slept on the old bull buffalo hide. "'ain't much interested in goin' nowhere without her now."

"We will be going into our third day without water, Katharane her second." Reid Stuart said. "How many more can we last?"

"'few." The gunman answered. "But we're gonna' last those few. 'let Katty see another couple of sunsets, if nothun' else."

Katharane whimpered, stirred and struggled to sleep, tormented by her thirst and the Kiowa's ceaseless cries and threats.

"I'll read to her from your Bible. She's used to being put

to sleep by that." The gunman said. He withdrew the Bible from the wooden crate, opened it and began to read in the dim reflected light of the moon from the Psalms. "He that dwelleth in the secret place of the most High shall abide under the shadow of the Almighty. I will say of the Lord, He is my refuge and my fortress; my God; in him I will trust. Surely he shall deliver thee from the snare of the fowler, and from the noisome pestilence. He shall cover thee with his feathers, and under his wings shalt thou trust; his truth shall be thy shield and buckler. Thou shalt not be afraid for the terror by night; nor for the arrow that flieth by day." The child lay still and began to snore softly.

The gunman offered Katharane the small bite of dried buffalo meat which he had chewed for her. She took it and put it in her mouth. But she could not swallow it. She gagged. She had not had a drink of water for three days. Reid Stuart and the gunman had not for four days. Katharane tried to wet her lips, but her tongue was almost as parched as her lips. "I'm thirsty, Pop. Katty thirsty."

Agony cut across the gunman's face. Reid Stuart felt sorrow for his partner. He knew the gunman could and would withstand almost anything for Katharane, but not her suffering. The gunman could not ignore her entreaty. He grabbed the rawhide handle of the empty wooden bucket with his right hand, set the hammer of his black pistol on half cock with his left thumb, stepped up out of the dugout and walked toward the spring.

Suddenly, time stopped and time raced. It seemed an eternity to Reid Stuart before the first two Kiowa charged. He could see the gunman was at the spring. Surely he could smell the cool sweet water of Katharane's spring. Then the black pistol spoke as if uninterrupted by the necessity of the mechanical movement necessary to cause the hammer to strike the heads of the brass shell casings. Both bucks went down. Reid Stuart was elated. His heart throbbed within his chest. He laughed out loud.

The gunman swung the bucket into the pool directly beneath the spring and brought it out with water pouring over its sides. Reid Stuart rubbed his lips with his tongue as he watched the water splashing down his partner's buckskin pant's leg. Another buck charged the gunman. He sent an arrow slicing toward the gunman. The arrow ricocheted off of the hard pan behind the gunman and Reid Stuart thought it must have passed directly through the gunfighter's body. But the gunfighter snapped off two rapid rounds and this buck, too, died. Then Reid Stuart heard it. The ground from beneath the spring threw up an echo of the hard pounding driving sounds of horses, many horses, running hard. Reid Stuart's heart sank. He raised his Sharps to his shoulder and dropped the lead Kiowa pony before it could clear the ledge beneath the spring where the first pool formed. Reid Stuart dropped the Sharps, its one round spent, and grabbed the gunman's repeating rifle.

The gunman killed the second horse as it tried to jump from the first pool's ledge. Now the black pistol was empty and silent. He glanced at the dugout, at Reid Stuart, then at Katharane, and he smiled.

Reid Stuart pumped two rounds into the mass of horses that burst from beneath the spring and onto the yard before the dugout. Then he stopped, seized by the gunman's eyes that flashed and danced, first with surprise, then with pride, then with despair. "No! No! No!" He screamed.

Katharane ran toward him, clutching both of her pistols in her hands. The Kiowa swung their horses into line, preparing to charge the gunman who now kneeled on his left knee and held the child in his arms. The gunman swung Katharane onto her knees behind his raised right leg and grabbed her pistols. His black pistol dropped into the dust. He fired both pistols at the mounted Kiowa. Reid Stuart worked the lever action of the repeating rifle with a fury. Their combined fire drove the Kiowa backwards. The braves circled back off of the yard and onto the first pool's ledge and regrouped. Frantically the gunman felt along his belt for ammunition. He had none.

"No more bullets, Pop." Katharane said.

The gunman looked down at the child sitting on her knees behind his leg. She held her empty hands up to him. He held her small pistols in his hands. Reid Stuart had his left foot out of the dugout. He held the heavy Sharps by the barrel. Katharane looked at the water and licked her lips. The gunfighter knew they were spent. Heavy tears welled up in his eyes. He put his right arm against Katharane's back. "Go ahead, Katty. Drink all you want." Katharane smiled with the peaceful happiness of a child grateful for an even simple kindness. She cupped her hands in the water and bent her face to them to drink. For a moment, one eternal second of damnation, the gunfighter reasoned to drown her in the water bucket. But he could feel Katharane taking the water into her. He could feel her breathing. He was a hard man, hard like the plains he lived on. He had killed with as little mercy as they had, but this was beyond even his strength of will. He heard a horse clamber up the steep trail behind the pool. He cocked the empty useless pistol. The sound of the hammer being cocked would buy a few precious seconds more for Katharane to drink. He trained his eyes on the first pool from where the buck would have to charge, and prepared his mind to make his body take the horse and rider to the ground. They would not come by Katharane easily.

"Mama!"

The gunman looked at the child who stared at the top of the half dugout. Reid Stuart stepped out of the dugout and turned to look above it.

"Mama, you've come back!" Katharane cried and ran toward the corner of the dugout. The Squaw Woman sat on a horse next to Kwanhah. She slid down and lumbered toward Katharane. Horses carrying naked and almost naked painted warriors seemed to rise up out of the plains, as many as the innumerable tufts of buffalo grass.

"Comanche?" Reid Stuart called to the gunman.

"There's never been this many Comanch' on these plains. I make their number at better'n five hundred." The gunfighter said. "And they're not all Comanch'. Stone Calf and White Shield." The gunman nodded at two of the riders. "Leaders of the southern Cheyenne. The two next to them I make to be Lone Wolf and Woman's Heart of the Kiowa. And it looks like Kwanhah has been chosen to lead this war party. The big mucky muck there." The gunman bent his head towards an Indian wearing a full headdress. "I don't know."

"Eeshatai, prophet to the Arapahoe, the Cheyenne, the Kiowa." Kwanhah answered. He was listening closely to what the gunfighter was telling Reid Stuart.

"And the Kwerhar-rehnuh?" The gunman asked Kwanhah.

153

"And the Kwerhar-rehnuh." Kwanhah answered.

"What does it mean for us?" Reid Stuart asked.

"It means Katty will be okay. Kwanhah will see to that. But I'm not so sure for me and you. This is definitely a raiding party. And from their size and look I'd say they aim to butcher every white they can find."

"They butcher the buffalo. We starve." Kwanhah declared.

"We don't." Katharane spoke directly to the Comanche chief from the front of the dugout where the Squaw Woman had carried her. Kwanhah nodded at her. She smiled brightly at him. Several of the bucks and Stone Calf laughed at this. But the leader of the Kiowa that had besieged the gunman, Reid Stuart and Katharane did not laugh. He led what was left of his band forward, stopping halfway between the upper pool and the dugout. There he demanded his right of conquest, the right to kill and scalp the gunfighter and Reid Stuart and to take Katharane.

Kwanhah explained how Katharane had stopped the hunters from killing buffalo on the Escadara and how she sent them away, and how the gunfighter and Reid Stuart had forced this upon the hunters.

"What are they saying?" Reid Stuart asked.

"That Kiowa wants our scalps." The gunman answered. "And Katty."

"The bastard!" Reid Stuart cursed.

"Kwanhah's tellin' him 'bout Katty runnin' those hide hunters off the Escadara. He's tellin' him that she's strong magic, good medicine. Stone Calf and White Shield agree with Kwanhah that Katty's not to be tampered with. Lone Wolf and Woman's Heart are stayin' silent. They're Kiowa and this ban we've shot up is Kiowa." The gunman explained to Reid Stuart. "'more importantly, the Prophet there ain't sayin' nothin', yet."

Reid Stuart looked at the silent, stone faced Eesahataii. The great medicine man did not return his look. The Kiowa, weary from arguing, screamed at Kwanhah, speaking partly in his dialect and the voice of the People, the Comanche. "At least let me kill the white men. They have killed many of my warriors. The spirit of my dead warriors cries for their deaths. The squaw can tend the child." Lone Wolf and Woman's heart nodded their approval of this plan. They could see no reason to spare the gunman or Reid Stuart.

The gunman jerked his knife from his belt. "Stinkin' dog eatin' Kiowa."

"What is it?" Reid Stuart asked.

"Our friend there is bargainin' leavin' Katty be as long as he can lift mine and your scalps. And the Kiowa chiefs are backin' him now."

The Kiowa raised his war club and screeched his challenge at the gunmn. Suddenly he fell silent. He stared at the lip of the dugout. Katharane stood there. She wore her white doe skins. The Squaw Woman had braided the child's auburn hair into a single braid. Around her neck hung Cynthia Parker's rope necklace, the one Kwanhah had given the child when Reid Stuart and the gunfighter had first carried her into his camp. Kwanhah stiffened on his mount and all fell silent around him. Whether he was remembering his mother, Cynthia Ann Parker, the captured white wife of Kwanhah's father Nocona, or his baby sister, Topsannah, as she was at eighteen months when Sul Ross's rangers captured her and Cynthia Ann along the Lower Tongue River, or whether he sensed Katharane's desperate ambition and knew it posed a dilemma he would have to resolve, the gunfighter could not know, but he did know that a crisis was at hand. He glanced at Reid Stuart, who was staring at his young daughter. Katharane raised her arms above her head and began to speak in the tongue of the Squaw Woman's people.

Lone Wolf and Woman's Heart had met to trade with Tafoya at the River of Tongues. They could understand what the child said and they translated for Eesahataii.

"What in the world is she doing?" Reid Stuart exclaimed.

"'tryun' to save our lives." The gunman answered.

"What is she saying?" Reid Stuart asked.

"She is tellin' them the buffalo come every year just as the great cold from the plains comes. They come because the hide hunters cannot, because her magic is strong, stronger than even the

155

hide hunters. That you and I are her magic. If they take us from her, they take her magic from her. Then the buffalo will no longer come because the hide hunters will come and butcher bulls, cows, calves, all of them. But with her magic there will always be buffalo on the Escadara for the Kwerhar-rehnuh to hunt and to kill and to eat."

"There will be no hide hunters left when we are finished." Lone Wolf reminded Kwanhah and the others.

Eesahataii rode his horse forward and confronted the child. "Then what need have we of your magic if there are no hide hunters?"

Woman's Heart translated Eesahataii's Cheyenne into the tongue of the Kwerhar-rehnuh.

"So that's what this is." The gunman said. "The Prophet intends to rid the plains of buffalo hunters. So he doesn't see much need for Katty's magic."

"That is not good for us, is it?" Reid Stuart asked.

"No." The gunman answered. "Look." He nodded at the dugout. The Squaw Woman whispered something to Katharane. The child turned and faced the canyon. She put her hands on her hips and raised her chin. The gunman smiled and Reid Stuart shook his head. The child stood calmly, stoically and self-assuredly in front of a nation of warriors that was ready to slaughter and torture her, her father, the gunfighter, even the squaw, waiting only for the Prophet's command. But she stood there as defiant to them as they were to her, buoyed by the Squaw Woman's gentle coaxing. Again in the tongue of the Kwerhar-rehnuh Katharane called out to the canyon.

"Jesus Christ, Katty! No!" The gunman exclaimed. But the child ignored him and continued to speak.

"What's wrong?" Reid Stuart asked.

"Katty's sendin' the buffalo from the canyon. If the Prophet doesn't buy it we're done for and Katty may be to."

But from the canyon came a sound, a sound non-distinct to unknowing ears, but to those that had listened to it and for it each year of their lives it was as clear as the words the child spoke.

It was the sound of the hooves of the great herd as they scraped across the shale rock floor of the canyon near its mouth with the large canyon. The herd was beginning its yearly pilgrimage out into the large canyon and from there up onto the plains. The buffalo were leaving just as the child had beseeched them to do. Several of the Kwerhar-rehnuh bucks began to wail for they recognized the sound and its source. Kwanhah silenced them. Katharane stopped speaking and turned and looked at the Prophet.

Kwanhah told Woman's Heart to tell Eesahataii that the buffalo were leaving as Katharane had told them. Eesahataii raised his right arm to gain attention. He said to Katharane. "Your magic is strong. But have you cursed the buffalo from this canyon for all the seasons to come?"

"If I am here." The child answered, still using the language of Kwanhah's band. "And they are here." She pointed at her father and the gunfighter. "My magic will bring the buffalo again." She turned her face from Eesahataii and beamed up at Kwanhah. "And the Kwerhar-rehnuh shall hunt them and have them, their meat, their hides, their bones, their hearts, for it is the Kwerhar-rehnuh and Kwanhah that gave me my mother."

Kwanhah smiled. The Prophet nodded. But the Kiowa leader, filled with fury, made a rash and fatal decision. He turned his horse at Katharane, raised his war axe high above his head and screamed. "Then let her magic save her!"

The gunman started forward to intercept the Kiowa, but he made only one step because Kwanhah's horse landed between him and Katharane and the mounted Kiowa, and the air exploded with the vibrations of the Comanche death cry. The Kiowa stopped, but withdrawing his challenge would not spare him for the Comanche war chief issued his own and again the dusky air of the high plains rang with the rising octaves of Kwanhah's cry. Kwanhah threw his shield to the ground, raised his war lance, the eagle's feathers just below its stone head twisted gently in the dying breeze of the day. He filled his chest with air which caused his tawny sun burnt shoulders to rise up and apart, and cried out loudly once again. Then he charged and drove his spear through the Kiowa's chest, killing him. There was silence as Kwanhah dismounted, walked to the Kiowa, put his right foot on the dead man's chest and jerked his spear free. Then the early evening erupted with excited cries, hoots and exaltations from the Kwerhar-rehnuh's bucks. They were in a frenzy of excitement from the girl's performance and their chief's daring.

Eesahataii sensed the danger to his expedition. The Comanche would turn on the Kiowa and fight them to the death if Kwanhah now ordered it and Kwanhah clearly would have no one tampering with the child. The Prophet raised his arms and silenced the bucks. He spoke directly to Katharane. "Your magic is strong. It has saved the two whites. As long as the buffalo come to your canyon no Cheyenne nor Arapahoe nor Comanche nor Kiowa will molest you. Your magic lies with the buffalo. Do you understand?"

Katharane raised her head and said in the Kwerhar-rehnuh tongue. "My magic lies with the buffalo and my father and my Pop and my mother." She paused, turned around and looked at the Comanche war chief and said. "And Kwanhah."

Again the Prophet nodded.

"We're gonna' be all-right, Stuart." The gunman said. "Katty's done it. She's saved us."

"Katharane and the Squaw Woman have saved us." Reid Stuart said.

"Damn squaw." The gunman cursed.

The plains rang with the cries of the dying during the summer of 1874. The buffalo died by the thousands before the hunters' guns. The hunters died, maybe a half dozen or more, beneath the Comanche lances. And the Comanche died, not by blood, at least not their own blood, but by the buffalos' blood and the hide hunters' blood. It brought soldiers, black soldiers wearing blue uniforms, with orders to drive the Comanche and the Kiowa from the plains. And now Katharane traveled daily with her father and the gunman. Her white mustang was never more than a few quick strides from the black filly and the gunman, whose eyes were more often on her than on the cattle he and Reid Stuart roped and branded. By September the black soldiers were positioned to strike deep into the canyon country, the heart of the Comancheria where custom and faith told the Comanche they were safe from any pursuer.

Katharane sat on her white mustang next to Kwanhah and his black war pony.

"'don't like leavin'." The gunman said as he jerked the cinch tight against the black filly's belly. Faint, muffled pops of distant rifle fire came from where their canyon met the big canyon.

"Do we have a choice?" Reid Stuart asked. He sat on the buckskin and held the filly's reins.

"'ain't never run from Yankee soldiers before." The gunman said and jerked the cinch again.

"I'm not speaking of the cavalry." Reid Stuart said. He glanced at Kwanhah. "I think he intends to take Katharane and the Squaw woman, whether you and I go or not."

"'makes sense." The gunman said. "He knows those damn black buffalo soldiers get the taste of blood and they'd as soon kill a squaw and a child mistaken for her offin' as they would him and his people." He swung up into his saddle.

"I do not believe officers of the United States Cavalry would condone the killing of a woman and a child." Reid Stuart said.

"'wanna' bet." The gunman said. "'ride down the canyon and look. Then you'll believe. Or if you're so damn certain, stay here with Katty and the squaw and wait for those officers."

"They would take the Squaw Woman to a reservation. I cannot do that to Katharane or her." Reid Stuart said as they followed Kwanhah and the Kwerhar-rehnuh away from the dugout. "I don't like going out onto the plains with winter this close on us. We haven't made our fall buffalo kill, and we are carrying more than half of our present rations on this mule." Reid Stuart said. He shook the rope by which he led the roan mule.

"We'll get our winters supply of buffalo meat and more, 'less I mistake our guide's intended destination." The gunman replied.

"That would be?" Reid Stuart asked.

"Canyons de amarillas, the Yellow Houses, below the Tule." The gunfighter explained. "'be filled with the winter herds by now, and they are a far hard ride for your Yankee troopers.

Maybe too far and too hard, Kwanhah hopes."

"Do you know this country?" Reid Stuart asked. For two days and nights Kwanhah had led the people, Reid Stuart, the gunman, Katharane and the Squaw Woman south by southwest, deep into the southern plains.

"A little." The gunman said.

"How little?" Reid Stuart asked.

"'little enough that I'm makin' note of landmarks so I can get us back."

"Are you certain that we are going back?" Reid Stuart asked as he stared at the broad back of Kwanhah.

"Yep. 'soon as the hunt's over. Comanch' only winter in the canyons." The gunman said. "And they, like I, know that Yankee soldiers have no stomach for stayin' and waitin'. They'll have come and gone before the first days of November."

"November!" Reid Stuart exclaimed. "That's almost six weeks."

"'be six to eight weeks before this hunt ends." The gunman said.

Reid Stuart looked at the cold dark faces that rode silently around him and the gunfighter. He found no comfort in the thought of eight weeks of their silent company, no comfort and little rest.

"Rescate." Kwanhah said and pointed ahead.

"What did he say?" Reid Stuart asked the gunman.

"Rescate." The gunman said. "'place where the Comanch' traded their white captives to the Comancheros and Mex's for bounty or horses. Rescate." The gunman repeated the name.

Reid Stuart watched the far distant canyons seem to rise up from the prairie, looking like so many large yellow houses that climbed up out of the flat prairie. Then he, too, used Kwanhah's name for the canyons. "Rescate." He murmured and wondered if they were as much in need of rescue or barter for their freedom as the kidnapped white captives which had been brought here.

"Fire?" Reid Stuart asked. He pulled the mule up to a short lead. He had no intentions of losing their winter's buffalo meat because the silly creature decided to spook at the smell of smoke. It had been too hard an eight weeks of hunting and living with the Kwerhar-rehnuh to be wasted on the stupidity of a mule.

The dark cloud boiled above the prairie like smoke from a prairie fire, churning and bubbling up into the plains sky, rolling over itself as smoke did when it was following a grass fire. But this cloud did not move. It just rose into the prairie sky, dropped quickly back to the prairie and seemed to vanish into the ground.

"'don't think so." The gunman answered. He moved his black filly in front of Katharane's white mustang and slowed the pace. "'ain't movin' like a fire would. 'smoke just seems to hangin' in 'bout the same spot." He pulled the brim of his hat down. "Damned if I can figure it. 'looks like it's comin' from about where the Tule should be."

"We're that close?" Reid Stuart asked.

"We're that close." The gunman answered. He swung the black filly at the distant cloud. Reluctantly Reid Stuart followed him.

"My God! What is it?" Reid Stuart asked.

"Horses." The gunman answered. "Dead horses and buzzards feedin' on them, what's left of them. More buzzards than they are blades of grass on this godforsaken prairie."

In the bottom of the Tule canyon the ruined remnants of a thousand swollen bloated rotting carcasses poked their rigid stripped legs to the sky, which pitched and rolled above them with what seemed to be a thousand buzzards for each carcass.

"How?" Reid Stuart asked.

"I don't know." The gunman answered. "Someone must've driven them in there and shot them."

'Why?' Reid Stuart began to ask, but did not. Instead he said. "The Army. They are trying to put the Comanche afoot."

The gunman nodded. "Brutal but effective." He said. "With winter comin' even the Comanch' cannot survive on these plains afoot."

161

The stench from the vomit of the gluttonous buzzards rose out of the narrow canyon and stifled their breaths. Katharane gagged. The gunman turned the filly. "Come on!" He yelled to be heard above the cloud of croaking buzzards that rose from the canyon, disturbed by the forced ingress of a new flock upon the almost barren carcasses that covered the canyon's floor. "Let's get home."

The squaw smelled them on the wind. She rolled her eyes and begged Katharane to come to her. Katharane refused. She rode beside the gunman.

"Soldiers." Reid Stuart said. "Union mounts above the dugout." He pointed at the four horses staked above the dugout.

The gunman hit the filly with his spurs and she trotted forward to the dugout. Katharane's white mustang matched her trot. Four black soldiers stood in the dugout. They had opened the wooden crate. A young officer, white, flanked by a black Sergeant and four more black soldiers, all mounted on large long gaited horses, sat on their horses in front of the dugout. They turned and each stared at Katharane.

"You niggers make it a habit of trespassin' in another man's home." The gunman said. He dropped the loop from the black revolver and shoved Katharane's mustang behind the filly.

Reid Stuart led the mule with the Squaw Woman and the buffalo meat to the dugout.

"They are soldiers, sir. Soldiers in the service of the United States Army and under the command of Ranald McKenzie." The Lieutenant stated proudly.

"Are they now?" The gunfighter retorted. "Soldiers, black soldiers. I don't see no black officers. Do you?" He looked about as if searching for a black officer.

The Lieutenant's face reddened.

"No. No black officer. 'gotta' be a gentleman to be an officer. Right, Lieutenant?" The gunman did not allow the young lieutenant to answer. Instead he answered for him. "Right, and since they can't be gentlemen, they can't be officers these black soldiers of your's. The best they can be is cannon fodder for your Yankee army." Now the gunman leaned heavily on the black revolver's grip. "Now take your niggers and git, Lieutenant. And tell your Yankee colonel it's been a while since I've had the pleasure of killin' any Yankee soldiers. But if he sends any back up this canyon I will be happy to oblige him."

"Colonel MacKenzie is not the kind of man to accept ultimatums." The Lieutenant tried to sound certain of his position and its strength. He was not.

"He ain't got a choice." The gunman stared the young lieutenant down.

The young officer cowered angrily. "You will regret this, sir." He cried at Reid Stuart as he ordered his detail to withdraw into the canyon. "You certainly will."

The Squaw Woman slid off of the mule and walked to Katharane's mustang. Katharane let the squaw lift her off of the horse. Together, they disappeared into the dugout. Reid Stuart stared at the gunfighter. The gunfighter met his stare and said. "I ain't got no use for your Yankee army using blacks as soldiers, Stuart."

"What I have no use for is a man that will fight and kill for something he does not believe in, whether he's black or white." Reid Stuart said.

The gunman did not respond. He turned the filly down the trail and followed the retreating soldiers. Reid Stuart stared at his back and watched now how stiffly he sat his saddle, watched him until he disappeared around the point. Then he followed him. It was basic military strategy, one rode point, the other rear guard. Near the mouth of their canyon Reid Stuart joined the gunman on a point of rock that overlooked the big canyon.

Hundreds of tepees lay burnt on the canyon floor. Blankets, hides, clay utensils, everything the Comanche would need to survive the winter, lay broken, burnt and scattered across the canyon floor. A long column of horses stood in line, facing away from Reid Stuart and the gunman.

"A regiment, at least." The gunman said.

"Yes." Reid Stuart agreed. "They're positioned for a long march. It appears Colonel MacKenzie is preparing to take his men out of the canyons now." They watched the young lieutenant as he rode to the front of the column. After a few minutes the Lieutenant's black troopers joined the long column. Reid Stuart and the gunman did not see the young lieutenant again. They watched the column move slowly forward like a long rope taking up its slack.

"Are they leavin'?" The gunman asked.

"Yes." Reid Stuart said. "We must not be important enough to Colonel MacKenzie to delay his departure."

"They'll be back." The gunman said.

"Yes. They will be back." Reid Stuart agreed. "But not before spring."

An unfamiliar quiet came to the plains and to the Escadara. That spring the buffalo did not come to the canyon or the Kiowa, but neither did the black soldiers. Kwanhah with the Kwerhar-rehnuh, fewer of them than ever before, watered once at Katharane's spring. But Kwanhah had not come again. Only the days came and went. Katharane grew and played and learned. The gunman patiently tutored her in addition and subtraction, and how to identify her letters, until she could read by herself from Reid Stuart's Bible. And he instructed her in using the small handguns. She quickly became a marksman with either hand. And they rode, the gunman and Reid Stuart, the gunman and Katharane. And they talked, Reid Stuart and the gunman, the gunman and Katharane, Reid Stuart, the gunman, Katharane and the Squaw Woman. And often, in the evenings, they laughed.

Slowly, imperceptibly, unknowingly the gunman grew happy. His eyes twinkled, and his voice, soft and deep, made kind and gentle sounds to the child he spent hour after hour either riding beside or carrying her on the front of his saddle. It seemed he had found peace with the plains and with himself. It seemed.

CHARLES GOODNIGHT
1875-1880

Charles Goodnight and Leigh Dyer allowed their horses to follow the path along the edge of the canyon. The horses and riders were hot, tired and thirsty. They and the rest of Goodnight's company had been without even the gypsum or flotsam water of the now vanished plains' playa ponds for two days. Goodnight placed his hand against the letter folded inside of his shirt. He and his brother-in-law were close to the place Bose Ikard had tried to describe in his scratchy hard to read handwriting as the place where he and Young Tom Hawkins had encountered a young girl and two men.

Leigh Dyer worried about the canyon below. He had thought that once his employer and brother-in-law had confirmed that the large canyon they had sighted from a distance was the one they sought he would immediately return to lead the others to it. Leigh Dyer did not understand why Charles Goodnight pressed their tired mounts along the narrow trail of this smaller canyon. Dyer earnestly wished they were using the last of their horses' reserves of strength to again cross the long flat miles of prairie to rejoin the others. He felt secure there, but not here. Here, alone with the plainsman, he was uncertain and nervous.

As the two riders rounded a giant boulder they were greeted with a large pool of blue water. Farther down the canyon wall, like blue steps leading down into the unseeable bottom of the canyon, they could see two more pools.

"Leigh. I wonder of this is how Adam felt when he woke up in Eden?" Charles Goodnight asked.

It did not appear nearly as safe as Eden to Leigh Dyer. "Someone stacked these rocks, Mr. Goodnight." He said as he studied the small spillway over which some of the clear sparkling water flowed, then raced down the canyon wall to the next pool. Leigh Dyer was a short stocky Irishman, a capable horseman and a trusted employee for Charles Goodnight. But he had an abiding fear of the marker at which Goodnight's partner, the Englishman Charles Adair, Adair's wife, Dyer's older sister and Goodnight's wife, Mary, a hundred Durham bulls and five good gun hands waited for them to return. A fear generated by the stories which he had heard about those markers in saloons in Pueblo and Trinidad, Colorado, and of the renegade Indians which still roamed the area at will. He longed for the comfort of having those five other guns much nearer.

"Yes. And if you look at the one below us, someone has stacked rocks in it as well." Charles Goodnight said. "It seems they were trying to control the flow of water from it." He added.

The two hot and thirsty horses ignored their riders' attempts to restrain them. They walked to the pool, lowered their heads and drank deeply.

"What do you call these pools?" Leigh Dyer asked.

"Tinaja." The girl's voice came from a stand of scrub cedar to the riders' right. Leigh Dyer's hand went to the butt of his Winchester. "Release your rifle or you shall never leave your saddle alive again." The voice stepped from behind the scrub cedar. The small girl wore dark buckskins and a holster, from which two pistols hung, one below each of her hips. The guns seemed to replace her legs. Her dark hair flowed down her back in a single braid.

"Lord above!" Leigh Dyer exclaimed. "It's a little girl." He stood up in his stirrups and shook his right foot free to dismount, but stopped when he heard the heavy click of a revolver's hammer being cocked.

"My Pop says life and death are the same. They each happen in seconds." The girl spoke slowly as she spread her feet apart. "You have not been invited to leave your horse. You are both trespassers."

Leigh Dyer's face reddened. He was angry and embarrassed, and he swore at the child. "No damn girl with a couple of pop guns is going to upbraid me!"

"Easy, Leigh," Charles Goodnight cautioned. "Those are not pop guns. Take a look at those casings in her gun belt. They appear to be hand loads, and notice their leads. They've been notched."

"Shit! Butcher loads." The Irishman cursed, again. But he sat back down on his saddle.

"My Lord's name will not be taken in vain! Not on my land and not by a couple of trespassers!" The girl's voice rose in volume and pitch.

Leigh Dyer started to argue, but he was interrupted by a high whining woman's voice which spoke in a mysterious chant like dialect, unknown to the Irishman. The voice came from above the upper pool. The child answered the woman's beseeching cry in the same strange dialect.

"What's that she's speaking now?" Leigh Dyer asked.

"Comanche, I think." Charles Goodnight answered.

"Jesus! A Comanche squaw and her papoose." Leigh Dyer snorted.

"I am not an Indian!" The girl retorted. "My name is Katharane Diane Stuart. And you are trespassers!"

"My God! He exists. He really exists." Charles Goodnight murmured, almost to himself.

"What is it? Who exists?" Leigh Dyer cried.

"Reid Stuart. We've ridden onto Reid Stuart's Escadara. It's not a myth. They've been here all along, tucked away in this upper canyon." Charles Goodnight answered.

"Oh! Damn the luck." Leigh Dyer wet his lips. "I wonder if those stories are true."

"You know my father?" Katharane asked Charles Goodnight.

"I know of him." He answered her.

"Mr. Goodnight. We have to have water for the bulls, the other stock and Mrs. Goodnight and the others." Leigh Dyer interposed. "Whether this child wishes us to or not."

"Mrs. Goodnight." Katharane repeated the words as if she did not understand their meaning.

"Yes, my wife." Charles Goodnight said. "She's waiting with the others out there on the prairie." He gestured with his right hand.

"She's with you!" Katharane cried.

"Yes."

"Is she a white woman? Like me?"

"Yes." Charles Goodnight laughed as he studied the dark tint of the girl's skin on her arms and legs and even her face.

"Will she come here? To the tinaja? Like you have?" Katharane asked and swallowed. She put her hands together and touched her fingertips to her lips.

"Well. I am not certain." Charles Goodnight said. He scratched his stubbly beard. "We must find water."

"You can have our water!" Katharane blurted out. "If you bring her here." She added quietly. "It's good water. The best water on the plains."

Leigh Dyer looked at Charles Goodnight and laughed and said. "You've traded a lot of things for water, Mr. Goodnight. But this is a first."

"Miss Stuart..." Charles Goodnight began.

"Katty. They call me Katty." Katharane interrupted him.

"Okay. Miss Katty. May Leigh Dyer and I have some of your water now?"

"Are you going to bring her here? You promise?" Katharane worked her fingers in and out of themselves. "Please." She whispered.

Charles Goodnight and Leigh Dyer stared at each other. The child was crying, silently. "Is it that important to you, child?" Charles Goodnight asked.

Katharane nodded. "I may never see another white woman if you do not bring her?" She stared, teary eyed, into Charles Goodnight's eyes.

Charles Goodnight met her gaze and said. "Yes. I promise, Miss Katty. I promise." He stepped down from his horse. Leigh

Dyer dismounted, too. He knelt in front of his horse and cupped his hands in the water.

"Don't drink that water, Mr. Dyer." Katharane said. She pointed at the spring. "That's the water we drink. Come on." She scrambled up the path to the spring. Charles Goodnight and Leigh Dyer followed her. She ran to the end of the upper pool nearest the canyon wall and picked up a dried gourd from several stacked there and scooped it full of water from the pool where the spring flowed into it. "Here. Drink this." She handed the gourd to Leigh Dyer.

The Irishman sipped at the water, tasted it, then he took a long deep drink. "Mr. Goodnight." Leigh Dyer licked his lips dry. "That's the sweetest tasting, coolest water I've ever put in my mouth." He handed the gourd to Charles Goodnight.

"Then she'll come! She will!" Katharane clapped her hands.

"Yes." Charles Goodnight chuckled. "She'll come."

"Child, how old are you?" Leigh Dyer asked Katharane as Charles Goodnight drank from the gourd.

"Nine."

"And you've never seen a white woman?" He asked incredulously.

"None, besides myself. I have seen myself in a mirror Pop brought from Tafoya's for me." Katharane answered.

Leigh Dyer started, again, to question the child, to ask her if she was indeed white. He doubted this. But he knew Charles Goodnight despised any hint of bigotry, so he repeated his question. "You have seen no other white woman, other than yourself in a looking glass?"

Katharane shook her head. "I never have."

He stared at her in disbelief.

"Before today." Katharane said and looked up at Charles Goodnight. "You promised, Mr. Goodnight." Again, the hope, the anxiety, the desperation glimmered in Katharane's brown eyes. Truly, she believed this to be her one chance to meet another white

169

woman.

"Miss Katty. I vow to you, that if I never do another thing in this life, that before nightfall you shall meet Mary Goodnight."

Katharane stared out into the hot shimmering plains.

"They no come." The Squaw Woman said haltingly in English.

"They will come, Mama. They will." Katharane retorted. She straightened her white doeskin dress and pulled at the single braid the Squaw Woman had made of her long auburn hair. "They must." Katharane spoke now in the tongue of the Kwerhar-rehnuh Comanche. "He promised. And Charles Goodnight is a good man, I think. He will keep his promise to me."

"Huh!" The squaw grunted. She, too, used the Comanche dialect. "Buck's promise to squaw not important, not bad to break."

"He will come, Mama!" Katharane snapped in English, abandoning her Comanche dialect. "He will come and he will bring the white woman." Much softer, she said. "He must. He promised me this." She stared at the remorseless prairie. "There! See!" She exclaimed and pointed at the empty prairie. She ran to her white mustang.

"Katty! Wait!" The squaw cried. "No go!"

But the child was already mounted, her white doeskin dress high above her knees, the pistols rubbing against the bare skin of her legs, riding toward the shimmering dancing movement beyond the far mirage.

"Rider coming, Mr. Goodnight." Leigh Dyer called to the angular figure that sat on his horse a hundred yards or so away from the caravan which Dyer led. Word of the rider's approach spread among the men that herded the restless thirsty Shorthorn bulls. They stood in their stirrups and strained to see who or what it was riding to them from the empty prairie.

A quarter of a mile before she reached Leigh Dyer and the cattle Katharane stopped. She surveyed the cattle, the two wagons and the men. Charles Goodnight lifted his hat and waved it. Katharane waved in response and trotted her mustang to him. "Is she here? Is she really with you, Mr. Goodnight?" She asked excitedly.

Charles Goodnight nodded and pointed at a wagon which moved up behind them. When it stopped before them, he spoke to a woman seated on the seat. "Mary. This is Miss Katharane Diane Stuart, the young lady that has never seen a white woman."

Mary Goodnight stood up and climbed down from the wagon. She walked to her husband's horse and stood beside it. When she removed her hat her long blonde hair fell about her shoulders. Katharane stared at her. Leigh Dyer walked to the white mustang. "Let me help you down, girl." He said and held his hands up to Katharane. She leaned out into his strong hands and he set her on her feet on the ground. Katharane straightened her white doeskin dress and held her hands in front of her with her fingers laced together.

Mary Goodnight held her hand out to Katharane. "My name is Mary Goodnight, Katharane."

Katharane stared at her hand, but she did not move to take it.

"Go on, girl. Take Mrs. Goodnight's hand." Leigh Dyer urged Katharane.

Katharane stepped forward and took Mary Goodnight's hand in both of her hands. She stared into the woman's eyes. "They call me Katty." She said softly. "I've never seen a white woman with blue eyes before."

Mary Goodnight smiled and said. "And I've never seen a girl as lovely as you, Katharane." The child smiled.

"Now, Miss Katty." Charles Goodnight said. "I have kept my end of this agreement. What about your's? We need water, and we need a goodly amount of it."

"Oh yes! You can have all the water you want. I will show you." Katharane turned to walk back to her mustang.

"I think my husband can find it, Katharane. Why don't you ride with Mrs. Adair and me on the wagon?" Mary Goodnight asked the child.

"Mrs. Adair." Katharane said slowly. "Is she white? Like

171

you and I?"

"Yes." Mary Goodnight laughed. "Come Katharane." She gripped the child's left hand.

"My horse." Katharane protested.

"I'll tie him on lead behind the wagon." Leigh Dyer offered. He took the little horse to the back of the wagon and tied its reins to the wagon.

"Katharane, I haven't seen a white mustang before." Charles Goodnight said.

"Chief Kwanhah gave him to me." Katharane said.

"What tribe claims your Chief Kwanhah, Katharane?" Charles Goodnight asked.

"The Kwerhar-rehnuh." Katharane spoke the name in its natural dialect.

"The Kwerhar-rehnuh?" Charles Goodnight anglicized the name.

"My Mama's people." Katharane explained.

"I thought you were white, Katharane."

"I am." Katharane said. "She's not my real mama. But she's the only mama I know. Pop and Dad traded some mustangs to Kwanhah for her. She takes care of me."

"Traded!" John Adair snorted. "They trade horses for human beings. What kind of men are these?" The Englishman demanded.

"The kind of men you hold your tongue around until know the why of a thing." Charles Goodnight warned the quick tongued Englishman.

"Men that condone slavery should not expect civility." Adair retorted.

"My mama's not a slave." Katharane said quietly. "She stays with me."

"Because, child, she's not free to leave." Adair snapped.

"Uh-huh. She can. She doesn't want to leave me. She

wants to stay with me." Katharane began to argue.

"She wants to stay because she was bartered for and placed in servitude to you!" Adair snarled.

"You no know!" Katharane cried. "You no know why my Mama stays!" Her grammar lost amidst her anger.

Mary Goodnight tightened her grip on the child's left hand. But Katharane's right hand slid quickly up to the butt of her pistol.

"That's enough, John!" Charles Goodnight intervened. "Katharane's right. You do not know why the woman chooses to stay, and you should find out before you start making accusations. You will get called for that real quick in this country, and called hard." Charles Goodnight watched the girl grip the pistol. John Adair rode silently away.

"Come, Katharane." Mary Goodnight coaxed. She led the child to the wagon where Leigh Dyer helped Mary Goodnight climb up onto the wagon's seat, then lifted Katharane up beside her. Mrs. John Adair sat on the other side of the seat. The child quickly forgot about the surly John Adair. She studied Mary Goodnight, her hands, her face, her voice, her movements. "How long have you lived here, Katharane?" Mary Goodnight asked.

"As long as I can remember." Katharane answered. "Dad brought me here. And we found Pop. Then Pop traded for my mama and brought us to the Escadara."

"What is the Escadara?" Mrs. John Adair asked.

"Our home." The child answered matter of factly.

"You found your Pop?" Mary Goodnight asked.

Charles Goodnight continued to ride alongside the wagon. The bulls had scented the water at the tinajas and were taking the most direct route to that water, without need of any correction of their course. Charles Goodnight left them to their determined march and he eavesdropped on the conversation on the wagon's seat.

"Dad found Pop camped on the plains." Katharane explained.

"Does your Pop have a name?" Mary Goodnight asked.

"Dad calls him Canada." Katharane said. "That's all the name he has. I guess."

"Do your father and Canada know we are coming to your home, Katharane?" Mary Goodnight asked.

"No." Katharane said, and caught her breath. She stood up on the floorboards beneath the wagon's seat. Mary Goodnight grabbed her arm and the child sat back onto the wagon's seat. She stared into Mary Goodnight's eyes. "Please don't let them bother my mama. She might get scared and run away."

Charles Goodnight answered for his wife. "No one will bother your mama, Katharane." He called to his brother-in-law. "Leigh. Leigh Dyer." Leigh Dyer drew his horse back to walk beside Charles Goodnight's mount and receive his instructions. "When we get to Katharane's dugout you see to it that no one disturbs her mama."

"Yes sir." Leigh Dyer said. He trotted his horse to the front of the bull herd.

"You have only bulls with you that I can see." Katharane said.

"Yes, only bulls." Charles Goodnight said.

"You can't grow cattle with only bulls." Katharane said slowly. She shook her head. Mary Goodnight laughed.

"I have cattle in the big canyon beyond..." Charles Goodnight began.

Katharane gasped. She stood up and gripped her pistols. "Those men who came into our canyon and argued with Pop, you're the Charles Goodnight they said would accuse us of stealing his cattle because Pop said any cattle found on the Escadara were mine."

Now Charles Goodnight laughed. "I am Charles Goodnight, and those were and are my cattle. And if you claim any stray upon your range I do think we have a problem." He said. "But you have no need of your guns. We can settle this without shooting at each other." He chuckled.

"Okay." Katharane said and returned to her seat next to Mary Goodnight.

The scent of the fresh water at the spring grew stronger and sweeter, and the bulls grew anxious. They pressed against the slow steady pace set for them by the two point riders until the riders could no longer hold them. The bulls broke passed them and ran for the water they could only smell.

"Get ahead of 'em. Dammit!" Charles Goodnight roared. He spurred his horse and raced after the running bulls.

Leigh Dyer and the cowboys were pushing the bulls away from the top pool when the wagon arrived with Katharane, Mary Goodnight and Mrs. John Adair. Katharane climbed down from the wagon and waited at the lip of the dugout until Mary Goodnight and Mrs. John Adair joined her. Then she stepped down into the dark dugout and called back to the two women. "Come on."

Mary Goodnight stepped down into the dugout. Mrs. John Adair followed her. The two women stood blind in the dugout, their eyes not yet adjusted to the acute contrast of the dark dugout to the bright sunlit plains. "Mama." Katharane called to someone they could not see.

Mary Goodnight heard a rustling in the far back corner of the dugout. A pair of wild animal eyes glittered in the darkness.

"My God!" Mrs. John Adair exclaimed.

Katharane spoke again, but the eyes did not approach. Then the child barked a command in a strange dialect that neither woman had heard before. Slowly the eyes came forth from the darkness. Mary Goodnight and Mrs. John Adair stared at the Comanche squaw.

"This is my mama." Katharane said.

Mary Goodnight extended her hand. The Squaw Woman shrank back. Katharane spoke in the strange dialect again. The squaw slowly reached her hand up and touched Mary Goodnight's hand. Then she withdrew back into the darkness of the dugout. Mary Goodnight rubbed her fingers against the oil left upon them from the squaw's hand. She sniffed her fingers. They smelled of a heavy thick smell of burnt grease and sweat.

"I am dying of thirst, Mary." Mrs. John Adair said. "And it is stifling in here."

"Let's go to the spring. You can drink there." Katharane said.

"A book?" Katharane asked.

The sun was setting on the plains. Goodnight's cowboys had pushed the bulls into a rope corral several hundred yards from the dugout and were staking their horses along the picket line they had made by tying two ropes together and to a saddle at each end. The Mexican cook was setting up the camp near the wagon and above the dugout. Mary Goodnight was unpacking a case that rode in the back of the wagon. She had laid a book on top of one of the water barrels which were strapped to the side of the wagon.

"Do you read, Katharane?" Mary Goodnight asked.

"Yes. I read the Bible. My Pop taught me."

"Do you read anything other than the Bible?" Mary Goodnight asked.

"I didn't know there was any book other than the Bible." Katharane said.

Mary Goodnight picked up the book and handed it to Katharane, who held it on the palms of her hands as if she was afraid to grip it. "Mo-bi." She began.

"Mo-be." Mary Goodnight corrected her.

"Mo-be Dick." Katharane read the title.

"It is about whales, Katharane. Do you know what a whale is?" Mary Goodnight asked.

"In the Bible one swallowed Jonah. And Jonah lived in its belly for days. Then the whale spit him up."

"Yes. In the Bible that is a story about a whale. But this is a story about hunting whales and killing them and taking the oil and fat from their bodies."

"Like my mama's people do the buffalo?" Katharane asked. "Or like the hide hunters do?"

"What is the difference, child?" Mrs. John Adair asked.

"Well, my Pop says the people live with the buffalo and only kill what they need. The hide hunters kill every buffalo they can find and leave the meat to rot. They take only the hides and sometimes the tongues."

"It is a story about both, I think, Katharane." Mary Goodnight said.

"May I read your book?" Katharane asked.

"Certainly, you may." Mary Goodnight said. "Come. Let's sit together on this buffalo hide." Mary Goodnight sat down on a buffalo hide Charles Goodnight had spread on the ground beside the wagon. Katharane sat next to her and opened the book on her lap. The sun set behind them, orange, purple, gold, fading to yellow against the ever darkening azure sky and crimson plains.

Charles Goodnight dug a shallow fire pit behind the wagon. And a cowboy carried some dry driftwood which he had found in the canyon to the fire pit. Mr. and Mrs. John Adair retired to a small tent which the cook had set up on the other side of the wagon for them. Katharane read very slowly, many of the words were strange to her. Mary Goodnight pronounced the ones she could not read. "Call me Ishmael. Some years ago—never mind how long precisely—having little or no money in my purse, and nothing particular to interest me on shore, I thought I would sail about a little and see the watery part of the world." These were new words for Katharane, and put together in a manner she was unaccustomed to reading. But she continued to read aloud in a voice, both soft in its youthfulness and strong in its vocal quality. Her voice floated with the fading breeze. "This is my substitute for pistol and ball. With a philosophical flourish Cato throws himself upon his sword; I quietly take to the ship. There is nothing surprising in this. If they but knew it, almost all men in their degree, some time or other, cherish very nearly the same feelings towards the ocean with me."

The cowboys listened to the music of the child's voice, attentive and appreciative, some lost in remembrance, others alert to each change in rhythm or octave or inflection in the little girl's voice and others following the lyrics of her song.

From the dugout the Squaw Woman called to the child. Katharane looked at the dark slit in the prairie. The Squaw Woman stood on the lip of the dugout, her stout frame outlined by the flat low glare of the setting sun. "May Mama come and listen?" Katharane asked.

"Of course she can." Mary Goodnight said.

Katharane laid the book on the buffalo hide, stood up and ran to the dugout.

"Will she come, Charles?" Mary Goodnight asked. She looked up at her husband.

"I don't know, Mary."

Katharane's voice rose. The squaw jabbered, pointed into the dugout and moaned. Then Katharane screamed, a violent rushing whirl of consonants held together by unnamed verbs, then she turned and stomped back to the buffalo hide. The squaw slowly, obediently followed the child. Several of the cowboys stood up and watched her. John Adair came out of his tent and stood beside Charles Goodnight. "So, that is a Comanche." John Adair said.

"Yes." Charles Goodnight replied.

"Not very impressive, I must say."

"She can find water on the plains when you can't. She can go for days without eating. She can walk behind your horse until he drops from exhaustion. Then she can strap his load onto her travois and drag it another forty miles. She can squat in the morning, have a baby and be back with her people by night fall." Charles Goodnight turned and glared at the Englishman. "And she can, apparently, raise and love a very intelligent and beautiful little white girl that the trade of a few wild mustangs took that unimpressive squaw from her people for. And do it without belligerence or jealousy or any of the other traits that so damn mine and your race, John."

"And you find that admirable?" John Adair snorted, turned to go back to his tent, then he stopped and added. "And do you truly believe that child to be white?" Then he stomped away.

"Charles?" Mary Goodnight touched her husband's arm. "Is Katharane white?"

He shrugged. "'hard to tell. But from the way she speaks

our language, I think she has to be."

Katharane sat next to Mary Goodnight. The squaw squatted on her ankles next to the child. She wore a worn stained deerskin shift which hung from her shoulders to her ankles. Her hair was black and matted, and it had not been cleaned nor combed for months. She smelled of buffalo fat, grease and dung. The odor almost gagged Mary Goodnight, but she swallowed her discomfort and smiled at Katharane and the Squaw Woman. Katharane picked up the book and began to read again. The squaw stared at the pages as the child turned them. "Kat-tie read." She said slowly.

"Yes, Mama," Katharane said. "I read words." She pointed at the printing on the page and said. "Words."

"Words." The squaw repeated.

"I'm sorry Mama interrupts." Katharane said very apologetically to Mary Goodnight.

"It's all-right, Katharane." Mary Goodnight said. "I think it is wonderful you are teaching your Mama your language."

The squaw wrinkled her nose, laid over on her side, pushed herself up onto her hands and knees, stood up and ran for the dugout. Katharane dropped the book and jumped to her feet.

"Charles! What's happening?" Mary Goodnight cried.

Rocks skittered across the ledge and into the top pool. The black filly leaped onto the yard above the spring. A cowboy reached for his Winchester that lay propped against his saddle.

"No! Pop!" Katharane yelled. She drew her pistols as the black revolver flashed out of its holster. Katharane's pistols cracked and dust danced between the black filly's front feet. The horse reared and spun sideways. The gunman held the black pistol above his head and jerked the filly's reins driving her around to face Katharane and the Goodnights.

"Stay away from those guns!" Charles Goodnight yelled. He stared at the black revolver which the gunman held above his head.

"Katty! What the hell?" The gunman cursed.

"No, Pop, no. There's a white woman with them. Two white women. Don't shoot them."

Charles Goodnight saw John Adair coming out of the tent carrying his hunting rifle. Goodnight stepped to the tent and wrenched the rifle away from Adair.

"By thunder, Goodnight!" John Adair shouted. "I'll have my gun back now, sir."

"Not unless you want to die." Charles Goodnight snapped.

The gunman spurred the black filly and she jumped onto the buffalo hide on which Katharane and Mary Goodnight stood. "Put those guns away." He commanded the child.

"Not until you put your's away." Katharane whined.

The buckskin lunged up onto the yard, the heavy Sharps waving above its head. The gunman shoved the black revolver back into its holster. "Hold up, Stuart." He called back to Reid Stuart.

Katharane shoved her pistols back into the holsters. For a moment the gunman stared at Mary Goodnight. He bent down and swung Katharane up onto his saddle in front of him. He took his hat off and laid it on the saddle horn in front of the child. His curly hair waved in blond ringlets down across his forehead. "Mam." He said softly to Mary Goodnight. Before she could reply he reined his horse around and rode back to Reid Stuart. He swung his filly around the buckskin and placed her to Reid Stuart's left, facing the cow camp.

"It's Charles Goodnight, Dad. The man the men in the canyon work for." Katharane explained to her father.

Reid Stuart watched a dark frown pass across the gunman's face.

"I told them they could use our water and camp here. He has two white women with him. White like us." Katharane said excitedly.

Charles Goodnight walked to Reid Stuart, the gunman and Katharane. He raised his hand to Reid Stuart. "My name is Charles Goodnight, Mr. Stuart. I apologize if our presence startled you." Reid Stuart shook his hand. Goodnight did not offer his hand to the gunman.

"And Pop." Katharane said. "Mrs. Goodnight has a book. And it's not the Bible. It's called Moby Dick. And we're reading it. It's about whales. Like the one that swallowed Jonah."

Mary Goodnight stepped next to her husband. She watched the gunman's face grow soft and pleasant as he smiled at the child.

"Can Pop read the book with us, Mrs. Goodnight?" Katharane asked.

"If he wishes." Mary Goodnight answered.

The gunman lifted the child and swung his right leg across the front of his saddle and stepped to the ground, carrying the child in his arms. He left his hat hanging on his saddle's horn.

"What are you doing?" Reid Stuart asked.

"'gonna' go read Moby Dick with Katty and Mrs. Goodnight." The gunman answered.

"Don't you think we should at least find out the purpose of Mr. Goodnight's encampment at our home first?" Reid Stuart grumbled.

"No. If I was worried about it I'd go ahead and shoot him now."

"Don't shoot him now, Pop. We won't get to read Moby Dick with Mrs. Goodnight." Katharane pleaded.

Charles Goodnight laughed.

"All-right, Katty." The gunman said. "I can always shoot him later." Goodnight's and the gunman's eyes met, neither one shirked or faded from the confrontation. Both pairs of eyes flickered with something, recognition, dislike or disdain. Reid Stuart was not certain as to what. Then the gunman walked away with Katharane and Mary Goodnight.

"Leigh." Charles Goodnight called to his foreman.

"Yes sir." Leigh Dyer answered.

"Tomorrow morning, first light, start the bulls down the trail passed the tinaja. Cook." Charles Goodnight addressed the

Mexican cook. "I'll leave a cowboy with you. Take the wagon along the rim. Maybe you can find a way down into the canyon."

"There's not." Reid Stuart said. "Only way to get a wagon down is to take it apart and carry it down."

Goodnight nodded. "All right, start taking it apart."

"Si', el senor." The Mexican cook answered. Several cowboys began to unload the wagon.

"'guess we'd best let these folks turn in, Katty. They have a busy day ahead of them tomorrow." The gunman said.

"But Pop, we haven't finished Moby Dick. And I won't get to when Mrs. Goodnight leaves." Katharane protested.

"'can't help that." The gunfighter said. He stood up and held his hand down to the child. "Come on." Reluctantly she stood up and took his hand.

"Katharane." Mary Goodnight said from where she sat. The little girl looked at Mary Goodnight. Mary Goodnight held the book out to her. "I want you to have this." The child looked at the gunfighter.

"Please." Mary Goodnight said. "It is my gift to my new friend."

Katharane took the book. "But I don't have a gift for you." She said.

"That's all right, Katharane." Mary Goodnight said.

The child looked up at the gunfighter, again. The gunfighter winked at her. "We'll make her one." He said softly to the child.

She said happily. "Okay."

"What do you say, Katharane?" Reid Stuart asked.

"Thank you." Katharane said to Mary Goodnight.

"You're very welcome."

Katharane, Mary Goodnight and Mrs. Adair followed Charles Goodnight and John Adair as they rode drag on their herd of bulls as it wound its way down the narrow trail to the floor of

Ceta canyon. The gunman followed close behind Mary Goodnight and Mrs. Adair. That they rode sidesaddle worried him, but they were expert horsewomen and they traversed the trail uneventfully. At the mouth of the Ceta where it flowed into the big canyon Charles Goodnight rode back to Katharane, his wife, Mrs. Adair and the gunman. "We've made it, Mary. I can see Bose Ikard and Young Tom Hawkins coming up the big canyon." He said.

"I never doubted, Charles. Not for a moment." Mary Goodnight responded.

"Well, Miss Katharane. We part here. I will return in the spring to check for my strays." Charles Goodnight said.

"If you're strays are not branded with the drooped E you will be welcome to them." The child said. "But if they are." She raised her head and aimed her chin at Goodnight and said boldly. "They are mine."

"But if the mothers that claim them are burnt with this brand, Katharane." Charles Goodnight said, and he stepped down from his horse and drew a capitalized J and A in the sand of the wash where their horses stood. "They are mine. No matter whose brand they wear."

Katharane frowned.

"So it would seem beneficial to both of us to be careful that we do not brand the other's strays." Goodnight said as he remounted. The gunman's stare drew his attention. The cold gray eyes said it would not be Reid Stuart and certainly not the child who would decide the issue of strays, it would be the gunman and no mark held any meaning, any respect nor any restraint for him save the Escadara drooped E. 'So be it.' Charles Goodnight thought to himself. 'You lay a runnin' iron to a JA branded steer and I'll hang you for it.'

Mary Goodnight's voice separated the two men. "When you visit, Katharane, you will have to tell me about your mother, your real mother. We did not get to talk about her." Mary Goodnight spoke softly, almost confidentially to the child.

Katharane did not answer. She looked to the gunfighter. He reached and stroked the back of her hair. "Katty don't know about her real mama." The gunfighter said quietly. "Good luck to you, Mary Goodnight." He touched the brim of his hat, turned the black filly between Katharane's mustang and Mary Goodnight's sorrel and forced the mustang to walk beside his filly. Mary Goodnight turned and watched them disappear back into their canyon.

"Who was my mama?" Katharane's question crackled through the late October afternoon as rare and as startling as a clap of thunder would have been. Reid Stuart looked to the prairie sky above the distant dugout as if he sought in it the source of such a bold disturbance. Then he lowered his eyes and set them hard and full against the gunman's gaze.

"She's been troublin' 'bout this for a month now, Stu'." The gunman said. "Ever since Mary Goodnight asked her."

"Who was my mama, my real mama?" Katharane repeated.

"She was just a woman, Katharane." Reid Stuart said, and he spurred his buckskin and rode for the dugout. "Let's head home." He called over his shoulder.

Katharane turned her white mustang and pursued her father. The gunman followed. "But who was she?" Katharane demanded as she overtook her father.

Again, harder, Reid Stuart spurred his horse and the buckskin stretched itself out into a long lope. Katharane lashed her mustang with her reins and the little horse raced after the buckskin. The gunman stung the filly's flanks with his Spanish spurs. The quick little horse overtook the mustang in a few strides. He reached down and slid his fingers through the mustang's hackamore. He reined the filly in the direction of the canyon.

"You turn a'loose of my horse!" Katharane screamed. "You no halter my horse, Pop! You no do that!" She cried.

The gunman held to the halter and led the mustang away from the dugout and to the edge of the canyon. The two horses stood on the edge of the canyon. The gunman waited until Katharane stopped sniffling, then he said softly. "I hated this canyon when I first came to it."

"But Pop! You love the canyon. You've always loved the canyon." Katharane said. She rubbed her nose with the back of her hand.

"You're probably right, little one. I always did. But I didn't know it at the time. I had to learn it."

The gunman and the little girl sat on their horses and watched the canyon. After a few moments Katharane asked. "How did you learn that you loved the canyon, Pop?"

"What if I told you how I came to love the canyon is not somethin' I can tell ya'?"

"Why?"

"Because if I told you maybe I couldn't keep on lovin' it."

"I don't understand." Katharane sniffed. She was quiet. Then she asked. "Dad never told you about my mama? He never said anything about her? What she looked like? What happened to her?"

"No."

"You never asked?"

"'wasn't for me to ask. 'reckon if Reid Stuart has something to tell me, he will. If he doesn't." He shrugged. "Then it's not for me to ask him about it." He shifted his weight in the saddle. He sat thinking for several moments, until he looked far across the canyon and said. "If Reid Stuart chooses to keep it his, then by me it's his to keep."

"Pop, are you telling me I shouldn't want to know about my mother?"

"No. That's not what I'm tellin' you." The gunman said quietly. "Wantin' something is okay. But asking someone to give up somethin' they don't want to give up so you can have it may not be."

"You've done it, Pop. You've even taken things you wanted with your gun. I've seen you."

"Maybe so, but I've never taken things just to have them. And I've always tried to be certain that my need for them was greater than whoever I was takin' them from."

"Well. I still don't see why Dad can't tell me about my

mother."

"I don't know the why of it, Katty." The gunman said. He turned his head and looked at the little girl. "Nor do you." Then he looked back out into the canyon and said. "Nor do either of us know what you might be makin' him give up if you goad him into tellin' you." He frowned. "Besides, what need do you really have to know?"

"Pop! Everyone needs to know who their mother is."

"'would seem to me to be much more important to know who loves you than who gave birth to you." The wind was dying in the canyon, lying down among the cedars, settling into the breaks, quieting itself on the canyon floor and preparing itself for the long silent night. The canyon beckoned to the gunfighter's spirit at this time more than any other. "I knew who my mother was, Katty. But I didn't know who loved me." The gunman stood up in his stirrups and looked down into the canyon floor as if he searched for someone who should be there. "Or at least, who I thought loved me. And I loved her so, Katty."

"As much as you love the canyon?"

The gunman nodded. "As much as I love the canyon, but she couldn't love me."

"Why not?"

The gunfighter shrugged. "She said it was because I am the way I am."

"That's not fair!" The child cried. "If you weren't the way you are, you wouldn't be you, Pop."

"You are so right, Miss Katty, so very right. But I gave up a lot to learn that." The gunman sat back down in his saddle. "So knowing who loves you seems a lot more important to me than knowing who birthed ya'." He said sadly.

"But I know who loves me, Pop. You do. I just don't know who my mother is."

The gunman smiled at the child. He reached to her and cupped his left hand around the back of her neck and said. "Reid Stuart loves you too, Katty, whether he tells you about your mother or not. He loves you."

Katharane lay asleep next to the Squaw Woman. Most nights now she slept with the gunman. But this night, driven maybe by doubts as to even the squaw's purpose in her life, she had climbed onto the old cot and curled herself against the squaw's large stomach and slept.

"You never told me about the girl you loved." Reid Stuart spoke to the darkness outside of the dugout.

"No." The gunman answered.

"Why did you tell Katharane?"

"I'm not sure." The gunman answered. "I thought maybe it would help her if I shared something with her I hadn't shared with anyone else."

"That assumes she understands a great deal, and she's just a child." Reid Stuart said.

"She's a very smart child." The gunman argued.

"Then you believe I should tell Katharane about her mother?" Reid Stuart asked.

"I think whether you do or don't's not my concern."

"Then what is your concern?" Reid Stuart demanded angrily.

"Katty."

From the light sleep he had become accustomed to on the plains Reid Stuart half heard, half felt the gunman's voice calling his name. He sat up on his buffalo hide bedroll. Above him the Squaw Woman and Katharane slept on the cot. The gunman squatted on his heels on the front edge of the dugout. Reid Stuart pulled on his boots, got up and stepped up and out of the dugout. "What is it?" He asked. He stared into the darkness, searching for the answer to why the gunman had disturbed his sleep.

"I didn't tell Katty everything about that woman I loved."

Reid Stuart rolled a cigarette and waited. He knew the gunman well enough now to know that if he continued he would do so whether or not Reid Stuart said anything.

"I was one of sixteen horsemen called to duty by J. E. B.

Stuart. I was leavin', not figurin' I'd get back. I so needed to tell her. So I told her. I told her I loved her, Stuart. And she got angry. She screamed at me that she didn't want that from me and that she had made that clear. How could she make clear to me that I couldn't love her? How could she do that for me, Stuart?"

"I don't know."

"'told me to go on with my life. Hell! I thought I was by tellin' her the truth. Tellin' her I loved her, wanted her. 'ain't never wanted anyone in my life." The gunman stood up as he continued. "I didn't tell her she loved me. I told her I loved her and she was angry with me for that. I ain't never told another soul that that I can remember, other than her."

Reid Stuart smoked his cigarette.

"'rode with Stuart. 'fought with him. Butchered, learned how to kill a man easier that you can light one of them loose rolled cigarettes. 'lived through the war and they turned me out. So I used what I knew how to do the best to make my way. 'did some hired gun work along the border. 'till it got to be I wasn't killin' for pay I was killin' cause that's what I did. Then I heard a story about an Indian range on the high northwest plains no white man knew. So I started ridin' and I didn't stop 'till I hit the Canadian. 'been here ever since." The gunfighter bowed his head. "There ain't nothun' worse than that God awful gut eatin' loneliness that comes when you finally realize they don't love you and they never did. It eats away a man's will like bein' afoot on those damn plains." The gunman nodded at the dark prairie as he spoke. "Until you're just at a place, any place and you might as well be there or in hell for the difference it makes you."

Reid Stuart inhaled the smoke from his cigarette. Slowly he said. "Well. It's not a bad place to live. And sometimes all we can hope for is a place to live." Reid Stuart ground his cigarette's leavings into the hard packed lip of the dugout and stepped back down into the dugout.

Winter came to the plains. For Reid Stuart, the gunman, Katharane and the Squaw Woman it was a time of hours spent together in the crowded dugout listening to the gunman's soft voice reading long passages either from Reid Stuart's Bible or Katharane's Moby Dick. Solitude could only be found in undisturbed thoughts.

For Mary Goodnight the cold seemed to imprison all living things. But it was the wind, the unceasing wind that mastered even the canyon, which frightened her. Surely this bitterly relentless and cold wind must be destroying the plains above the canyon and all that lived there. "I wonder what it is like for Katharane in that dugout." She voiced her fears to her husband as the wind howled across the cedar poles which covered the top of her dugout. She watched the wisps of snow that whipped passed the cracks between the poles.

"She's as safe, if not safer, in her dugout than you are in your's, Mary." Charles Goodnight said. He stepped behind his wife and squeezed her shoulders and sought to quiet her discomfort about Katharane and what Mary perceived to be her unkindness to the child. "Don't trouble yourself about Katharane. You had no way of knowing Reid Stuart had never told her of her mother."

"Oh Charles! Why wouldn't a man tell his child about her mother?"

"I don't know, Mary. But I believe Reid Stuart to be a good man. So he has his reasons."

"Only a man would find a reason to not tell a child about her mother." Mary sighed. The wind wailed. "How long, Charles, how long can it blow like this?"

"A while yet, Mary, a while." Charles Goodnight answered.

"'came a blow for my birthday." The gunman said. Reid Stuart nodded. "'be a good sixty days before we see spring this year, Stu'."

"Here, Pop. How is this one?" The child asked. She held up one of the white moccasins the gunfighter had helped her stitch together from the sun bleached doeskin he had cured during the summer.

The gunman inspected the last of the four holes through which the tan buckskin strand would be laced. He carried the moccasin to the stone hearth and picked up a running iron, holding it by the iron ring which was usually heated and used to roll the desired brand onto the hip of a calf, and shoved the slender straight handle into the hot coals of the fire. Once the end of the iron was red hot he withdrew it from the fire and seared the four holes. He blew the black singed pieces of hide away from the holes and handed the moccasin back to Katharane. "Now you can work the lacing through the holes and they won't tear." He said.

Katharane took the moccasin and sat on the floor in front of the hearth. She began to work the thick string of rawhide through the holes. The squaw squatted next to Katharane and watched the child struggle with the string. "Do you think Mrs. Goodnight will like them?" Katharane asked.

"She'll like 'em, Katty girl. She'll like 'em." The gunman answered. He looked at Reid Stuart who sat silently and sullenly on top of the wooden crate.

Reid Stuart held Katharane's "Moby Dick" and watched his child as she worked to lace the leather into the moccasins. With the gunman's help Katharane had read "Moby Dick" aloud, twice, struggling to be heard above the plains' winter winds which echoed against the dugout like the waves of some angry ocean around a wooden ship, making the words she read sound small and weak and misplaced against the wind's wearisome wailing, as misplaced as Ahab's wooden ship on an ocean pitted against the Leviathan.

"Riders coming, Mr. Goodnight." Bose Ikard said. He sat on his horse in front of the dugout.

Charles Goodnight and his wife stepped out of the dugout and stood next to Bose's horse. Warm days had returned to the canyon not two weeks before, and after the long winter's captivity Mary Goodnight sought any excuse for leaving the dugout.

Young Tom Hawkins led his horse to the group. "'want me to ride out and inquire of their purpose, Mr. Goodnight?" Young Tom asked. He was eager to please his employer.

"No need." Bose said. He dropped his hand from shielding his eyes. "That's Miss Katharane, Mr. Stuart and the man with the black gun."

"Katharane!" Mary Goodnight exclaimed happily. She could not conceal her joy.

Charles Goodnight smiled. And Bose said. "Yes mam. 'comin' to see you I imagine."

"You are a kind man, Mr. Ikard." Mary Goodnight said.

"No'm. 'just honest."

"Katharane. Reid Stuart." Charles Goodnight greeted Katharane and her father. He did not speak to the gunman.

"'mornin', Mary Goodnight." The gunman touched his hat and spoke to Mary Goodnight before she could protest her husband's shunning of him.

"Good morning to you." Mary Goodnight replied.

"'sorry to barge in so early on a spring mornin'." The gunman said. "But this child has been at us since before daylight to come."

Katharane slid off of her saddle. She held a bundle of white cloth. She carried her package to Mary Goodnight. "I have a gift for you." Katharane said and handed the bundle to Mary Goodnight.

"Thank you, Katharane. You did not have to do that." Mary Goodnight said. She took the bundle from the child, who watched nervously as she unwrapped it. "They are beautiful!" Mary Goodnight exclaimed. "Charles. Look at these." She held the moccasins in her right hand.

"Katty worked on 'em most of the winter." The gunfighter said.

"They are lovely." Mary Goodnight said, again.

"'good workmanship, too." Charles Goodnight added. "Awfully good."

Katharane beamed. "Try them on." She urged.

Mary Goodnight sat on a cedar stump in the yard in front of the dugout. She unlaced her shoes and pulled them off. Then she slipped a moccasin on each foot. They fit perfectly. "How could you know the size to make them, Katharane?" She asked the child.

"Pop told me." Katharane said. "He studied your feet

when you were reading "Moby Dick" with us. He showed me what size to make them."

Mary Goodnight blushed. The gunman sat quietly on the black filly. Charles Goodnight's eyes changed. Katharane saw them change and understood the danger to her mission in that change. "It's all-right, Mr. Goodnight." Katharane said. "They're a gift from me. Pop said he shouldn't be givin' Miss Mary a gift. It might not look right. And he didn't. He only helped a little."

The gunman smiled. Now Charles Goodnight's face flamed. But Bose's and Mary's laughter forced him to swallow his anger.

"Will you stay for lunch?" Mary Goodnight asked.

"Dinner?" Katharane asked.

"You are welcome to stay for dinner, also." Mary Goodnight said. "But we will have lunch before dinner."

"Lunch before dinner." Katharane repeated Mary Goodnight's words, trying to understand what she was being told.

"Dinner is what Katty knows the noon meal by, mam." The gunfighter explained to Mary Goodnight.

"Dinner is what they call the noon meal here, Mary." Charles Goodnight said as if the gunfighter's statement was not sufficient. "Supper is their evenin' meal."

"For dinner." Mary Goodnight said pleasantly. "One of the cowboy's brought me some chickens. If Mr. Ikard will wring one of their necks for me we will have fried chicken for dinner. Have you eaten chicken, Katharane?"

Katharane nodded. "Pop cooks prairie chickens for me sometimes." She said.

"I think this will be different." Mary Goodnight said.

"Okay." Katharane said.

"Good." Charles Goodnight said. "That will give Reid Stuart and I some time to talk. I have some thoughts about dealin' with strays on each other's range."

"Watch him, Dad." Katharane said seriously. "Pop says

he's an old horse thief. If he'd steal horses he might try to steal my strays."

"Horse thief." Charles Goodnight snorted. He spat tobacco juice between his boots.

Katharane looked at Mary Goodnight and asked. "Why does he chew something he doesn't want to swallow?"

"I have no idea, Katharane." Mary Goodnight laughed. "Young Tom, would you and Bose take Katharane with you to put their horses in the corral. I fear my husband and Mr. Stuart will conduct what I imagine will be a rather profane conversation which I wish to be outside of Katharane's hearing."

"Yes mam!" Tom Hawkins said quickly. He picked up the white mustang's lead and glanced at Katharane as he waited for the gunman to step down from the black filly. When the gunfighter did he took the black filly's reins in his other hand, and he hoped Bose Ikard would usher the girl between them.

"Mr. Ikard." Mary Goodnight spoke to the black man. "After the horses are corralled, may Katharane accompany you to bring me two pullets?"

"Yes mam." Bose replied. He held his right hand down to Katharane. "Come along, Miss Katty. We'll catch and pluck a couple of fat hens for Miss Mary to fry up for your dinner."

Before Katharane could respond, Tom Hawkins volunteered. "I'll help you, too, Bose."

Mary Goodnight smiled at Katharane and Katharane said, "Okay." She reached up and grasped Bose's hand. "But what's Pop going to do?" She asked.

"I think your Pop can help me with the fire." Mary Goodnight said.

"Oh." Katharane said. "Okay. But he doesn't know anything much about cooking inside." Again, Mary Goodnight laughed and Bose Ikard chuckled.

The gunman carried the wood into Mary Goodnight's dugout. "What do you know of Katharane's mother?" Mary Goodnight asked him.

The gunman shoved several short sticks into the rock hearth and said. "I don't."

"Sir. I find that hard to believe."

The gunfighter shrugged. "Believe it or not, it's what I know." He stood up.

"Then I suppose Katharane's mother must be dead. I cannot imagine a man taking a baby from her mother and bringing her here, alone." Mary Goodnight said. She set an iron skillet on the rock hearth and stood in front of the gunfighter looking into his eyes.

He shifted his feet and said. "Reid Stuart's not an ordinary man." Then he met Mary Goodnight's gaze and said. "And Katty's not an ordinary little girl, Mary Goodnight. Be kind to her. She needs the kindness and gentleness of a woman."

"It is not difficult to be kind to Katharane." Mary Goodnight said. "But it is difficult not to hurt her or disturb her peace of mind when I know so very little about her. And how can I learn about her when no one will discuss her family with me?"

The gunman chewed on the inside of his cheek, thinking, then he answered. "'learn about the canyons and you will learn about Katty."

"How will that help me understand Katharane?" Mary Goodnight demanded.

"The canyon is a living, breathing being. She can talk to you as plain as I am, once you learn her language. Her language is Katty's language." The gunman looked at Mary Goodnight. "Learn to listen to the canyon and understand what she is saying to you and you will understand Katty."

Mary Goodnight sat at one end of the makeshift table which Bose Ikard had set up in the yard in front of the dugout. Her husband sat at the other end. Reid Stuart, Katharane and the gunman sat to her left. Bose Ikard and Young Tom sat to her right.

"This is a wonderful lunch, Mrs. Goodnight." Reid Stuart said.

Katharane licked at the meal crumbs that stuck to her fingers where she had held the drumstick. "It's very good." She said. "I like fried chicken. Don't you, Pop?"

The gunfighter winked at the girl. "I surely do, Katty girl. I surely do." He said.

"Mary." Charles Goodnight said. "Reid Stuart and I have agreed. Monday next, we begin the first co-operative roundup on these plains. We'll work and mark our cattle together. That way each will have a say as to the strays."

"That's a splendid agreement, Charles." Mary Goodnight said.

"'seems uneven to me." The gunfighter said.

"Why?" Mary Goodnight asked. "Each ranch is sharing in the other's work."

"Your husband's got more'n a dozen hands workin' for him." The gunman answered. "There's just me and Stuart for the Escadara."

"And me!" Katharane cried. "Me too, Pop."

"And mostly you, Katty, mostly you." The gunfighter said.

"We are going to pay Charles Goodnight on a per head count of our cattle worked." Reid Stuart said.

"Is he going to pay for his cattle we work?" Katharane asked. "Pop and I are fast."

Charles Goodnight laughed. "That seems only fair to me." He said.

"I ain't much on payin' him for anything." The gunman said. "But it's just money. Do as you please."

"It's not my money to do anything with." Reid Stuart said. "I don't have any money. You're the one with the gold."

Everyone around the table fell silent until Katharane said. "It's okay, Dad. Pop will let us use his money."

The gunfighter's lips twitched. He almost smiled. He rubbed the back of the child's head and said. "Like I said, Stuart. It's just money. Do as you wish with it."

Charles Goodnight, Bose Ikard, Young Tom and a half-dozen other cowboys waited in the big canyon across from where the Ceta joined it. Daylight began to creep down the western wall of the big canyon.

"Do you think they will come, Bose?" Young Tom asked. He was anxious to see Katharane, again.

"Reid Stuart said they'd come. They'll be here." Charles Goodnight answered.

"There they are." Bose Ikard said. He pointed at a high point above the big canyon's floor.

Reid Stuart's tall buckskin turned out and across the point. Katharane's white mustang followed and walked beside the gunman's black filly. Behind them a red mule carried the Squaw Woman and drug a travois loaded with provisions.

"That damn Comanche squaw ain't campin' with me." Judson Willey grumbled. "She might decide to scalp one of us."

"She'll camp where she pleases." Charles Goodnight snapped. "And I can't imagine how it would ever please her to camp near you, Judson, even for a chance at such a pretty head of hair as your's."

Bill Henry chuckled. But Judson Willey did not appreciate the humor. He was serious. He was afraid of the squaw. He and most of the other cowboys had no knowledge of Indians, other than the camp fire horror tales about Comanche atrocities committed against whites on the plains.

"Bose." Charles Goodnight said. "You and Young Tom come with me."

"Yes sir, Mr. Charles." Bose Ikard said. He started his horse after Charles Goodnight's long gaited grey horse. Young Tom's sorrel almost passed Charles Goodnight's grey. Young Tom had to rein him up. Both his horse and the cowboy were anxious to meet the approaching riders.

"Reid." Charles Goodnight spoke to Reid Stuart as his grey horse stopped alongside of Reid Stuart's buckskin.

196

"Charles." Reid Stuart responded. The two men shook hands.

"I thought we'd start from here and work back down the canyon." Charles Goodnight said. "That way we'll hit a goodly part of your range in the big canyon first. Then we'll drop into the top of my range."

"All right." Reid Stuart said. "Canada, Katty and I have worked through the Ceta fairly well anyway."

For weeks the roundup progressed down the big canyon. The cowboys would leave camp before first light, throw themselves in a great loop and roust the Longhorn cattle from their bedding grounds among stands of the short cedars. The small groups of cattle would be slowly blended together until a herd was formed by the experienced hands that pushed the cattle into the rising early morning wind. Before noon the herd would be driven into a box canyon or against the high wall of the big canyon and turned around and around until the cattle milled amongst themselves without any sense of single direction to their movement. Then the work would begin: sorting, roping, dragging, castrating, branding, ear marking, which for the Escadara was an over cropping of the right ear and an undercutting of the left ear. It was all hard and bloody work.

The Squaw Woman had broken camp each morning and followed the riders, even on the mornings when the child had tried to convince her that they would return to the same site to camp that night. That did not matter, she thought. She could not chance to be absent if a kill should be made. The hunt was going very badly and she was concerned. For too many days now the small short horned 'buffalo' of the white men had escaped their every attempt to kill them. Though she was not certain how, because the white braves seemed very able to rope them and drag them to the ground. But when they tried to kill them with their knives they only succeeded in cutting off small parts of their bodies and always the small short horned 'buffalo' escaped with their lives. Each night for a week now the Squaw Woman had made long and vocal prayers to the wind and the sun, and even to the buffalo itself, to give up its life so she and the child and the white men might survive. Her prayers flowed like the wind through the canyon, rising up and down the canyon walls for long periods of time. She chanted the ageless entreaties of the Comanche to the spirits of the canyon and the plains. And to Charles Goodnight's ears her incantations were sweet and soothing, but they terrified his cowboys.

This morning Katharane had convinced her not to bring down their camp, but she could not convince her to stay away from the hunt. For hours without a pause for rest she had walked behind the riders. Two of the riders swung a large horned 'buffalo' from the herd. One flung his lariat across the 'buffalo's' horns and jerked it to the ground. He drug the 'buffalo' to a small fire where another cowboy sat upon it's shoulder and another one held it's hind legs. The squaw crept closer. Maybe, she thought, maybe if she could reach the 'buffalo' before it escaped as the others had she could slit its throat. Then, maybe the hunt would turn and find favor among the braves and the spirits. She feared the white braves. But she feared starvation more, feared the days and days without meat, the weeks of berries, bitter and rotting from the plain's sun, the months of hearing the babies cry for food and watching the old ones slowly falter, fall and die. She pulled the sharp skinning knife from her chamois shift. She was within two steps of the struggling 'buffalo'. Her shadow passed across the cowboys.

Judson Willey shrieked. He released the big bloody steer's front leg and leaped backwards. The steer rolled over. Bill Henry's boot slipped from behind the knee on it's bottom leg. The steer kicked him in the chest.

"Damn you Judson!" Bill Henry cursed. He fell away from the kicking steer. The steer jumped to its feet and ran away.

The Squaw Woman looked from Judson Willey, who sat on his butt behind her, to Bill Henry, who sat on his knees rubbing his chest, to the steer which trotted away. She held the skinning knife in her right hand. She worked her left hand open then closed. She was confused, childlike, almost stricken that the 'buffalo' had escaped her. She began to cry.

Charles Goodnight, the gunfighter and Katharane rode up. Katharane jumped from her horse and ran to the squaw.

"Bill! What in damnation hell is going on here?" Charles Goodnight demanded.

"She tried to sneak up on me." Judson Willey said. His eyes were still wild with fear.

"What?" Charles Goodnight roared.

"That damn fool Judson thinks that squaw was tryun' to scalp him, Mr. Goodnight." Bill Henry muttered.

"Jesus Christ! You are worse than a bunch of school children." Charles Goodnight swore.

"I've heard of it." Judson Willey defended himself. "Comanche squaw scalpin' a man alive while he was..." He stopped.

"That's ludicrous!" Charles Goodnight croaked. "Pure bullshit! They are totally submissive during intercourse." He stopped. His face burned bright red.

The gunfighter grinned and said. "'sounds like you know somethin' about that sort of thing."

"I know many things which I have not done." Charles Goodnight retorted. "Like how it feels to murder a man."

The gunman did not acknowledge Charles Goodnight's accusation. Instead he watched Katharane as she lead the squaw to them. He had heard Goodnight call him a murderer, but he did not care what was said of him. He cared only about what affected Katharane, and he did not see that Goodnight's words could hurt her. If he had Charles Goodnight would be facing him, the black pistol and death. Katharane picked up the braided buffalo hair reins of the mustang's bridle. "She thinks this is like the buffalo hunt and that all the buffalo are getting away and we will starve this winter." Katharane explained the squaw's behavior to the gunfighter and Charles Goodnight. "She says your braves are not good warriors, Mr. Goodnight. They can't even kill the little short haired buffalo." The gunman laughed.

"She's right. They'd be totally worthless as warriors. That's for damn certain." Charles Goodnight grumbled. "They're not even much good as cowboys." He glared at Judson Willey and Bill Henry. The two cowboys walked sheepishly to their horses.

"Mama is going with me. We'll return to camp." Katharane said.

"We could let her skin one of Goodnight's steers. 'might

make her feel better." The gunman needled the cowman.

Katharane stepped up into her saddle. "No Pop." She laughed. "She doesn't have to skin anything. Mama will be all right with me." She kicked her left foot free from the stirrup, and the squaw stuck her foot into the stirrup and drug her heavy body up behind Katharane's saddle. The mustang shifted its feet under the weight.

"Why are these horses still saddled?" Charles Goodnight demanded as he rode into his cow camp.

Bose Ikard pointed across the narrow stream of the Prairie Dog Town Fork of the Red River. The buffalo flowed across the high point beyond the shallow slender stream. The cowboys stood, holding their horses' reins, and watched the several hundred buffalo follow one after the other as if lead by an invisible force.

"'before the massacres I saw a herd in this canyon stretch out for twenty-miles and more." The gunfighter said.

"Is that true, Mr. Goodnight?" Young Tom asked.

"Yes." Charles Goodnight answered without looking away from the herd. "Less than a decade ago they moved through these canyons in the thousands. Now only a few hundred appear here and there. It is a pity."

The buffalo trace wound itself across the high point like the railcars of a dark engineless train and little puffs of smoky dust rose from the herd's collective hooves. The sun was setting, a large red and yellow oblique above the canyon's western rim spraying purple streamers across the brown motleyness of the prairie, and its reflection off of the humped black backs of the buffalo shimmered in a false halo. Behind the cowboys, above the eastern rim, at two o'clock in the darkening sky the rising moon shone clear and defined, blue and black forms dotted its surface. At the far edge of the high plateau upon which Charles Goodnight had established this day's cow camp Reid Stuart lay on his stomach, the long barrel of the Sharps propped upon the iron fork in front of him. Katharane stood to his left. The Squaw Woman stood to his right. The setting sun cut shadows through the front of the worn doeskin shift Katharane now wore. The cowboys stared at the outline of her slender legs which rose high up toward her thighs to disappear there where the doeskin was thicker, less worn.

Her long unbraided hair hung down her back in waves, and her bare arms hung next to the quick receding concaves of her waist. She was just beginning her transition from a lovely girl to a beautiful young woman. The wind had died away and the canyon lay quiet, soft and enchanting in its late afternoon stillness. The wind would rise again before midnight, but for now the canyon was quiet and still and soft and the sound of the movement of the buffalo played out across the canyon and ran up its walls to die before it could escape above the rim. The Sharps roared, defiling the quiet, shocking the assembly. Its heavy dull echo reverberated against the canyon's walls. A cow near the end of the buffalo herd dropped as if all four of her legs had been pulled from beneath her at once.

"What in the hell did he do that for?" Judson Willey whined.

"'for Katty and her mama." the gunfighter said almost to himself. Louder he said. "'squaw prefers buffalo to beef." He reined his black filly to ride to Reid Stuart. Katharane and the excited squaw trotted down the front of the plateau. Reid Stuart carried the Sharps back to his buckskin, swung with it up onto the saddle and turned to wait for the gunman.

"It seems such a waste just to kill one of them." Young Tom said.

"Boy, we've never wasted anything on the Escadara." The gunfighter growled. "Especially not the buffalo, it was your hunters that did that." He trotted the black filly across the plateau to where Reid Stuart waited for him.

"Why does he take everything so personally?" Young Tom complained.

"Because for him it is personal." Charles Goodnight said. "He came here just to live out his days in these canyons. Not to change them. Now it must seem to him everything he does changes them."

"Then why does he do it?" Young Tom asked.

"For the little missy." Bose Ikard said.

"Is there anything he wouldn't do for her?" Young Tom asked.

"Reid Stuart had best pray there's not." Charles Goodnight said slowly. "Someday he may have to call on that devotion just to protect Katharane from that damn gunfighter." He turned and snapped at the gawking cowboys. "Get those horses unsaddled and cooled out. Now!" He walked away from Bose Ikard and Young Tom.

"What did Mr. Goodnight mean by that, I wonder?" Young Tom looked at Bose.

"He meant what he said." Bose said quietly. "Now I'm going to unsaddle Mr. Charles' horse for him. You best tend to your's." He walked slowly after his employer.

Young Tom hesitated for a moment longer watching Katharane and the squaw kneeling beside the dead buffalo. Then he lead his horse away.

"Mr. Ikard." Katharane's voice was soft. It shook a little in the quiet night. She stood just beyond the illumination of the camp's fire.

"Yes, Little Missy." Bose Ikard answered. He stood up and walked towards the sound. Charles Goodnight, also, stood up. Young Tom and several of the cowboys sat up from their bedrolls and listened.

"Would you and Mr. Hawkins and Mr. Goodnight like to come to my camp and eat buffalo with my dad, Pop, Mama and me?" She asked very quietly. She spoke to Bose Ikard because of his gentle nature and soft tone with her.

"Yes." Young Tom blurted before Bose could answer. He picked up his hat, flinching at the snickers coming from the other cowboys. But he walked to Bose and Katharane.

"'been a long time since I've eaten buffalo." Charles Goodnight said. "And I would never turn down an invitation to dine with an attractive young lady."

Katharane smiled and danced on the balls of her feet. She led them back to her camp.

"That was some of the best buffalo I've eaten." Charles Goodnight said.

"Yes mam." Bose agreed.

"Thank you." Young Tom said.

"You're welcome." Katharane responded. She began to say something else when a wail, a lone and singular cry, broke the quiet darkness. The cry reached out with unseen fingers and touched ever so lightly upon their skin, making it tingle with unknown fears. Katharane moved close to the gunfighter. He put his right arm behind her back and squeezed her waist.

Young Tom wet his lips. When Katharane had moved he had hoped she would slide closer to him. Now he watched the gunfighter hold her against his side and massage her waist, and he longed to be as bold.

"He sounds like he's in our canyon, Pop." Katharane almost whispered.

"'could be." The gunfighter said.

"A wolf killed my nanny goat that first winter. Didn't it, Pop?" Katharane asked the gunfighter to confirm what she had been told as to the goat's disappearance.

"Yes." He answered.

"Do you think it was him?" Katharane asked. She stared into the darkness beyond the small campfire.

"'possible, I suppose. This one sounds like an old timer. 'sorta like his voice is hoarse and's been cracked by too much howlin' into too many plains' winds." The gunman said. "But more'n likely it was some she-bitch that got your goat. They get braver than the males in the winters. 'hurtin' for food, I suppose."

"Are you going to shoot him tomorrow, Pop?" Katharane asked.

"'pelt ain't no good in the summer." The gunman answered. "You want him shot I'll shoot him this winter when he's got a good coat on him."

"And in the meantime he may pull down three to four calves." Charles Goodnight said. "Before the sun is up I should send Bose and Young Tom to dispatch him."

"I'll get that wolf for you." Young Tom said eagerly.

"I do the killin' on the Escadara." The gunman said determinedly. "And I decide when it's to be done."

"Is that for man or beast?" Charles Goodnight asked.

"Both." The gunman stated.

The wolf called again, long and drawn far down through the canyon, its wail higher at the outset falling lower deeper with its long descent down the canyon to them.

"A tribute to you." Charles Goodnight said to the gunman. "For his life."

"For a while." The gunman said and pulled Katharane close, causing her to lay her head against his shoulder. "Don't fret, Katty girl. You'll sleep by my side this night. And he'll not disturb your sleep many nights passed November's moon."

"Okay, Pop."

Mid June's heat stopped the round-up. Blood loss from the castration and the searing heat sent the bigger steers into shock. That and the flies made losses too great to continue.

"Come fall. We'll begin again." Charles Goodnight said to Reid Stuart.

"Until then." Reid Stuart said. He extended his hand to Charles Goodnight and they shook hands. Reid Stuart led. The gunman and Katharane followed. The squaw trailed them. They rode slowly away.

Bose watched the melancholy creep across Young Tom's face as they faded from sight. "You will see her this fall. And she'll look prettier than ever." He consoled the cowboy. "Besides, she's still too young."

Charles Goodnight looked sharply at the young cowboy. "You have intentions there?" He barked.

"No. No." Young Tom stuttered. "No sir. She's just a little girl."

Charles Goodnight looked at Bose. Bose winked. The cowman shook his head and sighed.

Young Tom did not see Katharane that fall. Charles Goodnight sent him with three other cowboys to ride the western perimeter of the JA range. Bose waited outside the new bunkhouse. The late December air bit through his clothing and made him shiver. He did not care for the high plains' winters. Young Tom walked to him. "How was she?"

"Miss Katty's well. And she's coming into her womanhood." Bose clamped a large black hand on the cowboy's bony shoulder. "When you tellin' that girl of your feelin's for her?"

Young Tom walked silently into the bunkhouse. He and Bose slept head to head on cots against the southwest wall. This winter they spent much more time on their bunks than they cared to.

The horsemen waited outside of the partially completed house in the morning's new light.

"Who is it, Charles?" Mary Goodnight asked. She stood next to the iron footboard of the bed. She wore a white dressing gown.

"Reid, Katharane and that damn gunfighter." Charles Goodnight said. He pushed his pants down over the tops of his boots and stood up from the soft bed.

"'mornin' Mr. Reid, Mr. Canada, Miss Katty." Bose Ikard said as he walked across the soon to be weathered boards of the porch to where their horses stood.

"They're here, Bose. They are really here. Pop and I saw them. We really did." Katharane said excitedly.

Bose smiled and waited for the young girl to explain. Katharane's smile faded into a frown. "What is it, Little Missy?" Bose asked.

"The new calves, Bose." Katharane said.

"Oh Missy! Forgive this forgetful old fool of a fool." Bose said. "I certainly should have known what you meant."

Katharane smiled, happy again. "They are beautiful, Bose." She said.

"'scrawny little devils." The gunfighter said.

"No, they're not, Pop." Katharane said. To Bose she said. "We've come to see if you and Young Tom and Miss Mary want

205

to see them." She said very confidentially.

"Yes. We do." Young Tom said. He stood at the end of the porch.

"Yes what?" Charles Goodnight asked. He walked out onto the porch. Young Tom flinched and did not answer.

"Yes Young Tom and I want to see Miss Katty's new calves." Bose said. "She has come to ask Miss Mary, also."

"Good." Charles Goodnight said. "I've been intending to ride the big canyon with enough men to make a thorough sweep of the canyon. I want to know how many of our cattle are mixing in with Escadara cattle there." He looked at Reid Stuart. "That might interest you as well."

"It does." Reid Stuart said.

"And you?" Charles Goodnight demanded of the gunman.

"It doesn't." The gunman answered flatly. "I run a hot runnin' iron across the hip of whatever interests me." Goodnight scowled at the gunman.

"Mr. Reid can ride with us and the men." Bose interceded. "Mr. Canada can bring Miss Katty and Miss Mary. We'll be near their Ceta by the end of our sweep." Charles Goodnight hesitated.

"Oh yes! Please?" Katharane cried.

"All right." Charles Goodnight relented. "Bose, you and Young Tom get three of the men. I want to get there before noon."

Bose Ikard watched Tom Hawkins' shoulders sag with disappointment. But the cowboy silently followed Charles Goodnight's instructions.

Charles Goodnight squatted next to Bose. "Ain't no doubt, Mr. Charles. Eight to ten riders drivin' 'bout fifty head." Bose said. "'movin' 'em up the canyon. They're plannin' on takin' 'em to the territory. No other reason to their keepin' 'em together."

"They're headin' 'em for the big canyon." Charles Goodnight said to Reid Stuart who had dismounted and now stood beside the plainsman and the black cowboy. "Maybe fifty head and eight riders at least." He said, stood up and climbed back onto his horse. "We should leave a man here to warn that gunfighter not to bring Mary and Katharane on."

"No need to leave anyone." Reid Stuart said. "Canada will read the sign. He'll know."

"I hope you're right. But we damn sure may need every gun we've got." Charles Goodnight said. He looked at Bose Ikard, Young Tom Hawkins and his three other men. "All right." Charles Goodnight said. "Bose take the point and cut for sign. Young Tom, you drop back quarter of a mile or so. And keep you eyes open!"

"What is it, Pop?" Katharane asked.

"Your Dad and Goodnight have picked up a track. They're followin' it on into the big canyon." The gunman said. He held the filly's reins in his right hand and looked in the direction of the big canyon.

"Is there something wrong?" Mary Goodnight asked.

"From the looks of those tracks I'd say they're followin' 'bout a dozen rustlers and some forty odd head of cattle."

"How can you know they are rustlers?" Mary Goodnight asked.

"Who else besides your husband or my partner has got any business driving cattle up this canyon?"

"What are we to do?"

"We'll follow along behind sorta' slow and watch the sign." The gunman said. He remounted and led them forward. He studied the ground beneath the black filly. He reined her to a stop and stepped down. He held the filly's reins behind him and walked in front of her.

"What is it? What do you see?" Mary Goodnight asked.

"I'm not certain yet." The gunman said. He led the filly back to Katharane. "Here, Little Bit. Hold my horse while I make a circle on foot. I need to check for something." He ambled away from Mary Goodnight and Katharane, and walked a wide semi-circle in front of them. He stopped once, squatted and inspected the canyon floor. Then he completed his loop and walked back to Katharane. "They're smart this bunch. Damn smart." He said. He remounted.

"What do you mean?" Mary Goodnight asked.

"They've dropped back two riders. Let 'em fall out of the cattle they're drivin' and drift off into a ravine or gully and wait while your husband and the others pass. Then fall in behind them."

"How can you know this?"

"The sign." The gunman answered as he reined the filly forward. "'kept seein' a fresh track made after the last of the Goodnight horses. A track made over their tracks."

"How can you be certain its not one of our men's horses?" Mary Goodnight demanded.

"'same way your husband could, if he wasn't pushin' so hard to catch 'em." The gunman said. He frowned. "Maybe he'll catch it before they decide to make their move. What I can't figure is why whoever he's got ridin' rear guard ain't pickin' 'em up."

Mary Goodnight looked at the gunman.

"They're settin' an ambush." The gunman explained. "Sooner or later the ones drivin' the cattle will turn and stand. If your husband and Stuart don't know anybody's behind 'em they'll get caught in a crossfire. That old ranger you're married to is smart. He's got someone ridin' 'bout a hundred yards or so behind him and the others. But whoever it is, he ain't seein' what's happenin'."

"Can we warn them?" Mary Goodnight asked.

"'depends." The gunman said.

"It depends upon what?"

"Upon whether I can do it without puttin' Katty..." The gunman paused. Then he continued. "Without puttin' Katty and you in danger."

"You can do that. Can't you?"

"I can take two. That's all they've dropped back so far." The gunman answered. "Any more and it will depend upon the situation." He held the filly to a quick walk. He, Mary Goodnight and Katharane followed the rustlers' trail on into the canyon.

"Dammit! Why aren't they readin' it?" The gunfighter cursed.

"They still don't know they are being followed?" Mary Goodnight asked.

The gunfighter shook his head. "Not that I can tell." He remounted. "There's four behind 'em now, and we're gettin' damn close to those four." The gunfighter said. "You see that point?" He pointed at a high promenade of land.

"Yes." Mary Goodnight answered.

"You and Katty ride up on it. And wait." The gunman ordered. "If you see me leave this black horse for any reason, you go off the far side and ride. You'll be headin' for your ranch. You ride for all those horses are worth. Do you understand me, Mary Goodnight?"

"But..."

The gunfighter cut her off. "I'm trustin' Katty's well bein' to you, will you do it?" He looked at Mary Goodnight. "Otherwise, I'm takin' you and Katty and we're ridin' out now, and leavin' Reid Stuart and your husband to their own luck." The gunfighter frowned. "Whether it be good or bad."

Mary Goodnight watched deep lines crease the gunfighter's forehead. If she had been alone with him she would have argued. But she believed the gunfighter. For Katharane he would turn and ride silently away, even from his partner. And Mary Goodnight sensed that the gunman was at this moment a much needed, if unknown, ally of her husband and the others who pursued and were being pursued by the rustlers. "Yes."

Three men sat on their horses ahead of him. The gunfighter hesitated, but only for a moment. He drew the black pistol and shot the rider farthest to his left in the back of the head. He shot the next rider in the back of the neck as he turned his head, trying to find his unseen assailant. The third rider spurred his horse and fled through the scrub cedars. The gunman shot him in the back as he tried to escape. The Comanchero's dark eyes flickered as he watched the gunman execute the youngest of his three brothers. As each of his brothers had died while he watched from the thickest part of the cedars, where he had hidden from the gunman's unseen approach, his contempt for them and his wonder at the boldly efficient manner in which the gunman had killed them had increased. They were fools, he thought. So caught up in completing the ambush that they had not sensed the gunman's approach as he had nor even realized that the cowboys in front of them had turned from their pursuit of the others and were waiting for them and that 'the kid' would wait for their charge to draw the cowboys' fire before he moved to attack with the others, that 'the kid' would sacrifice them for his fifty head of stolen cattle. He knew he could kill 'the kid' when the time came, and it would come, but he wondered if he could kill the man with the black pistol who killed as mercilessly and recklessly as he did. He raised his rifle to try.

The gunman sought the fourth rider. He knew he was there, somewhere. 'Dammit! Where is he?' He swore silently to himself. Then a cold and disturbing chill shook him and he turned the filly and ran her to where Mary Goodnight and Katharane waited for him.

The Comanchero lowered his rifle as the black filly raced away. Another day, he thought. Now he must escape.

The rustlers raced away, abandoning the stolen cattle. Reid Stuart shot the horse from underneath one of them. Its rider went out and over the horse's head and down. The horse rolled over its dead rider and broke its back and neck and it, too, died. At their front Bose Ikard let them come within range. The stoic black cowboy aimed his Winchester and squeezed the trigger and a thief dropped from his saddle. Bose aimed again, fired and a horse went down, slamming its rider against a rock bursting his skull.

"Come on." Charles Goodnight cried. "We have to get to Bose before they figure out he's alone." He ripped at the great dappled gray horse and raced alongside of Reid Stuart's buckskin. The cowboys followed. The surviving rustlers fled.

Bose waited calmly as Goodnight and Reid Stuart reined hard to stop. "They're runnin', Mr. Charles." He said.

"Are you all right?" Charles Goodnight asked.

"Yes sir."

"Good. Take Judson and Bill Henry and see if you can tell

which way they are going. But go easy. You are not to try to overtake them. We are not going to engage them in a running gun battle until I find out what was going on behind us." Charles Goodnight said. Bose and the cowboys rode away.

Charles Goodnight, Reid Stuart and Young Tom waited as the gunman, Mary Goodnight and Katharane rode slowly across the open canyon floor to them. The gunman rode warily. He was still uneasy about the fourth rider he had not found. He stopped the filly next to Charles Goodnight's gray. "Who the hell was ridin' your rear guard?" He demanded, angrily.

"I was." Young Tom answered.

"Well boy. You damn nigh let 'em slide right under your nose and then slit your throat." The gunman snarled.

"But..." Young Tom began.

"'could've happened to anyone." Bose Ikard said as he hurried back to the group.

The gunman shook his head. "Not to me." He said, still angry. "And it damn sure shouldn't've happened to someone entrusted with making sure it didn't!"

"Where did they go, Bose?" Charles Goodnight intentionally interrupted the growing dispute between the quarrelsome gunman and the black cowboy. "You are back awfully soon."

The black cowboy cut his eyes in the direction of the Ceta canyon. "And another joined them there, Mr. Charles." Bose answered, allowing his own anger to slide quietly away.

"The fourth. Damn! I knew there was four." The gunman swore. Charles Goodnight frowned.

"What is it, Charles?" Mary Goodnight asked.

Her husband did not answer. He watched Katharane. Slowly the girl realized the threat now posed to the Squaw Woman, alone in the dugout. "Mama." Katharane said softly. Then she cried aloud, a wild trapped animal's cry for help and consolation. "Pop!" Katharane's cry broke the still canyon air like a gun shot.

"Give me your horse, boy!" The gunman demanded of

Tom Hawkins.

Young Tom looked at Bose. The gunman had already embarrassed the young cowboy. Now the belligerent gunman was demanding the surrender of his horse. Young Tom was not anxious to lend the hard eyed gunfighter his favorite horse. Bose stepped down from his horse and handed his reins to Reid Stuart. "Take my horse for your second, Mr. Reid. And God speed to you."

Now Young Tom dismounted and handed his reins to the gunman. "What are they going to do?" He asked Bose.

"Try to ride 'em down before they reach the dugout and Katty's mama." Bose said quietly, and added. "If they can."

"I'll take the lead, Stuart." The gunman yelled as he lashed the black filly and she jumped and began to run, drawing Young Tom's sorrel after her. Reid Stuart, leading Bose's tall roan, galloped the buckskin after him.

"We'll be pushing hard behind you." Charles Goodnight called after them. "If you have to make a stand and fight we'll get there to support you as quickly as we can."

Neither the gunfighter nor Reid Stuart acknowledged his call. They flashed in and out of the scrub cedars until they disappeared into the Ceta canyon.

Reid Stuart drew the buckskin up short causing him to stumble to avoid running into Young Tom's sorrel. The gunman pointed at the corpse. It lay on its back in the grass with its left shoulder shoved underneath a cedar tree, the heels of its boots still imbedded in the sod where they had battered through the soft sod as they had clawed at the sod trying to drive the already dead body away from the slashing knife. The corpse's eyes and mouth were open and its throat was ripped ajar.

"He's killin' 'em off and takin' their mounts." The gunman said. "'gettin' ready to make his run for the territory." A faint muffled pop came from far up the Ceta. The gunman spurred the hot filly and she charged ahead before Reid Stuart could ask him who 'he' was. The gunman knew 'him'. He had never seen 'him', never heard 'him' speak. He had only smelled 'him' in the stand of cedars, smelled 'him' even above the kerosene thick odor from the broken cedar buds. But the gunman knew 'him', knew 'he' had dark black eyes, black tangled greasy hair, stubby bloody fingers, knew 'his' nose was flat and knew 'his' mouth twisted when 'he' spoke, knew 'his' ears were too close to 'his' head and he knew this wild fierce thing had no heart, no soul. The gunman knew 'he' was an animal, an animal that killed, one of the last true Comancheros, bred by a Mexican renegade through an Apache squaw, hated by both races throughout 'his' life. At fourteen 'he' had killed 'his' father for a rifle. With that rifle and the New Mexico territory to vanish into, 'he' and the rest of the old Mexican outlaw's bastard half-Apache wolf pups that rode with 'him' had fed themselves upon the plains' horses, cattle and women. They took them or they killed them.

Two more corpses lay on the canyon floor. One's throat had been slashed like the first. The other had been shot in the back of the head. Reid Stuart saw the black filly drifting to a stop beside the two dead men. He knew the gunman had gone to the sorrel. Reid Stuart felt his buckskin's neck. The buckskin still had something left. Reid Stuart galloped on. He could hear the gunman lashing Young Tom's sorrel. He could hear the cedar limbs popping and snapping passed the gunman's buckskin chaps. It was a break neck ride. And if they ran onto what was left of the rustlers at this pace Reid Stuart doubted if even the gunman was fast enough to get the first shot off. But he rode just as hard. He felt the buckskin lose his stride, stumble, gather his feet and regain his cadence. He lifted the heavy Sharps, swung his left leg across the pommel of his saddle, shoved his left boot into Bose's roan's left stirrup and stepped across the roan's saddle and settled himself down into it. Bose's roan was a strong horse. He took long sure rhythmic strides that ate up the canyon floor.

The Comanchero eyed the 'kid' as they faced each other where they squatted near the spring and drank. He knew he could kill the 'kid' now. But he would not. Two men to be pursued across the plains instead of one could benefit him. He would separate himself from the 'kid' once they crossed the Canadian river. Any pursuers would have a choice, split their forces or follow one trail. It could give him an advantage. He stood up. "Bring your rifle." He commanded the 'kid'. "Kill their horses." He sniffed the air. He smelled the Comanche squaw. But he did not have time to seek her out. He knew the way. He would come back.

The squaw lay hidden in the tall grass above the dugout.

A rifle shot rang off of the Ceta's walls. "The squaw?" Reid Stuart yelled his question to the gunman who was now only some ten yards ahead of him. Young Tom's sorrel had been unable to maintain the brutal pace the gunfighter had demanded of him. Bose's roan's steady stride had slowly gained on the sorrel.

Two more shots rang out. "He's killin' our horses." The gunman yelled back.

The Comanchero and the 'kid' took fresh mounts and led their watered remudas out onto the plains. Distance would be their savior now. They loped away from the dugout.

Young Tom's sorrel stood at the first pool, his front legs spread, his head down, his sides trembling, unable to drink, but Bose's roan lifted its head from the pool when Charles Goodnight and the others arrived. The gunman stood with his hands on his hips and stared at the plains. Reid Stuart walked from the dugout to Charles Goodnight. "Our horses were played out when we got here." Reid Stuart said to Goodnight. "And they killed our remuda." Charles Goodnight glanced at he dead horses below the pools.

"We couldn't follow without fresh horses." Reid Stuart said.

"Mama?" Katharane's eyes begged her father.

"I don't know, Katharane." Reid Stuart dropped his head and his voice. "We haven't found her." He mumbled as the gunman approached.

"Do you think they took her with them?" Charles Goodnight asked.

"If they'd a found her they'd a killed her." The gunman said. "Runnin' like they are, they'd a never takin' her with 'em."

Katharane sobbed softly.

"Spread out. Ride in circles around the dugout." Charles Goodnight ordered his men. "And watch where your horses step." He cautioned them.

The cowboys swung their horses slowly out and spaced themselves a half dozen steps apart. They looked at the prairie because Charles Goodnight had ordered them to do so. But none of them wanted to find the body. None of them wanted the responsibility of raising his head, catching Charles Goodnight's eye and wondering all the while if the girl would notice, would know what it meant.

Bose slid down from behind Charles Goodnight's saddle and stood next to Katharane's mustang. One of the cowboys handed the buckskin's and the filly's leads to Bose. Goodnight had chosen to rest the two hard ridden horses and have Bose and Young Tom ride double, Bose behind him, Young Tom behind Katharane.

"Mama." Katharane at first pleaded almost silently. Then she screamed at the empty plains. "Mama! I want my Mama!" She cried.

Her sobs sent chills running across the shoulders of the cowboys. They dropped their heads lower and looked at the prairie but did not see it. They only heard the little girl crying for her mother, and whether or not the squaw was her mother her haunting cries left no doubt the child feared her loss as much as any child could fear the loss of a beloved mother.

"Oh Charles." Mary Goodnight whispered. "Is she dead?"

"If they found her." Charles Goodnight answered.

The horses moved slowly forward like a large scythe cutting across the plains. The Squaw Woman stood up as they approached her.

"Look!" Young Tom cried and pointed at the squaw where she stood above the dugout in the tall grass. He had to grab the back of the saddle to keep from being unseated as Katharane swung off of the mustang.

"Mama. Mama" The child sang as she ran for the squaw who in reply came to the top of the dugout.

"You stupid stinkin' gut worryin' Comanche bitch!" The gunman cursed. "I'll drive a boot through your fat butt for troublin' Katty so." He started for the squaw.

The squaw saw him. She stopped. She worked her hands. She wanted to go to the child. But she did not want to confront the angry gunman. She turned and trotted across the top of the dugout. The gunman turned along the front of the dugout, paralleling the squaw and cursing her with each step. The squaw stopped again. She faced Katharane and lifted her hands and beseeched the child to come to her with a wailing that made many of the cowboys tremble. She turned and went back across the top of the dugout again. The gunman turned and followed her along the front of the dugout. Several of the cowboys began to chuckle at the ridiculous dance.

Charles Goodnight laughed. "I wonder which one is going to give out first, Reid, the squaw or that gunfighter?" He asked.

"You would think he would have better sense." Reid Stuart grunted.

"I'm gonna' shoot your ass if you don't come down from there." The gunman threatened the squaw. That only caused her to trot faster and wail louder.

Katharane ran passed the gunfighter and up onto the top of the dugout and into the arms of the squaw. "Mama. Mama." She repeated as she buried her face into the squaw's hot smelly midriff.

To Katharane the gunfighter relented. He walked back to Reid Stuart and Charles Goodnight.

"Bose, Young Tom, Mary and I will stay here the night. Just in case..." Charles Goodnight began.

"Not needed." The gunfighter growled. "I can deal well enough with any that might choose to return."

"And not wanted?" Charles Goodnight asked.

"Wanted, and you are welcome here as our guests anytime." Reid Stuart said firmly. He glared at the gunfighter who finally shrugged and stalked away.

"I'll send the others back to pick up the dead. Otherwise the varmints will scavenge the bodies before daylight." Charles Goodnight said.

"All right." Reid Stuart replied. "Miss Mary can sleep in

the dugout with Katharane and the squaw. You, Bose and Young Tom can make your camp above the dugout. Canada and I will sleep here in the yard."

Goodnight nodded. He helped his wife dismount. Then he instructed his men as to his expectations of them. They turned their horses and rode down the trail away from the spring. Bose and Young Tom had spread their bedrolls just beyond the back of the top of the dugout. Bose was spreading Charles Goodnight's bedroll for him when his employer and Reid Stuart approached.

"I should take Bose and that gunfighter and be after them." Charles Goodnight said. He looked out onto the plains.

"To what end?" Reid Stuart asked.

"To bring them to account." Charles Goodnight said.

"Well. I'm afraid that will have to be left to someone else. Goodnight." Reid Stuart said.

Charles Goodnight nodded in response, but he did not speak and he did not take his eyes away from the plains.

"Goodnight, Mr. Reid." Bose said.

"Goodnight, sir." Young Tom said.

Reid Stuart walked down to the front of the dugout. The gunman stood between the dugout and the spring and he, too, studied the plains, his back to the dugout where the squaw, Katharane and Mary Goodnight prepared for bed. Reid Stuart stepped down into the dugout near the rock hearth, pulled a smoldering stick from the fire, stepped back up out of the dugout and walked to the gunman. Reid Stuart lifted his tobacco pouch and shook the dry flaky leaves out onto a paper he held pinched by his thumb against the inside of his first and second fingers. He hooked the tobacco pouch back around his buffalo hide belt. Then he licked the edge of the paper and twisted the ends together. He stuck the cigarette between his lips and touched the hot end of the stick to it.

"Those things are gonna' kill you." The gunman said, without looking at his partner.

"I know. You have told me before." Reid Stuart said. He smoked his cigarette.

"I should be after them, Stuart." The gunman said.

"Why?"

"'cause he knows where Katty is."

Reid Stuart smoked until the cigarette burnt his lips. Then he squeezed the fire from the butt's remnants with his thumb and forefinger. Mary Goodnight stepped out of the dugout. She wore one of the squaw's deerskin shifts. It hung off of her shoulders, dangerously close to sliding off of her slender frame. Reid Stuart walked to her.

"My husband and your friend are troubled over those two men who escaped, Mr. Stuart." She said.

"Yes mam." Reid Stuart said.

"My husband wants them dead for the wrongs they've done. Though it frightens me I can understand why he feels as he does. What I am wondering is, do you understand why your friend wishes them dead?"

Reid Stuart looked into Mary Goodnight's face. Slowly, quietly he bowed his head and said. "Yes. I do. And that frightens me, too." He raised his head and looked at Mary Goodnight again and said. "Goodnight, Mary Goodnight." He offered her his hand. She took it and he helped her step back into the dugout again. The western horizon rumbled, low, far away, but ever threatening.

VENGEANCE IS MINE

1881-1883

"Who are they, Mama?" Katharane asked as she and the Squaw Woman watched the dust rise above the lost horizon of the plains like a large gray cloud. They could not see the riders, only the dust from their horses' hooves.

The Squaw Woman took Katharane's hand and led her back into the dugout. The squat Comanche rolled the bulky feather mattress to the far side of the wooden frame. She pointed at the leather trampoline which supported Katharane's bed. "Katty stay."

"Why? What's wrong? We don't even know who they are." Katharane began to argue, but she stopped when she saw the desperate look in the Squaw Woman's eyes which the squaw's ancestors, bred, reared and destroyed with violence, had left with her, eyes which caught, mirrored and reflected hopelessness and resignation in their gaze. Katharane's father called it the look of the Kiowa that he had seen in the squaw's eyes that first morning in April in the canyon.

"Kiowa. Katty hide."

"But Mama, there are no more Kiowa."

"Kiowa. Katty stay." The Squaw Woman shook the mattress. "Katty stay. No move. No say."

Katharane knew that the unseen riders were not Kiowa. But the churning in her stomach, the Squaw Woman's insistence and her father's warning that many riders approaching from the plains meant danger frightened her. "We could ride out, Mama."

The Squaw Woman shook her head. "They look. They find."

"I have my guns. We can fight." Katharane pleaded, and she put her hands on the grips of her pistols.

The Comanche woman took the girl's face in her hands.

"Too many." The squaw, old by the ways of the Comanche, almost forty, spoke quietly, softly, and lovingly to the white girl who called her mama. "Katty stay. Katty no move. Katty no say. Katty do for Mama. Katty wait for black gun and Stuart."

Katharane surrendered and lay down on the leather trampoline. The Squaw Woman nodded at her daughter and folded the thick feather mattress back over her. Silence and darkness came to Katharane with the mattress. She listened. At first she heard only the sound of the Squaw Woman's moccasins scuffing the dirt floor of the dugout, then she heard the vague and indistinct voices of men, and then a curse, swearing, harsh and bitter and frightening and loud, almost as if it were uttered into her ear, followed by a crushing weight upon the mattress. She could barely breathe underneath the weight upon her and the grip of the fear inside her chest. She heard the Squaw Woman whimper. She could see nothing, she could not move and she could not shut out the voices of the men that cursed and that of her mother that prayed the Kwerhar-rehnuh prayer to the wind to carry her daughter safely away.

"Come on, Hank. Stick it in her dammit!"

"Shit! I can't find it for all the fat. Damn pussed up squaw."

"Here. I'll make it easy for you."

Katharane heard the Squaw Woman cry out, then she felt her body jerk, stiffen and become still where it lay on top of her.

"Christ! You ripped her almost to her navel. Ain't no good in it now."

"Then get off and let me at it."

Katharane felt weight rise from the feather mattress, then a heavier weight slammed the mattress down into her face, almost smothering her. The mattress shook, rose and then pounded down against her, against her spread legs, against her stomach and against her hot face. She tried to swallow, could not, heard the Squaw Woman try to begin again her prayer to the wind, and then a grunt, a groan and another curse drowned out her mother's voice.

"Did you get it done?"

"Damn right! I got it done. Now I'll finish it."

Again, Katharane felt the Squaw Woman jerk. She heard a snap, like a green cedar branch snapping, then the sound of something being ripped apart like the sound old well worn buckskin made when it was torn apart.

"Jesus! You done gutted the bitch alive."

Katharane smelled sweat, blood and a rancid scent of flesh she could not identify. Again the weight rose from the feather mattress. This time it did not return. She heard gun shots and shouts from outside of the dugout, a horse's agonized scream and old Casner's dog whimper and howl. 'Pop'. She prayed silently. 'Let it be my Pop.' But she knew it was not the report of the black pistol and she lay very still.

"The girl." The Comanchero demanded.

The two men hesitated. They feared the Comanchero, his look, his voice made them sweat and stutter. "They said some...sometimes she rode with them two. She...she must be with them 'cause she ain't here." The one holding the bloody knife stammered.

"Just my luck." The other one said more boldly. "I could sure stand me a young girly to go at." Then he fell silent before the Comanchero's cold eyes.

"She is the black gun's." The Comanchero said. "Do you wish a go at him?" He waited. No one answered. "No?" He taunted. "If you do not wish a chance before the black gun, leave her to me if you find her."

Katharane prayed softly until she heard a voice from outside of the dugout and she stopped. "Come on! Torch that dump and let's ride." A warm wetness now penetrated through the feathers of the mattress and moistened Katharane's cheek, mixing with her tears. More of the wetness penetrated the mattress and covered her hands and stomach. She began to smell smoke through the mattress and the dugout became unbearably hot. But she lay still and stopped, and she waited for the gunman and her father as the Squaw Woman had told her to do.

At first Reid Stuart thought it was a prairie fire danger-ously close to where the dugout was located. He hoped he was wrong, then, as the black filly began to twist in and out of the scrub cedars as she dashed along the floor of the Ceta, he began to pray it was a grass fire. "Grass fire?" Reid Stuart yelled ahead to the gunman.

"'can't be. 'not movin'." The gunman yelled back over his shoulder. The black filly surged up the steep trail leading to the pools and the dugout. The gunman drove her on, spurring her flanks between each jump, insuring she did not pause nor hesitate.

Reid Stuart lashed the buckskin's rump with his reins. But the large horse could not match the filly's quickness up the canyon wall. The gunman had disappeared down into the smoking burned out dugout when Reid Stuart's buckskin skittered up and over the edge of the canyon wall. Reid Stuart tried to call to his partner, but no words would form on his chapped lips. He sat stunned, silent and dry mouthed and stared at the dead stock, the burnt corrals and the dark smoking dugout. Katharane's white mustang lay in the center of the upper horse corral. The pony was dead, shot through its head. Old Casner's one eyed dog lay on top of the dugout's sod roof dying, its back was broken. The two yearlings which he and Katharane had gathered and penned for fattening and slaughter lay dead on either side of Katharane's mustang. They were already beginning to bloat. The cedar posts, black and smoldering near their bases where the raiders had poured kerosene to ensure their ignition, stood like failing tombstones above the dead animals. Reid Stuart looked and saw it, sniffed and smelled it, listened and heard it, licked his lips and tasted it, and remembered and knew it. Death.

The gunman stood in the smoky darkness of the dugout. The old cedar beams which Reid Stuart had used as rafters to stabilize the sod roof were blackened from the heat and the smoke which the poles that covered each end of the dugout had given off as they had burned. But the sturdy beams had not succumbed to the fire. They were intact and they steadfastly supported the roof. He blinked and tried to see. The table was broken. But the wooden crate which held Reid Stuart's instrument and his Bible was untouched and not damaged. Then he saw the feather mattress and the disemboweled dead Squaw Woman that lay atop it. "Katty!" He cried.

Katharane had heard his boots hit the dugout's hard pan

floor. She could barely breathe, her eyes burned from the smoke and her throat was raw and sore from swallowing her tears and choking back her sobs. She continued to lay very still and quiet until she heard the gunman cry for her. "Pop. Oh, Pop!" She cried and struggled to push the heavy mattress off of her.

The gunman stepped to the cot, rolled the mattress away from the edge, being careful not to tumble the Squaw Woman's corpse off the other side, and then he lifted Katharane into his arms. "Hold tight to my neck, child." He commanded. "And don't you open your eyes. Promise me." He held Katharane tightly in his arms, her back to the bloody body of the squaw and again he demanded. "Promise me." Katharane nodded her head against the gunman's neck. He turned and stepped up and out of the dugout.

Reid Stuart stared at the long blood soaked hair of his daughter. He began to choke. "Did they scalp..." He gagged.

"She's alive, Stuart." The gunman said. "Alive and unhurt as best I can tell."

Reid Stuart dismounted. The gunman handed Katharane to him. "Take her to the spring and clean her up." He said to Reid Stuart.

Reid Stuart looked at him and asked. "The Squaw Woman?"

The gunman shook his head. "Don't bring Katty back 'till I tell ya'." He cautioned his partner as he turned and went back into the dugout. Reid Stuart carried Katharane to the spring.

Slowly they appeared among the scrub cedar, the long buckskin with Reid Stuart in its saddle, the buffalo gun resting across its lap, the mule on lead behind the buckskin, its sad cargo, wrapped and tied securely within a dusty white buffalo hide, draped carefully across its harness, followed by a paint pony with Katharane, her head bent, eyes fixed upon her hands on the saddle's horn, and at Katharane's side, close, very close, the gunman, his hand at ease against his black pistol. So, they came out of the Ceta and into the big canyon and toward the marker and Mary and Charles Goodnight and Goodnight's men.

Charles and Mary Goodnight, Bose Ikard and Young Tom Hawkins rode out to meet them. Mary Goodnight leaned out from where she sat on her side saddle and put her left hand on Katharane's right shoulder. "I am so sorry, Katharane."

Katharane did not look at her. She spoke to her hands stacked on her saddle's horn. "Yes mam."

"They were twelve of them." Charles Goodnight said to Reid Stuart. "'passed by Tascosa last night. Headin' west and ridin' hard. They'll split up if we don't catch them before the New Mexico territory." Reid Stuart nodded. 'It's a hard thing, Reid." Charles Goodnight continued. "But if we are to have any hopes of catchin' 'em, we've got to start right now."

"No!" Katharane's voice crackled through the morning air, startling horses and riders. Charles Goodnight's big gray shuffled its feet and blew through its nose. Every rider now looked at Katharane. "No." She repeated, and let her silent suffering settle over the group. No one spoke. It seemed as if they must now remain quiet until she gave them permission to do otherwise.

Until the gunman's gentle drawl filled the air, brushed against their ears and released them from their unspoken pledge of silent attendance. "We've got tendin' to do for Katty's mama first." The words died away, swallowed by the big canyon.

Charles Goodnight glanced at Reid Stuart. "If we give them another day's lead, you know we'll never catch them." He warned.

"It's not for you, nor anyone, but my father and Pop and me to go after them." Katharane's eyes burned with anger as she glared at Charles Goodnight. Anger which was quickly washed away by hot tears that fell upon her hands as she dropped her head again, her untied auburn hair falling across her cheeks and catching there upon her tears, and said. "It was my mama they killed."

"Katharane. Surely you know that everyone hates what has happened and wants to do whatever they can to see those men punished." Mary Goodnight said. She squeezed Katharane's shoulder.

"Do I?" Katharane raised her head and stared big and empty eyed at Mary Goodnight. "Do I, Miss Mary? Where are they?" She turned her head, as if looking about the canyon for other riders. Then she brought her eyes back to Mary Goodnight. "They knew as well as you the way we would come, where we would take my mama. I don't see any other riders coming. Do you?" She swallowed her tears and continued. "Where are they, Miss Mary?" She demanded. "I don't see them. I see you, and I see Mr. Goodnight and his men. And I know they would ride after those men if Charles Goodnight told them to. Maybe some of them, like Mr. Ikard and Young Tom." Katharane nodded at Bose and Tom Hawkins. "They'd be proud to go. But that is all I know that would, Miss Mary. I don't know if another soul on these plains gives a damn about a squaw killing." Katharane's voice grew thick and rich with the tears she gulped down her throat. She swallowed and cried out. "She was my mama, Miss Mary! Don't they know that? Don't they care?" She pleaded to Mary Goodnight to help her understand.

"Oh Katharane!" Mary Goodnight cried back. "I don't know how to explain all that has happened and why. I don't. But you must let my husband and these men help. You must."

"No." Katharane shook her head. "No. Only my father, Pop and I can go after those men. Only we know why they must die for what they've done."

No one spoke. The judgment Katharane had passed upon the Squaw Woman's killers had stunned them. The duty it carried to Reid Stuart and the gunman was great. All, save Katharane, knew it might well mean their deaths, too. All knew it would not be an easy thing to do.

Charles Goodnight eyed Reid Stuart. "How are you going to accomplish it?" He asked.

"I don't know yet." Reid Stuart answered. "First, we are going to tend to the Squaw Woman."

"I'm not going to let you say goodbye to your mama alone, Katharane. I am not." Mary Goodnight said fervently. "Charles and I are going with you to her place."

Young Tom swallowed. He stared at Bose. He was desperate to go, but he would not ask his employer and he dared not ask Katharane. It would not be appropriate he thought. His eyes asked Bose what he should do.

The Negro scout took his hat off and spoke slowly and deliberately. "Miss Katharane." He spoke so softly that the others looked at him to be certain not only who had spoken but if someone had spoken at all.

Katharane answered him. "Yes, Bose."

"Young Tom and I would take most kind appreciation if you should see fit to allow us to ride with you to your mama's sacred place."

Even Katharane's bitter sadness could not ignore the kindness in the quiet voice that asked without asking, that offered without offering and that gave without expectation. She looked at the scout and nodded. She mumbled faintly. "Thank you, Bose. Thank you, Tom."

Young Tom clenched his fists to keep from screaming.

"One thing more, Missy."

Now everyone listened intently to Bose Ikard.

"Yes?"

"The men. They need to pay their respects to you."

Katharane did not understand. She frowned.

"May I lead your horse over to them, so they can do that?"

"If you wish." Katharane murmured.

The black cowboy stepped down from his mount.

"That's a right long walk, Bose." Charles Goodnight said. "Your's and Katharane's horses are gentle, why don't you lead Katharane's horse behind your's?"

"When you lead a lady's horse, Mr. Charles, you lead it with respect and with dignity, and you always walk beside it, proper like." Bose Ikard said to his employer and friend. He grasped the paint pony's hackamore with his right hand. Then he turned to Young Tom and said. "Tom. You ride ahead. Tell 'em I am bringin' Miss Katharane for them to pay their respects. Tell 'em I'd best not see a hat on a head."

"Yes sir, Bose." Young Tom answered. He spurred his horse and trotted back to the other cowboys.

226

"Why is he carving a marker into the boulder?" Young Tom asked Bose. The two cowboys watched the gunman chisel at the hard face of the granite boulder. Young Tom's nerves still tingled from the ride through the narrows and the view from the platform above the far canyon, the place where the gunman had found Kwanhah and his band camped in April of 1868, the place where he and Reid Stuart had taken the squaw from her people and had given Katharane to her to care for. Young Tom continued. "They put the squaw up on that cedar scaffold. The vultures will scatter her bones far from this place."

"They put her up there because that is the way of her people, the Comanche." Bose explained. "They believe the closer they are to the sky the closer they are to the spirit world." Bose paused as the sound of the gunman's chisel paused, then he resumed when the gunman again began to hammer the chisel against the rock. "The marker's for Miss Katty."

The gunman worked on the rock for two hours. When he had finished Charles Goodnight, Mary Goodnight, Bose Ikard, Tom Hawkins and Reid Stuart formed a semi-circle in front of the granite boulder into which the gunman had carved the memorial. Katharane walked into the semi-circle. She read the inscription aloud. "COMANCHE SQUAW WOMAN, Killed 4 August 1881, She was Katty's Mama."

Katharane did not cry. Instead she asked her father. "Read something from your Bible for my mama, Dad."

Reid Stuart opened his Bible. He thumbed through the pages, stopped, studied one page and read from it. "And to the woman were given two wings of a great eagle, that she might fly into the wilderness, into her place, where she is nourished for a time and times."

"Yes sir, Mr. Reid." Bose Ikard exclaimed. "Yes sir." The black cowboy stepped to Katharane and gripped her shoulders. "Your mama has the wings of a great eagle, Miss Katharane. And right now she's flying to her place with the spirit of her people. Let yourself believe this child and be easy with yourself."

Katharane looked into the Negro's sad eyes. Still she did not cry. "Yes, Bose, I will do that." Bose winked at her, released her and walked away.

Katharane lay on a bedroll next to Mary Goodnight. Bose Ikard built a small fire downwind of Katharane and Mary Goodnight. Young Tom carried an old dead piece of driftwood he had found to the fire. Charles Goodnight checked the hobbles around the horses' hocks. Reid Stuart squatted on his boots' heels on the rock platform next to the gunman. He stared into the far canyon with his friend and asked. "How long you figure it'll take to ride 'em down?"

"A while." The gunman answered.

"Six months?" Reid Stuart pressed him.

"'more like a year. Maybe two. They'll scatter once they know they're bein' trailed. 'take some time and trackin' to get 'em all." The gunman answered thoughtfully.

"A year, two." Reid Stuart mumbled. "Won't be much left of the ranch by then." He paused. Then he cursed. "Damn. Twelve years of hard work gone." He shook his head and looked down at his boots. "But it can't be helped, I guess." He said quietly. He raised his head to stare into the bottom of the far canyon as it evaporated into the dusk. The gunman remained silent. "Katharane can stay with the Goodnights. Miss Mary will see that she's well cared for. And maybe Charles can sell our stock, so we'll have a stake to start over with when we get back." Reid Stuart stopped. "Think we'll get back, Canada?"

The gunfighter shrugged, but he said. "I reckon'."

"When we do, do you think we'll want to start over, again?" Reid Stuart asked.

The gunman smiled at the black canyon and said. "I reckon' you would. But you ain't goin'. You're stayin' here with Katty. This is somethin' I can do. I should have gone after him when we chased him out of the big canyon. Now he's come back and it's for me to go after him."

"Are you certain he was there?"

"I'm certain." The gunman said, without taking his eyes from the far canyon.

Reid Stuart rolled a smoke, walked to the fire, lit it and returned and squatted next to the gunman. He exhaled smoke through his nose. "You going after him or away from Katharane?"

For long agonizing seconds the gunman was silent. Finally he said. "Does it matter?"

"I don't know." Reid Stuart said. But it was the reason he did not argue with the gunman. And it was the reason he would let the gunman go alone. "Are you certain you can get him?"

'I'll get him."

Charles and Mary Goodnight stood in front of the dugout. Bose and Young Tom waited on their horses at the spring. Reid Stuart and Katharane stood next to Charles Goodnight's big grey which stood ground hitched to the yard in front of the dugout. No one spoke. Each waited and listened and wondered if the they would ever all be together again. Was this a parting or just a separation?

The gunman broke the tense silence. "What do you wake up for each morning, Katty?" The gunman asked as he dropped his saddle across Goodnight's grey's back.

"What do you mean, Pop?"

"Why do you want to wake up each morning?" The gunman asked. He reached underneath the grey and grabbed the cinch.

"For you and Dad and the ranch."

"Reid Stuart wakes up for the ranch." The gunman fed the cinch through the iron ring on his saddle. "You don't have a reason, one reason, for waking up each morning. Not yet."

"So?"

"So, when you do, and you will, don't let anything or anyone come between you." The gunman turned and looked at the girl. "The reason I'll wake up in the morning is to find the men who killed your Squaw Woman. And I'll keep on wakin' up each mornin' till I find each and all of them. Nothing, not one thing upon these high prairies can or will stop me." He turned away from her and pulled the cinch tight.

"How will I know it's done?" Katharane asked. She stared at the toes of her moccasins.

The gunman worked the leather cinch, first lifting it up

against the grey horse's belly, then pulling it down against the iron ring on the saddle, as he answered her. "You'll know, Katty. I've thought about it since we left the Comanch's canyon. When I get him I will send you a sign, a Comanche sign. And then there will be no doubt that it's done and he's dead." He jerked the cinch one final time. Then he laced it in and out of itself three times.

Reid Stuart tied the sorrel's lead rope through the heavy leather loop holding the lariat to the saddle. He tied the tall roan on lead behind the sorrel. Then he turned to the gunman and said, "They're the best mounts we can muster." Reid Stuart rubbed his bony elbows. "I'll pay Charles Goodnight for the grey."

The gunman nodded his head. Leaving moved in and around Katharane, the gunman and Reid Stuart. Each wanted to say something, but the silence of leaving overpowered them because it was time for the gunman to go. He reached his left hand out to Reid Stuart and grasped his partner's arm above the wrist. Reid Stuart wrapped his long skinny fingers around the gunfighter's arm. "Stu', I'm not gonna' be here to do it. Remember. The one who pulls the trigger first is the one who's right." The gunman said and squeezed his friend's arm. Then he pulled his arm away. He put his hands on his hips and stared across the grey's saddle at the far prairie. He looked at the prairie for several moments. Then he reached for the saddle horn with his left hand.

"Pop?" Katharane's throaty voice croaked through the silence. She cried tearlessly.

The gunman hesitated. Then he released the saddle horn and turned to Katharane, caught each side of her face between his hands and kissed her on the mouth. "I love you, Katharane. Take care of that old black filly for me." It was the first time he had kissed Katharane on the mouth. It was the first time he had called her Katharane. And it was the only time he told her that he loved her.

Katharane opened her mouth to speak but he was gone, in the saddle and riding away. She chased after him, crying, calling to him. "I love you, Pop. I love you. You come back. You come back to me!" She screamed as she collapsed onto her knees. She sat on her knees amidst the sparse buffalo grass of the Llano Estacada and watched the gunfighter slowly disappear, there, but lost, he blended from her vision into the bear grass and just the sheer openness of the prairie. Katharane kept crying and calling after him. "You come back, Pop. You come back to Katty. You come back."

"It's as if he's always been gone." Katharane said.

"Just a month, that's all." Reid Stuart said. He sat on the gangly legged buckskin colt for which he had traded four good steers to Charles Goodnight. Katharane sat on a small dark bay gelding Bose Ikard and Young Tom had brought to her with the buckskin. Supposedly, the bay was a gift from all of the Goodnight cowboys, but Katharane suspicioned it was only Bose and Tom that had purchased the animal, though at a reduced price. Miss Mary would have seen to that. Still she had spent hours trying to think of a gift she could give all of Charles Goodnight's men. But he now had almost two dozen cowboys and she could not fashion a gift for each. So the debt went without being repaid, but not forgotten. The two horses stood above the dugout and, as their riders did, they stared out into the unbending prairie. Each day, late, they stood at the same spot and waited, for what they had no knowledge. But if they tried to drift from their stations their riders were quick to draw tight rein.

"He will come back, Dad. He will. He has to."

"If he can, he will." Reid Stuart said.

"Why did he come out here, Dad, so alone and so far from everyone?"

"Because of a woman."

"Men do such silly things because of women. I don't understand."

"You're young. You will." Reid Stuart said. "With a woman a man has a reason to get up each morning. He may not tell her that. He may not even know it. He may even be mean to her or hurt her. But he has to have her." He pulled a cigarette paper from his shirt pocket and untied his tobacco pouch from his belt, built a thick round cigarette, stuck it in his mouth, fished two small flint rocks from the pouch and struck them against each other. On the third strike the dry paper took the spark and began to smoke. He sucked air slowly through the cigarette until its far end burned red with fire.

"Pop said I would find someone to wake up for each morning."

Reid Stuart nodded, exhaled and spoke through the smoke. "And as long as you can see yourself in his eyes you will get up each morning and go on. But when you leave his eyes, you will not do that." Reid Stuart slowly smoked his cigarette.

Father and daughter were quiet until Katharane spoke again. "Then why do you think Pop has stayed here so long? He doesn't have a woman."

'Because of you, Katharane.' Reid Stuart thought, but he said. "Because we found him. We didn't give him a lot of choices, daughter."

"What do you think he was doing when we found him?" Katharane asked.

"Just waiting to die."

The plains night began to roll across Reid Stuart and Katharane. Silently, they watched it come, until Katharane spoke again. "Then we saved him, Dad."

"Yes. He would say we saved him."

"Dad?'

"Yes."

"Do you think he wanted to be saved?"

Reid Stuart sucked hard on the soggy end of his hand rolled cigarette. Its ash glowed red and yellow, and its lonely light cast a soft shadow on Reid Stuart's face. "I don't know, Katharane. Maybe I want to think he did. But that may be more for me than for him."

"Well. I think he did. I'm glad we saved him." Katharane said and leaned against her father's thin bony shoulder and watched him smoke his cigarette.

Katharane tried to listen through Bose Ikard's soft voice. She desperately wanted to hear Charles Goodnight who was speaking pointedly and emphatically to her father. Charles

Goodnight and Reid Stuart stood at the spring. Katharane, Bose and Young Tom stood at the front of the dugout. Bose's slow monotone muted his employer's words.

Young Tom watched Katharane's every move. It had been nine months since he had stood at the spring and watched Katharane weep as the gunman had ridden away, nine long months of lying awake, of wondering about the slender young girl who had sat on her knees and wailed her love for the gunman. Could she ever love just a cowboy? Would she?

"Bose." Katharane cut the black cowboy off in mid-sentence. "What does Charles Goodnight know of my Pop?"

Softly, politely Bose Ikard said. "Can't say, Missy."

"Can't or won't!" Katharane snapped.

"Can't and won't." Bose answered quietly.

"Well someone can and will." Katharane said. She walked quickly to the spring. But Charles Goodnight noticed her approach and let his words drift away from her and fall unheard into the Ceta below. "You have news of my Pop." Katharane demanded.

"He's alive." Charles Goodnight replied.

"And?"

"And that's all I care to say about it to you." Charles Goodnight snorted. He looked at Reid Stuart. "Do with it as you will, Reid."

"Dad?"

"Mr. Goodnight has invited us to join the round-up again this spring." Reid Stuart said.

"I want to know about Pop."

"Like Mr. Goodnight said, he's alive, Katharane. And that's all I will say about this now."

Katharane glared at her father, but he did not yield and she knew she could not force him to do so, now. So she turned on Charles Goodnight. "So without my Pop the Escadara's welcome on the round-up. Is that it?"

"The Escadara is welcome." Charles Goodnight said.

Again, he looked at Reid Stuart. "Welcome in the round-up and the Association."

Katharane watched her father. He met Charles Goodnight's look, nodded and then turned to her. "Mr. Goodnight and some of the others have formed the Panhandle Stock Association and put up two-hundred and fifty dollars for any rustler that is caught and prosecuted. The two-hundred and fifty dollars came from the Association's members. Each has paid fifty dollars as membership dues. He wants us to join the Association, Katharane?"

"Does us include Pop?"

"Reid Stuart would be the Escadara's member in the Association." Charles Goodnight said.

"Even if the fifty dollars is Pop's fifty dollars?" Katharane asked. "Or are you less particular about whose money it is?" She looked full into Charles Goodnight's eyes.

"I care about having Reid Stuart in the Association. That's what I care about, girl." Charles Goodnight snapped. "I will put up his fifty dollars."

"No." Katharane said. "No, you will not. Pop will. I will get it, Dad." She turned to go to the dugout.

But Reid Stuart stopped her. "There is another thing, Katharane."

"Yes."

"Mr. Goodnight is taking a herd north to the railheads. I'm sending our cattle with him."

"How many of our cattle, Dad?"

"Every one I can find, brand and throw into a herd."

"Dad!"

"It's time, Katharane. We've held some of them for twelve years. There is no market in Texas for them. We've got steers with moss growing on their horns. And we've got to get our cattle on the trail before the southern herds reach our range or our cattle will die by the hundreds to their tick fever."

"But, Dad! What would Pop say if the herd doesn't make it? We would have lost everything you and he worked all these years for?"

Reid Stuart sighed. "I am aware of that." Then he smiled. "But I doubt he would be troubled by that as long as you are well."

Katharane blushed.

"I will make it," Charles Goodnight interjected. "That much I will assure you."

"My God, Mr. Charles." Bose Ikard whispered. He sat on his horse next to Charles Goodnight. Young Tom and those of Charles Goodnight's drovers who he had not sent to assist Reid Stuart and Katharane stood in their stirrups and strained to see through the dust that rolled and boiled above the rumbling bawling cattle that seemed to flow out of the mouth of the Ceta like waves upon a shore. "I haven't seen a herd that size since we first drove the buffalo out of the big canyon." Bose said.

The cattle spread across the big canyon like fast flowing water across dry earth, fingers bubbling and then running ahead of the masses or out to its sides, some drifting behind, but the ever growing inner circle swelled across the bottom of the big canyon below the butte from which Goodnight and the drovers watched.

"Where did they all come from?" Young Tom murmured, astonished by the number of cattle he saw.

"Thirteen years of work, of holding on against blizzards and drought." Charles Goodnight's deep voice began to boom forth. "Thirteen years of watching a baby girl grow into a young woman, and always, always, hoping. First, hoping the Kiowa or the Comanche didn't take her and the cattle. Then hoping a horse didn't drop a foot in a prairie dog's hole and bust its rider open beneath his saddle. Hoping it rained and the grass grew, hoping, working and gambling on weather and animals and each other, when it didn't make since to bet on tomorrow even. That's where they came from." Now Charles Goodnight stood in his stirrups, but he did not look at the great herd of cattle, he looked at his men, knew them to be good men, and believed that good men succeeded, especially when they were charged with a trust hard earned by someone else. He boomed forth his charge to his men. "And now Reid Stuart and Katharane are betting all that on this drive, on us, gentlemen. Close to four thousand head, every steer, and almost every cow above four years of age he and Katharane own. Let us not fail them." He let his voice die away into the canyon and into his drovers' psyches. Then he said. "Bose. Break these men into four groups, count those cattle and brand them with Katharane's drooped E."

"Every one, Mr. Charles? 'gotta' be some of your strays mixed in." Bose protested.

"Every one." Charles Goodnight said. "That's the deal I cut with Reid. He's throwing everything he has in with us. But no questions are to be asked as to their heritage. So rope them, burn their hides with the drooped E and throw them into our trail herd." Charles Goodnight picked up his reins, hesitated and said loudly. "And Reid Stuart says there's a buck bonus per man for every hundred head of Escadara cattle above twenty-five hundred that we get to the railheads." Goodnight paused, then he added. "And I imagine Miss Katharane might throw in a smile, too."

"Reid Stuart can keep his money. But I'll take all the smiles from that pretty daughter of his I can get." One of the cowboys chortled.

Charles Goodnight chuckled. "Cowboys, Mr. Ikard. They have simple desires."

"Yes sir, Mr. Charles." Bose replied. "And few of them."

"'bet that gunfighter ain't as fast as all that." Jim Eckwright said.

"He's fast." Tom Hawkins argued. "Isn't he, Bose?"

Bose Ikard knelt at the small fire around which the Goodnight cowboys squatted or rested against their saddles listening to Jim Eckwright's story about the Escadara gunfighter. "'fastest I ever seen." Bose affirmed quietly.

"Not from the story I heard. I bet I could take him." Jim Eckwright scoffed.

"Try me first, Pig Farmer."

Young Tom recognized the voice. "We meant no offense, Miss Katharane. We were just passing the time. We didn't realize you were here." He said cautiously.

Bose Ikard stood up and said. "Get your hats off, boys."

The other cowboys grabbed their hats from their heads. A couple of the cowboys picked their hats up and held them in their hands as if that was somehow more proper than leaving them on their saddles and standing empty handed. Even Jim Eckwright took his hat off. But he was not pleased to have been called out in front of the others. "It's not a good idea to go callin' someone out. 'specially when it's dark enough the fact that you're a girl might not be recognized." He grumbled.

"You seem very willing to call someone's hand who you know is not here to oblige you. And I doubt that I am in much danger from your ability with a firearm if you cannot make me for a woman. You must be almost blind." Katharane led her dark bay horse into the camp's fires' lights. "Any doubts now, Pig Farmer?" She taunted Jim Eckwright.

"No." Young Tom mumbled, as if answering for Jim Eckwright.The cowboys stared at Katharane. They had heard of her, heard tales of the beautiful auburn haired girl who roamed the Escadara range. A few had caught glimpses of her from the edge of Goodnight's home range where it abutted the Ceta canyon. A lucky few had met her when she came to visit Mrs. Goodnight at the JA's headquarters. But now, in the quivering light of their camps' fires, her beauty overpowered the darkness and made the hot dusty air too light to breathe.

"You have news of my Pop, Pig Farmer." Katharane demanded.

"I'm no pig farmer." Jim Eckwright growled.

Katharane weakened. She longed for any information about the gunfighter. It had been months since any word of him had found its way to her. "Can you give me any news about him?" Katharane asked. "Please."

"Tell her what you know, Jim." Tom Hawkins said. He would not let Katharane be forced to beg.

Jim Eckwright smiled sourly. "Sure. I'll tell her. Just like it was told to me." He broke off each word, making each a separate and distinct sound, instead of his usual easy rolling drawl.

Katharane gripped her left wrist with her right hand and waited. The cow camp grew quiet and still, as if the cowboys had become a part of the prairie, no more independent of it than the last sighs of its wind or the almost imperceptible sounds of its grass. Every ear listened to Jim Eckwright, but every eye watched Katharane's face.

"He's like a crazed wolf, they say." Jim Eckwright began. "He hunts 'em down. Then he kills them. Without question, without even giving them a chance to draw or run, he shoots them. Front, back, 'makes no difference to him."

Katharane chewed her bottom lip. She remained silent. More than her need to defend the gunman she needed to hear the rest of what Jim Eckwright had to say. Hoping that in the story she would find an answer to why the gunman was spoken of only in hushed whispers when she approached. Why Charles Goodnight stared silently through her when she asked about the gunfighter. Why her father refused to discuss the gunman with her. Maybe if she endured Jim Eckwright's insinuations she would find within his story some reassurance, even if unintended, that her Pop was alive, was well and was coming home to her, to the Escadara.

"But that ain't the worst of it." Jim Eckwright continued. "Not by far. They say he's sick, evil sick. That he defiles the bodies after he's killed them. And that he, himself, is rotting away from the doing of it."

A muffled sob, another, then a cry came from Katharane's throat.

"That's enough Jim." Young Tom commanded. "You've said enough."

The other cowboys waited. None drew a breath, as if they too, by breathing, might inflict more pain upon the trembling girl who hid her lovely face in her hands and sobbed.

"Missy." Bose Ikard said gently. "Why are you here, Missy?"

Katharane took her hands from her face and her tears shown in the firelight, diamonds dancing upon her face's flawless skin. Cowboys shuffled their boots against the hard packed earth. All of their throats tightened. A few stared at her. Most of them looked at the stars above her head. "To thank you men for your gift of this bay horse." Katharane said. She raised the bay's head. "He's a beautiful sweet tempered animal." Katharane breathed deeply. She tried to shake free the strands of her hair which clung to the tears on her face. And, again, every deprived cowboy fastened his eyes upon that face, but now each prayed silently. 'Don't let the fire fade.' "I have a gift to give each of you. And before the break out tomorrow, I want to give it to you." Katharane looked at Bose Ikard and Young Tom Hawkins. "I know most think it is very inappropriate for me to be in a cow camp. But you were kind to me. And I want to repay that kindness. May I do that?"

"Yes, Katharane Diane Stuart, you certainly may." Charles Goodnight's voice walked from the darkness with him. Reid Stuart walked beside Charles Goodnight.

"It's a poem from the Bible." Katharane said. She licked her lips and began. "To every thing there is a season, and a time to every purpose under the heavens." Katharane sucked the dry light air deep into her lungs and continued. "A time to be born, and a time to die. A time to plant, and a time to pluck up that which is planted. A time to kill, and a time to heal. A time to break down, and a time to build up." The cowboys stood motionless and listened. "A time to weep, and a time to laugh. A time to mourn, and a time to dance. A time to cast away stones, and a time to gather stones together. A time to get, and a time to lose. A time to keep, and a time to cast away." The fire began to fade. "A time to rend, and a time to sew. A time to keep silence, and a time to speak. A time to love, and a time to hate. A time of war, and a time of peace." Katharane swallowed. No cowboy moved. "He hath made everything beautiful in its time." The fire flickered, almost went out, gathered the last bites of fuel and flashed brightly. Quietly, Katharane continued. "There is nothing better, than that a man should rejoice in his own works." Then and in a stronger voice Katharane said. "Good luck to you, Charles Goodnight, to your men and to your drive. Do well what you do and get my father's and my Pop's cattle through." She turned and stepped into her father's arms.

The trail herd began to string itself out into a long and wavering line across the bottom of the big canyon. Reid Stuart and Katharane sat on their horses next to Charles Goodnight and Bose

Ikard on a point above the mouth of the Ceta. They watched the herd unwind itself from its bed ground.

"'mixed herd will be hard to trail, Mr. Charles." Bose Ikard said. "Those steers will keep a quicker pace than the mother cows."

"I know." Charles Goodnight sighed. "I vowed I would never take a mixed herd to the trail. But I have no choice, Bose. It is the herd I have. I have to take it."

Dust rose from a commotion near the rear of the herd. "'cow with a newborn calf fighting the drovers." Bose observed.

Charles Goodnight pulled his Winchester from its saddle scabbard. He handed it to Bose. "Kill the newborn calves."

"You can't do that!" Katharane cried. "Dad!"

"There is no choice, Katharane." Reid Stuart said. "A newborn cannot keep up with the herd. And a mothering cow will not leave it." Reid paused, then he added. "Unless it's dead."

"'bloody business, Mr. Charles." Bose said quietly.

"Would you rather I have Young Tom or one of the others do it?" Charles Goodnight asked.

"No. No. I'll do it." Bose said sadly. He touched his horse with his spurs.

"God bless you, Bose." Katharane said.

The Negro turned his face to Katharane and allowed a sad stoic smile to crack across it. Then he rode silently away.

"A hundred and eighty days, Reid." Charles Goodnight said. "I should be back in a hundred and eighty days."

Reid Stuart extended his hand to Charles Goodnight. "Anything I can see to for you while your away?" He asked.

"Mary." Charles Goodnight said. "I would sit this saddle much easier if I knew you and Katharane could spend some time with my Mary. And this." Charles Goodnight placed a four corner folded letter in Reid Stuart's hand. "You had best read that now." He told Reid Stuart.

Reid Stuart unfolded the letter and read it aloud:

Que Ti Qua Ranch, 1881

Dear Sir:

I send Mr. Reid Stuart to turn your cattle so they will not pass through his and my ranges. He will show you around these ranges and guide you until you strike the Canadian River. From there you must find your own way. The way he will show is ultimately nearer what must be your destination, the railheads to the north, and it is a shorter drive to water than any contrary route. Should you attempt to cross our ranges you would face a drive of 35 miles before you could hope to find any uncontested water.

I hope you will take this advice, as yourself and I have always been good friends. But even friendship will not protect you in any drive through Reid's or my range. And should you attempt to pass through, be kind enough to tell your men what they will have to face as I do not wish to hurt men that do not understand what they will be very sure to meet.

I hope you will not treat this as idle talk, for I mean every word of this, and if you have any feelings for me as a friend or acquaintance, you will not put me to any desperate actions. I will not perhaps see you myself, but take this advice from one that is and always has been your friend. Many cattle just to the east of our ranges are now dying of the fever contracted from cattle driven from Fort Worth; therefore, do not have any hope that you can convince me that your cattle will not give mine the fever, this we will not speak of. I simply say to you that you will never pass through here in good health.

Yours truly,

C. Goodnight

Reid Stuart looked up from the letter and asked. "Why not the Association?"

"It has to be you, Reid. You chose not to join the Association." Charles Goodnight raised his hand to silence Katharane's attempted remonstration. "Whether you did so from loyalty or for your own reasons, that is your concern. And I have left it as such." He said softly. He doggedly continued, "And the Association will not back me or you in this. But it must be done. It is the only way

241

to spare our stock from the tick fever."

"Then I will see to the doing of it." Reid Stuart said. "And Katharane will look in on Miss Mary."

"Good." Bose's first shot accented Charles Goodnight's word. More shots echoed down the canyon. Reid Stuart and Katharane sat on their horses and watched Charles Goodnight ride to the front of the herd. For an hour and a half the herd had been stretched out into its traveling length. As the herd moved slowly away small corpses lay in its wake. The long hard drive had begun.

"Dad. Shouldn't we get some of Mr. Goodnight's men to go with us?"

"That herd will hit the bottom of Charles' range day after tomorrow unless I ride hard for it right now, Katharane." Reid Stuart said. "And that's what I am going to do." He dropped the stirrup off of the buckskin's saddle horn. "You ride to Mary Goodnight. Ask her to send four men with Winchesters to the Lower Pease crossing. Goodnight's men will know where that is." He mounted the buckskin.

"But Dad?"

"Go on, Katharane. Do as I say."

As Reid Stuart turned the buckskin away from the new cedar corral he had built Katharane's bay flashed passed. "I will be there with Goodnight's men as soon as I can." She called over her shoulder as she dropped down onto the Ceta's trail.

Reid Stuart waved his acknowledgment and thought, 'Let her make the bottom first. Then I will put this buckskin to covering ground.'

"There are only three men here now, Katharane." Mary Goodnight said as she stroked the hot bay horse's nose. "And Joseph is ill. He cannot ride."

"Then have the other two get their rifles and ride with me. Please, Miss Mary. Dad's out there all alone."

"All right." Mary Goodnight sighed. "Andrew." She called to the bunkhouse. A young cowboy stepped out of the bunkhouse and ambled toward her. "Hurry." Mary Goodnight commanded. The cowboy trotted to her and Katharane.

"Yes mam."

"Get Charlie Murphy and two rifles. Saddle good mounts and put my side saddle on the sorrel."

"Mam?"

"Do as I said. And do it quickly."

"Yes mam."

"Well, Mr. Stuart." The trail boss said as he folded the letter Reid Stuart had handed to him. "This only seems to reaffirm a lot of peoples' belief of how overbearing prosperity has made Charles Goodnight." He handed the letter back to Reid Stuart. "I didn't bring this herd this far to be sent back by one Charles Goodnight. And you appear to be the only one very interested in making me do his bidding." The trail boss looked across the empty range to emphasize Reid Stuart's singleness in the endeavor.

Reid Stuart slid the letter back inside his buckskin shirt.

"Are you planning on sending me about by yourself, sir?" The trail boss asked.

"I intend to try." Reid Stuart said quietly.

"Then you're fixin' to die." A young cowboy that sat on a gray gelding that stood next to the trail boss's roan said. Before he could pull his pistol and so quickly and effortlessly that several of the other cowboys who had gathered behind the trail boss whispered their amazement, Reid Stuart swung the yawning hole in the muzzle of his Sharps against the young cowboy's side.

"Right after you do, son." Reid Stuart said.

"Riders coming in fast, Mr. Reynolds." One of the other cowboys warned the trail boss.

Charlie Murphy touched his horse with his spurs and swore aloud. "We're too damn strung out to do much good."

Katharane's bay flew across the ground in front of him, and Andrew and Mrs. Goodnight trailed behind him. Katharane's bay pitched to a stop beside her father's buckskin. The cowboys murmured and whispered to each other and stared, not at the

Winchesters which Andrew and Charlie Murphy carried, but at the beautiful auburn haired girl on the bay horse and Mary Goodnight, who sat erect and alert on the sorrel horse.

"Will you take your herd about, sir?" Katharane asked George Reynolds.

"Well, Missy. I have read the letter Charles Goodnight wrote demanding that of me. And this gentleman has already made that request of me. And I have refused." The trail boss said. "Why should I be more gracious to you?"

Katharane hesitated. She felt the weight of her pistols against her hips. But George Reynolds had too many men with him. Each of these men was staring directly at her. A thought came to her and she spoke aloud that thought. "Because if you do, you and your men will have the pleasure of mine and my father's company while we will ride your point until we put you on the trail Mr. Goodnight mentioned in his letter."

"Good enough by me." One of Reynolds' cowboys blurted, unsolicited.

George Reynolds sat silently for several moments, and then he said to Katharane. "Well. I'm not certain my men would back my play if I challenged you. And even if they would I am not anxious to kill a creature as lovely as you just to drive a bunch of cows across Charles Goodnight's range." He removed his hat. "I am not inclined to gunplay anytime. And your company would most assuredly be pleasant." He turned in his saddle and commanded. "Start putting them about boys." He turned back to Katharane and said. "Show us the way, pretty miss, and when you see him again tell Charles Goodnight you are much more effective at this than any Winchester quarantine."

Katharane blushed.

"What does it say, Miss Mary?" Katharane asked. She and Reid Stuart stood on Mary Goodnight's veranda as she opened the small envelope which had found its way to her through many hands.

"Oh Katharane! It's the most wonderful news." Mary Goodnight said excitedly.

"My Pop's coming home!" Katharane exclaimed.

"No." Mary Goodnight said. "I'm sorry, Katharane. It's not that wonderful."

"Oh." Katharane looked at her hands.

"But it is good news." Mary Goodnight said. "They made the drive with less than an eight percent loss."

"What? Less than eight percent, are you certain, Mary?" Reid Stuart asked.

Katharane looked up at her father. She had never heard him call Mary Goodnight by her first name.

Mary Goodnight nodded, as she continued to read the letter. "Yes. That is what Charles writes here." She pointed at the script. "And that the prices were exceptional, nine dollars and thirty-five cents per hundred weight. That is what he sold the herd for."

"My God." Reid Stuart murmured. "Nine dollars and thirty-five cents per hundred weight."

"What does that mean, Dad?"

"It means Charles Goodnight will be heading back with enough gold in his saddle bags to buy these plains and everything on them." Reid Stuart said. "And a good part of that gold is ours, Katharane."

"There is more." Mary Goodnight said. "He wishes you to meet him in Fort Worth, Reid."

"Fort Worth." Reid Stuart said.

"We can't go to Fort Worth, Dad." Katharane said. "What if Pop returned and we were gone?"

Reid Stuart looked at Mary Goodnight. The sadness in his eyes told her of the heavy weight that hung upon his heart for his daughter. Mary Goodnight knew that Reid Stuart, too, had heard the rumors about the gunfighter. But she did not know why he shielded Katharane from these rumors? But she offered her kindness to them both. "Katharane can stay with me. I would enjoy her company. And we can check on the Escadara while you are away."

"Yes. Yes." Katharane said excitedly.

Slowly Reid Stuart nodded his consent.

"To Philadelphia." Mary Goodnight said as she dried her hands on her apron. She stepped beside Katharane and put her hands on Katharane's right shoulder. Katharane did not flinch. During the weeks she and Mary Goodnight had waited for Charles Goodnight and Reid Stuart to return she had become accustomed to Mary Goodnight's gentle touch.

"Yes." Charles Goodnight said. He hung his hat on the peg beside the door. "He had business there."

"What business?" Mary Goodnight asked, and she looked hard at her husband.

He looked back and did not yield. "His business."

"How long will he be gone?" Katharane asked.

"Four to six months."

"Six months!" Katharane exclaimed.

"It's a long trip and he has much to do." Charles Goodnight said.

"But winter is coming." Katharane argued. "What about the Escadara?"

"I am sending Bose and Young Tom and the Romero family to throw your cattle down into the Ceta. The Romeros can stay in your dugout. They will see that your cattle winter fine."

"And me? Where will I winter?" Katharane asked. Before Charles Goodnight could answer, Katharane cried. "My pies, Miss Mary, my pies!"

Mary Goodnight pulled the steaming round iron pie dishes from inside the wood stove's cavernous oven. She set them on top of the stove.

"They're ruined." Katharane moaned.

"No, Katharane. They will be fine. And every bite of them will be eaten at the evening meal." Mary Goodnight looked at her husband long enough that he understood he was to instruct Young Tom and Bose that an extra helping of pie was to be asked for and eaten this night. "And you will stay here until your father returns."

"How can I, Miss Mary?" Katharane asked. "I have been here so long already. I will be overstaying my welcome."

"No, child. You cannot stay passed your welcome here." Mary Goodnight said. "Charles."

"You are always welcome on the JA's, Katharane." Charles Goodnight said.

Eating the evening meal on Mary Goodnight's veranda became a regular occurrence, interrupted and forced into her kitchen only when the coming winter's wind was too cold. Most evenings Bose and Young Tom joined Katharane, Charles Goodnight and Mary Goodnight on her veranda near her kitchen's door. Bose and Young Tom would carry the table and the two benches and the one arm chair from the kitchen to the veranda. Mary Goodnight and Katharane would bring the food. And Katharane would prod Bose Ikard and Charles Goodnight into recounting tales of the drive and of the days when they served with the Rangers. Young Tom listened, seldom entering the conversation, but enjoying its flavor and warmth. Early night after early night the conversation dragged on until cold forced Mary Goodnight, Charles Goodnight and Katharane into the house and Bose and Young Tom back to the bunkhouse. All became easier and more comfortable being a part of this company. Comfortable enough that Young Tom would ask Charles Goodnight questions about the ranch and its management. But still he did not dare to speak directly to Katharane, even though he lived for these meals, to listen to Katharane laugh, to watch her eyes and her hands and to be near her. Mary Goodnight and Bose noticed his attentiveness to Katharane.

Charles Goodnight stood up from the arm chair and ex-cused himself. Mary Goodnight waited until the kitchen door closed behind him, then she said. "Tom."

"Yes mam."

"I believe Katharane would enjoy a ride before winter condemns us to stay inside."

Young Tom sat stupefied.

"Would you be so kind as to accompany her?"

"Well." Young Tom said very slowly. "Yes mam, I will."

He wanted to hug Mary Goodnight. But he waited. Katharane had not indicated that she was interested in riding with him.

"Oh yes! Miss Mary." Katharane exclaimed. "Tom is riding to the Mulberry's tomorrow. It is so beautiful there."

"How..." Young Tom looked at Bose who grinned his guilt at Tom. Katharane giggled.

"Well, Tom?" Mary Goodnight urged him.

"Sure." Young Tom said. "Sure. Katharane can ride with me."

"You need to ask her." Bose quietly instructed the novice suitor.

"Thank you, Mr. Ikard." Mary Goodnight said.

"Would you care to ride with me to the Mulberry's tomorrow?" Young Tom asked to his hands.

"Yes." Katharane answered immediately.

"Where is that young fool going with Katharane?" Charles Goodnight asked. He held Mary Goodnight's laced curtains away from the kitchen window and watched Young Tom trying to help Katharane saddle her bay horse. He smiled. Katharane allowed Young Tom little discretion in saddling her horse. She was accustomed to saddling her own horse.

"Tom and Katharane are riding to the Mulberry, Charles." Mary Goodnight said.

Charles Goodnight frowned and asked. "What in the hell for?"

"For a nice ride on a lovely late fall day. They're young, Charles. Let them share the day and each other."

"To what end?"

"To whatever end."

"Don't see much sense in it."

"Charles!"

"But one thing's for damn sure. He is not taking Katharane all the way to the Mulberry's without at least a saddle gun.

This country's not that settled." Charles Goodnight said and jerked the kitchen door open and stepped out onto the veranda. "Tom Hawkins." He bellowed.

"Charles." Mary Goodnight protested as she followed her husband out the door.

"I will not have you take Katharane to a remote watering pen on the Mulberry Creek without any means of protecting her." Charles Goodnight said loudly.

Young Tom stared silently across Katharane's saddle. He had no idea how to respond to his employer. His heart sank. 'Damn!' He cursed to himself. 'If she had just let me saddle her damn horse we would have been gone before that old bastard found out.' Now, he assumed, it was too late. The ride he had lain awake all night anticipating, just he and Katharane being together and alone, Charles Goodnight appeared to be curtailing. For a moment Tom thought of challenging the cantankerous old man. But he did not.

"We won't be unprotected." Katharane called as she ran passed Charles Goodnight and disappeared into the house. She re-emerged fastening her pistols about the new tan buckskin pants she wore.

"I had it more in my mind that this simple minded boy should care for you, Katharane." Charles Goodnight snorted.

"I know how to care for myself. Pop taught me how to use these very well." Katharane said. She put her hands on the grips of her pistols.

"I'm certain he did." Charles Goodnight said.

Young Tom felt Bose's hand on his shoulder. He turned. Bose handed him a Winchester sheathed in a leather scabbard and a box of cartridges. Tom took the scabbard and cartridges. He tied the scabbard onto the right side of his saddle and he slid the box of cartridges underneath the white cloth which covered the satchel of food Mary Goodnight had prepared for his and Katharane's ride. The Mulberry was four hours away and four and a half hours returning on tired horses.

The canyon was wide and the sod sure and soft beneath Tom's and Katharane's horses' hooves. The horses walked easily through the short grass.

"Pop said the grass used to touch the belly of a horse for miles and miles without break here in the canyon."

Tom listened intently. He wanted to hear every word, to understand each syllable, to catch each vowel. They were all important because Katharane said them. "It must've been something." Tom struggled to make conversation.

"Oh, it was." Katharane said. "Dad and Pop said the buffalo were like the blades of grass. Can you imagine a herd a mile wide and ten miles long? Can you?"

Tom shook his head. 'Could you imagine I would be here with Katharane Stuart?' He thought to himself. It all spun within his head. Thoughts of moments alone and then years spent together. A small ranch, their own herd, children, spun unsaid through his mind. Tom had little conception of his thoughts, his hopes and his desires, and he knew no way of telling the arrogant, assured young heiress of the awesome Escadara that she was part, if not all, of these thoughts, these hopes and these desires. He justified his hesitation by telling himself that Katharane was still too young, and, maybe, a working cowboy held no interest for such a confidant, accomplished young woman.

"Tom. Tom. Tom!" Katharane spoke his name louder each time and leaned near him.

"What? Yes." He stammered.

"Mr. Goodnight is remarkable. Isn't he? He has built reservoirs almost to the section and crowding pens at each reservoir."

"'never knew another man like him." Tom said. He watched Katharane's face.

"I have." She said and she looked directly at Tom, smiled and said. "My father and my Pop."

Tom wanted to return the smile but he failed to do so. He only watched her face and wondered if she had any thoughts of him. The conversation, carried by Katharane's exuberance, and the horses carried them on to the Mulberry pens. The day passed too quickly for Tom. But the chill of a late autumn day forced him to urge the little sorrel to quicken its gate. He and Katharane reached the JA headquarters an hour before dusk. Bose and Charles Goodnight stood in the horse corral. The gunman's old black filly knelt on her front knees her nose against the ground. She heaved and coughed. Bose held a Winchester.

"What is it? What's wrong?" Katharane asked. She slid down from the bay horse, crawled between the cedar rails of the corral and knelt beside the black filly.

"She's down, Little Missy." Bose said softly.

"Get her up, Bose. Please! I promised Pop." Katharane pleaded. Her eyes glittered with a desperate fear and an even more desperate hope.

"For the life of me I would if this old soul could, Missy." Bose said, almost tearfully. "But it's not to be. I've tried for better'n two hours now."

The horse coughed again and she trembled and heaved and wretched fluids through her nose.

"Hand me the Winchester, Bose." Charles Goodnight commanded.

"Why! Why!" Katharane cried as she jumped to her feet and confronted Charles Goodnight.

"Because the animal's down, girl, she can't get up and she'll never be able to get up." Charles Goodnight said. "Now hand me that goddamn rifle, Mr. Ikard, and let's be done with this." Charles Goodnight reached for the rifle Bose Ikard held.

"I'll do it, Mr. Charles." Bose said. As he drew the long action of the Winchester open with the lever below its handle, Katharane screamed. "No one shoots my Pop's horse! No one!" Her hands swept the small pistols free of their holsters. Both spoke simultaneously and together two bullets struck the black filly, one behind each ear, killing her instantly.

"Christ, child." Charles Goodnight grimaced. "This was not something I meant for you to do."

"Come away, Little Missy." Bose Ikard said. He gripped each of Katharane's wrists and slowly helped her guide the black pistols back into their holsters. Katharane laid her head against his bony shoulder and wept. The black man gently led the sobbing girl to the veranda and to Mary Goodnight's arms.

They waited in their chairs on the porch. The table set
before them, Bose, Young Tom and Charles Goodnight. Mary
Goodnight led Katharane from the kitchen to the table. Together,
they ate in silence. The meal was finished and the group began to
take up their places about the porch. Bose carried Mary
Goodnight's rocker out onto the veranda. She sat in it and began to
darn the crotch of a pair of cotton bloomers she was knitting for
Katharane. Young Tom blushed when he realized what Mary
Goodnight held in her hands. Charles Goodnight leaned against
the far post of the steps leading up to the veranda. Katharane sat
next to Mary Goodnight. Young Tom squatted on his boots' heels
next to Bose. Katharane was sullen and troubled. She stared at the
corral where she had destroyed the black filly.

"Little Missy, have you ever heard a whip-o-will?" Bose
asked. Katharane shook her head. Bose trilled the call through his
thick dark lips, light and high, tuned by his tongue, until it faded
away into the vast canyon. "Have you ever heard a Will-of-the-
Woods?"

"No." Katharane said softly.

Bose's throat quivered. "I learned that along a river as
wide as the big canyon."

"What river is as wide as the big canyon?" Katharane
asked.

"The Mississippi." Bose answered. "Have you ever seen a
cotton field?"

"No." Katharane said. And with each of Bose's questions
her voice grew stronger, her eyes brightened and her answers
came more quickly and eagerly.

Then, "Who was your mother?" It was gone, passed his
lips before the faint ticking in Young Tom's mind could warn him.
He had lowered his guard, accustomed to the unrestrained flow of
nightly conversation on the porch, lulled by Katharane's comfort
with each question Bose had put to her, Tom had asked the
question that had bounced around in his head all afternoon while
he and Katharane had ridden back from the Mulberry Creek pens.
But he realized the moment the words left his tongue that he had

trespassed. He knew by the quick cut of Charles Goodnight's eyes at him, by Mary Goodnight's rocker ceasing to rock, by Bose Ikard's knees popping with the sound of frozen cedar breaking against ice coated chaps as Bose rose from where he, too, squatted on his heels on the porch and by the anger which danced, wet and full, in Katharane's eyes and the hurt that climbed from her throat.

"Why would you ask me that!" Katharane demanded. "You were there when we placed my mama in her sacred place. You know where my Pop is and why." She stood up and she trembled. "Why would you ask me that, Tom Hawkins!" All the anger, the resentment with the unfairness of the black filly's need to be put down, with the almost religious insistence of Charles Goodnight that the sick animal be put down, with her Pop having to be gone and with her father choosing to be gone broke through the dam of pride which had forced her tears to evaporate earlier. She cried aloud as she stared down at Young Tom.

And with each of Katharane's tears a sickness churned in Young Tom's stomach and a dark and pervading fear clawed at his mind. Had he lost whatever chance he had for her affections? Katharane turned and ran into the house.

"Damn boy!" Charles Goodnight swore. "Don't you know you can't just ask a woman any damn thing like you would a man."

"And what do you mean by that, Charles Goodnight?" Mary Goodnight asked. She stood up and went into the house.

"Goddamn goat headed boy." Charles Goodnight mumbled. "I'm liable to catch hell for this for a week."

The three men stepped off the porch as the door opened and Mary Goodnight returned. She picked up the cotton bloomers she had been darning and sat down in the rocking chair. Then she pulled the bloomers to her mouth. Her shoulders trembled.

"Mary. What is it?" Charles Goodnight asked. He stepped onto the veranda and stood in front of his wife.

"She's leaving us, Charles. Oh, Charles, our Katharane is leaving us." Mary Goodnight swallowed her tears. "She says she must. That she has to go back to the Escadara to be there for her Pop when he returns."

"You knew this had to be sooner or later, Mary. You had to know Katharane would return to the Escadara. It's her home. It's where she belongs."

"But not yet, Charles, not yet, please!" Mary Goodnight dropped her head against her husband's right leg and wept.

Bose led Young Tom away, leaving Mary Goodnight alone on the veranda as Charles Goodnight marched into his house.

"I can't stop you from returning to your home, Katharane." Charles Goodnight said slowly. He stood next to the bed on which Katharane lay. Katharane remained silent. She pushed the side of her face deeper into the goose feathered pillow. "But I did promise Reid to look after you."

"Why should I care what Charles Goodnight promised Reid Stuart?" Katharane snarled into the pillow.

"No reason. No reason at all." Charles Goodnight took a deep breath, sat down on the edge of the bed and looked at the girl's tear streaked face. "No reason for you to give a damn what Charles Goodnight promised any man. But there is a lot of cause for you to care what Mary Goodnight promised your father."

Katharane turned her shoulders and laid the back of her head against the pillow. Loose strands of her long auburn hair clung to her face, penned there by the residue of her tears. Mary Goodnight's night shirt fell off of her shoulder. "What do you mean?" She sniffed.

"My God child! But you are beautiful." Charles Goodnight murmured. For a moment his eyes bore across and into Katharane's uncovered shoulder. As his age overcame his passion they softened and so did he. "Mary promised Reid Stuart you would not sleep unattended while he was gone. If you leave she will feel she has betrayed your father's confidence."

"So what." Katharane snapped. "I've betrayed Pop's." Fluids gurgled in her throat.

"No. No, Katharane, you have not betrayed him. He would have shot that horse and you know that. But if you leave you will force Mary to betray Reid Stuart."

"Who cares?" Katharane's young vanity smirked.

"I care." Charles Goodnight said. "Do you have any idea what it took to make me come to you like this?"

Katharane did not answer.

"It took not wanting to disappoint the kindest, gentlest nature I've ever known. And I'm hoping that same need not to disappoint someone who has been so very kind to you, also, will overcome your pride, like it has mine, and you will stay with us until your father returns."

"So it's not because you are worried about me or what Reid Stuart will think of you if I go back to the Escadara that you're asking me to stay?"

"No. I'm not worried about you at the Escadara. That damn gunman and your mama taught you enough that you can survive a winter at the Escadara." Charles Goodnight said. "And I don't give a damn what Reid Stuart or any man thinks of Charles Goodnight. I know what I am about. But I worry what Mary thinks of me. How she feels, her well being. I love her, child."

Katharane gazed at the old plainsman. She had never considered he had feelings of love for anyone, not even for his wife, hearing him avow that love moved Katharane. She raised her head from her pillow, kissed Charles Goodnight and said. "Then for Miss Mary, I will stay until Dad or Pop returns."

"Damn girl!" Charles Goodnight recoiled from her bold kiss. He stood up and stalked from the room.

It had been ten days since Charles Goodnight had ordered the black filly shot. And now for the first time they had eaten together on the veranda again. Young Tom had almost whispered a prayer of thanksgiving. Instead he had told Katharane about the two year old black filly Tom Bugbee's line rider had told him and Bose about two days earlier. Katharane's eyes had glittered and danced and her voice had cracked with excitement and enthusiasm when she had asked him about the horse. Young Tom could tell her little more, just that it was black, black from its nose to its hooves. But that had been enough to send Katharane chattering to Miss Mary about the horse, about what her Pop might think if she had the filly at the Escadara when he returned. As Katharane had held Mary Goodnight's hand and talked about Bugbee's black filly Mary Goodnight's eyes had caught Charles Goodnight's eyes and silently spoken to him in a language Young Tom could not translate, and now Charles Goodnight's eyes seared into Young Tom.

Tom swallowed. Was he to be banished to the western line camps again this winter? If so, he might not have the opportunity to see if his two dollars and the four Bose Ikard had given to him would be enough to buy the black filly. He cursed his poverty and waited for Charles Goodnight's pronouncement.

Charles Goodnight swore, not at Young Tom, not at any particular thing. He just swore, loudly and profanely. "Goddamit it, Bose, hurry up!"

"Yes sir, Mr. Charles." Bose answered. But he did not take one quicker step as he approached Charles Goodnight and Tom.

'Hurry up, Bose.' Young Tom screamed silently in his mind. He yearned to know if he was to be forbidden any chance to make amends to Katharane, if he could.

"Take Young Tom, for what good his damn worthless hide is to you." Charles Goodnight growled. "Take him and enough staples to make Bugbee's Quarter Circle T. Buy that second summer black filly this young fool slobbered all over himself about at dinner last night." Charles Goodnight glared at Young Tom. "Buy her. Bring her back."

Young Tom stared, dumbstruck. How could he know, neither he nor Bose had spoken about purchasing the filly with their employer?

"Young Tom and I haven't enough money to buy that filly, Mr. Charles." Bose said politely.

Charles Goodnight shoved a leather pouch against Bose Ikard's stomach. "You do now. There's five twenty dollar gold pieces. Get that damn horse." He turned to walk away.

Bose stopped him. "How many do I give Mr. Bugbee for that filly, Mr. Charles?" He and Young Tom stared at the leather pouch he held in the palm of his right hand.

"As many as it takes, dammit." Charles Goodnight cursed. "Just don't come back without that horse or I'll skin you both. I vow it." He limped away.

"She is the most beautiful horse ever." Katharane said this over and over. Almost daily, at each breakfast, and after she had helped Mary Goodnight clean and put away the dishes and the utensils, Katharane had raced to the corrals where Bose and Young Tom waited with the haltered young black horse.

"She's beautiful. Isn't she Bose, Tom?" Katharane asked. She stroked the black horse's sleek nose.

"Yes mam." Bose agreed.

"She is." Tom joined Bose in agreeing with Katharane.

"She should be." Charles Goodnight grumbled. "I paid more for this damn horse than I've ever paid for a four legged creature."

"She's not a creature." Katharane said softly. "She's a lady. She's Pop's new lady."

"Well step that pretty lady out here." Charles Goodnight said. He unraveled a long braided lead rope. "And let's see if she remembers her leads and her manners."

And so the winter went. Only on the bitterest of days did Katharane fail to work with the black filly. Even in the midst of a three day norther she walked to the corral to visit the black horse.

"Why in the world is that child going out in this blow?" Charles Goodnight asked his wife.

"It is her way of visiting with her Pop, Charles." Mary Goodnight slowly stirred the simmering milk she was heating for Katharane to warm herself with.

"And what of Reid Stuart?" Charles Goodnight asked. "Damn silly girl should think of her father, not that gunfighter."

"You will not curse Katharane in this house, Charles Goodnight." Mary Goodnight snapped.

Charles Goodnight pulled the old buffalo cape over his head and tied a bandana over his head and underneath the stubble on his chin.

"What are you about to do, Charles Goodnight?" Mary Goodnight demanded.

"Somebody has to see to that fool girl." The wind chilled the house before Charles Goodnight could pull the door closed behind him. But a warmth glowed in Mary Goodnight, fueled by her husband's concern for Katharane.

Winter broke in the canyon in early March, a week later on the plains. Riders began to come and go from the JA's headquarters. And Charles Goodnight watched the dread build in his wife's eyes as she realized that Reid Stuart would soon return and Katharane would leave the JA's for the Escadara.

"Someone is coming home, Katharane." Mary Goodnight said.

"My Pop!"

"No." Mary Goodnight said softly. She took Katharane's left hand in her left hand and rubbed the back of it with the fingers of her right hand.

"It's your father, child." Charles Goodnight said. "Reid Stuart's coming home."

"When?"

"'hard to say." Charles Goodnight answered. "An outrider for the Matadors saw him at the old Comanche camp at the Springs Lake between the Prairie Dog Town Fork and the Lower Pease two days ago. 'told my man today and he brought word to me." Charles Goodnight ran his hand through his silver hair. "He's leading two loaded pack mules. That means two, maybe three more camps to make. Maybe the day after tomorrow, I would guess."

Charles Goodnight sat upright in the bed. The sun had not yet risen, only its pre-dawn glitter gave any illumination to the room.

"What is it, Charles?" Mary Goodnight asked. She sat up in the bed, too.

"Do you hear that?" Charles Goodnight asked.

Mary Goodnight listened. The soft slipping sound passed

through the quiet dark and invaded the bedroom. "Yes." She said. She reached for her long cotton robe.

"What is it? I've never heard it before."

"It's Katharane. She's combing her hair."

"At this hour! What in tar nation for?"

Mary Goodnight stood up and pulled the robe around her. "Because she is a woman and one of the men in her life may be coming home today." Mary Goodnight said as she walked from the bedroom. She stopped in the kitchen door. "Katharane, would you like some breakfast?"

Katharane sat on a chair in the center of the dark kitchen. She turned her head and looked across her shoulder upon which her long wet hair hung. "I didn't mean to disturb you, Miss Mary."

"You didn't, child."

"Dad might come today and I wanted to be ready for him."

"I know." Mary Goodnight said as she shoved one of the stumps Bose had gathered for her into the stove. She picked up the heavy iron poker and stirred the coals in the bottom of the fire box. They began to glow, the stump began to smoke, then slowly it took fire and a gentle flame lit the kitchen. Mary Goodnight went to Katharane and took the comb from her and began to draw the comb slowly through Katharane's long auburn hair, smoothing its silken softness back against Katharane's head with the palm of her left hand.

Charles Goodnight leaned against the kitchen door's jam and watched his wife and remembered what she had said to him through her tears only hours before. 'I'll never have a daughter, Charles. We'll never be closer to having a child than we are with Katharane. I so want her to stay.' His Mary had asked so little of him, and he had given her so little. 'Damn you, Reid Stuart. Lay over another day at the springs. Another day, give my Mary one more day of knowing the love of child that I cannot give her.'

Somewhere in the darkness of Charles Goodnight's lower JA range that love of child caused a weary Reid Stuart to ride on through the night.

"'rider comin', Mr. Charles."

"I know, Bose. I've been watchin' him for the last ten minutes. It's Reid Stuart. Go get Katharane." Charles Goodnight paused. He put the side of his face against the oak four by four that supported one corner of the veranda's roof and said. "And Mary."

Young Tom stepped up onto the porch. "Are you ill, sir?"

"Yes." Charles Goodnight said and pulled his face away from the post. "I am heartily sick of men and ranches."

"It's all right, Charles." Mary Goodnight said. She put hand on her husband's shoulder.

"Who is it?" Katharane asked.

"It's your father, Katharane." Mary Goodnight said. She put her face against her husband's back.

Katharane leaped from the porch. She ran towards the buckskin. Reid Stuart dropped the mules away to be gathered later and poured his spurs into the buckskin and the horse galloped forward. As he approached Katharane Reid Stuart gripped his reins and slammed his hands against his right hip. The buckskin drove his front feet into the ground and slid to a stop, unaccustomed to such harsh bridle work. Reid Stuart swung his right leg over the horse's rump and walked out of the saddle. Katharane flew into his arms. "You're home. You're really home!" She cried.

"You missed me?" Reid Stuart asked.

"Yes." Katharane bent her head back and kissed her father on the lips.

He smiled and watched her eyes. "I haven't seen that look in your eyes for a long while."

"And what look is that, Mr. Reid Stuart?" Katharane asked gaily.

"The look your eyes used to dance with when you looked at the Squaw Woman and Canada." Reid Stuart swallowed as he continued. "I didn't know if I'd ever see it again."

"Oh, Dad!" Katharane said, and took a step back and gripped the backs of her father's wrists. "It's for you, too."

260

Reid Stuart smiled.

"And it will still be for you, too, when you see it again when Pop gets back."

Reid Stuart's smile faded.

"Dad." Katharane stared into her father's face. "Have you heard from him? Have you?"

Reid Stuart studied the toes of his boots, shook his head and lied to his daughter. "No. Just rumors of him."

"As far away as Philadelphia?" Katharane asked.

"No, only as far away as Fort Worth."

"You stopped in Fort Worth again! What for?" Katharane demanded.

"To confirm with some stonemasons that they would be here this spring to build a house, a home, Katharane. Our home."

"A house, a real house?" Katharane giggled.

"Yes." Reid Stuart answered.

"But where should we build it, Dad?"

"Only one place for a house on the Escadara." Reid Stuart said. "Above the dugout."

"Yes, yes! Above the dugout. Oh, won't Pop be surprised." Katharane bounced with excitement. "How soon will it be finished? How big will it be? Will it have a veranda like Miss Mary's?"

"It will take maybe a year to complete. I wish it to have two stories. But you decide how you want the rooms. And, yes, it will have a veranda like Mary Goodnight's." Reid Stuart answered. "Now let's pick up my mules." He swung Katharane into his arms and set her on the saddle. He swung up behind her on the saddle. He did not ride in the saddle with her as the gunman had.

"We're going to have a house, Miss Mary, a real house like your's." Katharane rattled the words at Mary Goodnight as Reid Stuart helped her down from the buckskin.

Mary Goodnight smiled despite the melancholy that filled

her heart. "Yes, Katharane, that will be wonderful." Mary Goodnight said.

"And you will come? You and Bose, and Young Tom, too?" Katharane asked.

"I will come." Tom Hawkins answered too eagerly.

Reid Stuart eyed the cowboy. Bose grinned at Reid Stuart, and he handed one of the mule's leads to Tom and said. "Bring Mr. Reid's horse, too. He needs grainin' and waterin'."

"You will come?" Katharane repeated her question to Mary Goodnight.

"Yes." Mary Goodnight said. "We will come."

Katharane danced across the porch and put her arms around Mary Goodnight.

Reid Stuart chuckled and said. "Well. I see Mary Goodnight has done well by you child."

"Better than that!" Katharane exclaimed. "She has taught me to cook. I can bake pies even Charles Goodnight likes." She stuck her tongue out at Charles Goodnight.

"I'd give you a hidin' if Reid Stuart wasn't here to do so himself." Charles Goodnight fumed. But Reid Stuart saw the laughter in Charles Goodnight's eyes and caught the softness in the inflection of his voice and knew he need not reproach his daughter for she had intended no offense and Charles Goodnight had taken none.

"It's here! It's here!" Katharane cried as she ran from the spring to the top of the dugout.

"What's here?" Reid Stuart asked as he followed Katharane. Two wagons slowly grew out of the prairie.

"My house." Katharane clapped her hands. "It's on those wagons. Isn't it, Dad?"

"The tools to build it and the hands that know how to use those tools are on those wagons." Reid Stuart answered. "Come with me and I will introduce you to the Scotsmen."

The Scotsmen, five of them, aided by Juan Romero's three

sons built Katharane's house and a two room single story flat roofed bunkhouse where Juan Romero, his wife, three sons, two daughters, a nephew and Juan Romero's mother-in-law would live.

The Romeros had come to the plains with sheep. The sheep left with the fencing of the open range but the Romeros had stayed. Charles Goodnight introduced Juan Romero to Reid Stuart, and the prospect of five good, strong caballeros had lured Reid Stuart to extend an invitation to the Romeros to stay and for Juan Romero's boys to help the Scotsmen build Katharane's house and Juan Romero to ride with him. The Romero family quickly demonstrated their eagerness to work. So Reid Stuart added the bunkhouse and a rock corral to the Scotsmen's contract and enticed the Romero family to live on the Escadara despite Katharane's protests against this.

Katharane appointed herself the overseer of the construction of each stage of the house, of the placement of almost each board used to build its two and one-half stories. The old dugout, unchanged and undamaged formed its basement. The first floor sat two feet above the old dugout supported by six inch by six inch piers tied together with four inch by four inch oak beams.

The Scotsmen had been amazed by the foundation Reid Stuart had drawn to scale on the hard packed prairie in front of the dugout. They wondered from where the mass of material which would be needed to build a house upon the scale the foundation called for would come. But as Reid Stuart added instructions to lay a rock stairway from the dugout up to the expected kitchen above it, the first two wagons from Dodge City loaded with oak timbers, square twenty-penny bridge nails and number one ship lapped planking, ten inch by one inch by twenty feet had arrived. And they continued to arrive at regular two week intervals. The craftsmen realized that Reid Stuart would supply them with as much and as good of materials as could be bought. So they worked with enthusiasm to insure that their craftsmanship matched the quality of the materials and the scope of Reid Stuart's vision of his daughter's home.

Sixteen months later the testament to their skill and the permanence of the Escadara rose above the lip of the Ceta canyon. The house was solid. Its ship lapped walls were rocked on the outside. It had four turrets, one on each corner, thirty four feet tall at their peaks. An eight foot wide veranda, ten feet from floor to roof, circumnavigated it. Two ten foot tall four foot wide oak doors, each swung on five solid brass hinges, led into an open room that ran the entire length of the house and occupied the front one-half of its width. A five foot wide staircase led from this area up to the landing ten feet above the floor. From this landing four rooms opened to the back upstairs of the house. The landing, to the left of the staircase, turned and opened twice into one large room which was nearest the staircase and above the kitchen. This room's oak beam girded floor formed one-eighth of the ceiling of the large downstairs room. The rest of that downstairs room reached all the way to the four by four oak rafters which supported the roof twenty four feet above the main floor; at the back of the downstairs, beneath the upstairs room, was the kitchen and two more rooms. Another stairway led from the first floor to the landing. A round rock fireplace stood between this staircase and the kitchen. It served in the kitchen as oven and hearth, in the master room as a corner stove, in the first downstairs room as again a corner stove and on the landing above as heat for the upstairs. Another rock fireplace stood at the far end of the master room and encased the flue from the old dugout's fireplace and carried it up to and through the high roof.

Reid Stuart had planned well to heat Katharane's home against the arctic cold of the plain's winter. To cool his daughter's house, two pairs of three foot by eight foot windows opened from the master room onto the veranda to receive the prevailing southwest winds of summer.

The house swallowed Reid Stuart's and Katharane's meager furnishings. Katharane's brass bed with its goose down mattress and a vanity with a beveled mirror, gifts from Mary Goodnight, seemed like a doll's furniture in the large room above the kitchen. The gunman's and Reid Stuart's cots were the only disruption to the clean swept planks of the two downstairs bedrooms. The old plank table and the three cottonwood stumps looked like a tiny lost island in the great front room. The wooden pegs hewn into the walls on each side of the twelve inch facings of the tall front doors held Reid Stuart's Sharps, his hat, a leather duster and his spurs. The four pegs to the left of the door held Katharane's hat, her holsters and pistols, and on the last peg the gunfighter's old bull buffalo cape hung.

Katharane and Reid Stuart walked through the empty kitchen, out its door and onto the veranda. There they stood side by side and watched the Scotsmen and their wagons disappear into the prairie.

"Now, daughter, with your house built, what do you and I do?" Reid Stuart asked Katharane.

She rubbed the small of his back and said. "Now we wait for Pop to come home."

"Leave it go, Stuart." Charles Goodnight said. "He was born to an ending like this, and you know it."

The old wanderer, who had brought the news that the gunfighter was ill, that he was in New Mexico still pursuing the Comanchero, the only one of the Squaw Woman's killers he had yet to find and kill, watched Katharane.

Reid Stuart looked at Charles Goodnight. "Maybe so, but am I the one to decide?" He asked.

"Dad! You can't! You can't do that to Pop." Katharane cried.

"A lot of people in this room say I should, Katharane." Reid Stuart said as he looked from Young Tom to Bose Ikard to Charles Goodnight and finally to his daughter. "They say it's not only the right thing to do for him. It's the best I can do for him."

"They don't understand him. They can't. They don't know him. We do." Katharane pleaded with her father.

"We know him, Katharane. But understand him?" Reid Stuart shook his head. "You may. I don't. I never have." He sighed and stood up. "But I do understand this. He's out there as much because of me as himself. And for that reason I can't leave him." He turned to the old wanderer and asked. "How much to lead me to him, old man?"

"Not interested."

"Then maybe you'd damn well best get interested." Katharane cursed the old wanderer. "See that mule." She pointed through the glassless window at the old man's gray mule.

"Jennifer?"

Katharane took Reid Stuart's buffalo gun down from the pegs. "If you don't get interested in leading us to my Pop before I walk out that door, Jennifer will be stew meat tonight and buzzard bait in the morning."

"You shoot my mule, my Jennifer?" The old man gasped.

"I'll shoot her. I'll skin her out. I'll butcher her. I'll cook her. And I'll feed her to you." Katharane threatened."

"You put down that gun." The old man's voice trembled. "I'll take you to him."

"Reid." Charles Goodnight said. "That's a hell of a ride under any circumstance. Better than four hundred miles across a dry plain. And the whole territory is working alive with scum. You run into a pack of them with just you, him." Charles Goodnight looked at the old prospector. "And Katharane." He did not say the rest of what he thought. He looked at Reid Stuart and he knew Reid Stuart understood what he was thinking.

But Reid Stuart would not relent. "The Romeros wouldn't be any help in a fight." He said. "Katharane and I are what we have. We'll make do."

"I'll send Bose and Young Tom with you." Charles Goodnight offered.

"No." Katharane said. "Only Pop could go after the men that killed my mama, and only Dad and I can go after him."

Tom Hawkins was heartsick. His mind screamed at him. 'Go with her!' But he forced himself to stay silent.

"Reid." Charles Goodnight tried again. "Do you think he would bring Katharane with him to look for you?"

"I don't know." Reid Stuart said. "But I know he would come. And Katharane won't stay."

"Katharane." Charles Goodnight turned his entreaty to her.

"We are going. And we are going to bring my Pop home." Katharane said.

"I should have killed that son-of-a-bitch the first time I saw him." Charles Goodnight cursed. "I don't know why I didn't."

"Because." Katharane said. "You knew you couldn't. Not you or any other man can take my Pop alone. And you know that." She hung the Sharps back across the wooden pegs. "But there is something you can do." She looked at Charles Goodnight. "You can ask Bose and Tom to check on the house and things until Dad and I get back with Pop."

Charles Goodnight sighed. "I'll do that."

From the gunman, without knowing she was, without his intending it and maybe without even his wanting it, Katharane, the child, had learned to care for her father and the gunman, to love them. These things the gunman had not set out to teach her, as he had her letters and to cipher with numbers. But his and Reid Stuart's being there, always being there for her, had nurtured within her a deep and true love for them. Now that love drove Katharane, the young woman, to go to the gunman. Across the Canadian, west into the New Mexico territory, the old man led Katharane and Reid Stuart.

"It's a blue hole, Dad, a blue hole of water." Katharane said excitedly. She stepped down from the bay horse. Twenty feet below the escarpment, led down to by four tiers of solid rock shelves, a pool of water, maybe thirty feet in diameter, shimmered in the late day sun. Katharane scrambled down the giant steps formed by the rock shelves. She stood on the bottom shelf five feet above the surface of the pool. She stared into the water. Reid Stuart and the old prospector sat on their mounts and watched her. "Where does it come from?" Katharane asked, still staring into the pool.

"From the soul of the earth, girly." The old man answered. "It's as pure and cold and clear as new snowfall."

Suddenly Katharane reached with both of her hands and gripped the shoulders of her buckskin shirt and pulled the shirt over her head. She dropped it onto the rock floor behind her. Reid Stuart could make out the outlines of her maturing breasts as they bubbled out beneath her arms. She kicked off her moccasins, unfastened her belt and slid her pants down to her ankles. She straightened and stepped out of her pants. For a moment the sun captured her and held her, framed against the translucent surface of the pool. Reid Stuart stared at his daughter. 'Look away.' He thought. But he did not. He could not. Katharane dove into the water. Her butt, white and shining, a flash of dark between her smooth thighs, then her toes vanished beneath the water.

"Oh Lordy!" The old man cried. "Lordy, I seen. I seen." He repeated. He jumped from his mule, grabbed a rope and bounced wild and catlike down the shelves until he stood above the pool. "Come up, girly! Come up!" He cried. "There ain't no bottom. It goes to the center of the earth."

Slowly Katharane's head reappeared from the water. The old man dropped the rope over it as Katharane spit water. "It's cold!" She squealed.

"Put the rope around you, girly." The old man coaxed.

Katharane pulled the rope over her head and snugged it around her stomach. She sucked in all the air her lungs would accept and dove again. The old man played the rope out. He was so excited that his left boot slipped off of the ledge and he had to sit down quickly on his butt to avoid falling into the pool. Reid Stuart laughed. The old man's eyes never left the pool, the spot where Katharane had vanished underneath the water. His head bobbed about and his hands fed the rope through themselves. The rope stopped. The old man held it, feeling it with his fingers. Reid Stuart frowned. "Here she comes!" The old man shouted and reeled the rope in hand over hand. Katharane's form appeared, clear and distinct deep underneath the imaging water, seconds before her head broke through the water's surface.

"I can't reach it." Katharane gasped. She brushed the water from her face with her hands. "I can't reach the bottom. I can't even see it!"

"Ain't no bottom." The old man informed her. "'comes from the center of nowhere, girly." He held the rope in his hands and pulled on it slightly, coaxing her shoulders above the water, staring at her all the while.

"Quit that!" Katharane grabbed the rope and pulled. The old man sat back. "I'll pull you in." Katharane threatened and laughed.

"Dunk him, Katharane." Reid Stuart chuckled. He picked up the leads on Katharane's bay, the old man's mule and the pack mule and clucked his buckskin into motion. "I'll make camp." He called down to the old man and Katharane.

"Okay, Dad." Katharane called back.

The camp established, Reid Stuart walked back to the base of the ledges where the surface of the pool was only two to three feet below them. Katharane swam around the pool. The old man watched her, mesmerized. As Reid Stuart watched his girl woman child swim nude in the clear and opaque water of the deep strong spring he understood why the gunman had left, and now he understood why he had not returned. The gunman's not returning had troubled Reid Stuart for a long time. Done or not, the gunman could have ridden home. He knew the way. He had the will to do it. Why did he fail to do so? Why had he stayed away from them and the Escadara? Now, watching Katharane swim, Reid Stuart understood. The gunman wanted Katharane. He wanted the woman she was to be. He wanted it more than anything he had ever known, just as he had wanted the woman that was married. And he could not have her. He did not have the restraint of family as Reid Stuart had. Katharane was not his daughter and no convention of society or rule of blood forbade his having her; nor did time or age make it physically impossible for him to have her as it did for the old wanderer. And the gunman was not forestalled by any naive romance such as that which held Young Tom at bay. Only the gunman's love held him away from that which his mind and body cried for. To have it would destroy Katharane. Not to have it was destroying him. The heavy burden of this knowledge saddened Reid Stuart. He loved his daughter. He loved his partner as well. And now he understood that someday he would have to choose between them. He turned and walked back to his camp.

When he felt her hand on his shoulder, Reid Stuart glanced up at Katharane. She wore only the long tailed pullover buckskin shirt. She stood barefooted on the dry prairie, her long wet hair drying in the afternoon breeze, sunlight dancing against the beads of water on her tanned smooth slender legs, and life, warm and hopeful, shining in her eyes.

"I've been thinking, Katharane. Thinking I want to go home."

"We will, Reid Stuart." Katharane put her hand in the middle of his back. "We will go home just as soon as we find Pop." Reid Stuart looked into the far New Mexico desert and thought. 'I meant home without him, Katty.' But he did not say this and the old wanderer's mumbling approach of, "I seen. I seen, Jennifer," forced Reid Stuart to leave this thought buried silently in his mind. "Do you think I did him any real harm?" Katharane asked.

Reid Stuart looked up at his child standing above him and realized she had become less of a child and more of a woman, and that she was becoming more a woman with each day. "Maybe not." He said quietly.

"I seen." The old wanderer mumbled repeatedly to himself as he drifted into the camp.

"Nasty old bugger." Katharane said. "You would think he had never seen a woman before."

"Are you a woman, daughter?"

Katharane blushed and said. "I think so."

"So do I." Reid Stuart said softly. "That's why I want to go home." He said even softer.

"We will." Katharane said. She put her arms around Reid Stuart's right arm and squeezed it between her breasts. "When we find Pop."

"I seen." The old man chanted as he stirred about the camp.

"Do you think he may not have?" Katharane asked her father.

"May not have what?" Reid Stuart asked.

"That he may not have seen a woman before?"

"It's possible in this country, Katharane." Reid Stuart answered. "A man could live a lifetime here and not see three women. I doubt Canada has seen a white woman here, other than Mary Goodnight." 'And that's why he came here.' Reid Stuart thought silently. He sighed and said. "There are so few things we really control, so few."

"Well he's seen one now." Katharane's assertion broke

270

through Reid Stuart's silent thoughts.

He nodded. "Probably made his whole life worthwhile."

"Oh, Dad." Katharane laughed. She rubbed her cheek on his bony shoulder.

"What is that?" Katharane asked. She stared at the distant visages in the western sky.

"Mountains." The old wanderer said. "Sanny' Fe is just beyond them."

"Is that where Pop is, Dad?"

"I don't know, Katharane. But that's where he goes to pick up supplies and money."

"You've known that for a while?" Katharane asked.

Reid Stuart nodded. He looked at the dim mountains and not his daughter.

"And you couldn't tell me that?" Katharane demanded angrily.

"I chose not to."

"Why?"

"Because I didn't want you to get your hopes up that he was coming back." Reid Stuart turned in his saddle and looked at his daughter. "You need to know this, Katharane. He may choose not to come back with us. And if he does I want you to leave it at that."

Katharane glared at her father. "He will come back. He will." She said fiercely. "He will come back because he will want to come back. He will."

Reid Stuart sighed. "Then let's keep traveling. We are a long three to four days to Santa Fe."

"More like five." The old wanderer said.

"Is he here?" Katharane asked.

"No." Reid Stuart answered. "But he was here three weeks ago." He swung up onto the buckskin. "He picked up supplies and ammunition and rode north. They believe he is going to Taos."

271

Reid Stuart looked at the old wanderer. "Can you get us there?"

The old man mumbled. "I seen." He glanced at Katharane, then he looked at Reid Stuart. "They say he's mad. Why you want to go all that way for a madman?"

"They don't know my Pop." Katharane interrupted. "He'll be fine with me." She watched the old wanderer. He wavered. He was weary. And Jennifer was foot sore. She leaned toward the mule and said very softly. "Remember. You've seen. You take us to my Pop and maybe you'll see again."

The left half of Reid Stuart's top lip rolled outward into an angry snarl. A fury rose in him, then just as suddenly that fury quit him and it was replaced by an old and weary hurt. He looked at his daughter through sad tired eyes. But she kept her gaze on the old wanderer who stared at her with unrepentant excitement. "For that I'll take you to the end of the land where the great water rolls, girly." He said thickly.

The old wanderer led them north into the mountains. Reid Stuart was uneasy in the mountains. He did not understand them like he had grown to understand the plains. On the plains distance was flat and straight. It radiated away from him in vanishing straight lines that only seemed to converge on the far horizon. In the mountains he crossed his own track a dozen times and could still see the spot from where he had begun and the point across the next valley to where he wished to be. On the plains he was the center of his universe. In the mountains each peak formed its own center and held its own universe. Truly he was trusting to the old wanderer's sense of direction and his honesty of purpose to get them to Taos.

Katharane was excited. The mountains were new and different, and she was still young enough to feel certain that the old wanderer truly was leading them towards her Pop, that they would find him and that he would eagerly ride back to the Escadara with them. She believed that all the things she had grown up with would be again as they had been, unchanged and static.

"Where did you come from?"

"From Santa Fe. Through the mountains."

"I hate those damn mountains."

"So do I."

The gunman raised his head. Reid Stuart caught his breath. The gunman was emaciated. His breath came to him in haggard wheezes. His eyes were puffy and swollen. His lips were dried pieces of leather, weather cracked and fevered. "I didn't get him, Stu'. I didn't get that damn Comanchero." The gunman muttered.

"It doesn't matter. It's done, done as well as any man could." Reid Stuart said. "What happens to him doesn't matter anymore."

"He still knows where we are." The gunman coughed. "He still knows, and he still ain't dead."

"Don't trouble yourself." Reid Stuart pleaded with the gunman.

"You better get him in the saddle and riding." The old wanderer warned. "That crowd." He nodded at the one gathering in the street in front of the mercantile building. "Looks to be planning on troubling him for certain."

Reid Stuart helped his partner onto his bay horse.

"That's the Eagle's Nest." The old wanderer pointed at the pass high above the mountain lake where the horses drank. "Other side of it is the Cimarron gap. Once in it only way out and that's onto the eastern plains below the Raton. From there you gotta' cross open plains all the way."

"You're not coming with us?" Katharane asked.

"No, girly." The old wanderer shook his head. "You're not going to make it with him." He pointed at the gunfighter. "And I choose not to be with you when you don't."

The gunman sat in the saddle with his hands stacked on top of the saddle horn, his right hand stacked first then his left hand stacked on it. Katharane had watched him sit with his hands as they were now many times. But she had never seen him with his shoulders humped forward and his head down. He seemed so very small, almost like a sleepy small boy sitting in the saddle.

"Stuart, are you there?" The gunman's voice was weak and hoarse and faint.

Reid Stuart leaned over to his friend and answered him. "I'm here, Canada."

"You wouldn't've asked this much of any beast of burden." The gunman raised his head slowly and stared straight ahead. His eyes were gone. Only two deep blackened pools seemed to sit in his face where his eyes had been. "I'm done in, Stu', either have the kindness to shoot me or leave me to die as the Comanch' would. But in the name of mercy do one or the other."

"No!" Katharane screamed. "No, Pop! No!" She looked at her father. "No, Dad. No! You can't let him quit. You can't! He won't if you ask him not to. Please! Please! For me."

"How much would you have me do to him for you, child?" Reid Stuart cried out. "How much? Don't you know he's given you everything he's had, his land, his dreams? Would you have me take away his dignity and give you that, too? Would you, Katharane?" Tears ebbed and flowed along the deep wrinkles just below Reid Stuart's eyes.

Katharane had never seen her father cry. She could not look at him. She swung her left foot out of her stirrup, pivoted across her saddle and sat down in the gunman's saddle in front of him and facing him. She lifted his chin. "I love you, Pop. Do you hear me? I love you. And I will always love you. You will never have to leave me, Pop. I'll never send you away. I'll always be with you."

"Katharane." Reid Stuart pleaded with his daughter. "In God's name don't do this to him, don't make him fight himself for you! Don't promise him something which he can't let himself have. Don't do that just so you can have him awhile longer. It'll come back to haunt you and him both."

Katharane ignored her father. "Do you understand, Pop? Always. Always." She pushed her lips against the cracked sores which were the gunman's lips.

The gunman tried to open his eyes. They were just two slits in the black pools. But they were there and they understood.

"Always. Always." Katharane whispered to him. "But you've got to ride, Pop. You've got to make the Ceta. Remember the water at the Ceta? Remember how good it tastes?" Katharane felt the muscles along the bay horse's ribs tighten as the horse reacted to the gunman's spurs which goosed his flanks. The bay horse began to move forward. Katharane looped her horse's reins around the gunman's saddle horn which was behind her. "Come on, Dad." She looked at her father. "Take the lead."

Reid Stuart tapped the tall buckskin's right shoulder with the ends of his reins. He eased the horse and the pack mule in front of the gunman's and held it to any easy walk.

"I seen, girly. I seen." The old wanderer called after them as their horses labored up the steep grade to the pass.

As Reid Stuart led the mule and Katharane's and the gunman's horses into the pass, and the lake and the old man and Jennifer began to disappear below them, Katharane yelled. "You seen, old man, you seen!"

At the bottom of the long Cimarron Reid Stuart called a halt to their march. The gunman had to be held in the saddle. He sucked his breath through his swollen silent lips. "We'll lay up here for a few days and regroup before we strike out across the plains." Reid Stuart stared at the vast Llano Estacado which stretched before him. The Escadara waited at the far edge of this dry prairie where the canyon broke its seamless surface. He looked across his shoulder at the sick gunfighter and thought. 'For him it could as well be a thousand miles. He'll never make it.' Then he glanced at this daughter. 'Can she deal with it when he doesn't?' Katharane bent over the still gunfighter, tucking the blanket around his shoulders.

"He comes."

"Who comes?" The old wanderer asked the nervous Caballero who stood before the single plank which formed the bar in the Taos tavern.

"He comes. He wants the girl and to kill the one with the black gun." The Caballero said cautiously to the barman. "He knows the black gun is weak and that the girl has come for him. So he comes for them." The oily haired rider turned to the old wanderer and said. "And he knows you are the one who knows where they have gone."

The old wanderer's eyes widened. "No. No. I don't know!" The old wanderer argued.

"He knows and he's coming here for you. Whether you know or not will not set with him. He will kill you and everything you have to get to them."

"Kill my Jennifer." The old wanderer whispered. "Kill my mule." He mumbled to himself. "And the girly I seen. I seen." He turned and wobbled stiffly out of the bar and to where he had left Jennifer standing wearily in the street. "I seen." The old man mumbled again. He crawled up onto the mule and cried into the night. "I seen!"

"Damn drunken old loony." The barman cursed.

Back through the first pass and down into the valley of the eagle beneath its nest at the lake Jennifer trotted steadily eastward. She climbed to the rim of the nest and trotted down into the Cimarron. Broken to the saddle, knowledgeable of the trail and indefatigable in her march the mule carried the sleeping old wanderer through the Cimarron and unerringly onto the trail, east by east southeast toward the far canyons, onto the same trail upon which Reid Stuart, Katharane and the gunman had rode slowly out upon two days before.

"Could be real bad for Mr. Reid and Miss Katharane, Mr. Charles, if that Comanchero catches them." Bose Ikard said.

Charles Goodnight stared across the Canadian River at the open prairie. He held the post dispatch from Fort Sumner which he had intercepted in his left hand: ...Stuart, girl and gunman left Taos....Comanchero pursuing them....Old prospector believed between....Routes unknown... Charles Goodnight knew Reid Stuart's route. He knew it better even than Reid Stuart. But was there time? "I don't believe anyone is going to catch them, Bose."

"I don't rightly see how he can keep from it. They don't know he's chasing them and they must be going slow, with Mr. Canada sick and all." Bose said sorrowfully.

"That's why they won't catch them." Charles Goodnight said. "I think that old pilgrim found them and they know the Comanchero's after them. And if that gunman's as sick as they say they're coming day and night across those plains, Bose." He pointed at the vast plains beyond the Canadian River. "Young Katharane will not rest if that gunman is still alive. She believes that if she can get him home, home to his Escadara, she can save him. And for her Reid Stuart's sailing them straight on at that canyon without rest."

"If that be so we should be making a crossing tonight." The Negro said. He touched his horse with his spurs.

"Crossing a flooded Canadian at night is too risky." Charles Goodnight said.

"For Miss Katharane I'll risk it, sir." Bose said calmly. He stepped his big roan off of the loose mud of the river's bank. Tom Hawkins moved his sorrel horse in line and followed Bose. The other four cowboys followed him. Charles Goodnight brought up the rear.

"Dad?"

"I've been watching him." Reid Stuart said.

"Who is it? He's following right on our track and he's gaining on us." Katharane said.

"I don't know who it is." Reid Stuart said. He slipped the Sharps from its cover. "But I intend to." He trotted the buckskin out to meet the approaching rider.

Katharane watched her father stop the rider. She watched him turn and lead whoever it was toward her. As they approached she recognized the old wanderer. The old man slid down from his mule. "I've been on Jennifer for three days, maybe four, best I can remember. My Jennifer's been trailing you on her own." The old wanderer put his hand on the top of his mule's nose. "He's coming for you, girly." He said confidingly.

"Who is coming for me?" Katharane demanded. She glanced at her father. He stared at the prairie in the direction from which the old wandered had come to them.

"The one he didn't get, girly." The old wanderer said. "The bad one, he's coming out of the desert after us." The old wanderer rubbed his mule's neck. He looked up at the sick gunman. "Too bad he's dying. He could kill him for us."

"Is that all anyone wants from him, to kill someone for them?" Katharane cried. "And he's not dying." She said angrily. "He's just sick. He will be okay once we get him home."

"He's dying, sure and certain." The old wanderer said. "No matter though. He's coming. And he'll get us all long before we reach your Escadara." The old man sucked on the insides of his mouth. "Too bad he'll kill my mule, too." He rubbed the mule lovingly.

"There's three of us and only one of him. Why are you sure he will kill us instead of us killing him." Katharane demanded.

"The hunter kills and the hunted die. He's hunting us. When he finds us he will kill us." The old wanderer continued to stroke the mule's neck. He looked up again at the gunman. "Sure too bad this one's sick. We can't kill him but he could."

"Oh! You're just a silly old fool!" Katharane snapped.

"Old man." Reid Stuart said. He did not take his eyes away from the flat eastern New Mexico plains. "We are two, two days and a half's, hard ride from the Canadian. Right?"

"That's right."

"From the Canadian can you find the Escadara?"

"Should be able to, I've been that way once." The old wanderer answered.

"Take my daughter and my partner and go there." Reid Stuart said as he mounted the buckskin.

"What are you doing, Dad?" Katharane asked.

"What he would do." Reid Stuart nodded at the gunman. "I'm going back and kill that Comanchero."

"Can't do it." The old wanderer shook his head. "You ain't like him nor this one either." He patted the gunman's leg. "And because you ain't you can't do it."

"Whether or not I can is not your concern." Reid Stuart said. "Your concern is getting my daughter and my partner home. Now can you do that?"

"Yep."

"Dad."

"The old man's right, Katharane." Reid Stuart picked up his reins from the buckskin's neck. "The hunter has the advantage. This will give me a couple. First, I will be hunting him. And he won't know it."

"Won't matter, he'll kill you, sure." The old man said.

"Shut up!" Katharane screamed at the old wanderer. She looked at the sick gunman, then her father.

Reid Stuart saw the torment in his daughter's eyes. "It's not that way, Katharane." He said softly. "You're not choosing him over me. There is no other way."

"But...."

"It wouldn't matter, anyway." Reid Stuart continued. "Even if you chose him, it wouldn't matter." He stared at her. "You're my daughter and I love you."

"Only be one when he hooks up with that Comanchero." The old wanderer chimed in, uninvited. "Better be sure, girly." He said. "This dying one." He rubbed the gunman's leg, "Or your daddy."

Katharane drew her right pistol and cocked the hammer. "You shut up, old man." She snarled. "Or you'll be catching her brains in your hat." She shoved the barrel of her pistol between the mule's eyes. The mule raised its ears and crossed its eyes, focusing on the barrel of the pistol.

"Not my mule!" The old wanderer screeched. "You got no cause to mistreat my mule!"

"You shut up then."

The old man smacked his lips shut and nodded his head."Dad." Katharane said, again.

"It's not your doing, child." Reid Stuart said. "It's mine. Now go on." Reid Stuart goosed the buckskin. The horse stepped away. Katharane stared at her father's back as it slowly grew smaller and smaller as the buckskin carried him back into the eastern New Mexico desert. But she did not call after him.

"Who they be?" The old wanderer mused as he studied the distant riders.

"It's Bose and Tom!" Katharane cried. She spurred her tired horse. "Bose! Tom!" She yelled as she raced into the far mirage.

"Hold up, girly!" The old wanderer called after her. She

ignored him.

"That's Katharane." Young Tom said. He lashed the sorrel with the tails of his reins.

"You take young Katharane, the old man and Mr. Canada, Tom, and ride back to Mr. Charles. Tell him where you left me." Bose said.

"What are you going to do?" Tom asked.

"I'm going to Mr. Reid."

"But Bose." Tom protested.

"Go on now, Tom. Tell Mr. Charles. He will know what to do."

Katharane put her hand on the black cowboy's cheek. "Thank you, Bose." She leaned to Bose and kissed the black skin that bubbled between her thumb and forefinger.

"Go on now!" Bose almost screamed. He had never been kissed by a white woman and it frightened him. He looked about as if he expected either the gunman to revive and shoot him or some forgotten overseer to bring the lash down upon his shoulders. He heeled into his tall roan and loped away following Katharane's, the old wanderer's and the gunman's track.

Reid Stuart knelt beside his horse. The Comanchero squatted beside his. Between them the shallow valley darkened. When only a thin crescent of orange sunset shown in the western sky Reid Stuart cocked the heavy hammer of the Sharps and crawled away from the hobbled buckskin. The Comanchero waited until he could not see beyond the barrel of the old Army Infield. Then he, too, crawled away from his horse.

Bose Ikard's roan moved slowly through the darkness. The tracks Bose followed in the faint early night were fresh. He was close to Reid Stuart.

The dirt smelled of heat and parched grass and sweat, Reid Stuart's sweat. Fear, he was sweating because he was afraid. He swallowed his breathing, steadied his chin on the stock of the Sharps. He had fought in pitched battles, more than most men alive, and survived. This was different. He was feeling his way through the New Mexico desert at night trying to find just one man, not riding into a wall of smoke and noise and fire. Was the old man right? Could he not kill the Comanchero? Was this something that only the gunfighter could do? Were there such men who could not be killed singly, only obliterated within an advancing regiment or by a mortar's blast or a salvo of a hundred guns fired at once? Reid Stuart lay with the dust packing his nostrils and tearing his eyes. His hands cramped as they gripped the Sharps. His knees ached from crawling, and somewhere before him in the dark, maybe only a dozen strides away, lay the killer patiently waiting to make his kill. What kind of man was this? He had never known a man so nerved, except for the gunman. The outlaw waiting to kill Reid Stuart was that dark and foreboding part of the gunman's psyche Reid Stuart had seen at Tafoya's, incarnate, living, breathing, and killing. The old wanderer was right. Only another like him, only the gunman could kill him. Reid Stuart realized he was waiting to die.

Bose studied the markings beside the hobbled buckskin. Then he lay down beside them, slid the Winchester in front of him, cocked its hammer and crawled along the track as best he could.

The Comanchero eased to the base of the rise and rested there. He was close to the man he would kill. He could smell his sweat. He would wait a few minutes until the night swallowed whatever signs of movements there might be. Then he would crawl across the rise, kill the man that had ridden back to kill him and be after the old man, the sick one and the prize, the girl.

As he listened to fabric, hard coarse fabric, scraping over the packed New Mexico desert dirt, Reid Stuart felt his skin go cold and numb. He forced himself to concentrate on the sound. The scraping continued. But he was not certain from where. It was behind him! He rolled onto his back and swung the Sharps over, resting its long barrel on his knees. If he fired it from this position it would probably shatter his chin, but doing so might just save his life for it seemed that the Comanchero had flanked him and was moving in to kill him. He might just have a chance. All Reid Stuart could do was pray that fortune and fate lay with him and that he got one shot before the Comanchero closed on him.

"Mr. Reid. Mr. Reid." Bose's whisper was only a faint and soft and timid breath. "Mr. Reid."

'Bose.' Reid Stuart formed the name on his lips but no

sound came. He licked his lips and whispered hoarsely. "Bose."

The Comanchero felt the voices more than he heard them. He stopped and lay completely still, sunken almost into the impenetrable desert floor. How many? Two? Three? Too many to crawl into with just his knife, and he had left the Infield behind so could move more quickly and much more quietly. He waited. He heard two bodies roll onto the sand side by side. 'Mother of Jesus.' He swore silently. He hated the unseen men. He hated the gunfighter. He hated the girl. He would have her, but not this time. He turned and crawled away.

Charles Goodnight sat on his gray horse and studied Reid Stuart's buckskin and Bose Ikard's roan that stood at the crest of a rise which lay before a shallow valley. Beyond, in the valley, Bose Ikard and Reid Stuart or their corpses waited, and the Comanchero and how many men? The old pilgrim had babbled about one Comanchero, but cutthroats seldom traveled alone, especially when they were on a raid. There was only one way in, across the rise. If the Comanchero and his cutthroats were waiting it would take a heavy toll on Goodnight's cowboys. He knew this. He also knew that if Reid Stuart and Bose were waiting on a dawn assault, or if they had been wounded in the night, he had not time to lead his boys around the rise and up from the end of the valley if he was to be of service to Reid Stuart and his dear old friend, Bose Ikard.

"What are we going to do?" Young Tom asked. He looked at Charles Goodnight and the hairs on the backs of his hands tingled and the skin beneath crawled. His throat tightened. Charles Goodnight's eyes glittered. They glowed with a strange and bright brilliance as if he saw something far away up close and immediate. Young Tom had never known battle. None of the young cowboys had. And the look of the warrior readying himself, his mind, his body, his soul, for combat thrilled and frightened and confused them. The readiness to fight that now shown wolf like in Charles Goodnight's knowing eyes, brave, determined, sad, excited, committed, reconciled, and along the set of his stubborn jaw baffled them. To them Charles Goodnight was the benevolent old taskmaster. Never before had they seen him as plainsman and Indian fighter.

Charles Goodnight reached into his saddle bag and pulled

his extra pistol out. He rolled the cylinder, then gripped the pistol in his right hand and held it above his head. He picked up his reins in his left hand. "Put the spurs to them, boys, if you're going with me!" He roared and drove his spurs into the gray horse's belly. The horse farted and leaped forward into a run. "I'm coming in to you, Bose! Damn that Comanchero to hell I am!" Charles Goodnight cried as he raced for the rise.

They were young. But not a one faltered. Their horses took up the chase of Charles Goodnight's gray, and every cowboy gave them the bit and urged them on. Young Tom's eyes watered from the dry wind that whipped passed his little sorrel's flying mane and the fright in his heart. The ground rumbled beneath their horses' hooves and wild elation and fear made them scream and cry and curse, and loyalty and devotion carried them on after the reckless old plainsman that rode before them.

Young Tom swallowed. "Oh God! The rise." He whispered. Then he screamed. "He'll shoot the first one over that rise for sure. Mr. Goodnight! Rein in!" If Charles Goodnight heard him he ignored him Young Tom could only suppose because as he reached the rise Charles Goodnight ripped long bloody rows down the great gray's flanks driving the last beats of strength and speed from the desperate horse. Then Young Tom understood. "He's going over that rise first on purpose!" He yelled to the other cowboys.

The cowboys threw spurs deep into their already gasping horses' flanks and cursed themselves for their cruelty. The old iron willed plainsman crested the rise first like an old bull buffalo on a blind charge roaring. "Bose! Bose! Where are you?"

Young Tom began to cry. Then it was over. The battle cry echoed away into the desert. The horses' hooves were silent. Charles Goodnight's gray stood, sides heaving, in front of Reid Stuart and Bose Ikard. And Charles Goodnight leaned forward against his hands which rested on his saddle horn and talked to the two of them as if passing the time among friends on a casual meeting on any early morning. Young Tom was angry.

Bose's gentle voice calmed him. "Tom. Tom."

JUSTICE

1883

The gunfighter's fever rose rapidly. His shirt and his pants were wet from his sweat, but still he shivered. Katharane pulled back the hand stitched blanket Mary Goodnight had given her with which she had covered the gunman. She took a deep breath. Then she stripped the gunfighter naked.

"Damn." Reid Stuart said. He stood up from the chair next to the bed where the gunfighter lay, walked into the kitchen, lit a smoke and carried it out onto the veranda.

"Dad." Katharane called to him. "Bring me another bucket of cold water from the spring."

Reid Stuart picked up a wooden bucket and stepped off the veranda without answering Katharane and walked to the spring. He did not know many things about the worn thin ill man that lay naked on his daughter's bed and trembled each time she touched the wet rag to his feverish skin. But Reid Stuart did know that the gunman would not knowingly have come to this place where he now lay. He might have come home to the Escadara, but he would not have come to this place beneath Katharane's hands. He had spent years going away from this, trying to hide from it, trying to change himself to where he could never again be brought to a place such as this where his heart was so close to the surface, so close to being vulnerable, exposed, chanced and lost. The gunman would not be able to go back from this, not now. If he survived he would not be able to change what would be between himself and Katharane. These seemingly vengeful increments of time during which Katharane would be with him, caring for him, nursing him, would bring him closer and closer to her. Possibly if the gunman had returned well and able to ride and work and, therefore, could only spend an occasional few hours with her instead of the long days and days, the unbroken and continuous time he would now by necessity spend with her, his feelings for her, so long suppressed, would have bloomed and faded quickly like a late season cactus rose. But these feelings, shared or unshared by Katharane, Reid Stuart was uncertain as to which, but he sensed they were at least common between them, would have grown slowly and deeply within the gunman, so slow and so deep as to become a part of him, as much as his hand or his foot, and the gunman would be incapable of separating himself from these feelings without a pain more unbearable to his psyche than that of having his hand or his foot torn from his body. Reid Stuart also knew that he, Reid Stuart, would not after this be able to change these feelings or even affect them. And Reid Stuart knew he could do even less about the inevitable pain these feelings would bring to his partner and his daughter. This troubled him most. It would have been both a wondrous relief and an unrelenting grief for Reid Stuart if he thought these feelings were the gunman's alone. But Reid Stuart knew they were not, not completely, not yet, someday when Katharane married, but not now; therefore, he knew if the gunman survived the future would bring whatever it brought for them no matter how he or they acted now, disrespectful even of their sincerest efforts. If the gunman lived Reid Stuart now understood, as Goodnight had first understood, there was a great danger for Katharane in these feelings which the gunfighter would most surely have for her. What man could turn away from the chance to be close to a spirit such as Katharane's, close to her thoughts, close to her heart, close to her body, to know that she might think of him when she least realized that was what she was doing and he could think of her when he most needed her easy warmth? The gunman had shared his pasts, his hurts, his hopes and his dreams in his moments with Katharane. And it was only in these moments, not in the day in and day out going away of his life, that the gunman was most nearly someone to be loved and who could love. During his other long hours of living he was only sometimes bearable. Reid Stuart walked across the veranda and into Katharane's room. He set the bucket filled with the spring's cold water next to the bed.

Katharane laid three long strips of white cloth along the edge of the bed. "Dad, we have to bring Pop's fever down. We..."

"Let him die, Katharane." It came from somewhere distant, long hidden within Reid Stuart, from a place made immune to death by war and never before shared with his daughter.

Katharane shivered. It frightened her. She pretended not to

hear him. "We have to bring his fever down." She repeated. The sound of Reid Stuart's boot heels against the oak floorboards answered her. They stopped next to the hearth in the kitchen, paused there, then continued slowly out the door, the smoke from the cigarette hanging in the air behind them. Katharane sighed. "All right, Dad, all right. Maybe this is something I must do by myself." She said softly. She dipped one of the strips of cloth into the cold water and wrung the excess out. She bathed the gunfighter's arms, neck, chest, abdomen and legs with the cold wet cloth. She rolled him over onto his stomach, picked up another cloth, dipped it into the bucket and washed his shoulders, back and legs. For an hour and a half Katharane bathed the gunfighter, until she was satisfied that his fever had either peaked or, at least, slowed. Then she covered him with the blanket, dipped a cup of fresh water from the bucket and lifted his head. "Come on, Pop, you have to drink. You have to keep some fluids in you." She held his head off of the pillow and carefully tipped the cup against his cracked lips and coaxed him to drink.

It took her half an hour to get him to take three swallows of the water. She waited an hour, laid the blanket back and began the long slow bathing again. Around three in the morning fatigue overcame Katharane. She stood up, looked at the bucket, the wet cloths and the naked gunfighter. She trembled with tiredness. She pulled her dress over her head. Her naked nipples stood out. She slid into the bed next to the gunfighter and pulled the blanket up and covered them with it.

The gunfighter slept the fever's sleep, unaware that Katharane lay naked next to him. He was barely semi-conscious, immersed in a struggle for his life. A struggle fueled more by Katharane's will than his own.

Reid Stuart did not come to the house to have meals with Katharane the next day nor the next nor the next. He had one of Juan Romero's boys, Miguel, bring the food Katharane prepared for him to the veranda. Katharane did not join him on the veranda. She stayed at the gunfighter's side. She did not see her father inside the house, but she knew that he had been there because each morning and each afternoon there was a fresh bucket of spring water at the head of her bed and Miguel had refused to carry water into the room where the gunfighter lay.

By the fifth day the gunfighter appeared comatose. The fever had caused most of the solid food that Katharane had almost forced down him back up. Only her determined spooning of water into him had avoided his total dehydration and, thereafter, kidney failure. His lungs were heavily congested. But Katharane's faithful bathing of him had prevented a sustained fever high enough to damage his mind.

Katharane was tired and haggard. She leaned against the door jam and watched her father set the bucket of water next to her bed. He laid the back of his hand against the gunfighter's forehead. Streams of fire ran up and down against the thin skin on the back of his hand. Reid Stuart lifted his hand and place it close to the gunfighter's lips. "He's just sleeping, Dad."

Reid Stuart looked at his exhausted daughter. "His fever hasn't broken, Katharane. If anything it has gone up." He said gently.

"It will break. It has to." Katharane said.

"No, child, it doesn't have to." Reid Stuart said more forcefully. "Two weeks on the trail, five days here. And still he hasn't changed."

Katharane folded her arms across her stomach. The tears did not flow from her eyes, they marched out of the corner of each eye, one teardrop obediently following the other. "Tonight, Dad, tonight it will break." Katharane turned her face away from her father. Her body shook from its desperate tiredness. "It has to." She whispered.

"No. No it doesn't have to." Reid Stuart repeated, as he slowly walked passed his daughter.

Katharane walked to the bed, sat next to the gunfighter and looked at him. The gunfighter lay on his back. His face was hollow. His eyes were sunken. His slender body was racked and rail like. He had lost twenty pounds from a body which had never carried an extra pound. His breathing came in shallow rasps. She bent to pull a wet rag from the bucket beside the bed, then she stopped. "It's now or never, Pop. Oh God! Forgive me, Pop. We can't go on like this." Katharane removed all of her clothing. She lifted the naked gunfighter by his shoulders and sat him up. Then she slid his feet off of the bed and onto the floor. She put her left arm underneath the gunfighter's right arm and gripped his left side and stood him up. His weight staggered her and she had to spread her legs to keep herself and the gunfighter from collapsing onto the floor.

"Come on, Pop. Walk with me." Katharane coaxed. Slowly she led the gunfighter across the floor and into the kitchen. She pulled the heavy oak door which led from the kitchen onto the veranda open and stepped the gunfighter out onto the porch. Going down the three steps from the porch to the ground the gunfighter's knees buckled and Katharane had to throw her arms around him and clutch him to her to keep him from collapsing. Once on the hard packed clay of the yard she was able to steer him step by step by step to the spring.

The buckskin raised its head from drinking at the spring. Reid Stuart turned on the horse's saddle and stared at the two naked bodies that seemed joined in some slow dance as they approached the spring and the first reservoir. He pushed against the buckskin's neck and the horse stepped up onto the flat packed grassless prairie above the spring, Reid Stuart rode to his daughter and his partner.

Katharane did not look at her father who turned the buckskin to hide her and the gunfighter from the house where the Romero family was finishing their evening meal. He sat in his saddle and watched Juan Romero blow out the lantern in their one window. Reid Stuart stared at the square dull one room structure as if his careful watching prevented anyone within from watching Katharane and the gunfighter.

Katharane stepped down into the reservoir, dragging the gunfighter with her. She sat down and held his head against her shoulder. The water was cold. The night air made her ears tingle and any of her skin that was above the insulation of the water rippled with chill bumps. She dozed and awoke and dozed. Somewhere passed midnight Katharane awoke and felt the gunman's body pressed against her body. He lay with half his body atop her body, her leg cradled between his legs. Katharane felt a firm warmth against her right thigh. He was aroused. She felt his face, his neck. The fever was gone. She placed her ear next to his lips. For the first time in weeks his lips were naturally damp. Katharane laughed quietly, clutched her fingers in his curly hair and kissed his forehead. Katharane looked to the house. Between the spring and the house Reid Stuart still sat in the buckskin's saddle, very much asleep. The buckskin, ground hitched, stood with its head down, also asleep. Katharane pulled the gunfighter close to her and waited for dawn.

The gunman recovered slowly at first, then each day brought renewed strength and an old and restless desire to be out and about stirred him to rise to his feet before most men would have raised their heads from their pillows.

"You wait here, Pop." Katharane left the gunman balanced against the door facing. "Watch Pop, Dad. Please." She said to her father as she crossed the veranda.

Reid Stuart got up and carried his tin cup filled with coffee to the door and stood next to the gunfighter. "I gave you up for dead." He said.

"I was dead." The gunfighter acknowledged. "I keep stamping my feet just to convince my mind that I'm not." He grinned at Reid Stuart.

Reid Stuart nodded. From the corrals Katharane's unseen voice floated across the veranda. "Andale', pronto'."

"Katty's not bashful 'bout bossin' those Mex's." The gunman said. His right shoulder bumped against Reid Stuart's left biceps as they stood side by side in the open door.

"No. She's not." Reid Stuart said.

"It's good to hear her voice. It makes me glad I am alive."

Reid Stuart put his left hand on the gunfighter's right shoulder and, without looking at him, said. "Be glad you are alive for yourself, my friend."

"Hell, Stu'." The gunman said. "There ain't nothun' to me but you and Katty and this black pistol." Even in his weakness from his illness the gunman still wore the black revolver. "You know that."

"Yes. I know that." Reid Stuart said quietly. "I know."

Katharane led the Bugbee black filly across the yard. The filly carried the gunman's saddle. She stepped high and walked in place as Katharane turned her and stopped her in front of the kitchen door. The gunman limped across the veranda and eased down the steps to the yard. Reid Stuart followed him. The gunman put his left hand on the horse's nose and looked across his arm at Katharane. "What happened to that old filly of mine?" He asked. Katharane bit her lip.

"Katharane shot her." Reid Stuart said.

The gunman turned his head to look at Reid Stuart. "You let Katty do that?" He demanded.

"I had to, Pop." Katharane said shakily, mistaking the gunman's anger as being about the killing of the horse instead of her having to do it.

"I wasn't here. She was alone." Reid Stuart answered for Katharane.

"She was down and Bose said she would never get up." Katharane swallowed. "Mr. Goodnight was going to shoot her. But I couldn't let anyone shoot your horse. I couldn't!" Katharane pushed her forehead against the filly's neck. "So I shot her with my pistols like you told me. One shot behind each ear." She whispered into the silky hide of the young horse.

The gunman reached to Katharane and put his left hand underneath her hair and cupped it around the back of her neck. "You done good, Katty girl." He said to her like he had so many times when she was a child learning to read or write or shoot. "You done real good." He took the filly's reins from her.

"What are you doing?" Reid Stuart asked.

"'goin' for a ride on Katty's black, she got for me." The gunman answered. He gripped his buckskin pants behind his left knee with his left hand and began to lift his left foot into the stirrup.

"Wait Pop!" Katharane cried. "I'll make us a picnic." She turned to her father. "Can we, Dad? Can we?"

"Why not." Reid Stuart smiled.

"Yes!" Katharane shouted and she ran for the kitchen. "Tell Juan to saddle my bay for me, Dad." She called as she vanished into the kitchen.

As Juan Romero led the saddled bay horse to the house Katharane reappeared from the kitchen. She carried a large piece of white cloth, doubled and tied at its corners. She had stuffed a chunk of the dried buffalo meat from the lone old cow her father had shot the fall before near the mouth of the Tule. Maybe he had done so because he had known the old cow would not survive the winter or maybe because he had been remembering the early winters on the Escadara with her and the squaw woman and the gunman, Katharane did not know. But she was glad now that he had. Buffalo meat would be their special treat on this picnic. She had added eight strips of beef jerky, half a loaf of yesterday's dark bread the Romero's had baked for them and four boiled eggs. She looped the tied corners of the cloth around her saddle horn. Reid Stuart tied the goat skin water bag he had filled at the spring around his. Then they mounted side by side. The gunman already sat on the black filly.

"She's young and skittish, Pop. Watch her." Katharane cautioned.

Reid Stuart laughed and the gunman smiled. "I taught you to ride, Katty girl. 'reckon I remember enough to stay atop this filly." He said and winked at Katharane.

Juan Romero handed Katharane four fresh hot corn tortillas. "For your breakfast, la senorita." He said softly.

"Gracias." Katharane replied. She handed one of the tortillas to her father and one to the gunman. She kept two for herself. The gunman stared at the flat piece of hot meal. "Roll it up, Pop. Like this." Katharane said. She rolled the two tortillas together, end to end, and took a bite from one end. The gunfighter and Reid Stuart did the same. The three tortilla eaters turned their horses and started them down the trail into the Ceta.

The black filly reached the bottom first and the gunman stared up at the high spires of the house which seemed to rise by themselves out of the prairie as he waited for Katharane and Reid Stuart to join him.

"Things have changed." Reid Stuart said as he reined up next to the gunman.

The gunman nodded. "'couldn' t see the dugout from here." He said. "That's one of the reasons I put it there." He frowned. "But you can damn sure see that house you built."

"With the Comanche and the Kiowa gone, being hidden didn't seem as important." Reid Stuart said. "We have neighbors closer than two hundred miles now."

"'bein' hidden from neighbors may be more important than bein' hidden from the Kiowa." The gunman grumbled.

"Oh Pop." Katharane laughed. "Quit your griping and ride with me." She heeled into the bay and he loped away.

The gunman turned the black filly and stuck her with his spurs. She tried to rear. He pushed his knuckles against her neck and rippled her flanks with his spurs. She shot forward. Down through the Ceta they rode. Reid Stuart did not urge the patient buckskin to keep up. Katharane and the gunman rode away from him and disappeared into the stands of cedar. Katharane's laughter floated back to Reid Stuart and her voice followed her laughter. "You can't catch me, Pop. I have more horse."

"'ridin' the horse you gave me." The gunman's voice responded. "'you give me a slow horse?" He asked plaintively.

Reid Stuart turned the buckskin through the last of the scrub cedars. The big canyon lay open before him with Katharane a half of a mile ahead of the gunfighter and galloping away from him. "You're a rich man, Pop. Buy a faster horse." Katharane's retort drifted back to Reid Stuart.

The gunman slowed the filly to a walk. Reid Stuart loped the buckskin to him. "Katty thinks I'm a rich man." The gunman greeted Reid Stuart.

"You are a rich man." Reid Stuart said.

The gunman let the filly angle off of the line he would have taken with her if this had been a serious ride. "Yes. I suppose I am." He said. "'got a beautiful horse between my legs. 'got Katty." He looked at Reid Stuart. "I am a rich man, Stu'." Then a cough, deep and rattling, escaped from his chest.

"Are you okay?" Reid Stuart asked.

"I'm okay. Just a little tired."

"Let's rest a while then." Reid Stuart said. He reined the

buckskin back to a slow meandering walk. The gunman rested in the saddle, more comfortable there than on the ground, eased by the gentle gait of the filly. Reid Stuart had watched him do it a hundred times. But it never looked better to him than it did on this quiet noon day as they drifted out of the mouth of the Ceta and into the big canyon. Katharane loped across the top of the mesa midway across the big canyon from them.

"There was a day we would not have let her ride half that distance from us." The gunman said.

"She's older now." Reid Stuart said. "And it is a different canyon now."

"Are we different, too? As to Katty, I mean." The gunman stopped the filly, but he continued to look at Katharane as he asked this.

Reid Stuart did not answer as he reined the buckskin to stand next to the filly.

"During the sickness I kept seeing this horse approaching, always approaching, never reaching me, just always approaching."

"Just a horse?" Reid Stuart asked.

The gunman nodded. "'best I could tell. But there was something else. Something I've always wanted, a presence. I was naked and I could feel it touchin' my body, touchin' the tips of my fingers, against my lips, my tongue, against..." The gunman's voice faded. He turned in his saddle and faced Reid Stuart. His eyes were undone, haunted by this ghost of his mind. "What does it feel like to kiss a woman you love, Stuart? To know her?"

"Hell! You've known a woman."

"No." The gunman said very slowly. "No. I haven't. Not really. Not one I loved. Just in my mind. What does it feel like?"

'Christ!' Reid Stuart thought. He stared into his friend's eyes. Never had he wanted more to be able to put words together to make something so much of the spirit real and tangible.

Before Reid Stuart could answer, the gunman blurted out. "Oh God, Stu'! I thought it was Katty. So help me I thought it was Katty." Their eyes searched the other's, knowing, not knowing, wondering. The difference was that the gunman's eyes trusted

293

Reid Stuart's. "Was it, Stu'? Was it Katty?"

Reid Stuart hesitated. Then he lied to his partner. "No. It wasn't Katharane."

"Good." The gunman sighed. He looked back at Katharane. "I prayed it wasn't. I really did."

Reid Stuart put his hand on the gunman's hands that were stacked on the filly's saddle horn and said. "Being with a woman you love feels like it felt in your mind, compadre, just as it felt to you."

Katharane returned. She worked her bay in between the filly and the buckskin. "Let's eat." She said cheerfully as she dismounted. She pulled the four cornered white cloth from her saddle horn and set it on the ground and untied it.

Reid Stuart watched the gunman slowly chew the tough dried buffalo meat. A first cross heifer with her new calf crept out of the scrub cedar and grazed on the new tender grass along the stream of the Prairie Dog Town Fork. A new calf season was with the Escadara, and changes, too; new black Angus bulls, buffalo bulls the gunfighter called them, better stock and the defining and limiting of ranges made management of those ranges a necessity. And now on the Escadara quickly, so very quickly, Katharane was becoming a young woman. Reid Stuart chewed the buffalo meat, thought of these changes, and watched his friend, his partner, and worried. Too many changes, too many people were not things which would benefit the gunfighter. And the changes in Katharane would only confuse him. It would be a long season of change for the old warrior.

Charles Goodnight frowned as the gunman walked through the door and into the kitchen.

"'hopin' I'd died. Were you, old man?" The gunman tipped his hat to Mary Goodnight who stood next to Katharane and Reid Stuart. He did not speak to Bose Ikard or Young Tom.

"It would have made things a hell of a lot simpler." Charles Goodnight retorted. He relented before Mary Goodnight's reproving look. "There's talk of convening a grand jury in Clarendon to inquire as to indicting Canada in three of the Squaw Woman killings." Charles Goodnight spoke directly to Reid

Stuart.

"They can't do that!" Katharane cried. "Those men Pop killed murdered my mama." Mary Goodnight put her arms around Katharane.

"A lot of this stems from jealousy over the Escadara range, Reid, whether they will admit it or not." Charles Goodnight said. "But I'm afraid they're very serious. Grand jury will convene at the White Hotel in Clarendon two weeks from Friday. If you have anything to say, be there. Otherwise, indictments and warrants will issue."

"Indictment nor warrant will help the man who tries to serve it." The gunman warned.

"As I hear it they anticipate that will be your response." Charles Goodnight said as he turned and faced the gunman. "Reportedly they are bringing in lawmen known for their ability with a gun. If they ride on you more than just your life will be at risk." The rancher glanced at Katharane. "That's why they made certain I heard of it. They knew Mary and I would ride here to warn you. They're betting you'll ride in, to protect Katharane if nothing else. And they will be waiting." Now Charles Goodnight stared at Katharane and his wife, but he addressed Reid Stuart. "One other thing, Reid, the Association is backing this."

"Are you?" Reid Stuart asked.

"I told them I would have no part in it."

"Losin' your nerve, old man?" The gunman taunted Charles Goodnight.

"It's not my nerve that is troubling me, gunman." Charles Goodnight said, still without taking his eyes from his wife and Katharane. "It's my heart. I am afraid it's stronger than my nerve and my sense of justice." He picked up his hat. "Now I've done what I can, Mary." He said to his wife. "It's time we were leaving."

"Not before lunch." Katharane protested. "It's been so long since we all ate together. Please."

"Yes, Katharane, you and I will prepare lunch and possibly these intelligent gentlemen can discuss this further on the veranda and arrive at something more meaningful than calling each other names and threatening to shoot up the place." Mary Goodnight said.

The gunman smiled. Bose Ikard chuckled. Young Tom swallowed. Charles Goodnight cursed under his breath. And Reid Stuart said. "Come on, Charles. We're out manned and outgunned in here." He led their retreat to the veranda.

Katharane stood at the kitchen door and watched Juan Romero walk across the yard. Her father and the gunman had ridden across the yard and down the trail into the Ceta the afternoon before as the sun set against the plains' far horizon. 'We may be a day or two bringing those old 'horns out of the Tule.' Her father had said to her as he sat in his saddle on the buckskin. Then he had reached down and rubbed her cheek with the backs of the fingers of his left hand. The gunman had not said a word. Now she said aloud. "There are no wild cattle in the Tule. The Tule's too narrow. And even if there is Pop always said there is only one way to bring them out and that's in your belly." She called loudly to Juan Romero. "Juan Romero."

"Si, la senorita, Katty."

"When were Mr. Goodnight and Miss Mary here?"

"Dos amonos antes de ayed."

'Today's the day Charles Goodnight said the grand jury would convene in Clarendon.' Katharane thought silently. 'They've gone. Oh God! They've gone to face them.' "Juan Romero. Saddle my bay. Quickly, por favor." She urged Juan Romero. He hesitated. "Hurry, amigo."

"Pero, la senorita." Juan Romero said slowly. "El senor Reid say no."

"Then they have gone to Clarendon. Haven't they?" Juan Romero did not answer. "Do as I say. Saddle my horse now!" Katharane commanded.

"Rider coming, Mr. Charles." Bose Ikard said. He stood below the porch.

"'comin' hard, too." Tom Hawkins said. "I can't make him out." He shielded his eyes with his hands and stared at the horse and rider which seemed to be so slowly climbing out of the canyon to them, but which in fact was coming to them at a gallop.

"That's because it's not a him, Tom." Bose said. "That's Miss Katharane on that bay Mr. Charles gave her. And she's riding fast." He swung up into his saddle and rode to meet her. Tom followed him. They escorted Katharane to where Charles and Mary Goodnight waited on the porch.

"What is it, Katharane? What's wrong?" Mary Goodnight asked.

Katharane took a deep breath and said. "They've gone, Miss Mary. Dad and Pop, they've gone to Clarendon. I know they have." She struggled to steady her breathing. "Dad said they were going to gather the old Longhorns from the Tule. I trailed them to where they would have cut off if they were really going to try to bring those wild cattle out of the Tule. They didn't. They went on." Katharane reached out and caught Charles Goodnight's hand. "Please. Please. Mr. Goodnight." She begged. "I don't know if I can find Clarendon. Not in time. They are going to hang my Pop without even knowing why he rode after those men." Her eyes fixed Charles Goodnight's eyes. "You know. You do. Please help me. Just take me to Clarendon and make them listen to me. That's all I'm asking."

"I'm sorry, Katharane." Charles Goodnight chewed on the inside of his cheek. "I have done all I can. I cannot interfere. I gave the Association my word."

"But they'll hang him!" Katharane cried. "And they may kill my Dad doing it. You know that." Charles Goodnight did not blink. He did not speak. Katharane dropped his hand and turned to Bose Ikard. "Please, Bose. Please." She whispered. "You're not part of the Association. You didn't give them your word. Just lead me to Clarendon. Please."

A sadness bred of generations of silently watching those he loved suffer moved across Bose Ikard's dark features. "It's not for me to say, Miss Katharane." He said softly, sadly.

Young Tom had retreated several steps. His mind swam. If Katharane asked him, would he take her to Clarendon? Would he defy Charles Goodnight?

"Charles will go with you, Katharane." Mary Goodnight said.

Bose stepped to Young Tom and spoke into his ear. "Saddle Mr. Charles' big roan, take Miss Katharane's horse and put her saddle on your little soft footed sorrel." Young Tom looked confused. Bose winked and handed Katharane's bay's reins to him.

"Mary! I gave the Association my word." Charles Goodnight exclaimed.

"You gave me your word long before there was a cattlemen's association, Charles Goodnight, and I followed you here believing in that word." Mary Goodnight wiped her hands on her apron. "You promised to love and honor me as long as we both shall live." Mary Goodnight began to untie her apron. "Don't disgrace me now by refusing to accompany Katharane." She folded the apron. "I am not asking you to go against the Association. I am asking you to do no more than a kindness for Katharane." She laid the apron aside. "And if you cannot find the courage in your heart to do so I will find it in mine."

"Dammit! God dammit!" Charles Goodnight cursed. "Bose! Where are you?" He yelled.

"I'm right here, Mr. Charles." Bose said patiently.

"Get my horse, Katharane a fresh mount, Young Tom and two Winchesters." He commanded.

"Your horse is being saddled, Mr. Charles." Bose said. "And Young Tom is saddling his sorrel for Miss Katharane. He'll bring both horses soon. You have the Winchesters locked in the house."

"Why in Hades did you have my horse saddled before I told you to?"

"You told me to a long time ago, Mr. Charles." Bose answered politely.

Charles Goodnight studied the calm leathery black face. He tried to see if Bose Ikard thought what he was about to do was right or wrong. But all he could be certain that he saw in the dark eyes was an unblinking loyalty and an unerring knowledge of his employer that a long and often tested friendship had given the Negro. "Well. Don't stand there. Go in the house and get the damn rifles." Charles Goodnight grumbled.

"Here are the rifles, Mr. Ikard." Mary Goodnight said. She held a Winchester in each hand and she had a box of cartridges balanced in the crook of her right arm.

"That's New Clarendon." Charles Goodnight nodded at the dozen wooden buildings divided unequally by three dirt streets. "They're convened in the lobby of the White Hotel. That's that building there." Charles Goodnight pointed at a large unpainted wooden two story structure midway of the second street.

Katharane slid from Young Tom's sorrel. She untied the heavy buffalo robe from behind her saddle and laid it on the ground. She kneeled beside the robe and unrolled it part way. A pair of white doeskin leggings, a white doeskin shirt stitched together by buckskin lacings, the necklace Chief Kwanhah had given Katharane and a pair of white moccasins lay on the robe.

"Girl, when did you braid your hair?" Charles Goodnight asked.

"She's been doing it the last few miles." Young Tom answered.

Katharane stood up, raised her arms above her head, gripped the back of her buckskin shirt and pulled it over her head.

"Damnation!" Charles Goodnight cursed. "Cover yourself." He commanded.

Bose Ikard looked away, but Young Tom stared at Katharane's naked breasts.

"I am covering myself!" Katharane retorted as she struggled to slide the white doeskin shirt over her head. As the shirt slid over her breasts she said, "I don't have time for modesty. I am going to change my britches now. You are welcome to watch or not."

"Girl! Don't you drop those pants 'till..." Charles Goodnight began and he just managed to turn his head before Katharane wiggled free of her buckskin pants.

Bose Ikard's elbow cracked against Young Tom's ribs.

Tom flinched, blushed and looked away. Katharane struggled into the tight leggings. Then she draped the necklace over her head and shoved her feet into the moccasins. She rolled the buffalo robe up and, carrying it under her left arm, she remounted. "We must hurry." Katharane said. She goosed the sorrel. The little horse stepped forward into a quick trot.

Katharane pulled a string of what Charles Goodnight took for animal pelts from the buffalo robe and tied it to the back of her belt as Bose Ikard stepped through the side door of the White Hotel. Young Tom followed him. Charles Goodnight led Katharane through the door and into the large noisy lobby and he noticed quickly that this grand jury was not in the least secret. The room was filled with people. The noise in the room seemed to be absorbed, ate up by the common attention given to Charles Goodnight and the auburn haired girl dressed in white doeskins at his side.

"I thought you wanted no part in this, Charles." Judge White said.

"I want less part in this than you can imagine, Judge." Charles Goodnight answered. "But I have brought someone who has something you need to hear." Charles Goodnight took a half step back and Katharane stood alone. She glanced at the old rancher. His steady eyes did not waiver. He had brought her, but he would not stand beside her, not for this, not for the gunman.

"I am not certain this is proper." Judge White began.

Katharane sensed that her chance to speak was passing from her grasp and Charles Goodnight's ability to command the group's attention. She took a deep breath and began. "I came to tell you about a man you don't know." Her voice was shaky and soft.

Murmurs began to rise from the back. A voice asked, "How do you know we don't know him?"

In a stronger voice Katharane said. "Because only I know him."

The murmurs rose in volume and the same voice from before again challenged her. "We know he rode down, shot and butchered maybe a dozen men."

"And do you know that he rode after men that you would have hanged?" Katharane responded.

"We may hang him, too." The voice taunted Katharane.

She pressed on. "Men that killed my mother. If not for Canada these men would still be here, still be feared and still be killing us. If not for Canada and my father some of you would not be here. I know how lucky I am to have him and my father, and to have had them here for me. I never dreamed I would be so unlucky that I would hear anyone say that Canada should be hanged for being there, for riding down men that murdered my mother."

A wooden chair grating across the wooden floor interrupted Katharane. A young man with wavy sand colored hair stood up from his seat next to Hank Cresswell, owner of the Bar CC. His deep green eyes flashed as he surveyed the room until he focused them upon Katharane. His jaws were set, hard and square. He raised his chin and pointed it at Katharane as he spoke loudly, ensuring everyone would hear his words. "And they marked them. Two men on horseback who carried the law loaded into their guns and saw fit to carve a bastardized letter into their victim's foreheads. You are more fortunate than you realize, Miss Stuart. We are gathered here to determine if one man should face a properly convened grand jury for these crimes. We should be here to decide if both should face indictment." He turned his gaze upon the gathering in the lobby. "There may have been a place for such gunmen on the plains in 1869." He said very loudly. "But there is not now. Now it is the legacy of these gunmen that confronts us each time we try to establish a proper system of justice, a legal system."

"Yes." The loud nameless voice that had taunted Katharane shouted. "That's right." Several more voices echoed their approval.

Katharane shook her head. She struggled to be heard. "There was a place in Texas for your father in 1836. I wonder if there's one here for him now, Mr. Houston. Or would you seek to hang him, too?" Katharane raised her voice again. "I can't speak like Temple Houston can. But I know in my heart that when there's no longer a place here for men like my father and Canada, then there's no place here for men like Mr. Goodnight or 'Cap' Arrington." Katharane looked at the old ranger who sat at the far end of the first row of chairs. "Or you, Hank Cresswell." She pointed at the man seated next to Temple Houston's still empty chair. "They were fierce men on horseback. Two savage riders who rose out of the mysterious canyon to pursue any trespassers. I've heard the stories too, Mr. Houston." Katharane licked her lips and plunged on, her voice trembling from her effort to be heard and to try to express her feelings for her father and the gunman. "But my first memory of one of those savage men is of Canada standing knee deep in a pool of water, wearing only his buckskin shirt, his hat and his black gun, standing there while a baby girl floated on her back in the cool water, holding his hat over her to shade her from the broiling August sun." Katharane struggled on, trying to say what was in her heart and why. "I've seen those men sit on their horses as the sun set, after fourteen hours of hard riding, standing guard against the open plains, so a little girl could run and jump and play before going to bed. That black pistol you hate, meant safety for me. It being there meant I could grow up on our land, Mr. Houston."

"Miss Stuart, not a man here questions anyone's right to defend their home and family. But exacting a man's life for any trespass upon one's range is far harsher than any sense of justice can tolerate."

"It was a harsh land, Mr. Houston." Katharane's throat tightened. She strained to control the emotion in her voice. "Our first winter on the plains it snowed and blew so hard and was so cold that Dad and Canada couldn't ride up the trail from the canyon to the dugout for days. I could hear them shouting to me from below. And the Squaw Woman would carry me out of the dugout, hold me up so they could see me and wave to me. Then she would carry me back in and keep me warm during the freezing nights, wrap me in buffalo hides heated by the warmth of her body."

"No one has ever claimed that they did less than their most by you, Miss Stuart." Temple Houston interrupted Katharane. "But to purposefully execute twelve men without trial for the alleged murder of a Comanche squaw living off the reservation and away from her own people." The tall young lawyer hesitated. He had blundered and he knew it. Charles Goodnight straightened and scowled at Houston. Reid Stuart's boot struck a hollow thud against the timber of the wooden floor.

A ripple of anticipation stirred the room. Its occupants knew Temple Houston was dangerously close to crossing a border from which Reid Stuart and the gunman would not allow him or them to retreat.

"The Bible says he that killeth with the sword must be killed with the sword." Katharane said. Her eyes glistened. But she stared defiantly into Temple Houston's eyes. "Mr. Houston, none of you would have let me talk here today if Charles Goodnight had not ridden all this way with me to tell you to hear me before you judge my Pop for riding down my Squaw Woman's killers." Katharane used her childhood name for the gunman publicly for the first time. Boots shuffled against the rough yellow pine boards of Judge White's hotel floor. "Yet none one of you." Katharane raised her hand and passed it across the sea of faces before her. "Not one offered to ride after them!" She dared them to dispute her. They did not. "My Pop went. He went for me. And he went alone, because of me and because Dad had to stay with me because my Squaw Woman was dead. Dead!" Katharane stared into stoic sun burnt faces. The eyes in these faces were not unkind to the beautiful girl before them, but they were stern and set and not swayed, as yet, in their conviction that an excess had been done which it was their duty to redress. So Katharane took a deep breath and plunged ahead boldly, angrily. "To you my Squaw Woman was just a stinking, dog eating Comanche bitch, and what happened to her or her kind didn't matter."

Several coughs protested Katharane's accusation. But it was Thomas Bugbee who challenged it. He spoke directly to Charles Goodnight, ignoring Katharane who stood between him and the cattleman. "All-right, Charles. We didn't come here to fight Indians. Everyone knows the Escadara's thinking on this. They'd've as soon seen mine, and maybe your, scalps swingin' from a Comanche lodge pole as see those lodge poles forced on to the reservation."

"I can't say I totally disagree with them on that, Tom." Charles Goodnight growled in reply.

"For me, Mr. Bugbee, that Indian squaw was the only Mama I ever knew." Katharane spoke directly to the rancher. "The second day I was with her I sucked at her teat, hiding in the shadows of a high crevice in the wall of a canyon. Hiding from the

Kiowa that Dad and Pop were riding down because those Kiowa had butchered a group of mustangers at the mouth of the Ceta on our land. They did. Then they came back for me and I was there and I was okay because of the Squaw Woman." Katharane pulled breath into her lungs and continued. "She fed me every day of the thirteen years she was with me. And when she saw the riders coming she shoved me beneath the feather mattress Mrs. Goodnight had given me and told me to stay there and not to make a sound no matter what I heard. She knew what they were going to do to her, Mr. Bugbee. She knew, Mr. Houston." Tears danced in Katharane's eyes. "And I laid there listening to them laugh and curse her and feeling them slamming her against me through the mattress. Listening to her moan and whisper prayers to the winds and the sky and the sun and the buffalo as they ripped her apart." Katharane turned her gaze upon Temple Houston. "I could hear her flesh tearing, Mr. Houston. I heard a bone break. I could smell their stench. I knew they were killing her, Mr. Houston. Do you know what it's like to be lying underneath someone you love and know they being butchered alive. Do you?"

Temple Houston mutely shook his head. "Well I do, Mr. Houston." Katharane swallowed and continued. "I laid there wearing my pistols, and I didn't make a sound because I was afraid and because she had told me not to and because I loved her more than anyone and knew only to obey her. I laid there with her blood soaking through the feathers in the mattress and feeling warm and thick against my face and in my hair. I laid there sweating from the heat and the fear and the dread and the weight of the dead body of my Squaw Woman on top of me, afraid to cry out because the men that had ripped her from her pelvis to her belly button would show me no more compassion than they showed her, knowing that they could come back and find me. Wondering who would help me, and vowing with each shallow frightened breath I took that if I lived they would pay for her death. I lay there until I heard Pop calling my name, felt him lifting the mattress and pulling me out from under it, carrying me outside to Dad's arms where I could smell the cedar posts of our corrals burning, see the dead stock, my pony shot through the eye, the Escadara, my home, thirteen hard years of work and danger and believing in only ourselves, in ruins. And not one of you offered to ride after them for me." Katharane turned the fury and fear in her eyes upon face after face in the room.

The weathered redness of years in the sun left most of these faces as Katharane's eyes flashed upon theirs. Many eyes polished the toes of their owner's boots. "Not one!" Katharane crossed her arms underneath her breasts and hugged herself. "Damn you all to hell for that!" She fought to hold back her tears. Several escaped and trailed down her cheeks. Her voice grew thick from the unseen tears she swallowed. "She was my Squaw Woman and I loved her, and you would have let her death go unavenged because she was a Comanche and because she lived on the Escadara. My Pop rode them down. For two lonely years he lived without us and we without him to do what everyone of you would have ridden together to do if it had been a white woman. He brought them justice, Mr. Houston, Comanche justice!" She cried out, and she swung the string of scalps from behind her back and let them dangle between her deerskin clad legs.

The shriveled wads of hair, held together by the dried, wrinkled, cracked meat of the scalp, seemed alive, seemed to rise and fall between the wonderfully beautiful young girl's legs as she breathed. Hanging between the soft velvety white of Katharane's doe skins they looked like dark cankerous sores, leaking some venomous stench, cruelly attached to the soft underbelly of a newborn calf.

"This is Comanche justice! And it is good and right and they deserved it, each and every one of their damnable souls, for what they did to my Mama!" Katharane screamed her defiance at the silent still faced men seated in the lobby of the hotel. The flow of tears down her cheeks increased. She coughed. But she managed to speak through the anguish choking her. "You, Pat Garrett." Katharane pointed a trembling finger at the tall, black haired, tallow complexioned man standing next to Cope Willingham, the Tascosa sheriff who leaned against a window sill on the far side of the lobby. "You're the only one with stomach enough to try Canada. You're the one they'll pick to do their shit work." Katharane felt for the butts of her pistols. But they were not there. She had not brought them. She knew she was, again, powerless to defend someone she loved. Her heart cried out. "I'm begging you!" She coughed. "I want my Pop. I want my Pop. Just leave him be. You do that for me and I'll do anything you ask of me."

The room gasped at the audacity of the beauty before

them. And the hard heavy click of the hammer of old Sharps broke the stillness left by Katharane's proposition as Reid Stuart set its hammer back, ready to be fired. And the all too familiar sound of the leather loop dropping from the gunman's black revolver's hammer followed this. The men in the lobby still sat dazed and dumfounded.

Cope Willingham stood up very slowly from the window where he sat and stood behind Pat Garrett. John Siringo, the Pinkerton detective, stepped nest to the Tascosa sheriff. And 'Cap Arrington rose from his chair. "I'm afraid they were too smart to set any one gun against your Pop, Miss Katharane. They brought four." The old ranger spoke very slowly and deliberately.

"Are you one of them, 'Cap?" Katharane asked.

"I'm afraid I am, Miss Katharane. I'm afraid I am."

"I should have known. Why else would you be here, 'Cap.'" Katharane said. She tried to stop crying, to blink dry the tears in her eyes.

Pat Garrett took two steps toward Katharane.

"No, Garrett."

"You tend to your part in this, Houston. And I'll tend to mine." The tall New Mexican lawman growled as he pointed at the lawyer. He took one more step and stopped. He crossed his arms in front of him.

"Please." Katharane begged.

"All-right, Miss Katharane Stuart, I won't draw against your Pop." Pat Garrett said softly to Katharane. Then louder he said. "And if anyone here should doubt the reason I'll make it clear now. I would have faced that gunman. And he might have beaten me. Just might have. But I have little fear of that anymore." The lawman said matter of factly. "But I do fear the kind of love any woman has for a man that would drive her to come here and to say what you've said today. You have shamed us all as we should be shamed. If you love that old gunfighter this much, my hand will be no part in his hanging, though hang he should. You can have him. I'll do that much for you." The tall quiet man paused. Then he said. "And for your Squaw Woman."

Katharane's sobs came fast. The hurt that had hung in her heart since the Squaw Woman's death rattled from her throat. She wept until she felt Charles Goodnight's hand on her left shoulder and heard him speak softly to her. "It's all-right now, Katharane." Then she heard the beat of boots against the floor boards and knew the rhythm of their owner's gait. "Oh Pop!" Katharane flung herself into the gunman's arms. "Please! Please! Don't let them do this to you!" She cried.

Her tears tasted salty sweet to the gunman as he pressed his lips against her cheek and whispered. "Don't fret, my little Katty girl. We're goin' home, home to the Escadara."

Chairs clattered as ranchers and settlers stood as the gunman passed among them carrying Katharane in his arms with the scalps still dangling between her legs and Charles Goodnight, Bose Ikard and Tom Hawkins following them.

Reid Stuart sipped his coffee and wished they had left the day before. The gunman leaned back in his chair. Charles Goodnight tore a chaw of tobacco free from its plug. Katharane beamed at the German matron who ran the hotel in the White House. The matron carried Katharane's second glass of fresh milk to the table where the three men and the child sat. Young Tom sat on the White House's veranda, near the open window and the table where Katharane sat. He and Bose had eaten on the veranda where Charles Goodnight had carried their breakfasts to them earlier. Judge White and others, including Tom Bugbee, had prevailed upon Charles Goodnight to delay his and the Escadara's departure. "At least give un the semblance of respect." The judge had demanded of Charles Goodnight. "Let this grand jury vote. You and I both know what that vote will be. Stay over at my hotel. Leave in the morning."

Goodnight had waited for the old judge to offer the accommodations as a courtesy. When he did not Goodnight had offered them to Reid Stuart at Goodnight's own expense. Reid Stuart had declined his charity, but Katharane had prevailed upon her father and the gunfighter to spend the night with her in the hotel. They had finally agreed, and much to the matron's disbelief and Charles Goodnight's dismay, Katharane and the gunfighter had shared one room and he and Reid Stuart had shared another.

Now at breakfast in the lobby before the open window the

German woman scoured the girl with her eyes for signs of misplaced affections from the night before. Katharane mistook the inspection for appreciation and smiled at her. Katharane was enjoying the ham and eggs. She seldom had them.

Young Tom stood up from where he squatted on his boots on the veranda and said. "Here they come, Mr. Goodnight."

"I see them." Charles Goodnight said. "Let them walk to us. I don't have the stomach for spending my legs walking to meet the likes of them this morning."

Old Judge White, Temple Houston, Pat Garrett and the Reverend Lewis Carhart entered the White House and walked to the table where Charles Goodnight and the others sat. "This grand jury has adjourned without returning an indictment against you, sir." Judge White said to the gunman. "But I would advise you that its actions do not preclude the possibility of later grand juries doing just that if you come back to this town under similar circumstances."

"I won't be comin' back to this town." The gunman said. He let the front legs of his chair fall back down onto the wooden floor with a thump. "And the next time I see any of those grand jurors of your's they'll be lookin' across this at me." He put his hand on the black revolver. "And shortly thereafter I'll be puttin' a mark on 'em so you all will know by what way they came to know their ends."

"You are a murderer!" Temple Houston said angrily. "And you should hang. And if I ..."

"You don"t and you won't." The gunman interrupted him. "You ain't got the stomach for it."

"Don't, Pop." Katharane said shakily. "Please don't fight."

Reverend Carhart turned from where the German woman whispered to him and confronted Katharane. "If any woman worships the image of the mark in the forehead, the same shall drink of the wine of the wrath of God."

"By God, Preacher! You're a damned sight out of line saying that to this girl!" Charles Goodnight cursed Reverend Carhart. Goodnight stood up.

Judge White stepped back. Though anxious to be seen chastising the gunfighter, he had no desire to challenge Charles Goodnight. Goodnight used a power when he fought that the judge feared much more than the gunfighter's black pistol. Goodnight could and would muster votes and opinion in favor of his selected candidates, even in Clarendon. He had political influence throughout the region and the state and the Judge knew this and feared it. "She slept in this house with a man to whom she's not married, a man that kills and marks other men." The Reverend Carhart accused.

"What the hell!" Charles Goodnight roared. "She's slept with him since she was a baby. You babblin' silly old bastard!" Goodnight was screaming at the preacher now. "Get the hell out of here! All of you!"

Judge White led the Reverend's retreat. Temple Houston followed. Pat Garrett tipped his hat to Katharane and said. "Good day, Miss Katharane Stuart." He walked away.

"What's wrong with me staying with Pop?" Katharane asked.

"Not a thing." Charles Goodnight snapped. "At least nothing those rotters have any say as to." He walked to the door. "Bose! Tom!" He called. "Bring the horses. We're leaving."

"What the hell?" The gunman stared at the young doe entangled in the barbed wire.

"Bob-wire." Katharane said, using the name the cowboys used for J. F. Glidden's wire.

The doe opened its eye and stared at Charles Goodnight, Bose, Young Tom, Reid Stuart, Katharane and the gunman.

"Sons-of-a-bitches are cuttin' these plains to hell and gone with this cursed stuff." The gunman complained. He drew his pistol and shot the doe. "Too bad it ain't that Comanchero hung up in it. He's the only livin' creature I'd wish that on." He slid his pistol back in the black holster and rode ahead, searching for a break in the wire to pass through.

"Why does Pop still trouble himself so about that Comanchero, Dad? Even if he is alive, one Comanchero is no longer a threat to us." Katharane said.

"Some things about himself a man believes in completely, Katharane. He believes he has within himself the will to do that thing which no other man can do. He knows it as much within his heart as within his mind. When he fails at that he fails himself. Failing yourself, Katharane, that's damnation. That's nothingness."

"Failing to kill a man is not damnation, Reid." Charles Goodnight said.

"Mr. Goodnight's right, Dad." Katharane argued. "It's not like he broke his word."

"For some men, failing is not owning a ranch, not building a home, not knowing a woman. It depends upon the man, Katharane. For Canada he's always known he could kill any man he chose to kill. Brutal as that sounds, it is what Canada has been about for a very long time. The Comanchero took that away from him."

"And the woman he told us about. She took that from him, too. Didn't she, Dad?" Katharane asked.

Charles Goodnight cut his eyes at Reid Stuart. "I suppose." Reid Stuart said. He did not return Charles Goodnight's look.

"But it doesn't have to be that way, Dad. Pop could find someone."

Reid Stuart frowned. "It's not that simple for him, Katharane. He let's things run so deep with him. If it comes to that, I'd send him after that Comanchero, again."

"Why?" Katharane demanded.

Reid Stuart knew why, but he answered. "Because that is something he can still do."

"He can still love someone, Dad. He can still do that, too."

"Maybe." Reid Stuart did not believe it, but he repeated. "Maybe."

Katharane put her hands on her hips and said. "Men. They are impossible." She trotted her horse ahead to overtake the gunman.

Bose chuckled. Charles Goodnight moved his horse alongside Reid Stuart's buckskin. "I was glad to hear you say you would send that damn gunman from the Escadara before you would let him jeopardize Katharane."

"I didn't say anything about Katharane. Not a word, Charles." Reid Stuart said slowly. "But I would send him away before I saw him destroy himself." He looked at Charles Goodnight and said. "Even for her."

Mary Goodnight stood in her foyer where she, Reid Stuart, Katharane, the gunman, Bose and Young Tom listened to Charles Goodnight recount the events which had transpired in Clarendon, except for the encounter at the hotel.

"Scalps?" Mary Goodnight asked.

"Yes." Charles Goodnight answered.

Mary Goodnight looked at Katharane who stared at the floor. "Katharane?" Katharane looked at Mary Goodnight. "Do you still have them?"

"Yes Mam." Katharane said very softly.

"And what do you intend to do with them?"

Katharane shrugged her shoulders.

"They are an abomination, a false tribute to your mother."

A tear came to the corner of Katharane's eye.

"They are a sign. A Comanche sign." The gunman argued.

"Whatever their value may have been as to informing this child of her mother's killers' fate, they are now a curse to her, sir." Mary Goodnight spoke directly to the gunman. "They can only serve to remind her of an experience better forgotten, not reflected upon." Mary Goodnight turned to Katharane. "Katharane, what are you to do with them?"

"I don't know, Miss Mary." Katharane murmured and looked at the floor again.

"Does anyone?" Mary Goodnight demanded of the men gathered in her home.

The men stood silent and motionless, all but the gunman, who said. "They're Katty's to do with as she chooses."

Mary Goodnight took Katharane's hands in her hands. Katharane stared into her eyes and whispered. "I don't know what to do, Miss Mary. I don't."

Mary Goodnight took a deep breath and said. "I do." Not a person moved nor seemed even to breathe. Everyone listened to Mary Goodnight, to what conflict her words might bring between her and Katharane. Young Tom prayed silently her words would not occasion a rift between her and Katharane. He relied on their attachment to afford him chances to see Katharane and to be near her. "The Escadara will dine on my veranda tonight." Mary Goodnight stressed 'my veranda'. "Katharane will sleep in her room tonight." 'Her room' echoed through the foyer. "And I ask that you make accommodations for Reid Stuart and Canada, Mr. Ikard."

"Yes mam." Bose Ikard answered politely.

"In the morning Bose, you and Young Tom will bring the horses to the house and we will all deliver those scalps to your mother's sacred place, to be left there, for only she can accept them without stain or commission, and to be forgotten there." Mary Goodnight released Katharane's hands and took the young girl's face in her hands and spoke softly, but firmly, to her. "And tomorrow, Katharane, you will make your peace with that fine and noble woman that reared and loved you, and then you will go on with your life."

Katharane's body trembled as she stepped into Mary Goodnight's arms and buried her face into Mary Goodnight's strong right shoulder and emptied all the sadness she had left for the Squaw Woman onto it.

Katharane and Young Tom stood at the edge of the far canyon. The scalps hung from the bottom of the Squaw Woman's raised sepulcher. Bose Ikard tended the campfire. Charles Goodnight, Reid Stuart and the gunman leaned against their upright saddles. It had been a tiring day for all of them. The decision to camp for the night in the far reaches of the upper Tule canyon, even with the unearthly shadow of the Squaw Woman's funeral pyre moving slowly across the canyon's floor, was welcomed by all. Mary Goodnight sat down beside her husband. "Someday Katharane may marry some young man such as our Tom, Charles." She said.

"Katty ain't gonna' marry no cowboy." The gunman muttered.

Charles Goodnight straightened up. "She may." He said angrily.

"No." The gunman said.

"What do you find so objectionable with cowboys, sir?" Mary Goodnight asked, interrupting the two men. Something she seldom did. But her husband's quick anger disturbed her. And she knew that the gunman would not yield.

"Cowboys are dead men." The gunfighter said. "'waitin' for the right horse, the one that will break their back. The right cow, the one just locoed enough that she hangs a horn through their bowels and leaves 'em bleedin' to death from their guts."

Mary Goodnight worked her lips as a thought came to her. Quietly, but loud enough that both her husband and the gunfighter would hear her, she said. "Maybe she will marry a Yankee officer."

"Shit!" The gunman snorted.

Reid Stuart laughed. "It would serve you right if she did." He said to the gunman and goosed him in the ribs with his elbow.

"'rather she married a cowboy than that." The gunman grumbled.

"It was wired care of Charles Goodnight." Charles Goodnight said. "And delivered as you see it, a single flat sheet of paper." He stood in the front room of the Escadara.

Reid Stuart folded the paper once. "Then you have read it?" He asked Charles Goodnight.

"I have." Charles Goodnight said. "What are your intentions?"

Reid Stuart chewed on the inside of his cheek. "If you and Mary Goodnight will be so gracious as to have Katharane as a guest for a month or more, then I intend for my partner and I to ride to Fort Worth and meet Mr. William Harrell's emissary, as it requests."

Before Katharane could protest her father's intention to

leave her behind, Charles Goodnight answered. "Katharane is welcome at the JA's for as long as she cares to stay. But Mary has suggested that she and Katharane should accompany the three of us to Fort Worth. And that we should travel by train as much as possible." He looked at the gunman and Reid Stuart.

"To Fort Worth!" Katharane exclaimed. To Katharane Fort Worth was the east, a city, a great city. "Dad, can we?" Katharane asked, as if she doubted even their ability to do so.

Reid Stuart frowned and he glanced at the gunfighter.

"You wanna' go to Fort Worth, Katty girl?" The gunman asked.

"Yes."

"'buy you a blue velvet dancin' dress and go to the ball?"

"Oh yes, Pop! Yes!"

The gunman looked at Reid Stuart, grinned and said. "Let's go to Fort Worth then."

Reid Stuart smiled, too. "All-right." He said.

Katharane clapped and squealed.

"They say the track has reached Harrold." Charles Goodnight said. "That's still a hundred and thirty miles east of Clarendon. We will have to travel slowly. I will not exhaust Mary."

"Oh, we will go as slow as Miss Mary likes." Katharane exclaimed. "Won't we, Pop?"

"As slow as Miss Mary likes." The gunman agreed.

Katharane stood by herself, almost out onto the dance floor. She bounced on the balls of her feet as she watched the couples dancing. She held her arms crossed at her wrists behind her back and she smiled at each young man as he crossed the floor to ask one of the bowed and bound young ladies lining the wall to dance.

"Those silly little bastards!" Mary Goodnight hissed.

"Mary!" Charles Goodnight exclaimed. "I've never heard you curse before."

"Did someone offend you, Mrs. Goodnight?" Reid Stuart asked. The gunman leaned in to hear, also.

"Yes! They all offend me, everyone one of them. Not a one will ask Katharane to dance because those silly jealous little twits have ostracized her." Mary Goodnight glared across the room at the decorated girls who congregated against the far wall.

"Well Mary, there's not much we can do about that." Charles Goodnight said.

"Yes there is." Mary Goodnight said. "Each of you will ask Katharane to dance." She looked at the three plainsmen.

They would have rather she had told them that they were to face off with each other. Reid Stuart stared at his new boots as if they were nailed to the wooden floor. Charles Goodnight rubbed his lower back as if now it hurt him a great deal. The gunman swallowed his drink with one large gulp. The band finished the song and the couples began to walk from the floor. Mary Goodnight turned upon the three men next to her. Before she could speak the gunman stepped to the middle of the room and with a voice soft and rich and strong, a voice that filled the room, stilled the crowd and sang with a gentleness of nature, a kindness of purpose that was his and Katharane's alone, he called. "Katharane Diane Stuart."

Katharane stepped forward. "That's me." She said and held her hand up as if anyone could have mistaken her.

"Will you dance with me?" The gunman asked in the same strong sultry voice, and he bowed low and swung his right arm in front of him.

"Oh yes! Yes!" Katharane cried and skipped across the floor to the gunfighter.

With a dark steely eyed glance of disdain and contempt the gunman silenced the few giggles and snickers from the young couples that had surrounded him and Katharane on the dance floor. He turned to the orchestra leader and said. "Play a waltz." With his left hand the gunfighter swung Katharane into the center of Charles Paddock's parlor floor, with his right hand he raised her left hand above her shoulder, laced his fingers through her fingers and pulled her arm away from her side. Her golden cleavage caught the sunlight that flowed through the open French doors which lead out to the garden, and her skin seemed to dance and sparkle beneath the blue velvet of the dress which the gunman had bought for her. Several of the older women whispered among themselves. The young girls, with collars buttoned to their chins, gaped at Katharane's sun darkened skin which shone deep down between her breasts. Unlike the high collared dresses of the other young women, Katharane's beautiful blue velvet party girl's dress fell off of her strong shoulders and slid dangerously far down her chest. Her dazzling brown eyes mirrored each ray of sunlight that caught upon them and threw the rays back out even brighter and more alive. She was the loveliest of all at the dance.

William Harrell counted the last few stanzas of the waltz. He balanced on the balls of his feet ready to walk out onto the dance floor when the beautiful young girl and the strange gray haired gentleman with the black holster and pistol stopped dancing. For a dance with someone as pretty and alive and different as this young girl he would overcome his shyness. The orchestra stopped. But before he could step onto the dance floor the gray haired man led the young girl to another gray haired gentleman and the girl offered her hand to him.

Reid Stuart stepped out onto the floor with Katharane, and the West Point trained former Calvary officer quickly reclaimed the grace of movement which had been drilled into him at the academy. He swept his daughter around the floor as if she had danced a thousand waltzes rather than just the previous one. Katharane laughed and gazed into her father's eyes.

Again William Harrell counted down the waltz. And again before he could step forward to ask her for the next dance the beautiful young girl was handed over to another gentleman, a white haired one.

The dignified old ranger accepted Katharane's hand from Reid Stuart, bowed stiffly to her and stepped bravely onto the floor with her. Charles Goodnight was not as skilled or as graceful as Reid Stuart, but his composure carried him through, and Katharane rewarded his courage with a warm kiss on his cheek which set the room to buzzing and his cheeks to blazing with color. Mary Goodnight laughed at her embarrassed husband.

William Harrell was within two steps of the young girl

and she was smiling at him, when a deep base voice speaking in a strange dialect caused her to turn from him. Katharane answered Kwanhah Parker in the tongue of the Kwerhar-rehunuh Comanche. She stepped to him and looked up into his face. The gunman dropped the loop from the black revolver. Reid Stuart grasped the gunfighter's hand as it closed around the butt of the black pistol. The room was silent. Katharane stared into the black eyes of the Comanche chief who stood before her dressed in a suit. Then she laid her head against his chest. Someone coughed. Katharane raised her head and spoke to the orchestra leader. "Play for us." And she and the last Comanche war chief danced together. William Harrell retreated and stood next to Mary Goodnight.

"You should ask Katharane to dance." Mary Goodnight said to the handsome young man.

"Mary." Charles Goodnight admonished his wife for her forwardness on behalf of Katharane. "Leave the young man be."

"He was trying to ask her, Charles, when Chief Kwanhah interrupted him."

"Oh."

"Then you are Charles Goodnight, sir?" William Harrell asked Charles Goodnight.

"I am. Why do you ask?"

"My name is William Harrell, sir." William offered his hand to Charles Goodnight, who shook it. Reid Stuart turned and looked at the young man. The gunfighter watched Katharane. "I am from Philadelphia. My father sent me to find a man named Reid Stuart. My father told me that Mr. Stuart might be in your company, if I should find you."

Charles Goodnight smiled and said. "William Harrell meet Reid Stuart." He put his hand on Reid Stuart's shoulder. "And by the way, that young lady you fancy is his daughter."

"Oh." William said as he extended his hand to Reid Stuart. "It is a pleasure to meet your, sir. My father considers you a very special friend."

"He should." Reid Stuart said as he shook William's hand. "My and my partner's money made him a very rich man."

"And you as well, sir." William said. "My father has invested your money well."

Reid Stuart nodded. "So he has. But not without exacting his own share of wealth from it."

"Do you feel he has been unfair?" William asked.

Reid Stuart watched his partner watch Katharane. "No. He has not been unfair."

"I'm glad to hear that, sir. My father speaks highly of you. He says you were a valiant soldier in the war."

"I was a soldier." Reid Stuart said flatly.

"I wished I had been old enough to have fought against the South." William said.

"Why?" Reid Stuart asked just as flatly.

Now the gunfighter turned and looked at William.

"Because it was a noble and just cause the North fought for, sir."

"'would've liked to have killed some Rebs, would ya'?" The gunfighter asked.

"I would have liked to have fought for the North and to have fought beside men like my father and Reid Stuart. Would you not have been proud to serve with them, too?"

The gunman turned his face back to the dance floor and Katharane and said. "I was proud to have fought against them."

The waltz ended.

"That is enough talk about the War. It's over and done." Mary Goodnight said. "Go now William. Ask Katharane to dance."

William smiled and said. "Yes mam." He walked to Katharane as Kwanhah Parker disappeared into Charles Paddock's garden with Charles Goodnight following him.

"Where's Katharane?" Reid Stuart asked.

"She's in the garden with Mr. William Harrell." Mary Goodnight said.

"I thought you would be there with her." Reid Stuart said to the gunman.

"He would. But I have forced his attention to be with me." Mary Goodnight said. "Katharane and William are supervised enough."

"All-right, Miss Mary." Reid Stuart relented.

"You two are too restless" Mary Goodnight said. "If you wish to leave I will see to Katharane."

"I thought you wanted to do some gambling." Reid Stuart said to the gunman.

The gunman frowned, puzzled by Reid Stuart's willingness to indulge his desire to gamble which Reid Stuart had scorned him for before they arrived in Fort Worth, but he answered. "'do."

"Then this would be a good time for you to do so, with Katharane occupied and Mary Goodnight willing to see after her."

"Good enough." The gunman said. "Goodnight, Mary Goodnight." He smiled at her.

"This is too much damn goodnight my husband would say." Mary Goodnight said and she returned the gunman's smile. "But, goodnight to you, sir. And to you, Mr. Reid Stuart."

Reid Stuart bowed from his waist. Then he and the gunfighter left Mary Goodnight.

Katharane and William Harrell stood ankle deep in the heavy mud in front of the dull blank two story building. They could smell the vapors which rose from the fresh piles of manure which steamed beneath the three government horses, the paint pony and a red mule which were tied to the rail in front of the weathered gray unpainted ship lapped planking of the saloon. Laughter, cursing, the frog voice of a cowboy trying to sing, and from the second floor, mixed with the voices of men, women's voices emanated from the saloon. When a woman screamed Katharane and William looked at each other in alarm. Neither had been inside a bordello. Katharane had been inside of the saloon at Tascosa, but this was a much harder place, and at Tascosa the gunman had eliminated any danger for her. Katharane moistened her lips and spoke to William. "Mr. Harrell." William Harrell stared at one of the second story windows. Katharane touched his shoulder and said. "William."

He looked at her and at first his eyes were troubled, then they glittered with anticipation as he stared at her, and he smiled.

Katharane smiled back. She could not help herself. He was young and handsome and interested in her. "William." She repeated his name. "Stay close to me." He moved against her left shoulder. For a moment Katharane thought about leaving. She had promised Mary Goodnight she and William would be mindful of where they went and that they would return within an hour. But she was now almost desperate to find her father, and the man with the Bolder hat had told her that Reid Stuart was here. She believed that man. So Katharane led William into the brothel.

To their left a bar ran the length of the wall. A Mexican man stood behind the bar. Three soldiers leaned against the bar. Two of the soldiers were young slender built boys, but the third soldier was tall and heavy set and his hair was graying at its ends. A landing overhung the bar for three-fourths of its length. A stairway descended from the far end of the landing to the wooden floor. Midway of the landing a hallway disappeared into darkness. Tables and chairs were scattered about on the planking of the floor. Men sat in the chairs and almost all of the chairs were occupied. Half-naked women, mostly girls, walked about among the tables. Katharane glanced at William. He was watching one of the almost naked girls.

The girl noticed William staring at her. She walked to him. "Hello, cowboy." She crooned and wrapped her arms around William's right arm and pressed herself to him.

William stared at his shoulder which was wedged between her naked breasts. The three soldiers now stood with their butts against the bar and watched William and the girl. Most of the men in the bar were now watching William's seduction.

"Well, cowboy?" The girl asked and pressed her pelvis against William's hand which was pressed palm flat against his holster. As she did she noticed the ivory grip of the pistol. "Pay me good and I might let you play with me with your pretty pistol." Several of the men snickered. "Well, honey?" The girl hunched herself against William's hand. "Come on, honey. I need it." The girl whispered audibly and bit his ear.

William told her and the barroom the truth. "I don't know what you mean." Laughter floated out into the hall from every corner. William prayed the girl would be merciful and would just walk away from him.

She was not merciful and she did not walk away. "Well, honey. Since you're such a pretty boy and so innocent maybe I'll show you how for free." She rubbed her nose against his cheek.

The men in the bar, bored with playing cards or sporting the girls, urged her on. This was big fun for them.

"No thank you, mam."

The bar exploded with laughter this time.

"Come on, love. Let me do it for free. I'll give it all to you."

Katharane saw the Mexican bartender's eyes move before she heard his voice. "Puta es el breed's."

The girl vanished from William's arm. The breed was a buck negro's bastard son by a quarter Choctaw and a quarter Cherokee white squaw. "Nothing is for free with one of my girls, simple boy."

Again William spoke truthfully. "I don't want anything from her."

"Sheree! My girl is not good enough for you. Eh?" The breed's eyes were cold and black and set deep into his head above his high proud Cherokee cheekbones. His father's heavy forehead rolled out over his eyebrows and his black hair was popped against his head in tightly wadded curls. "My girl is not fit to suit you, eh? You think?" He spoke with a thick and ugly borrowed Cajun accent. The dark suit he wore did little to hide the heat and smell of anger as it rose in his body.

"Your girls are fit to rut with anything." Katharane said as she caught William's arm and stepped between him and the breed, "From pigs to even you." She brought the sharp heel of her right riding boot down on the breed's left instep and steered William to the bar.

Several of the men snickered and the girl forgot herself and giggled. The breed turned upon her. She fled to the stairs and up them. The breed followed leisurely behind her. He eyed each table as he passed it. None of the men met his eyes.

"Si', la senorita." The bartender said to Katharane.

"Two beers, please."

William glanced at Katharane. She winked at him. She did not know if he had drank a beer before in his life, she had not, but she hoped that ordering the beers would take some of the attention away from her and William.

The older soldier at the bar introduced himself to Katharane. "Sergeant Miles McClinton, mam."

"Sergeant," Katharane acknowledged him. "I am Katharane Diane Stuart and this is Mr. William Harrell of Philadelphia."

The sergeant shook hands with William and as he did noticed the pistol which William wore. "'mighty fine lookin' piece you're wearin' on that right hip, son." The sergeant said as he leaned on his elbows, his back against the bar.

"Thank you, sir."

"Ever use it?"

"No sir."

The sergeant frowned. "This ain't no place to be packin' a gun you've never used. You go easy here, son."

"Yes sir."

"'mighty fine lookin' piece you've got next to you, too." The soldier closest to the sergeant said. "She your sister?"

"No." There was no change in the softness of William's voice, but he did not dignify his response with his usual 'sir'.

"She your girl?" The solder asked.

William did not answer.

"Well, she damn sure ain't your ma'." The soldier croaked.

The youngest soldier laughed. William spoke to the mirror

323

behind the bar. "No. She is not my mother either. But you would be best advised to treat her as if she is." He turned and glared at the soldier.

"Remember what I said 'bout goin' easy here, son." The sergeant said and he turned his back to the young soldier next to him and blocked his path to William.

"Yes sir." William said. He picked up his mug of beer and took a swallow and coughed.

The soldier hooted with laughter. He was anxious to provoke William. "Tastes just like horse piss. Doesn't it, sonny boy?"

"He wouldn't know. He has more sense than to drink downstream of his horse." Katharane said. She placed her left hand on William's right shoulder.

The youngest soldier laughed delightedly. "Looks like she's got you figured, Sidetrap. Once a private always a private, right, Sarge'?"

The sergeant chuckled.

"Corporal Demond Wilson of Vicksburg, Mississippi, at your service, mam." The youngest soldier said in a heavy southern accent. He swept his duck billed cap from his head.

"Thank you, corporal." Katharane said. She extended her hand to the corporal.

He took it and held it. "Now, mam, It's obvious he's not here for the sport." The corporal grinned at William. "And it's even more obvious that you're not here to work. Though, and beggin' your pardon, if you were there wouldn't be a dime left among the company here for the privilege." He continued to smile.

"There are not enough dimes among you to afford you even the privilege of holding my hand." Katharane said, and she withdrew her hand from his.

The corporal nodded. "Yes, mam. I truly admire a lady who knows her worth. Don't you, sarge'?"

The sergeant nodded and said. "And one that knows a wet eared pup when she sees one."

The corporal laughed. "So, mam, what are you here for?

Maybe we can help you?"

"I doubt it, but you might. As I said, we are looking for Reid Stuart."

"Beggin' your pardon, mam, who is Reid Stuart?"

It had not occurred to Katharane that they would not know who Reid Stuart was. "He's my father. He carries a large rifle."

"You mean that mean old coot carryin' that buffalo gun?" Corporal Wilson asked in disbelief. Before Katharane could answer a girl's piercing scream, followed by wild and panicked pleading, silenced the noisy barroom. Everyone looked at the hallway midway of the landing. William started forward.

"No, William, that isn't our concern." Katharane said and placed her hands against William's chest. She sensed that neither she nor William could stop what was happening upstairs.

The sergeant blocked the corporal's path with the back of his arm. "You boys listen to the young lady. You get in between that mongrel breed and his bitch and he'll cut your spleens out."

Another piercing scream shattered the stillness, followed by a moan and a gagging plea. "No. No. Please, please. Take it out." Then only the sounds of the sobs of the girl as she cried broke the silence in the barroom. But quickly the busy barroom again filled with its customary noise and drowned out the sounds of the sobbing girl.

"Well. There's your man, mam." Corporal Wilson pointed at the bottom of the stairway where Reid Stuart limped from a doorway beneath the landing's stairway He carried his old Sharps rifle to a table almost hidden behind the stairway. He sat at the table, laid the Sharps across his knees, moved a half empty whiskey bottle to one side and took his tobacco pouch from his shirt pocket. He studied the empty pouch and frowned.

He looked up and called loudly. "Barkeep, tobacco, por favor." Then he saw William. "William Harrell, is that you?" He asked incredulously. "What in the world are you doing in this whorehouse?"

"William is in this whorehouse because he is helping me find you!" Katharane cried.

"Damn boy! Why'd you bring Katharane here?"

"I didn't, sir. She brought me." William replied.

The sergeant chuckled again and shook his head and said. "You sure tell it straight out. Don't you, son?"

"Yes sir."

A heavyset colored woman rumbled down the stairs and hurried to the bar. "Miguel! Send for the sheriff. The breed says he is going to kill the old man." She pointed at Reid Stuart. "Be quick with you now! Soon as he is finished with Carla he will be down."

"Why does he want to kill my father?" Katharane asked angrily.

"Because the old man has had two of the breed's youngest girls and has not paid, not once! He even talked Carla into it twice. The breed is raging mad." The old negro midwife warned.

"You best get your father and leave, Miss." The sergeant advised Katharane who stood staring silently at her father.

"Yes. You are right." William replied for Katharane. "Katharane, get your father and we will go." He touched Katharane's arm as he spoke. Together they started to go to Reid Stuart.

But the breed stepped from the stairway and stood between them and Reid Stuart. He was furious, but he spoke calmly in his acquired accent. "But Sheree. You would not want him to leave without paying me. After all I have done for him."

"I did for myself, that's what I did. And I didn't have to use a device to make them cry." Reid Stuart taunted the breed, hoping to draw him away from Katharane and William.

The anger rose in the breed. But he knew that Reid Stuart carried the buffalo gun. "Quiet, my friend. Your time to die will come soon." He called over his shoulder, but he did not turn his head. He would have to play the hand out further if he hoped to have his chance to kill Reid Stuart. The breed smiled. Maybe the old man would be foolish enough to come to the girl. "But Sheree, I have forgotten my manners. This is not your concern, is it?" The breed crooned. "Forgive me, Sheree." He extended his hand to Katharane.

Katharane noticed a thick cord of blood on the back of his hand. The breed saw her looking at the bloody cord. "Sorry,

Sheree, I should have cleaned myself better." He raised his hand to his mouth and slowly lifted the bloody cord from the back of his hand with his lips.

Katharane felt the nausea come up into her throat. But she stopped it there. Then she felt her face flush. She was suddenly keenly aware of William's presence, and she was embarrassed, as if he had witnessed some perverse intimacy between her and the breed and now she stood accountable to William for what he had witnessed. This thought humiliated her. Anger, blind, bitter and more personal to her than any biological intimacy, flowed through her mind. From one of the few truly dark places in her psyche a fury swelled in her, as uncontrollable as the tide is to the sea. She slapped the breed in the face. It was a stinging cracking slap. It was as powerful a blow as Katharane could throw unarmed. Her open palm cracked against the breed's left cheek and the color came up under his eye instantly.

The barroom was spellbound. This bold young woman had crossed all boundaries now. The breed might have accepted a blow from a man. But he would never accept being slapped by a woman. He mastered women by physical intimidation, by brutality, by torture if necessary. He could not allow any woman to strike him and walk away. He moved at Katharane. Katharane took a step back and stood beside William.

"I'm not holdin' with any man doin' over a lady." Corporal Wilson said. He started for the breed. The breed's left hand moved from his side to his waist band and at the advancing soldier like the strike of a snake, movement without motion. And the snake's tongue was smoke, burnt powder and hot lead. But it took the second barrel of the Derringer to stop the young corporal. He fell face forward onto the wet muddy floor boards of the bar, dead.

Reid Stuart slammed the butt of the Sharps against his shoulder and cocked its hammer. But he could not shoot the breed without the risk that the bullet would pass through him and hit Katharane or William. "Kill the son've a bitch, boy! Kill him now!" Reid Stuart cursed.

William's hand was on his pistol. He cocked its hammer. Then, he hesitated. Before the dead corporal's body hit the floor, as Reid Stuart cursed him and William hesitated, the enraged breed moved on Katharane. He held the smoking empty Derringer in his left hand, with his right hand he drew a gleaming white steel stiletto from his waist band. "Let's see how well this whore ruts with the blade." The breed sneered as he dropped his right hand to his side.

William saw the flash of the stiletto's steel. "What?" The word formed on his lips. But he could not speak.

"Kill him! Dammit, boy! Kill him!" Reid Stuart screamed. He jumped to his feet, but he was too far from the breed to stop him.

The breed was within a step of Katharane. She placed both of her hands on the top of the table behind her which barred any retreat. She stood as if to receive the knife. But still her eyes flashed hate and spite at the breed and her proud voice spit curses at him. "Bastard!"

"Baudet debaucher." The breed snarled into her face.

"Bastard." Katharane spat the word at the breed again, straight into his face, damning him, humiliating him and infuriating him.

The blade started forward. But the breed was not as quick with his knife as the black hatted man who had walked quickly from the bar's door to Katharane was on his feet. As Katharane felt the man move between her and the breed, as she saw the thick tangled curls that wove their way down the back of his head and onto his shirt collar, as she smelled the sweet familiar scent of his body she knew him and she screamed. "No, Pop! No!"

The knife ripped into the gunman's right hip. The breed set his feet to jerk the knife free. But the gunman locked the breed's hand and the knife against his hip with his right elbow and gripped the breed's right arm just above the elbow. Katharane could smell the stink of the breed's sweat as it mixed with the residue of the young whore's wetness he had just left. She could feel the firmness of the gunman's shoulders, the warmth of his buttocks and the softness of his hair.

The breed twisted the knife into the gunman's hip. He would cut his way free of this fool. And then he would gut him. The pain would slacken the man's grip and fear would speed his surrender. The breed knew this. He had killed men with his knife. He met the gunman's eyes, and the breed caught his breath. There was no fear there, only hate, a hate deeper and truer than the breed had ever seen in any man's eyes. He had seen such hate in a woman's eyes, but never in a man's. Such a hate could only come from love. Suddenly the breed realized that the man in front of him was not some 'good Samaritan' interloper, but this man knew this beautiful girl and he loved her, not a love garnered from lying with her, not a love known to the girl nor even the man, but still a love that was real and that was powerful. Now fear, deep and weakening, shown in the breed's eyes. This man felt no pain. His grip did not slacken. He did not cry from the searing pain of the stiletto ripping his flesh apart. Panic danced in the breed's dark eyes.

Katharane saw the breed's eyes change and she misread this change. She thought the breed had another weapon. "Kill him, Pop. Kill him for me." Katharane breathed the words into the gunman's ear.

The breed's eyes opened wide. His mouth dropped open. He stared, open mouthed as he watched a softness pass across the gunman's eyes at the sound of the girl's voice in his ear, the touch of her breath upon his face. The breed cried out, a trapped dying animal's cry, wild and anguished and devoid of hope. The gunman jammed the barrel of his black pistol into the breed's right side and squeezed its trigger. The breed's knees popped and locked straight. He lost his grip on his knife. The gunman pushed the breed back a step. He recocked the black revolver, shoved the hot barrel into the breed's right eye and against the bridge of his nose and squeezed the trigger again.

Katharane clasped her arms around the gunman and buried her face into the back of his head. The sergeant, kneeling above his dead corporal, turned his head away and whispered. "Christ." The young whore at the railing on the landing above the bar moaned. "Oh God. Oh God. Oh God." The bartender gasped and crossed himself and prayed. "Sweet mother of Jesus protect us."

The breed lay on his back, the top right one fourth of his head was blown away.

It had happened in less than a minute and a half. In less than ninety seconds the breed had hated, killed for that hate and died for that hate. The gunman had loved, hated and killed for that love.

KATHARANE DIANE STUART
PHILADELPHIA, 1886

"How will Pop take it, Dad?"

Reid Stuart frowned.

"Surely he knew I would marry someday."

"I suppose he did." Reid Stuart said. "But just because he knows something does not mean he accepts it." Reid Stuart rubbed at the hard dirt with the toe of his boot.

Katharane adjusted the tight buckskin leggings which the gunman had made for her. "He will accept it, Dad. He will. I know he will." Katharane said. "And he will be happy for me." She squeezed her father's left arm against her chest.

Reid Stuart tried not to smile, but he did smile. He smiled and said. "Maybe so." The sound of a horse climbing up the trail from the Ceta interrupted Katharane and Reid Stuart. The bay colt, hot and tired, walked slowly to the spring. The gunman swung down from the colt, dropped his reins and ambled slowly around the back of the colt. The gunman let his left shoulder bump against the colt. The young horse lifted its left hind leg to kick at the gunman. The gunman's left hand shot into the colt's flank. The horse set its left hind foot back onto the hard packed ground. The gunman moved slowly on to Katharane and Reid Stuart.

"Pop. Let's ride out to the point above where the Ceta meets the big canyon."

"I've been a horseback twenty miles today, Katty."

"Twenty." Reid Stuart chided him.

"Ten anyways." The gunman grumbled. "'sides. 'gonna' need that filly fresh tomorrow."

"She'll be fresh enough." Reid Stuart said. "You rest a minute while I unsaddle that colt and saddle your filly."

"'unsaddle and saddle my own goddamn horses, thank you very much, Reid Stuart." The gunman muttered as he limped back to the colt.

The gunman could not believe he could feel it again, as acute, as real, as brutal as before. The gunfighter sniffed the air and smelled it. His skin prickled and bumped up from it. His throat grew hot and dry from it. His heart and his mind ached from it. The old ghostly vapors of desperate loneliness rose up from the prairie beneath the black filly's hooves and settled around the tired gunfighter. He looked out to the Ceta, the canyon to which he had come to escape it the first time, and ... "Our canyon is beautiful. Isn't it, Pop? Do you think William will learn to love it like we do?" ...it was gone, taken from him by Katharane's words. "Pop?" There were no other canyons to escape to this time. The plains were littered with the sod turners now and the barbed wire turned a horse every twenty miles or so. "Pop? Did you hear me?"

"Yes, Katty, yes, I heard you."

"Well! Do you think William will love our canyon, too?" Katharane demanded.

The gunman reached down and felt the smooth hard walnut grip of the black pistol. It was still there. It was still his. He squeezed it. It felt good. He still had it. He could still use it, and probably better than any man alive. He could still do that. "Maybe, Katty, maybe he will." The hurting gunman answered the girl for whom he had given up all he had, everything that was a part of him, everything but the black pistol.

Katharane put her hand on the gunman's left shoulder. "He will, Pop, I know he will." Katharane said happily. For a breath or two, a short few tastes of air, the gunman took in the touch for which he lived. "It will be so nice to have William with us." Katharane took her hand away. "Do you think he will want to live here?" She asked worriedly.

The cruel hope which their time together had festered within him that this touch and these moments of their lives might be his alone wavered away from him down into the canyon's lost crevices to be forever hidden from him, but not his love for the girl. Quietly, gently, sadly he said. "He'll come." He tried to smile at her in his flinching manner. "For you."

"Oh, Pop! You're so sweet." Katharane laughed. "Come on. Let's ride the edge of the canyon together."

"Move away from the edge a little, Pop." Katharane called to the gunfighter. "You're too close. You're frightening me."

The gunman ignored her. He pushed the filly out of her long lope and into a strong gallop. Her hooves scattered dust and pebbles off of the lip of the canyon and sent them clattering down the steep sides of the Ceta.

"Pop. Please!" Katharane pleaded. She chased after him, keeping her mustang safely away from the rim of the Ceta.

The black filly's hooves seemed to hang suspended above the deep canyon as she gathered them beneath her in her wild gallop, just to find the slightest grip along the canyon's lip as she stretched out to gather her feet beneath her again. Katharane cried and pushed her hands against the mustang's neck. But she knew her little horse could not catch the flying filly. Reid Stuart stood at the horse corrals with Juan Romero and Juan's boy and watched the gunman slowly turn away from the edge of the canyon and lope into the corrals.

"Vamalos! Andale pronto." Juan Romero said to his son. He followed slowly after the boy who ran to the stone bunkhouse beyond the corrals and the barn.

"Damn you! Pop." Katharane cried. "You did that on purpose. You did it just to frighten me!" She jumped from the mustang and ran to the house.

Reid Stuart caught the mustang's reins. "You know better than to run that horse that close to the edge of the canyon." He said to the gunfighter.

The gunfighter jerked the cinch on the black filly's saddle loose. "'don't need you pissin' at me 'bout riskin' my neck, too, Stuart." The gunman muttered.

"It's not risking your neck that I'm pissing at you about. It's about risking that horse, needlessly." Reid Stuart said. "And Katharane's feelings."

The gunman spun around and faced Reid Stuart. "I'd never do anything to hurt Katty and you damn well know it." He gripped the black revolver. "Or you damned well better learn it. And quick."

"You just did." Reid Stuart said. He watched the gunman's hand on the pistol. "If you intend to use that thing get to it." He said. "I will not wait all night for you to decide."

The gunman released his grip on the pistol. "'don't see what I did to hurt her feelin's, no how." He turned his back to Reid Stuart and continued to unsaddle the filly.

"She wants to marry William." Reid Stuart said.

"So she told me."

"Do you think he will ask her?"

"If he's got a lick of sense in that feeble head of his, which is damned suspect, he will." The gunman answered. He pulled the saddle and the blanket off of the filly at the same time. The filly stepped forward. "Whoa! Damn you." He cursed the little horse.

"It won't matter if he does if she thinks you're opposed to it." Reid Stuart said. He put his hand on the filly's nose.

"You askin' me to give my blessin's to Katty marryin' that Yankee?" The gunman asked as he flung the saddle and blanket over the top cedar rail of the upper horse corral.

Reid Stuart dropped his head and said. "I guess I am asking you to do that. I wouldn't ask as much from any other man but I am asking that of you, my friend." He put his right hand on the gunman's right shoulder. "And Katharane is. Katharane is asking you to do that for her." Reid Stuart squeezed the gunman's bony shoulder. "It's all she knows to do. She cannot be certain of this. How could she, with just you and I to teach her about these feelings? And you and I, Canada, are damn short on expertise or successes in these matters."

The gunman sighed. "That's for sure."

"What Katharane does know is to ask you to tell her its okay for her to do this. That's all she knows to do. That's what she needs to have any confidence to travel more than fifteen hundred miles by herself..."

"What the hell you mean, by her self?" The gunman demanded. "You're goin' too."

"No."

"Why, in the name of what's holy, not?"

"There's reason."

"Dammit! Stuart!"

Reid Stuart took his hand from the gunman's shoulder and cupped both of his hands around the gunman's neck, trapping the heavy curls that hung there against the leathery neck beneath them. He bent forward until his face almost touched the gunman's face and said, "Do you remember that night we hid in the crevices and listened to the Kiowa torture that old mustanger and the boy?"

"I remember." The gunman said slowly.

"You told me there were things about us we could not ask each other. There was no reason for it, that it was just that way and had to be left that way."

The gunman nodded.

"I cannot go back. Not with Katharane. That is one of those things even you cannot ask me about. But Katharane must go. It is not for the likes of you nor I to decide this for her. Right or wrong, she must go. I cannot go with her. I cannot even help her decide to go. But you can." Reid Stuart bowed his head. "Forgive me, my old friend. I vowed I would never ask anything of you for Katharane which you did not willingly give. Not after she brought you back from New Mexico. And until now I don't think I ever have."

"You were there too, Stuart."

"Yes. I was. But I would have left you to die." Reid Stuart raised his head and looked into his partner's eyes. "Do you understand? I would have rode away and left you to die."

The gunman chewed on the inside of his mouth. "So? I'd a shot you, Stuart. Then I'd a rode away."

"I know you would have. Because that's the way you are. You would have done what you saw to be the right thing to do. I let Katharane bring you back with promises of things she could not give to you, whether those promises were spoken between you or not. Promises of things she could not even have comprehended then. But I did. I comprehended. I knew what she and her body were telling you. I knew."

The gunman stiffened.

"I knew how much that would tempt you to live, even if within your heart you knew it would never be. Just the slightest whisper of it made you cheat eternity when a thousand others would have died the first day. And now she's taking even that whisper away. And now I'm asking you to help her do it. And I know you would not ask that of me. Forgive me for this or not, I am asking you to do this for Katharane."

The gunman raised his chin and listened. "Do you hear it, Stu'?"

Reid Stuart listened to the silence.

"The wind's layin', Stu'. The wind's layin'." The gunman gripped Reid Stuart's wrists. "I never thought you could ask more of me than I could give when it came to Katty." The gunman shut his strong hands around Reid Stuart's wrists. "I never thought you could find something of me I couldn't bear to give to Katty." He swallowed. "But to ask me to give her up, would you ask that of any other man?"

"No." Reid Stuart said. "But I am asking it of you. I have to."

The gunman released Reid Stuart's wrists. "Then you may ask too much, too much." He turned again to the filly and unbridled her. Reid Stuart walked to the spring, knelt upon his knees and drank from his cupped hands. Finished with the filly the gunman unsaddled Katharane's mustang and gently rubbed its back, peeling away the sweat and the loose hair and the dirt, currying Katharane's little horse with the rough worn outside edge of his hand. The gunman's black filly stood hot and unkempt and pawed at the corral's hard dirt.

The guests turned in their chairs which sat twelve abreast, separated six and six by the wide aisle carpeted by the tutored grass which covered Harrell House's back yard and stared at the beautiful young woman who stood next to Charles Goodnight at the back of their assembly. She wore the whitest of doe skins, tied loosely at her sides with buckskin lace the color of sun bleached driftwood, the lace leaving glimpses of bronze luxurious skin between the laces and each edge of the buckskins which these laces struggled to hold together across her bosom and her buttocks. Her hair was pulled back into a single woven auburn braid. She wore roughly crafted white moccasins on her feet. And around her neck, on a length of buckskin, hung three brightly colored stones, which seemed to disappear between her almost exposed breasts as she breathed.

Katharane looked at the gathering of people, dressed in tailored finery, staring at her. She raised her eyes to the sky, folded her arms across her stomach and allowed her mind to drift to the edge of the Ceta, where the spring trickled out of the canyon wall and ran down into the first rock reservoir. She could feel the gentle eastern breeze tuck the soft doe skin gown around her legs which stretched its gentle touch across her buttocks. Again in her mind, she could see the rising sun shoot its rays across the far canyon and up the Ceta. She began a soft rhythmical chant that grew louder and stronger as she remembered how the sun rose out of the canyon and the early morning wind came up off of the plains. It was a strange and mournful chant, filled with the lyrics of the wind as it played through the strings of the canyons, rising and falling across the sandstone formations, losing itself in the small box canyons, but always rolling farther and farther and father down the belly of the big canyon, across the Prairie Dog Town Fork to the place where the black buffalo soldiers had engaged the Comanche's, crying as the Comanche's had cried when their wild mustangs had screamed from the hurt and the surprise of the buffalo soldiers rain of gunfire upon them, then rumbling low and distant like the sound of the hooves of the great herds of the buffalo, rumbling till it was gone or renewed by a new and piercing wail which echoed against the high canyon's walls.

"Katharane!" William Harrell, Sr. stood and tried to interrupt her symphonic chant.

"Be silent." Charles Goodnight commanded.

"What is she doing?" William Harrell, Sr. asked.

"She's praying." The old plainsman said softly.

"But I've never heard a prayer like this." William Harrell,

Sr. whispered.

"It is a Comanche prayer, a prayer to the new sun, the early day wind and to the spirits of the buffalo and the canyon." Charles Goodnight explained.

"My God! Where did this child learn such a thing?" Margaret Harrell exclaimed. She had moved to her husband's side.

"From the Squaw Woman." Charles Goodnight answered without taking his eyes away from Katharane. "You're son is a very lucky young man, Mrs. Harrell. I hope he has the good sense not to thwart that luck by seeking to change what he doesn't understand about this beautiful young woman." Now Charles Goodnight spoke directly to William Harrell, Sr. "Katharane will love your son. But he must not expect her to love him alone, be he her husband or not." The old man walked to Katharane and took her hand and drew it through the crook of his arm. "Come Katharane. We have your wedding to attend to."

Katharane gazed at Charles Goodnight and said. "My mama would have sung it had she been here."

"I know, child. I know she would. Now it is left to this old plainsman and you. Let us make your mama proud." Together Charles Goodnight and Katharane Diane Stuart marched forward to meet William Harrell, Jr.

The gunman's little black filly was game and blessed with quick early speed. For the first couple of miles the gunman had to glance over his shoulder and rein the filly in to keep from becoming separated from Reid Stuart and the big long gaited buckskin horse he rode. But by the time he and Reid Stuart had caught sight of the high point above the Canadian River the gunman's filly was behind Reid Stuart's buckskin and losing ground to the buckskin with each stride. When Reid Stuart reached the point above the Canadian he eased his horse to a stop, turned and waited for the gunman. He sat with his hands folded on top of the saddle horn as the filly stumbled to a stop next to his buckskin. The filly was almost done in, her flanks were white with sweat and she sucked for air.

"'guess you were right, I should've left 'em go with those three horses of our's they had stolen. But I never could stomach a horse thief." The gunman said. He pushed his hat back and said.

"'sure pissed 'em off when I shot our horses out from under 'em. Too bad I didn't notice the other dozen of 'em comin' up over the rise before I did my shootin'.'"

Reid Stuart nodded and said. "Too bad."

The gunman looked over his shoulder, again. The renegades were closing on him and Reid Stuart quickly now. But, as men accustomed to battle do, he moved and spoke slowly. "Maybe they'll stay bunched." The renegades did not stay grouped. They broke into three separate units. "That cuts it for us staying here, Stu'." The gunman said.

"Yep."

The three groups of renegades had positioned themselves so that they isolated Reid Stuart and the gunman on the bluff. The Canadian River was behind and maybe twenty feet below them. It carried maybe three, three and a half feet of water and it ran about twenty yards wide. All along the high point where Reid Stuart and the gunman sat on their horses its bank was a sheer dirt bluff. The gunman and Reid Stuart walked their horses to the edge of the bluff and looked down at the river. Reid Stuart looked at the gunman and asked. "Well?"

The gunman looked at Reid Stuart and said. "Hell."

The two men, so long at one another's side, bound by a myriad of common thoughts, acted as one man, their spurs hit their horses' soft underbellies simultaneously. The buckskin slid down the straight off river bank on its side and hip. The little filly seemed to fly down it. She hit the water before she slowed. By that time the buckskin was charging through the water. "Come on!" Reid Stuart yelled to the gunman.

"Bless her heart, she's tryun'!" The gunman yelled back. The filly might have made it, too, if she had not hit the quicksand. She was only ten steps from the other side of the Canadian when the bottom fell out from under her. She was belly deep in the quicksand before the gunman realized what had happened. He should have quit her then, but he hated to let her go like that, so he ripped her with his Spanish spurs. The filly surged against the relentless sucking of the quicksand. The gunman felt her go. She gasped, her entire body shuddered and her head dropped into the roiling water. The gunman jerked his Winchester free from its saddle scabbard and slid face first into the water upstream of his horse. The filly rolled and for just a moment freed from the quicksand by her roll her belly glistened wet and reflective in the high sun above and then she was gone. The gunman was waist deep and sinking deeper into the water and the quicksand when Reid Stuart's lariat hit him across his shoulders. The buckskin made the far bank, carrying Reid Stuart and towing the gunman. Then he quit. He stood with his legs spread and his head down and his body trembling.

The gunman leaned against the buckskin's rump. "I lost her, Stu'." The old gunfighter said. His eyes showed his sadness. "I lost my little filly that Katty gave me." He said it like it was a confession.

Reid Stuart put his hand on his partner's shoulder. A bullet splattered into the murky rolling water of the Canadian behind them. The renegades milled along the edge of the bluff which the gunman and Reid Stuart had just careened down. They shot at the buckskin again. Reid Stuart drug the buckskin by the reins and the gunman pushed and slapped the buckskin's rump until they got the horse behind two large boulders and out of the reach of the renegades' rifles. They crawled back to some smaller boulders nearer the river. Reid Stuart laid his big Sharps rifle in front of him and between two of the boulders. The gunman laid his Winchester at his side. They watched the renegades on the bluff.

The renegades were arguing. Their leader, a short stocky Indian, waved his arms and gestured at the river. The argument continued for several minutes. Finally, a young Indian turned his mount and rode away from the edge of the bluff. The young Indian raced past the group and off of the bluff at an angle. But he was not as lucky as Reid Stuart and the gunman, halfway down the cliff his horse began to roll side over side. The young Indian managed to stay separated from his horse and slide on his butt and back down the cliff. He and his horse hit the bottom together and again the young Indian was unlucky. He came to his feet between his horse and the river.

Reid Stuart had already leveled the big Sharps gun on the horse. But he hesitated when he saw the young Indian's back in his sights. The Indian was a boy, maybe in his early teens, but no older than fourteen. The gunman did not hesitate. The Winchester

339

slug was slow and it dropped quickly. But the gunman had allowed for a four to six inch drop by aiming at the base of the boy's skull. The bullet hit the boy between his shoulders like a sledge hammer. It drove him into the side of his horse. The horse bolted away. The Indian boy fell forward onto his hands and knees. He crawled to the base of the bluff and pulled himself to his feet and tried to climb the bluff. He could not. His back was covered with blood and dirt. He almost blended into the red and brown clay of the bluff. He bent his head back and looked to the top of the bluff and a wild, piercing, frightened cry echoed against the bluff and reverberated back into the canyon of the Canadian. The renegades on the top of the bluff answered him with several yelps and some derisive hoots, and then they turned and rode away to the south. His fate had deterred them from trying the bluff.

"Are you going to finish him?" Reid Stuart asked.

"We can't afford to waste any bullets. They rode south. They're headin' for the crossin' nearer the Walls. They ain't given up, yet." The young Indian boy had slumped to his knees. "And he ain't no threat to us. That bullet knocked a hole in his back you could put your fist in. He's dyin'. And I ain't sparin' another bullet killin' a dyin' Indian when we may need all we got to kill some live ones." The Sharps' report almost deafened the gunfighter and it ended the boy's suffering.

Reid Stuart and the gunman waited until dark to avoid pot shots from any of the renegades who might have dropped back for that purpose. Then they eased their way back to the buckskin and led him up a dry draw to a high mesa above the river. The draw would be between them and the morning's rising sun and they would be on the highest ground. It was the best place from which to fight. They sat in the dark, back to back. The gunman had the Winchester across his lap and his black revolver in his holster as always. Reid Stuart had the old Sharps across his lap. The gunman had one shell short of a full magazine in his Winchester, five rounds in the cylinder of the black revolver and six more rounds on his gun belt. Reid Stuart had twenty-four rounds of the fifty caliber shells in the old leather pouch tried to his belt and one round in the chamber of the Sharps. The gunman felt Reid Stuart's bony shoulder blades against his. He leaned the back of his head against Reid Stuart's.

"Do you think we will see another sunrise?" Reid Stuart asked.

"Hell, Stu'." The gunman answered. "I never figgered' on makin' it past forty and since I have I sorta' figger' it's like I'm cheatin' on my mortality anyway."

"Not me. I intend to live to be a hundred and forty."

Each rested the back of his head against the back of the other's head.

"Stu'?"

"Yes."

"Who would you rather have with you on this godforsaken point?"

"I can't think of anyone."

"Yaw, 'guess we'd both stick out to the end in a fight."

"No. You would. That's the difference between you and me. I might stick with you as long as you were alive. But if you were dead I'd ride out of here on that buckskin. Not you. You would fight it out to the death."

"You wanna' ride out, Stu'?"

"You're damn right I want to ride out."

The gunman chuckled. "Then why don't ya'?"

"Because you are not dead, not yet."

"Maybe I am. Maybe I am."

"No, you're not. You are hurting too much to be dead."

"'never said I was hurtin'."

"I know when you're hurting. I've been there before with you. You're in love with Katharane. And because you are, you are hurting. But you will live. And when you're seventy, and despite what you think now, you will be seventy, you will look back and see these as the best of our times together as long as you don't cut Katharane and me off from you in the meantime."

"'reckon Katty's married by now?"

"I 'reckon." Reid Stuart said. Over the years spent riding with the gunman Reid Stuart had acquired a few of the peculiarities of the gunman's speech. Occasionally he dropped a preposition from the beginning of a sentence or a consonant from the end of a word.

"Damn."

"What could you do about that now?"

"I could kill him."

"No."

"You gonna' stop me?" The gunman asked. "'cause if you're thinkin' about tryun' me you'd better hurt me quick. If I get inside I'll kick your scrawny ass." And with his left elbow the gunman goosed Reid Stuart in the ribs.

Reid Stuart flinched, chuckled and said. "I don't doubt that. But I'm not fighting you. No more than you will kill William. You could not do that to Katharane."

"Then what do we do?"

"What we are good at. We raise cattle."

"And that's gonna' be enough?"

"No." Reid Stuart said. "But it's something."

The gunman could feel every breath he and Reid Stuart took. He could hear the river as it warbled below them. He could see the prairie as it evaporated into blackness all around them and the stars which seemed to be everywhere in the night sky. And he felt an emptiness within greater than the one he and Reid Stuart sat in the midst of, an emptiness filled only by an aching doubt. "Am I really so hard to love, Stuart? Am I?"

"Yes. You make it pretty damn hard."

"How do I make it hard? I'd give 'em anything. I put everything I am into it."

"I know you do." Reid Stuart said.

"Then why?"

"You're like that black filly. She was a fine animal. She

put my buckskin to shame. She put everything she had into that run. But she gave too much. She put too much of herself at risk. Her heart burst. She was dead before she went under in that quicksand. You just cannot do that. You must not do that." Reid Stuart was silent for a moment, then he said, "Yes. That filly was a fine animal. But a lot of whether we get out of here alive depends on my buckskin having held enough back to carry us out of here tomorrow."

"Maybe, but if we do get out of here alive, it will be the black filly we talk about five years from now. We'll remember her and the run she made, and we'll have to scratch our heads and think in order to remember whether it was a buckskin or a bay that you were riding."

A lone coyote called from far out on the dark prairie. Reid Stuart and the gunman listened to its repetitive lyrics as they rose high then fell soft and low as they floated across the plains.

"When do you think they will hit us?" Reid Stuart asked.

"You know the answer to that as well as I do, Stu'. If they're comin' back, they'll send a couple in tonight. 'try to catch us nappin', 'slit our throats. If we get those two before they get us, then the rest of 'em will come hellin' in here 'round half past sun up."

A soft wind came up off of the prairie and brought the smell of sage and the odors of the buffalo wallows at the bend of the Canadian slowly wafting across Reid Stuart and the gunman. Reid Stuart bent his head forward and said. "I always wished I could be like you. Just not give a damn what anyone thinks. Always be able to stand just beyond the fire."

The gunman sighed. "Sometimes standing just beyond the fire hurts more than being in the fire."

The breeze rose up and over the mesa and Reid Stuart and the gunman, and fell down into the rising river behind them. "The fire hurts plenty, my friend." Reid Stuart said slowly. "It can keep a man away from his daughter's wedding."

"But at least you know how it feels. I've managed to stay away from it for the most part. But for that stayin' away, I've only come close to knowin' a pretty lady once, and never as you've known one."

The night and the two men became quiet. Reid Stuart and the gunman were able to be with each other and at the same time to be alone. It was a gracious solitude built upon many years of trust, upon enumerable incidents of placing their well being completely in the other's care. This solitude and Reid Stuart's and the gunman's common spirit brought long buried feelings to the surface. The gunman spoke first. "When I fuck up, I fuck up royally."

"That's true. But that's just you. You can't help that."

"This ain't easy for me, Stu'."

"I know that, too."

"I don't know how not to be in love with Katty. I don't know how to do that."

"Again, that's not something you can help. It's just the way you are. But you can learn to live with it."

"Can I, Stu'?" The gunman sighed. "God, for Katty, I pray I can."

Reid Stuart did not answer. He dropped his chin against his folded hands. The darkness and the waiting would have worn out most men until they cradled themselves in their own arms and whimpered until their failing nerve finally caused them to wander out into the night and perish. But the feel of their shoulders against the other's held the two old friends posted on that high ground, waiting patiently for morning to free them or destroy them.

"Do you see that star on the far point of the bigger dipper?" Reid Stuart pointed at a bright star on the end of the handle of the big dipper.

"Yes. I see it."

"Do you know the first time I noticed that star in this country?"

"No."

"The night you rode out after the Squaw Woman's death. I had stayed up thinking most of the night. It was probably about this time and I was wondering if you had left for good and wondering when you fucked up who would back your play, and I looked up and saw it, brighter than the other three and the farthest out, running the point, a little more distance between it and the third star than there was between any of the other three. And each early summer while you were gone when I would first spot it in the constellation in the lower part of the northern sky I would start watching the horizon and wondering." Reid Stuart paused. "You are that star, old friend, a little farther out on the point than the rest, you have to burn a little brighter than the rest or you get lost."

The breeze died away. The gunman felt inside of his shirt and found the smoke that he had rolled for Reid Stuart and shoved there when he had spotted the horse thieves. He took it out and pulled a match from his other shirt pocket. He put the smoke between his lips, bent his head down to his chest, struck the match on his thumb nail and lit the smoke. He handed the smoke across his left shoulder to Reid Stuart.

"What the..."

"Smoke?"

"Christ! They may spot the glow."

"Fuck 'em. By now they know we're here or they're not gonna' know."

It was all the excuse Reid Stuart needed. He took the smoke and pulled a drag on it.

"How many times have you hated me, Stu'?"

"Just once. Just once." Reid Stuart took another puff from his smoke.

The gunman felt him exhale it slowly. "Well, that's fewer times than I've hated myself."

The night was everywhere. "You owed me better and you knew it. That's the only reason, you know?" When the gunman did not answer Reid Stuart continued. "You could not accept being you. What you thought you saw in Katharane was just a reflection of your own needs and you managed to get blinded by the light of that mirror."

"Like hell, Stu'. One thing I did do was to look myself in the eye."

"But you didn't see what was really there, all you saw was Katharane not being there the way you wanted her. You never once saw that you were still there and that's what counts. Being there, going on, doing something because you can, loving someone just because you could." Reid Stuart shook his head. "You take off after a bunch of killers alone because you're in love, stay gone two years chasing them down, killing them and what did it get you? You damn nigh hung for it. And I'll be damned if you did not come back still in love with her. You have sure spent a lot of time and effort being in love not to be any better at it than you are." Reid Stuart drew a deep drag from his smoke and let it out slowly. "Goddamn you." He cursed the gunman softly. "You did it. You loved her in spite of yourself and her. I couldn't have done it. I wouldn't have done it. I admire you for that."

They sat there, waiting the night out, and at last the gunman saw himself as he was: much weaker than most men, searching, always looking for something from those around him that even he did not have the strength to give. At last he knew as Reid Stuart knew, it was Reid Stuart's strength the gunman had drawn on all these years. At last the old gunfighter knew that whatever future he was to have it was to be had with Reid Stuart.

"I cannot believe we are spending our wedding night on a train." William complained. "What difference would one day make?"

"It would mean one more day before I reach the Escadara." Katharane said. "Besides we have a sleeper cabin. What more do you want for your wedding night than me and a place to sleep together?"

"And you spent so much just to buy that black filly. You could have saved us half again and bought the sorrel and she has a better blood line."

"Pop does not ride a sorrel. He rides a black. And I spent not one dime of your's, William."

Now, if he persisted, they would argue. William had no desire to fight with his beautiful young wife on his wedding night. He wanted something very different from her and this he could and did demand. He reached for her and pulled her to him and this time she submitted.

Katharane folded her arms underneath her breasts. She trembled. It had been her first time. No great revelation had come from it, but one, that she was before and remained Katharane Diane Stuart and that was whom she wished to remain. "William." Katharane stared into the passing darkness beyond the window of their sleeping berth. "William." She called louder.

William Harrell stirred from his satiated sleep. "What? What is it?" He mumbled.

"I have decided."

"You have decided what?"

"I have decided to remain Katharane Diane Stuart."

William ground his teeth. "You are my wife."

"Yes. I am."

"My wife's name is Harrell."

"Your wife's name is Katharane. Katharane Diane Stuart."

"We will talk about this later." William said. He had not the courage to challenge Katharane, not this night. This was his night and he wanted her body, again. He reached for her.

Katharane yielded, but only her body. As William took her she growled. "I am Katharane Diane Stuart. I will always be Katharane Diane Stuart."

The train's whistle ricocheted off of the sage brush and bounced across the prairie the mile and more to where Reid Stuart and the gunman sat on their horses. "Blowing its whistle for the Goodnight crossing, it will be stopping soon." Reid Stuart said.

"Told ya'."

"Told me what for Christ's sake!" Reid Stuart snapped. He was angry, not so much with the gunman, but with the uncertainty he felt as to how the gunman would deal with William.

"Told ya' we were gonna' be late if you kept piddle assin' along." The gunman retorted.

The gunman appeared at ease, eager to meet the train and Katharane and...Reid Stuart turned to the gunfighter. "Are you really that eager to meet Katharane's William?"

The gunman's dead grey eyes flashed. Then they settled back to quietness, to control and to emptiness. "Katty's comin' home. That's all that matters." He gathered Katharane's mustang's reins. "And by God I aim to be there waitin' for her!" He slapped the white mustang's rump. The mustang broke into a run. "Come on, old man, ride! We've got a train to catch!" The gunman yelled.

"You damn fool! You are going to get us killed!" Reid Stuart yelled back, but he spurred the buckskin and rode after his friend.

"Next stop Goodnight." The conductor advised Charles Goodnight and William Harrell as he walked across the platform at the rear of the passenger car where they and Katharane and Mary Goodnight stood.

"I don't see them, Miss Mary. They're not here. They're not here." Katharane whispered almost tearfully.

Mary Goodnight squeezed Katharane's arm, but she did not say anything. She, too, did not see Reid Stuart or the handsome gunman standing among the cowboys at the water tower which bore her married name.

"I see Bose and Young Tom." Katharane whispered again. She pointed at the old black cowboy and the graying man standing next to him beneath the water tower.

"Katharane." Charles Goodnight called. Katharane and Mary Goodnight stepped across the passenger car's transom and stood next to Charles Goodnight and William Harrell. "Look." Charles Goodnight said. He aimed his blunt whiskered chin at the two distant images which seemed to be rising up out of the flat dry dust of the prairie.

"It's them! It's them!" Katharane cried. "It's Dad and Pop. No one else rides like that."

"Crazy damn fools. They're going to break their necks for sure, running those horses like that." Charles Goodnight cursed.

"Oh! But look how they ride, Charles." Mary Goodnight exclaimed.

"Yes, Mary." Charles Goodnight said. "Nothing on the plains approaches quite like horsemen. They rise up from the flatness of the horizon until they meet you eye to eye."

Almost everyone on the train had spotted the two horsemen by now. And they too watched them advance on the train.

"I have never seen men ride the way they do." William Harrell said.

"They're plainsmen." Charles Goodnight said.

"And what does that mean?" William asked.

Charles Goodnight chuckled. "And you haven't lived on the plains yet." He patted William on the shoulder. "See how straight up they sit their saddles."

"Yes. But doesn't that endanger their balance if their horses should take a jump?"

"On the plains lateral movement is more likely. Lateral movement, firing on the run while dodging being shot at."

"From the way you say that, Mr. Goodnight, it would appear you have had experience with being shot at on horseback." William said.

"I've probably been shot at more than any other man alive on these plains, William, except maybe for that damn gunman. But it doesn't mean a tinker's damn now. Now we've got to diversify our herds. We've got to save the grass from being over grazed into oblivion. And we've got to come to grips with the fact that the plains are changing and we have to change with them if we are to survive. Even the Escadara must change." Charles Goodnight rubbed the back of his neck. "That's your job, William. Change the Escadara. Keep her strong, keep her alive, for Katharane's sake."

"But I thought..."

"Look! Look how they ride!" Katharane interrupted her husband.

"Yes, watch close all of you. There will never again be men on horseback on these plains to match the likes of Reid Stuart and that gunman." Charles Goodnight agreed. And they watched, Charles Goodnight, Mary Goodnight, Katharane, William and the passengers that struggled for a view from the windows of the passenger car as on and on the riders came, two men most alive astride a horse. Their horses crossed the prairie in full long strides, racing for the front of the train. The black hatted man on the white mustang sat a part of the running horse, each of his movements were in sympathy with the little horse's struggle to fly free of the sage and brush which cluttered its way. The man on the tall buckskin balanced a long rifle encased in a doeskin sheath across the saddle in front of him. His horse appeared to be able to overtake the smaller mustang, but its rider held it in check and just behind the other horse. The two riders were beside the train as it continued to slow in its approach to the Goodnight water tower.

As the train slowly passed them the gunman yelled. "Take the lead, Stuart!" Reid Stuart spurred the buckskin passed the tiring mustang. The gunman handed his reins to Reid Stuart as the buckskin passed him. The transom on which Charles Goodnight, Mary Goodnight, William and Katharane stood drew alongside of the close running horses. The gunman kneed the mustang dangerously closer yet to the steps below the landing, on which steps Katharane now stood. He raised his arms to her. Katharane leaned, unafraid, into the familiar arms which she trusted completely.

"Katharane! No!" William cried.

But the gunman swung Katharane onto the saddle in front of him. She straddled his lap, facing him. Reid Stuart eased the running horses away from the train.

"Damn fool stunt, Stuart!" Charles Goodnight bellowed as the train left the slowing horses behind.

Reid Stuart stopped the horses. "Charles Goodnight was right. That was a damn fool stunt." He said to the gunman.

"I got her. Don't I."

Katharane leaned out and kissed her father's reddening cheek, making peace between him and the gunman as she had so many times. As they rode to the water tower Reid Stuart watched his friend lose himself in Katharane's voice, her laughter, in her eyes, in her happiness. He watched the gunman let himself once more succumb to all those dreams of the woman whose legs straddled his lap from where she sat on the front of the gunfighter's saddle. He watched his daughter wash away the cold unyielding veneer behind which his partner kept all the doubts and hopes, misgivings and compromises with which his complicated psyche tormented him hidden. Then he watched it all drain away from the gunman.

"Pop. Hand me down to William, please." Katharane laughed.

Slowly, wearily, painfully the old gunman lifted Katharane and lowered her to her husband and watched Katharane kiss William. "Dad. Pop." Katharane said as she held William's hand. "This is my husband." She kissed William on the cheek. He blushed. "And your new partner."

Mary Goodnight caught her breath. Charles Goodnight spilled tobacco juice down his chin. Bose and Young Tom stared at Katharane. They looked at the gunfighter and waited to hear his response. But Reid Stuart spoke first and his voice was hard. "A man chooses his own partners, Katharane. You may ask this of me, because you are my daughter. But I cannot let anyone, not even you, my daughter, ask that of my partner."

Katharane's eyes filled with tears. Her chin quivered. "But Dad, Pop understands. He..."

William stared at the hand which reached down from the white mustang to him. He took it in his and looked up into the dark grey eyes of the gunman. "Never thought you were much of a bargain as a partner alone, anyways, Stuart." The gunman said to Reid Stuart without looking at him. He shook William's hand. "'sides, 'can't see how it much matters whether I got one Yankee partner or two. I'm either twice blessed or twice cursed."

The tension was broken. Reid Stuart retreated and sat silently on his horse. William released the gunman's hand. The gunman stepped down from Katharane's white mustang. He handed her the reins. He cupped his hands together and held them mid-thigh next to the mustang. "Step up, Katty girl." He said and he winked at her.

The tears vanished from her eyes. She laughed and placed her left foot in the gunman's hands and swung up into the saddle. "Come William." Katharane said. "We'll get your horse and tack."

"Where'd you get a horse?" The gunman asked William.

"Mr. Goodnight was kind enough to sell me one of his." William answered.

"Kind!" The gunman chortled. "How many Yankee dollar kind was that old horse thief?"

"And what are you going to ride home?" Katharane teased the gunfighter. "At least William has a horse."

The gunman snorted. "'sure he didn't sell him a donkey or somethin'."

"He never thought of what he was doing to ride back, Katharane. He was so hell bent to get here." Reid Stuart said. He looked at his partner. "Looks like you may not only have to buy a horse from Charles Goodnight, you may have to buy a saddle from him, too. Doesn't it, as you haven't anything to ride on but your butt?"

Katharane laughed. "Come on, William. Help me." Katharane said and she rode to the back of the train to the last stock car which carried the horses. There she dismounted and William joined her.

"I hope you're gettin' a damn lot of satisfaction outta' watchin' me walk, Stuart." The gunman grumbled as he limped after the buckskin.

"I am." Reid Stuart replied.

"Give her to me, William." Katharane said. She took the reins of the young black filly William led down the gangway of the stock car. The gunman stood still. He said nothing. He stared at the horse. "Go on. Take her, Pop." Katharane encouraged the old gunfighter. "She's your's."

The gunfighter hesitated. "Mine." He murmured. "Mine. She's mine." He repeated softly. He walked to the black filly and took her face between his hands. The filly dropped her nose and pushed her forehead against his shoulder. "You got her back for me, Katty. You got her back." He stroked the horse's neck.

"Lord, Katharane. Did you raise that black from the dead?" Reid Stuart exclaimed.

Katharane stared at her father. "Dad, I don't understand. I bought her from Colonel Harrell."

"Of course. Of course." Reid Stuart stammered. "You could not know that we lost his black in the Canadian."

"The Canadian?"

"I will explain later." Reid Stuart told his daughter. "But for now this will do. We had to swim the Canadian to avoid some renegades. The black you had given him did not make it." Reid Stuart watched the gunman stroke the horse's neck.

"You got her back for me, Katty. You got her back." He spoke to the horse's face, his eyes fixed upon the horse's eyes.

"No, Pop. She is a different lady, but she's black and she's your's."

"She's mine. And she's from you." The gunman whispered into the horse's nostrils.

"Yes. She's from me to you, Pop."

"Why, William? Why is it so important?"

"Because I want it, Katharane. I want to own my land and my cattle."

"You have me. Isn't that enough?" Katharane tried to laugh away the seriousness in William's voice. She leaned provocatively against one of the timbers which supported the roof above the veranda.

"No." William said. He turned and stomped back into the house.

For the first time in her life Katharane faced a man who did not place her every whim above even his basic needs. Her husband chose to demand from her part and parcel of the Escadara. Her nature cried out against any demand, and more so the claim of right or privilege as to the universe her father and the gunman had built for her. But instead of the gunman's sad acquiescence to her or her father's benevolent tolerance of her, William demanded recognition as an owner of the Escadara, the wealth and prestige that would bring, and to have Katharane seed this demand with land, her father's and the gunman's land. Katharane heard the gunfighter's boots against the oak planks of the veranda. The gunman walked to Katharane. "Hello, Pop." Katharane said. She took a deep breath and swallowed her tears.

The gunman stood beside her, silent. "I suppose you heard."

"I heard." The gunman answered.

"Will Dad deed any of the land to William?"

"No." The gunman placed his hands on the railing of the veranda.

"Will you?"

"'never considered any of it mine to give, Katty."

"Oh, Pop. It is as much your's as mine and Dad's."

"Maybe so, but the idea of a ranch, ownin' land, that was always your father's. 'meant somethin' to him. 'still does."

"I know." Katharane laid her head on the gunfighter's shoulder. "But there is so much land. And it means so much to William to own some of it. Why can't Dad just deed the far plains, above the Ceta, to William. You and Dad both say it's the poorest land we have."

"It is. But its part of the Escadara and the Escadara is Reid Stuart's. That's the way your Dad sees it. He ain't gonna' give it up." The gunman paused. Then he said. "No. Reid Stuart won't give up an acre of the Escadara, not for anyone. He's given up too much and fought too hard to get it. It's his."

"His and your's."

"His and mine."

"And how do you see it, Pop?" Katharane rubbed her cheek against the gunman's bony shoulder. "Would you deed it to William?" Katharane raised her head and looked at the side of the gunfighter's face. "If I asked you?"

"Reid Stuart's my partner, Katty. And I would never go against him." The gunman looked at Katharane. "Unless you asked me to."

Katharane knew if she asked, the gunman would do anything for her. When she was a girl she had tested him. Always, always, he had honored her wishes, even when she and he knew they were only her childish conquests of his spirit.

"Would you ask me to go against your father for your

husband?"

Katharane touched the weathered worn cheek of her bene-factor. "Yes. Yes, I would do that. If it was what I wanted." She rubbed his cheek with her cheek. "But it's not, not now, six months ago, but not now, not for William."

"He's still trailin' 'bout five head." The gunfighter said as he stood up. "Passed by here more'n two hours ago from the looks of the sand that's fallin' back into those tracks."

"You think he's onto the LS's." Reid Stuart's question was a statement.

"No where else for him to be, ridin' the direction he is." The gunman answered. The two men stared at the dry cold miles of prairie which lay between them and home and Katharane. Then they looked at the tracks beneath them. "One of us gotta' find that damn boy." The gunman cursed. "The other best ride for home and see to Katty. She'll be worryin'."

"You're the best tracker. I have the strongest horse. You find William and I will see to Katharane." Reid Stuart heard only the first two of the vulgarities the gunman hurled at him and his son-in-law before the long strides of his tall buckskin carried him out of earshot of the gunman. He was leaving the gunman to find William purposefully, hopefully. The gunman must accept William and making him responsible for his well-being might, Reid Stuart thought, force him to act in the boy's best interest, at least for awhile.

Reid Stuart lifted his hat and used it to shade his eyes from the sun as he stared at Katharane standing on the veranda. He thought of his daughter as a beautiful young girl, but now she was an unusually attractive woman, even to her father's eyes. "Miss Stuart." Reid Stuart greeted Katharane as he eased the buckskin to a halt in the yard.

"Mrs. Katharane Harrell Stuart." Katharane informed him as she stepped down from the porch to greet him. She pressed her hands against the baby she carried inside of her belly.

"Yes. I had heard you had married a Yankee gentleman."

"I married a gentleman, sir."

Reid Stuart smiled and accepted the hug his daughter gave to him.

"Miguel." Katharane called to one of the two small Mexican boys resting in the shade of the barn. "Take my father's horse, let it drink, then see that it has grass to graze."

The boy winced for finding grass during the drought that now gripped the high plains, even after the heavy blizzards of January and February, was no easy task, but he took the reins and led the buckskin away.

"I don't know if I will be as welcome, once I state my purpose." Reid Stuart said.

Katharane hooked her arm into her father's and led him into the house. "What is that purpose, sir?"

"To tell you that that fool partner of mine and I have lost your husband."

"What?" Katharane stopped and looked at her father.

"Nothing serious. Will, apparently, is tracking strays onto the LS's. Canada's riding him down. They should be in before noon tomorrow at the latest."

"Are you certain Pop will try to find him?"

Reid Stuart laughed as he poured himself a glass of water from a crock pitcher which sat in the middle of the heavy oak table. "He was cursing William and me both when I left him. But I have found the best way to get to him is to make him responsible for someone. Maybe this will get him to open up to William a little. His silence with that boy is deafening."

"Maybe it will." Katharane agreed. "Dad?"

"Yes."

"Do you think William is in danger?"

"No. No. He has water, some beef jerky and his rifle." Reid Stuart reassured his daughter. "Besides, Canada will find him by dark."

"Dad?"

"Yes." Katharane hesitated. For a moment she considered

asking her father to deed the land above the Ceta to William. But she did not and she would not. The gunman was right. The Escadara was Reid Stuart's, and she, like the gunman, would not ask him to share that with anyone. "I hope William is safe."

"He is. Canada will see to that."

The gunman frowned. "Damn that boy. Don't he know Reid Stuart or I gotta' be trailin' him?" He muttered to himself. "Why's he pushin' so hard? He's got to be almost on 'em. 'sides, those strays'll bed down come night." The answer began to be written out on the prairie beneath the black filly. It was etched in the hard sod and reflected in the gunman's grey eyes. Three riders had crossed onto and stayed with William's track. A quarter of a mile farther, a wagon had joined these riders. The gunman leaned down, kept the filly in a steady walk and studied the three horses tracks, marked their signature in his mind, a signature which would tell the gunman sure and certain when he found these particular three horses, and from finding the horses he would be able to find the riders. He had done it many times. Then all the tracks merged, William's, the strays', the three horses' and those of the wagon.

The gunman stepped down from the filly. There had been a confrontation. The three horses had surrounded William's horse. The strays had flushed in different directions. There had been an escape. William had bolted the trap. The gunman could see the deep cuts in the prairie sod where William's horse had driven off of his hind feet and burst into a run. The three horses had responded in kind, and the wagon had even joined in the chase, its wheels flopping wildly on its dried axles and leaving long slashes in the earth where the wheels' rims had cut into it as they fought to circumvent their axles. Katharane's William was no longer following a few wayward strays. He was running, and running hard.

"Dammit!" The gunman cried. "Katty'll never forgive me if that damn boy gets himself killed." He swung up into his saddle and spurred the tired filly. She broke into a hard lope. He hit her again with his spurs and the lope lengthened and smoothed itself. He knew better than to waist the horse. He might need her for the fight, if he could overtake them in time.

"Our father, who art in heaven, hallowed be thy name."

William's voice cracked with the whip's singing snap and he cried out in agony as the whip cut through his flesh hissing with its bite.

"Boy. You'd best not stop prayin' agin'. This be your final chance for redemption." A hard, smoke starched voice of an older man snapped.

"Yaw! Sooner you say all them words, sooner the Reverend let's me cut your throat." A younger voice chortled with excitement.

"The words, you craven cur dog, are our Lord's prayer." The older man snarled. "And at least this young'un knows 'em. 'more'n I can say for you, you slobberin' goat worshippin' heathen." The whip snapped high on William's shoulder, only its tip tasting his flesh, but William cried again. "Now, son, calm yourself. You know the words. Go on with 'em. You'll be proud you did, when your demon-ridden soul meets our Lord. For had you not spooked 'em, we'd a had those fine steers for the Lord's own supper and our's. Now you must pay for that sin against the Lord's servants." He slashed the whip through the wonderful late light of the fading sunset and it curled itself around William's ribs.

William wailed. He raised his head, struggled futilely against the strips of hide which bound his wrists to the wagon's wheel, and gasped. He was staring into the gun barrel grey eyes of the gunman. Quiet, cold, calculating eyes, which watched and waited as the Reverend's whip ate into the bloody torn flesh of Williams's butchered back again, again, and then again, and once again. "Why? Why?" William screamed at the gunfighter.

"Because only through pain can penitence be had from the Lord." The Reverend patiently explained as he cleaned William's bloody flesh from his whip by pulling the whip between his thumb and forefinger.

"If that be so, then boy you'd best tie the Lord's hand there to that other wagon wheel, 'cause his time for penitence is at hand." The gunman's soft cold voice flowed across the wagon, passed William's sobbing, dropped head and straight at the Reverend and his accomplice.

The Reverend's eyes shot across the wagon bed and glowered at the gunman who now stood just beyond. "Lord takes no kindness to those who impede his work." He said slowly. He studied the gunman's hand which hung beside the black pistol and the hammer loop which lay freed from the pistol's hammer. The slobbering boy glanced at the rifle which leaned against the other wagon wheel.

"Go on, son. It's the only chance you're goin' to have." The gunman said gently.

The boy did. He dove for the rifle. The gunman's first shot blasted through the rotten side boards of the wagon and sent angry wooden splinters slashing into the boy's eyes and face. He dropped the rifle, clutched at his face with his hands as the gunman's second bullet tore through his left eye and killed him. The Reverend had coiled his whip. But instead of lashing out at the gunman with it, he turned and tried to flee. The gunman shot him in the back of his left knee. As the old man swore the gunman rolled him onto his back, tied his hands together and drug him to the back of the wagon where he looped his lariat through the Reverend's bindings and tied the other end to the undercarriage of the wagon. "What be your plan for the Lord's servant, demon?" The old man snarled at the gunman.

The gunman ignored him. He walked to William untied him and eased him down beside the wagon wheel. William leaned his shoulder against the wheel and sobbed. The gunman squatted on his heels next to William. He urged his canteen into William's hands. "Drink, boy, drink."

William sucked at the canteen, then he gagged, vomited and whimpered. "I shit myself."

"What?" The gunman asked.

"They told me I would shit myself and I would beg, and I did. I did." William sobbed into the canteen.

The gunfighter felt the panic rise in him. He had no skills with which to help William. He did not know how to comfort anyone. He rubbed the black butt of his pistol, but it could not help him with this. He cursed at it under his breath. His mind raced. He had to say something. He had to get William to stop crying. He took a deep breath and said. "No shame in that, son. Any man would have done the same."

William coughed. His sobs slowed. "Even you?"

It caught the gunfighter like a hot iron, unexpected, sharp and painful. He flinched. He ground his teeth together and swore to himself. 'Bastards'd starved for water before they heard me beg 'em.' But he said aloud. "Yes, even me."

"Why?" William cried softer now. "Why did you wait? Why did you let them do this to me?" He gagged and choked up more of the water he had just swallowed.

"Take it easy, boy. Just drink." The gunman eased the canteen back to William's lips. "Slow. That's it. Don't you worry. Reid Stuart'll make 'em pay for this."

"And you? Who will make you pay?" William sobbed through the water that splashed off of his lips. "Who will make you pay?"

"They whipped him, Stu'." The gunman said matter-of-factly as he helped Katharane lift William and slide him on his butt to the edge of the wagon's bed. "Tied him to the wheel and the old Reverend there." The gunman kicked dirt at the old man collapsed on the ground behind the wagon. "He took that cat-a-nine tails." The gunman nodded at the short whip which lay with its ends still bloody in the bottom of the wagon. "And cut William with it."

Reid Stuart stared at the bloody torn streaks that seemed to flow from William's shoulders and down to the lower part of his back. Suddenly, Reid Stuart gripped his stomach, gagged and fell to his knees.

"Dad!" Katharane cried. She clung to William to keep him from falling forward from the wagon and onto his face in the dirt.

Reid Stuart knelt on his knees and hands, his head between his arms and wretched again. The gunman squatted next to him. "Who did this?" Reid Stuart heaved again. He spat the last drops of vomit from his throat.

"The old Reverend there." The gunman nodded at the old man who now lay on his back and sucked breath through his cracked, blistered, bloody lips. "'half addled boy I left dead on the prairie and three I don't know. They were gone when I found the wagon. But I know their horses. I studied their sign real good. I can find their horses for you, Stu'."

"In this country if you can find a man's horse you can find the man." Reid Stuart said. He stood up. "Let's help Katharane get William into the house."

As Reid Stuart and the gunman lifted William beneath his armpits and walked him up the steps to the veranda Katharane called loudly. "Juan Romero! Come here!"

A Mexican boy trotted to the veranda. "Si', la senora. Que es..." He began, but stopped when he saw William's bloody back.

"Take the big bay, the fast one. Ride hard to Mr. Goodnight's. Don't spare the horse, ride hard all the way. Tell senor Goodnight that William is hurt. He will give you a fresh horse and send someone with you to help bring the doctor from Clarendon."

The boy vanished. They heard a horse snort and stamp its feet in protest, and a few minutes later they could hear the sharp report of its hooves as they echoed up and out of the canyon.

"How ya' gonna' lay him down?" The gunman asked as Katharane and Reid Stuart lowered William onto his and Katharane's bed on his stomach. William groaned. Then he whimpered.

"Like that." Katharane said. "On his stomach."

"Too bad he don't wear a sidearm. He'd at least had a chance to keep his dignity." The gunman said from where he stood in the doorway leading onto the veranda.

"His dignity? His dignity, Pop?" Katharane shook her head. "What about his life? If he hand been wearing a sidearm they would have killed him, just as he would have been killed in Fort Worth if he had tried to use it then. Is his dignity more important than his life?" The gunman stared silently at Katharane. "I hate that damn black gun, Pop. Do you hear me? I hate it." Katharane raged. "I pray for the day you lay it down and never pick it up again. I pray for that day, Pop."

The gunman turned silently away and walked from the house. Reid Stuart walked to the large oak doors and lifted the heavy bandoleer of fifty caliber cartridges from the pegs beside the door. "Pray as you wish, child. I have need of that black gun." He said as he fastened the bottom of the old bandoleer to the front of his belt.

"He let them whip me." William whispered at first. Then he screamed. "He let them whip me! Why? Why?" He began to sob.

Katharane stared at her father who stood beside the door and looked empty eyed at her.

"'want me to ride 'em down, Stu'?" The gunman asked Reid Stuart who leaned the long Sharps rifle against the top rail of the horse corral.

"No." Reid Stuart said flatly. "That is for me to do. But I do need you to find them for me." He stood with his hands on his hips and stared across the corral. He did not look at the gunman.

"'somethin' eatin' at you, Stu'?"

"Why do you ask?"

"'cause when you got somethin' on your mind you stand with your hands on your hips and you don't look at me."

Now Reid Stuart turned and looked at the gunman, looked hard into his eyes. "William says you let them whip him." Reid Stuart watched the gunman for a reaction to his accusation. There was none. "He wants to know why?"

"You askin' me why, Stu'?"

The two men watched each other and waited, waited for the other to make his move and wondered deep within their heart what they would do when the other did. It was Reid Stuart who made the move. "No. No, my friend, I am not asking." He said. He pulled his smoke from his shirt pocket, lit it and sucked the smoke deep into his lungs. "But if you think you waited for William's sake, you lie to yourself. You waited for your own. You have never waited for any two men, however armed and however ready for you. You could have taken them from the first moment. You know that and so do I."

"Yes. I know that, Stuart. And so do you." The gunman pursed his lips. "But all that matters is whether Katty knows that."

"How many?" Jim East, the sheriff of Tascosa, asked.

"Five." Reid Stuart said. "Those two." He nodded at the body of the boy the gunman had shot which lay in the bed of the wagon and the old Reverend stretched out in the dirt behind the wagon, barely visible in the light cast from Fant's tavern. "And three more. Those three are here, in Tascosa."

Pat Garret lifted a lantern above the wagon bed. "This boy's been shot through the eye." He told Sheriff East.

"That the boy you shot to free William?" The sheriff asked the gunman.

The gunman nodded.

"And the old one, in the dirt there," The Sheriff pointed at the now dead Reverend. "How did he die?"

"'forgot how to walk." The gunman replied.

"If you drug that old man to death..." Pat Garret began.

"Like I said, he forgot how to walk. That was a bad mistake, like accusin' someone of draggin' him to death." The gunman warned Pat Garret.

The Sheriff cut in. "How do you know the other three are in Tascosa, Reid?" He asked Reid Stuart.

"Their horses are tied right there to Fant's rail." Reid Stuart pointed at three saddled horses tied to the hitching rail in front of the saloon.

"Again, Reid, how can you know that? Canada said he never saw them." The Sheriff argued.

"Garret, bring that lantern." Reid Stuart demanded. He walked to the horses. Pat Garret reluctantly followed him.

The gunman knelt and looked closely at the track each horse left in the loose dirt. He stood up and said. "It's them, Stu'."

"How can you be so certain?" Pat Garret asked.

"'cause I can read sign. And 'cause I ain't readin' it on the LS payroll. That's how." The gunman answered.

"I read sign just as I see it." Pat Garret retorted. "And as I see it I'm not about to let three of my employer's men be locked up on what you say you read in a horse's track. Not when there are two other LS men backing their story that they have been here for two days."

"That just means there are six liars working for the LS's."
The gunman snorted.

Sheriff East tried to interrupt the rising anger between the
gunman and Pat Garret. "How do you get six out of three and
two?" He asked incredulously.

"I'm lookin' at the sixth liar." The gunman snarled. He
glared at Pat Garret.

"Not for long, you are not." Pat Garret threatened and
spread his feet.

"Right, soon as you draw, they'll be five again." The
gunman challenged.

"That's enough. There will be no gunplay here." The
Sheriff said. He stepped in front of Pat Garret. "Let's get those
boys out here, Pat, and ask them some questions."

Angrily Pat Garret stalked into Fant's cantina. In a few
moments he emerged leading five cowboys and Fant.

"Maybe you and Canada should wait by the wagon, Reid."
The Sheriff said.

Reid Stuart led the gunman to the wagon where he turned
and stared hard into the gunman's clear eyes. "I need to know the
right of this."

"That's the horses, Stu'. Ain't no doubt in that."

Reid Stuart nodded. He gripped the heavy Sharps tightly
and watched Sheriff East question the cowboys. Finally the sheriff
ended the interrogation by warning the cowboys that if the sign he
found verified the gunman's story they would all be arrested. He
walked back to Reid Stuart. "Pat and I are riding out in the
morning to look at those signs ourselves, Reid."

"Lock them up, Jim." Reid Stuart demanded.

"Reid, I can't do that. Not with them having alibis and not
without first seeing that sign myself. Nothing against Canada."
The Sheriff said, apologetically.

Each click of metal as Reid Stuart cocked the hammer on
the old Sharps seemed to ring out in the night air. Jim East
swallowed and said. "You did as much as anybody to bring law to

this land, Reid. You have to abide by it, too, or it doesn't mean a thing."

"Jim. Those were the horses that cornered William. The men riding those horses tied him to this wagon's wheel. Then they rode away while he was whipped near to death. I wouldn't tie down an outlaw horse and whip it like that. Now lock them up, Jim." Reid Stuart demanded.

"The only thing I have just cause to lock up right now is those horses, and that is what I am going to do." Jim East said firmly.

"You can't take our horses, Sheriff. We'd be afoot." One of the cowboys cried.

"If they'd be afoot it means the only horses they have been riding are those and those horses were there and the ones riding those horses were there, Jim." Reid Stuart said angrily.

"Tomorrow, Reid, after I have looked at that sign." Jim East stood his ground.

A cold darkness passed across Reid Stuart's features. Pat Garret took a deep breath. Someone was about to die. As Reid Stuart raised the great Sharps rifle the gunman stepped between his partner and Pat Garret and Jim East. The Sharps cannonade broke the night air apart. Six inches of red and yellow flame belched out of the end of its long muzzle, and one of the three guilty men's horses screamed and dropped to its knees, rolled onto its side and died, still tied to Fant's hitching rail.

"Jesus God Amody, Sheriff! He killed my horse!" The same cowboy screamed.

Reid Stuart breached the spent cartridge from the Sharps, jerked another long shell from the bandoleer, reloaded the Sharps and fired again and another horse screamed and died.

"Son've'a'bitch!" Another cowboy cursed.

"Stop him, Sheriff." Another cowboy begged. "In the name of God! Stop him. He's got no cause to kill the horses. There ain't no point to that."

Oblivious to the cowboys' pleas Reid Stuart reloaded.

"No. There ain't no point to it." Jim East said. "But I'm not going to die saving some horses for the likes of you. And I'm not going to kill a man as good as Reid Stuart to save them either. And that's what I would have to do to stop him."

The Sharps roared once again. The third horse coughed, knelt and died. Reid Stuart turned to face Pat Garret and Jim East. The gunman still shielded him from them. "Tell the LS's, the LX's, the Bar Double C's." He took a deep breath and continued. "And tell Goodnight at the JA's. Tell them all. I'm coming at round up. And they're all going to pay and pay and pay. Tell them that there is one brand, and only one brand, and it's the Escadara Drooped E. Tell them from now it is the old way. Anyone crosses that brand and they will pay for it with their life." Reid Stuart turned to walk away.

"Reid." Jim East called after him. "I'm still going to check that sign and lock them up if I can."

Reid Stuart did not stop. He dropped his head and said. "It doesn't matter anymore, Jim. It's done. This is the way it stands, the Escadara against all comers. The way it was before."

Katharane stood on the veranda beside her father. "If you or Pop or William are wounded or killed, someone will bring you back to me to nurse or bury. And if you die, Dad, it will probably be for some principal, at least as you see it, which you believe in, maybe even something which you understand. If Pop dies it will be because he runs out of bullets. I'm afraid that's the only principal he's guided by." Katharane rubbed her father's shoulders. "But William, Dad, William is an honorable man who believes all men are honorable. He will surely learn they are not, if he has not already." Katharane took a deep breath. She stared out at the prairie. "He's been damaged enough, Dad. And I don't mean just by the beating he took. He's been damaged down deep inside. Look after his soul, Dad. Don't let these Godforsaken plains take that from him, too." Her voice broke. She dropped her eyes as she felt her father's hand find her hand.

"I'll do my best for him, Katharane." Reid Stuart said. "And I ask that if it all goes awry that you do the same by the Escadara."

"Of course I will, Dad. I love the Escadara as you love

her."

"I hope that's true, Katharane." Reid Stuart released her hand and walked away without looking at her.

At each gathering Reid Stuart set the Escadara camp apart from the others. And at the beginning of each range's gathering came the same confrontation with Reid Stuart demanding that any unbranded calves that could not be placed with their mothers be branded with the drooped E, and the gunman sitting on his black filly next to Reid Stuart, ready with his black revolver to settle the confrontation. And the resentment of the Escadara outfit grew as the round-up progressed until Reid Stuart's onslaught reached a range which neither acknowledged his claims to the unmarked calves nor shied from the bloodshed threatened by the gunman.

The Escadara camp was quiet this night and ill at ease. All the cowboys knew that Reid Stuart intended to lead them onto Charles Goodnight's JA ranges tomorrow and they knew Charles Goodnight would not tolerate this. He would confront Reid Stuart and them with guns, and, if necessary, with bullets and death. They knew this would come. What they did not know was when or how it would come.

"Bose. Please step down and rest." Katharane greeted the black cowboy who sat on his horse which stood on the hard panned yard in front of her veranda.

"First maybe I should say what I was sent to say, Little Missy."

"No matter what you were sent to say, Mr. Bose Ikard, you are welcome in my home. Now, please, step down and have a drink of cool water." Katharane offered him a clay cup filled with the spring's water.

Bose dismounted, removed his hat and took the cup from Katharane and drank. When he had drank all the water he handed the cup back to Katharane and began to speak. "Mr. Charles sent me..."

Katharane interrupted him. "Who sent you, Bose?"

Bose smiled. "Well, Miss Mary had Mr. Charles to send me."

"That I believe."

"Mr. Charles will see that any Escadara strays are marked with the drooped E and cut out and returned to the Ceta. But he will not let the Escadara outfit come onto the JA's, Little Missy." Bose said gravely.

Katharane stared at Bose. But she did not say anything.

"Mr. Reid. He's gonna' come. He is." Bose licked his lips which were suddenly dry again. He looked into her eyes. "He will come and Mr. Charles will stop him. You understand what that means, Little Missy?"

Katharane nodded.

"Well, then I will be leaving now." Bose gripped the saddle horn. Then he hesitated and looked at Katharane again. "Young Tom and me, Little Missy, we want you to know this is not of our choosin' or likin'. But we ride for Mr. Charles."

Katharane walked to the black cowboy, put her hand on his arm and said. "Nor is it by my choosing nor is it to my liking, Mr. Ikard. Please, tell Tom for me that I understand."

"Thank you, Katharane Stuart. I will." Bose Ikard said and swung up onto his saddle and rode away.

Side by side, a dozen mounted men holding Winchester rifles blocked the big canyon. The Escadara cowboys were tired and hungry, and distrustful of the gunman and doubtful of the rightness of Reid Stuart's purposes. Reid Stuart and the gunman rode silently passed them and on to Charles Goodnight and his armed men.

"Charles."

"Reid." Charles Goodnight returned Reid Stuart's greeting. Then he spoke directly to his purpose. "You and your men are not welcome on the JA's. Turn about. I will have my men cut out any Escadara strays. Any others whose ownership is questionable I will allow you and William to have your say before they are branded."

"'been a damn sight since I've asked any man for allowance for any thing on these plains, old man." The gunman snarled.

Charles Goodnight ignored the gunman. He looked straight at Reid Stuart. "I am asking you, Reid. Turn about. Your point has been made."

"Rider coming, Mr. Goodnight." Tom Hawkins called out.

"That's Miss Katharane, Mr. Charles." Bose Ikard said. His horse stood next to Charles Goodnight's horse.

Katharane forced her white mustang between her father's buckskin and the gunman's black filly. "Dad?" She tried to lean forward and look back into Reid Stuart's eyes, but her large stomach made this impossible. She sat up straight, astride her horse. She still refused to ride side saddle even in her advancing pregnancy. She stared at the side of her father's face.

He ignored her and glared at Charles Goodnight. He slung the old deerskin sheath from the Sharps and pointed the long barrel at Charles Goodnight. "I am coming through," he said firmly.

"No. You are not." Charles Goodnight replied just as firmly.

Bose Ikard cocked the hammer on his Winchester. Young Tom breached the long action of his Winchester, loaded a cartridge into the barrel and said. "You had best move away, Katharane."

The gunman dropped the loop from the black revolver.

Katharane drove her heels into the mustang's belly. The little horse jumped between and passed Charles Goodnight's and Bose Ikard's larger horses. Katharane reeled her mustang around, drove her heels against his ribs again and he leaped between Charles Goodnight's and Bose Ikard's horses. She sat facing the gunman at point blank range. "You will have to draw against me, too, Pop." She cried.

The gunman's face twitched. He smiled and laid his left hand on his saddle horn and stacked his right hand on top of it. "No." He said. "No. I won't do that." He winked at Katharane. "But you go ahead, Stu'. Shoot that damned old bastard. And let them do what they may with you and me. But send Charles Goodnight to hell for sure."

Charles Goodnight stared down the long barrel of the great Sharps rifle of Reid Stuart.

"Dad! You can't! You can't!" Katharane cried. "It's wrong. And you know it. What's right or wrong may not matter to Pop. Maybe it is just the Escadara and the Escadara only for him, and nothing more. But you have always cared what was right, and you have always done this right thing. You always have! And this is wrong!"

Reid Stuart's mind swam with confusion and doubt. 'Damn you, Canada!' He thought. 'Damn you for not caring about the rightness or wrongness of a thing and making me do it for you.' He set the heavy cold hammer of the old Sharps back to safety and lowered the rifle. He picked up his reins and turned the buckskin. "Let's go home." He said to the gunman and rode away. The gunman followed him.

WILLIAM REID HARRELL

1887

KATHARANE CANADA HARRELL

1890

"Whosoever denieth the Son, the same hath not the Father: But he that acknowledgeth the Son hath the Father also." Katharane closed her father's Bible. "I have decided on our son's name, William." The baby slept against her naked breast.

"What name have you chosen?" William asked. He stood next to the bed.

"William Reid Harrell."

William smiled. He had worried that Katharane would seek to name his son after the gunman and her father. That she had not done so made him happy. "Mine and your father's name."

"Two of the best men I know." Katharane said. "Second only to my little man here." She cuddled the baby against her. "And to Pop, maybe. I wonder when Dad and Pop will get back."

William ground his teeth. The gunman was never far from his wife's thoughts. He traced the outline of the baby's ear. "Why are they riding almost to the New Mexico border to confront a problem that has not yet occurred?"

"Because they know if the XIT's turn out that many cattle, those cattle will drift around the fences and onto our western ranges and graze those ranges out."

"How can they know that?" William demanded.

"'cause those damn Chicago barn builders plan on settin' adrift more'n thirty thousand head." The gunfighter snorted. He and Reid Stuart stood in the door to Katharane's and William's bedroom. In a softer voice he said. "Whatcha' got their, Katty

371

girl?" The gunman stared at the baby lying on Katharane's bare chest.

"I have William Reid Harrell here, Pop."

"A grandson." Reid Stuart said.

"Your grandson, Dad."

William tried to draw the sheet over the baby and Katharane's chest. Katharane pulled the sheet away from the baby's face and frowned at her husband. William frowned back. But he released the sheet and turned to his father-in-law and asked. "Can their ranges sustain thirty thousand cattle?"

"Hell no! Not in a drought." The gunman cursed.

"We'll use the drift fences and the Romero's two youngest sons can ride them until the XIT's manager gets here next month." Reid Stuart interceded in the escalating confrontation between William and the gunman.

"'ride in and hail up that gentleman and make it known to him that we are gonna' start using him and his hands for fence posts if they let stock drift east onto the Escadara." The gunman growled.

"Oh Pop!" Katharane chided the gunman. "Maybe you should just stay here and baby-sit baby Will and me."

Reid Stuart laughed. "Little Will may not appreciate that."

William stalked from the room.

Katharane sat on the veranda. She held the baby close and wrapped her shawl around her shoulders and him. The late day was becoming cool and crisp. As she raised her gaze from her child she saw riders appearing up out of the Ceta. She stood to retreat into the house until she recognized the riders. "Miss Mary!" She cried.

Charles and Mary Goodnight, Bose and Young Tom rode to Katharane and the baby. "Oh Katharane! Is that our baby boy?" Mary Goodnight asked as she slid from her side saddle while Bose Ikard held her mount's reins. "I have been so anxious to see him since the word came. And Charles has just been atrocious and he would not accompany me until now." She glared at her husband.

"I have been a damn sight too busy to spend two days seeing a baby." Charles Goodnight snorted.

"Even my baby?" Katharane asked and smiled.

Charles Goodnight relented before Katharane's smile. "Well, maybe not your's, Katharane."

"I thought not." Katharane said.

Mary Goodnight held Will as Reid Stuart, the gunman and William came from the corrals. "Mary. Charles." Reid Stuart greeted Charles and Mary Goodnight. "Bose. Tom." He acknowledged the two cowboys.

"Mr. and Mrs. Goodnight." William said. "May I introduce you to my son." William reached for the baby in Mary Goodnight's arms.

"Our son." Katharane corrected William and stepped between him and Mary Goodnight and blocked him from taking the baby from Mary Goodnight.

"Excuse me, our son." William said curtly. "Since Katharane refers to him as her son it seemed appropriate that I should claim him as mine, also." He spoke of his wife in third person as if she was not standing in front of him.

Katharane bit her lip and forced a smile. The gunman stepped forward. He tipped his hat to Mary Goodnight He said nothing to Charles Goodnight or Young Tom or Bose Ikard. He forced his shoulder between William and Katharane. William retreated a step, yielding to the gunman who glared at him.

"I wish we were only here to meet young William." Charles Goodnight said, drawing the group's attention from William and the gunman to himself. "But there is another reason." He turned to Reid Stuart. "That damn fool Temple Houston is sponsoring a bill in the legislature to outlaw fences, new or old, around leased land."

"'don't see how that affects us." The gunfighter said.

"If it passes that means the western drift fences have to come down." Charles Goodnight said.

"They can't do that." Katharane said. "The winter drift

cattle would devour our ranges."

"I know that and so does Houston." Charles Goodnight snorted.

"'should've killed that half red nigger in Clarendon." The gunman muttered.

"Killing Houston will not help us now." Charles Goodnight said. "We have to kill that bill, and to do that I need you to come to Austin with me, Reid."

"Our fences are on the Escadara line. We own our range. They cannot make us take them down." Reid Stuart said.

"Are you going to leave me to this fight alone, Reid?" Charles Goodnight straightened. He was angry. "Just because your western line is not on leased ground."

"No. Of course we're not." Katharane said. "Dad and William will go with you to Austin. And Pop can stay here with Will and me. Maybe he will not find any need to shoot either of us." She teased the gunman.

"That boy don't quit pissin' down my leg ever time I hold him I may shoot him."

"He pisses down your leg because you bounce him around too much." Katharane scolded the gunfighter.

"'just tryin' to get a good seat under him so he'll be ready to ride." The gunman defended himself.

"He has several years before he will be ready to ride, Pop."

"Huh! 'had you ridin' at two."

"Well you will not have Will riding alone at two. Now you and Tom and Bose may come inside with Miss Mary and me and enjoy our gracious conversation. Mr. Goodnight and Dad and William can make their plans for Austin."

"Huh. 'gotta go inside with the ladies, do I?"

"Yes. You do." Katharane caught Mary Goodnight's arm and they each caught the cutting look William gave Katharane as they led the gunman, Bose and Young Tom into the house.

"If you don't want to go, William, don't." Katharane said. She stood in front of the chifarobe in their bedroom. "I only thought as you wish to have more say about the ranch you would want to be in Austin with Mr. Goodnight and Dad when they try to save our western ranges."

"Why?" William asked and before Katharane could answer he said. "I don't own any part of this ranch. Not one acre. I have no legal standing to speak for it and less cause to do so." He lifted the half empty whiskey bottle to his mouth and sucked at its contents. He drank almost every night now. He seldom came to their bed sober.

Katharane ground her teeth but remained silent. They had argued about his drinking and once William had struck her when she criticized him for drinking too much.

"But at least this will leave you ample time to spend with your Pop." William sneered and some of the whiskey dribbled down his chin.

Katharane snarled her defiance at him. "I spend and I will continue to spend as much time with him as I wish."

"I am certain you will. The question is how much time you will continue to spend with me, Miss Stuart." William took a large gulp from the bottle. Then he flung it against the wall, shattering it and sending the whiskey cascading onto the floor. Katharane caught her breath. "I will go to Austin, and then I am going to Philadelphia. From there I will wire you and you can send me my son."

"'quiet today." The gunman said.

Katharane watched Juanita Romero carry Will into the small rock house which was her's, her father's, her mother's, her brothers' and her sisters' home. Katharane shifted her weight in the saddle, found her seat and touched the white mustang with her spurs. The horse stepped forward and took the trail which led passed the spring and slid down into the Ceta canyon below. "It is a quiet day, Pop." Katharane said over her shoulder and rode on.

He followed her on his black filly. They rode across the Ceta's floor in silence. Spring was with the canyon and the canyon was with the spring, everything alive either giving birth or being borne or serving its purpose in the manner nature intended. "'seems like we've ridden this canyon a thousand times, Katty girl." The gunman said at last.

"I wish we could ride it a thousand more, Pop." Katharane replied without looking at the gunman.

"What's to say we can't?" The gunman asked. He brought the filly alongside of Katharane's mustang.

"Thing's change, Pop."

"'meanin'?"

"Meaning I have a child now to attend to." Katharane took a deep breath and said. "And a husband."

"'meanin'?"

"Meaning I have to spend more time with them, give them more closeness."

"And that's to come from mine and your's?" The gunman stared at the young woman he loved.

"Some." Katharane said. She glanced at him. She revered him, above even her father. He was her constant safe harbor. The hurt in his eyes overwhelmed her. "But not all, not all, Pop. We will still have our's." She pouted her lips, mimicking him. His eyes softened. She laughed, and she pushed away her thoughts of William, Philadelphia and William's threat. "And this day I am all your's."

His eyes glittered with happiness. "Then show me you still know how to ride like I taught ya'." The gunman said. He spurred the black filly into a gallop.

Katharane galloped her mustang after him. From the Ceta they turned their galloping horses south and southwest down the big canyon, slowed them to let them blow after half an hour and then struck up a steady trot on to the mouth of the Tule. There they stopped and dismounted and ate their lunch. After their lunch Katharane stretched out on the thick rug of untrodden grass which grew along the hidden stream just inside the mouth of the Tule canyon. The sun was warm on her face, the grass soft beneath her and the spring air which was funneled down across the grassy bottom of the narrows by the high close walls of the canyon cool and soothing across her body. She slept.

"'late, Katty girl." The gunman's voice broke slowly through her sleep. She stretched but she did not sit up. "'late." The gunman repeated. "We're gonna' have to ride hard to be home before dark."

"Let's not go home."

"What?" The gunman tried to shake away the hope rising in his heart, push back the surging panic in his mind that screamed. 'Take her now! Take Katty and ride away.' Could it still be? Could he still have her? "But the baby?" He almost whispered the words.

"Consuela will care for Will." Joy leapt at the gunman's soul like quick flames at dry brush. "She will give him enough teat for tonight. We will ride home first thing in the morning." Bitter disappointed bile boiled away the soothing wetness of his hope. The gunman swallowed his loss. "Tonight I want to be that little girl that used to sleep at your side again, Pop. We can sleep here and I can be safe with you, like I used to be."

The steady breeze out of the narrows hummed passed them. The blue early spring sky glided across the tops of the canyon. The lonely gunman pushed to his feet.

"Where are you going, Pop?"

"To gather wood for our camp tonight, 'still early enough in the season, the night will be cold." Katharane's weary benefactor said.

"Snare a prairie hen. A roasted hen would be so fine."

"'not so many anymore. But I'll try."

"Thanks, Pop."

The gunman nodded, laid the Winchester beside her and limped away.

Katharane bit her lip and stared out into the empty canyon. The gunman had been gone for several hours. The shadows were far out into the big canyon. It was dark at the bottom of the narrows behind her. The cool breeze was now cold and damp and heavy, and it swam across the grass and around her legs. She wanted the gunman to come now. She was angry that he had not already returned. When she was young he always seemed to reappear just as she began to miss him or at the moment she became fearful; predictable as the rising or falling of the sun over the canyon, he would arrive and vanquish her loneliness, her fear. She thought to saddle her horse and seek him out until she saw the movement and recognized his peculiar gate and her anger left her. The gunman began to emerge from the distance. He limped slowly toward her. As he neared she saw two fat prairie chickens dangling from a leather cord which he had laced through the fingers of his right hand. He carried three large pieces of drift wood in the crook of his left arm.

"You did, Pop! You did!" She called excitedly and waved her arms.

He raised the prairie chickens to his chest in response. She waved again and called. "They're beautiful, Pop, just beautiful."

"'got us a couple of fat hens to roast." The gunman breathed heavily from his exertion as he dropped the driftwood beside Katharane.

"They are lovely, Pop."

The gunman laid the prairie chickens on his saddle and removed his slicker which he wore tied around his waist.

"What do you have in there?" Katharane asked as the slicker fell open from the weight of its contents.

"Dried buffalo dung," The gunman said. He was studying the narrow's floor. "For the fire."

"I do not wish to have my supper cooked over buffalo shit. Thank you very much." Katharane scoffed.

He chuckled and continued to look about the canyon floor. "'not for cookin', 'put 'em on the fire when we go to sleep. 'keep the bitin' bugs away." He said. Then he saw what he searched for, one of the large silver dollar patches of rock which emerged from the thick grass at random across the canyon's floor. He picked up the driftwood and carried it to the rock. The rock's edge vanished down into the narrow slit that eons of running water had cut through the canyon's floor. A damp draft rose from the slit and across the rock. "Gather some dried grass and all the dead brush you can find and build the fire here." He instructed Katharane.

"Why here?" She asked. But she pulled on her doeskin gloves he had crafted for her and began to gather dried grass and bring it to the rock.

"'draft will make this rock act like a forced forge. 'fire'll get hot and fast and your supper, Katty girl, will be ready quicker that way." He pulled the monocle from his waistband and floated it between his thumb and forefinger until a single shaft of sunlight superheated the dried grass Katharane stacked on the rock. The grass smoked, then it flamed and he returned his monocle to his waistband and built a pyramid above the quickly burning grass with the three pieces of driftwood. "Put the brush around the outside of the driftwood, Katty. I will skin those hens and supper will be ready in no time." He left Katharane tending the fire and walked a short distance away to dress out the prairie chickens. When he returned he had the two hens skewered on his running iron. The pyramid had collapsed onto the rock. On each side of his makeshift cook fire he stacked several rocks and then he balanced the running iron across the rocks with the hens directly above the fire.

"Don't burn them, Pop." Katharane warned.

"How many times have I roasted prairie hens above a campfire for you, and have I ever burnt them?" He demanded.

Katharane giggled and squatted on her heels and stared at the cooking hens and said. "No. You never have, Pop."

He walked to the saddles and when he returned he carried the old buffalo hide which he carried tied to the back of his saddle for his bedroll. He spread it on the grass near the fire and sat down on one side. Katharane sat next to him. He lifted the running iron and turned the hens on the iron and returned them to the fire.

"Pop. Do people quit wanting each other?" Katharane asked suddenly.

He sat quietly chewing on his bottom lip. Katharane was not certain if he was contemplating his answer to her question or ignoring her. So she added. "You know. Do a man and a woman quit wanting to be with each other that way?"

"Passion does not beget passion. It consumes it." He lifted

the running iron and shifted the birds on it, again.

"Always?"

"'seems so."

Katharane took the gunman's right arm in her arms and pulled herself against his side. Always, he kept his left arm free and ready. Katharane lay her cheek against his shoulder. "Has your life been what you thought it would be, Pop?"

"'never thought it to be, I guess. 'just sort of lived it out." The gunman said slowly. "'saddled my horse each day and just rode into it." He was quiet for several moments. "Your's?"

"It hasn't been as grand as I imagined it to be." Katharane said. "But I have always been safe and fed and loved." She pushed her nose against the gunfighter's cheek. "But it's always been by your or Dad or my Mama."

"'squaw did right by you."

"Yes. She did." Katharane said. "But she's gone." She swallowed. "What happens when you and Dad are gone?"

The wild Comanche moon rose into the night sky and subsided into a white mirror. The stars came out.

"'got Will." The gunman said. Then he added. "And William."

"William is going on to Philadelphia after Austin." Katharane said quietly.

"What in the hell for?" The gunman snorted.

"To be away from me, I'm afraid, Pop."

Now the gunman chewed on the inside of his cheek. "This can be a difficult place. These plains can work on you if you let them. He'll be back, Katty." His voice was flat and without affect.

Katharane rubbed her cheek against the bony shoulder she knew so well. "Pop." She waited until she was certain he listened. "William must not take Will from me as my father took me from my mother." She swallowed and continued. "Vow to me, Pop. You will not let that happen, no matter what it takes." She leaned back, looked into his face, and the coldness which filled his grey eyes made her shiver for she knew it meant he would stop William and she knew how he would do it. She had known this before she had required his pledge to do so, but she could see the black pistol firing in his grey eyes and, though she had known it would be this way, it both frightened her and consoled her, for Will was her's now. The gunman would see to this for her without regard for what it meant for him. "Only you, Pop." She whispered.

"Only me what, Katty girl?"

"Only you could live here forever without caring what lay beyond the canyons and the prairie."

"'saw some of what lay beyond them during the war and I didn't care for it." He let his cheek touch the top of Katharane's head. So seldom had he been able to feel the warmth of someone he loved. It was everything and nothing. "'got everything I want right here."

She smiled. "For now you do, Pop."

He nodded. "For now." Time was the cruel crippler of his hopes. Tonight Katty was as close to being his as she would ever be and time would see that she was but only for a short while.

"I remember that April second night in 1868 when we first came to these plains, Katharane."

"Do you, Dad?" Katharane asked. She lay on the freshly changed sheets.

"Yes. I do." Reid Stuart said. "It seems so long ago, daughter, so long ago that I brought a baby girl to this place."

"And now we have another baby girl." The baby suckled at Katharane's right breast. "Another baby girl for Pop to love."

"If he can."

"He can."

"It's his mind, Katharane." Reid Stuart said. "His heart is still good. It is." He argued with himself.

"I know it is." Katharane reached for her father's hand. "You will see when he gets here. You will."

"I hope so." Reid Stuart said. If a man's mind could be

moved by his heart then his daughter was right, Reid Stuart thought, for it was the bitterness of his mind that made the gunman unpredictable. An old and lonely hurt so long thought over without resolution or understanding twisted his thoughts and tormented his soul. A hurt of which Reid Stuart feared his daughter had little suspicion. But troubling her so soon after the birth of her second child would not change it.

"Tell me about that April second night, Dad, while we wait for Pop and William."

"If you wish, daughter."

Reid Stuart's steady voice ate away the minutes, then the quarter hours, then the half hours and finally the hours of the late night. At last Katharane slept. But he did not. He sat in his wooden chair and wondered if he should have sent one of the Romero boys to fetch William from Fant's Tascosa bar instead of the gunman. William should not have left with Katharane so close to delivering, and he had lied to her that he intended to find her father and the gunman and summon them to the Escadara. He had ridden straight for Tascosa, hard liquor and harder women. Reid Stuart was certain of this, and it had angered him. So he had sent the gunman to return with William. All he was certain of now was that the gunman would return, with or without William. Things were not right between his daughter and her husband. The gunman was one thing of course, but William's drinking and whoring was another. And William's demand for title to part of the Escadara land. "It's mine." Reid Stuart cried aloud, startling himself from his half sleep.

The baby began to cry. Katharane awoke. "He's here." She said sleepily as she felt for the baby beside her.

"No one's..." Reid Stuart began, until he too heard the sound. The hoof beats were unmistakable. The black filly stopped at the porch. The gunman entered. A few moments later William staggered into the room and pushed passed Reid Stuart and to the bed.

"We have a daughter." Katharane said. The baby nursed.

"What we name her?" William asked, his voice still slurred from the liquor.

"Her name is Katharane Canada Harrell." Katharane said.

"'might at least have asked me?" William gurgled.

"You were not here." Katharane snapped. "And you are too drunk to be considered now."

"'never consider my wishes anyways." William whined.

The gunman pushed between William and Katharane. He lifted the baby from Katharane's teat. The baby protested. William protested. The gunman ignored them both. "'got me another little Katty girl, Stuart." He said and smiled at the baby and Katharane.

Reid Stuart did not answer, but Katharane did. "Yes you do, Pop."

William staggered out of the room.

The gunman spent hours with the baby. He left horses saddled and sweating upon his return from his day's work and marched belligerently away from the corrals, ignoring Reid Stuart's chastisements, and to the house to claim Little Katty.

The baby girl twisted in his hands and fretted. "What's troublin' you this day?" The gunfighter asked as he carried her out onto the veranda.

Katharane followed him. "She's spoiled."

"By whom?"

"You."

"Not me, not this girl." The gunman crooned to the baby. The baby continued to fret. He saw Consuela Romero rocking her newest baby in the doorway of the second bunkhouse which Reid Stuart had built beyond the corrals. "Maybe she's hungry." The gunman said as he stepped off the veranda with the baby.

"Pop. She just had her's." Katharane protested.

"Little Mexican teat won't hurt her." The gunman said as he carried the child toward the far bunkhouse. "'sides. Consuela has enough teat for two. She won't mind."

"You are impossible with her." Katharane said. "But it will give me some time with her father."

"Be careful. One Little Katty is enough." The gunfighter said without looking back.

"Now he's planning our family as well as deciding our daughter's diet." William said caustically. He stood in the open doorway which led from the house to the veranda. He held a drink in his right hand.

"Drinking already?"

"Already drinking," William reversed Katharane's words.

"You take him too seriously."

Consuela's baby's screams interrupted her confrontation with William. "Move to the other teat, you little heathen." The gunfighter's low commanding voice rumbled. "Get after it, Katty girl." It rolled back to the veranda.

"Katty girl." William scoffed.

"That's right!" Katharane snarled. "Would you rather he thought less of her or of me?" She demanded.

"I would rather you thought less of him and more of our family." William said. He emptied his drink and walked back into the house.

Katharane stood on the veranda alone until she heard William rattling the whiskey bottle as he lifted it clumsily from the breakfront nearest the kitchen. She turned and walked wearily back into the house. William stood between her and the kitchen doorway. He stared at her across his whiskey glass. "I want something from you Katharane."

Katharane did not hesitate. Maybe his lust for her could overcome his greed for liquor. She walked to him and pushed herself against him. William lifted his glass between them and drank without taking his eyes from her's. "The land, Katharane, I want the land, now. You said your father..."

"I will not ask that of Dad!" She pulled back from William.

"Then ask it of him." William looked at the far bunkhouse where the gunman stood.

"He will not go against Dad." Katharane folded her arms

across her stomach. "Don't you know that?" She shook her head. "William. They've seen and done things together no other two men on these plains have done or ever will do." She reached to touch William's arm. He lifted it away by raising the drink to his mouth. "Dad sat on a buckskin horse next to Pop's black filly and watched the sun dance on a hundred square miles of grass belly high to their horses and knew they were to be his, his, William. Grass belly high to their horses and Dad's dreams, dreams of a ranch and cattle and a home for me. Then he followed as that lonely man set an infant girl he had only known for three days on the front of his saddle and carried her through that grass to a home, his home. After that Dad followed that man into Comanchero trading camps on the River of Tongues, into canyons unnamed and unknown by white men. He followed everywhere that straight back led him. And every time Pop brought him back, back to me and to the Escadara. Pop gave Dad and I the Escadara, William. He gave us his home. And for it he asked nothing in return, nothing." Katharane repeated. "I cannot ask Dad to give up his dream. I cannot. I will never do that."

"Then you ask that gunman to do so, Katharane." William demanded. "You ask your precious Pop."

"Would you really have me ask that of him?" Katharane stared at William. "When do you think that would be appropriate to ask?"

"Maybe when you're hugging him, like you were on the veranda this evening," William glowered at his wife.

Katharane sighed. "Please, William. They're the only hugs Pop gets." She reached for William's arm again. Again he lifted the glass and drank to avoid her touch. "Everyone needs hugs, even Pop." She was almost pleading.

"They're more than hugs, Katharane. And you know it."

"What do you mean?" Katharane asked, angry now.

"I mean they're more than hugs. They mean a hell of a lot more than that to him." William lowered his glass and looked at his wife and said. "And maybe to you."

"You have no right to say that to me, now!" Katharane cried. "I told you about Pop. I told you that night in Fort Worth.

The very first night you met me. You married me knowing my feelings for Pop."

"Not knowing his." William glared. "Not knowing that his were all important to you."

Katharane glared back at her husband. She lifted her chin and said. "Don't make me choose, William. I won't do that. Not for you." She swallowed her tears and said. "I won't do that even for him."

"Come on, Katharane! You already have." William turned and walked away from Katharane.

It was as before, almost. The old gunfighter carried the baby girl cradled in his left arm, even when he rode. William angrily protested that his daughter was being placed in danger. But Katharane saw no danger. She, too, had ridden too many miles with the gunfighter when she was an infant to fear for her daughter's safety on a horse with him. So William drowned his ignored protests with whiskey and Katharane submerged herself into her children.

"What is today?" Katharane asked. She and the children stood beside Reid Stuart on the veranda. The gunman sat on the top step of the steps leading down to the yard. William had refused to join them. He asserted the late July heat was still too much for him even in the late evening. He sat alone and drank.

"July..." Reid Stuart hesitated. "Why it is July third, eighteen ninety-four, tomorrow will be the fourth of July. It's been more than thirty years since Gettysburg..." His voice drifted away. He glanced at the gunman. "There were some Texas boys there. With Hood as I recall."

"With Hood." The gunman agreed.

"Why do you ask, Katharane?" Reid Stuart asked, moving himself and the gunman away from hard memories which had not been softened by time.

"That glow in the sky. There in the West." Katharane said. "It's been there for three days now. But it seems brighter tonight." She rubbed Little Katty's cheek. Will moved to the rail and leaned against it beside his grandfather. "What is it?" She asked.

"'fire, grass fire, it's a big one. 'been burnin' out the LFD country of New Mexico, I imagine. 'wind has stood out of the west all day today. It's movin' onto the T's now. Spring Lake Branch'll be afire tomorrow." The gunfighter said. He stood up. "Those Chicago capitalists are gonna' loose ten thousand acres of grass and a thousand head of cattle." He walked up the steps to Katharane.

"Mommy, I'm afraid of the fire." Little Katty whined.

"'don't you fret, Little One." The gunfighter said as he scooped the young girl into his arms. She kissed him on the cheek. He smiled at her. "The Ceta'll stop it before it reaches us."

"Yes. It will." Reid Stuart said. "But we'll lose all the western grass and maybe the stock before it does."

"'throw the stock into the Ceta. They'll survive." The gunfighter said, quietly.

"We'll still lose the grass." Reid Stuart said.

"'grass'll grow back." The gunman said.

"It will take it a year or two." Reid Stuart complained.

The gunfighter did not respond.

"In the morning we ride for the XIT's." Reid Stuart said.

"'damn fool thing, Stuart, 'ridin' into that fire." The gunman said. "'best stay here with this pretty lady." He winked at Little Katty, who giggled at this.

Will looked to his mother. He longed to be asked to ride with the gunman and his grandfather. The gunman often carried Little Katty on his saddle all day. She balanced there, an unafraid tiny ballerina, completely adept on the front of his saddle, but Will was still a clumsy rider. His clumsiness provoked his father, who berated him for his ineptness, and this would bring Reid Stuart to his grandson's defense and Reid Stuart was always backed by the gunman. Katharane and her father each saw that these confrontations disturbed Will and they both knew the danger William would have placed himself in had he physically challenged Reid Stuart. The gunman would not tolerate this. So Will remained either with his mother or worked with the Mexicans.

Reid Stuart saw the boy look at his mother. He glanced at his daughter. Ever so slightly she nodded at him. "In the morning," Reid Stuart said again. "You and I." He paused and looked back at the gunfighter and said. "And Will ride for the T's."

"As you wish, Stu'." The gunman said. He bounced Little Katty on his arm. "But what you takin' that boy for?"

Katharane saw the hurt in Will's eyes. She hurried to erase it. "Because he is one of the men of the Escadara." She said. Will beamed at his mother for calling him a man, a man of the Escadara.

The gunman looked at Katharane and smiled. "Good enough reason." He said as he raised Little Katty high above his head. She laughed, gleefully. "'sides, he'll be a damn sight more use than his Papa would."

The smoke met the gunfighter, Reid Stuart and Will before they left the Escadara's western range. It rolled above them and settled around them. They wet their bandannas and tied them around their faces and urged their unsettled horses westward. They rode for almost an hour. Then the fire appeared. Like a great orange and yellow and gray and black sea it surged at them five miles and more on each side of them. Will's horse shied and the gunfighter grabbed its halter and wrenched the animal back into line between his horse and Reid Stuart's.

"'smoke'll reach the Ceta by dusk if this wind holds." The gunman said.

Reid Stuart nodded. "Katharane and Little Katty are safe enough for now." He answered the gunman's unspoken question. "If the fire breaks around us, we will ride for home immediately." He wondered if the gunman had been right when he said it was a foolish thing to ride into this fire.

Will's eyes burned from the smoke. He rubbed them with the back of his hand. The gunman took one of Will's hands, poured water from his canteen into the palm and Will rinsed his eyes and coughed. "Thanks."

The gunman did not respond. He led Will's horse and followed Reid Stuart into Red Tower camp where Mac Huffman and two dozen other XIT cowboys had gathered.

"We're tryin' to stop it at Blackwater Draw, Mr. Stuart." Mac Huffman said.

"You lead the way, Mac." Reid Stuart said. He and the gunman and Will followed Mac Huffman and the other cowboys forward, closer to the fire.

"What the hell do we fight it with, Mac?" Pres Abbott, one of the cowboys, asked.

The fire popped from grass cluster to grass cluster so fast it appeared to be one single wall of flame instead of the thousand separate explosions that made up the inferno.

"Shoot one of those big steers staggering out of it." The gunman said.

"What?" Pres Abbott stammered.

The gunman drew his black pistol and shot a big XIT steer behind the ear. "Cut its head off." The gunman ordered.

"But why?" Will coughed. The heat and smoke were choking him. The gunman ignored the boy. The XIT hands stared at the dead beef.

"Do it!" Mac Huffman shouted. "Do whatever he and Reid Stuart tell you to do. And do it quick or steers and grass may not be the only thing the XIT loses today."

The cowboys beheaded the steer. Will turned his face away.

"Now skin one side back from the center of its belly to its backbone." The gunman said. The cowboys complied. "You." The gunman pointed at Pres Abbott. "Drop a loop around its forelegs. And you." He pointed at another XIT cowboy. "Drop your loop around its hind legs. 'straddle the edge of that fire, one inside the fire line where its burnt and the other in the unburnt grass and drag like hell."

Again the cowboys hesitated. "Get to doing it, dammit!" Mac Huffman barked.

"And switch sides often." The gunman commanded. "Otherwise, you'll ruin the inside horse's feet."

The two XIT cowboys turned their horses and began to

drag the dead steer along the fire line. Other steers were shot, and soon the dead beeves left bloody but effective drags along the front of the advancing fire. The gunman, Reid Stuart and Will joined the other XIT cowboys and followed behind the dragging beeves, beating out smoldering ashes with their slickers and extra saddle blankets.

Five days later and bone weary Reid Stuart, the gunman and Will rode into the Escadara corrals. Katharane met them there. Reid Stuart dropped his saddle across the top rail of the corral and said "Gracias" to Juan Romero's youngest son who had immediately began currying the hot buckskin. He kissed his daughter on the cheek and limped on to the house. Will stopped next to his mother, grateful to leave his horse to the young Mexican boy.

Katharane noticed sadness still sat around the edges of her young son's eyes. "Was it a hard trip?" She asked her son.

He nodded. Then he blurted out. "He doesn't even talk to me, mama." The boy dropped his head and stared at his boots.

Katharane rubbed the back of his neck. She did not have to ask who, she knew he was speaking of the gunman. "It's just his way, Will." She said softly.

"Not with you and Little Katty, it's not." Will mumbled.

Katharane hugged her son. "Don't worry about it." She soothed him. "Go on to the house. I have a hot meal and cool spring water waiting for you there."

Dejected, the boy walked slowly to the house. Katharane rubbed the worn seat of the old saddle the gunfighter still rode. "I bought you a new saddle two Christmases ago. I've seen you ride it once." She chided the gunfighter.

He pushed the black filly's rump out of his way and walked to the fence where Katharane waited. "'like the old one better."

"It's worn out."

"So am I." He put his hands on Katharane's.

"Pop. I want to talk to you about Will."

"'boy ill?"

"No." Katharane gripped the gunman's hands. "He's troubled."

"'bout what?" The gunman frowned. "If it's 'bout that steer, there was no choice, Katty. We had to make a drag and damn quick."

"No. It's not about a steer. It's about you."

The gunfighter tensed. "What have I done to that boy?"

"You haven't done anything to him. You don't do anything with him. That's what troubles him."

The gunman frowned.

"You dote on Little Katty."

"She's a girl. He's a boy."

"A little boy, Pop."

"Damn nigh a man."

"He'll only be ten his next birthday. That is most certainly not a man." Katharane protested.

"Not a child, either." The gunman argued.

"Just pay him a little attention."

"That what you want?"

"That's what I want."

"Then you got it, Katty girl." He smiled at her.

She smiled back. "Thank you."

"That gunman's been taking Will with him almost everyday." William said. "Wonder why?" He followed Katharane to Will's and Little Katty's bedroom. Every night Katharane kissed each of her children in their beds. Seldom did William go with her, and even more seldom did he do so to check on the children, and only occasionally did he kiss his daughter, and never had he kissed Will. But this night William followed her into the bedroom.

Will sat up in his bed and spoke excitedly. "He measured my hands, Mom."

William began to ask who had done this. Then he knew. The gunman was the only one Will seemed to speak of anymore. William glared at his wife. Katharane ignored William. She smiled at her son and tucked the hand woven blanket around his shoulders as he lay back onto the feather mattress. "Go to sleep, Will." She kissed her son on his cheek. Then she walked to Little Katty's bed where her daughter was already asleep and kissed her very softly on the top of her head.

William sat on the side of their bed and drained his fifth glass of whiskey for the evening. "Why did he do that?" He asked Katharane as she entered the room. He stared at her through hollow intoxicated eyes.

"Why did who do what?" Katharane asked, hoping to avoid another angry confrontation with her husband about the gunman and his involvement with their children.

"Why did that damn gunman of your's trace my son's hands?" William asked again.

Katharane sat on her side of the bed, picked up her bone handled hairbrush and began to brush her hair. She remembered a childhood memory from so long ago that it had lapsed from conscious recollection into vague remembrance of gentle persistent hands which held a child's still and traced their outline onto worn leather.

"Well?" William demanded.

"Maybe he plans to make him some doeskin riding gloves for his birthday." She lied softly. But she knew, she knew, and it filled her with elation and dread.

"The boy's damn birthday is not for six months." William cursed.

Katharane brushed her hair and did not respond. William lay down and lapsed into a difficult drunken sleep.

Two days before Will's birthday Reid Stuart and William had taken him into Tascosa to fit him with new boots and a new hat. That morning the gunman had mysteriously left for the JA's. Katharane wondered what had drawn him to Mary and Charles Goodnight's ranch. He had no liking for Charles Goodnight. She worried to what end the gunman was going there. She stood on the veranda and stared at the evening sky which sat above the canyons.

"What'cha' doin', Mama?" Little Katty asked. She walked from the kitchen out onto the veranda where her mother stood. She reached with her left hand and grasped the edge of Katharane's skirt.

"What are you doing, Mother." Katharane corrected her daughter.

"What are you doing, Mother?" Little Katty pleasantly obliged.

"I am waiting for Pop."

The old gunfighter had just emerged from the Ceta. He dismounted and led the black filly that Katharane had given him a decade earlier to the horse corrals.

"He rode his black horse today. That makes him feel happy, doesn't it, Mother?"

"Yes."

"Mother?"

"What Katharane Canada?"

"Will he read to us from Grandpa's Bible tonight?"

"Maybe."

"Mother?"

"Yes."

"Does Mr. Canada believe in God?"

Katharane looked down at her daughter who watched the gunfighter unsaddling the black filly. She put her hand on the back of the little girl's head. "I don't know what Pop believes, Katharane Canada. But I do know he's seen God."

The child gazed up at her mother. "Mr. Canada has seen God, Mama?"

Katharane nodded.

"But how, Mama, I can't see God."

'In men's eyes just before he killed them.' Katharane thought to herself. But to her daughter she said. "Like he saw the Comanche and the buffalo, I suppose, and the plains. He has always said that being afoot on the plains would make a man understand eternity."

"What's eternity, Mama?"

"Eternity is God."

"Has Mr. Canada ever been afoot on the plains?"

"Yes."

"Then he believes in God?"

"No. I'm not certain that he does."

"But Mama, you said Mr. Canada said that being afoot on the plains would make you believe in God. And you said Mr. Canada has been afoot on the plains. So he has to believe in God." The child stared up into her mother's smiling eyes.

"No, daughter, the plains taught him to understand God. But even they have been unable to make him accept God. The only thing I am certain Pop believes in is Pop."

"Mother?"

"Yes."

"I don't understand."

"Neither do I, Katharane Canada. Neither do I."

The gunman walked from the corrals to the veranda. "Ladies."

Again and again Will sighted down the barrel of the rifle, first at the remainder of the cake Katharane had baked for his birthday celebration and then out the kitchen window.

"It's made by Remington Arms." William said. He was almost as excited as his son.

"'didn't know there was a Remington Arms." The gunman said.

William ignored him. At last Will was his. He was the center of his son's attentions for once. He reveled in it. "It is as fine a rifle as can be had. I had your grandfather ship it to me from Philadelphia." William took the rifle from his son. Carved into each side of the polished wooden stock were the initials "W.R.S.". "Dad had your initials carved into each side of the stock." He handed the rifle back to his son. "Want to shoot it?"

"Yes." Will said excitedly. Then he hesitated. He looked at his mother and said slowly without looking at his father. "But I haven't opened Pop's gift yet."

William grimaced. Before he could respond Katharane said. "Of course. Open Pop's gift to you. Then you men can do all the shooting you wish."

William stared at her. "He should open all his gifts before you and he abandon us." Katharane answered his stare. He continued to stare at her silently.

"I get to go too!" Little Katty mouthed through the spoon-ful of cake she held in her mouth.

"Later, maybe." Katharane said. "Now eat your cake."

The little brown haired girl wiggled her hips as she kneeled in the chair and dug her spoon into the large piece of cake on the plate in front of her.

The gunman's gift to Will was the last gift remaining on the table. Will began to slowly unfold the dark oilcloth which concealed it. As he did, Katharane gasped and Reid Stuart exclaimed. "Damn!" William stared at what lay on the oilcloth in angry disbelief. A heavy leather waistband folded around a black holster. The dull black walnut of a pistol's grip lay gently against the soft latigo leather.

"Pop's gun, give it back." Little Katty mumbled through the syrup and molasses sweetness of the soft candy which Katharane had also made for Will's party and for which she had now abandoned her cake.

Katharane glanced at the gunfighter to be certain his pistol still rested against his left hip. It did. "No. It's not Pop's gun, Sweetie." She said to her daughter.

Will touched the holster with his fingers. "It's just like your's. Isn't it?" His eyes danced with excitement and pride as he gazed at the old gunfighter.

"'close as that damned old gunsmith in Taos could make." The gunman said. "Put it on, boy."

Will grabbed the holster. He fumbled with the lacings that fastened the tongues together. The gunman knelt on his right knee and laced the belt fastened. It fit. He grunted with satisfaction. "'wasn't certain I cut enough notches in it to where it would tighten around your skinny middle."

Will beamed. "Can I shoot it?"

"'damn straight. Why else would I have given it to you." The gunman said. He winked at Little Katty who continued to work at the gooey candy with her wooden spoon.

She winked back at him as he followed the boy's vanishing figure out onto the veranda and onto the yard. Reid Stuart picked up the rifle. "Come on. Let's not let that fool partner of mine convince Will a handgun is more worthwhile than a rifle." He said to William and walked out the door.

William was stunned. He did not move. "He can't do this, Katharane." He turned to his wife. "My son will not be trained as a gunman."

"He is not going to be trained to be a gunman. He is just going to learn to shoot a pistol."

"A pistol, Katharane? A pistol?" William shook his head. "No. Not just a pistol. A black pistol. A black pistol that hails from the Escadara. Don't you see? Don't you realize how dangerous this is for Will? Don't you care?"

"Yes! I care. And I will see to it that Will does not wear that pistol except when he is with you or Pop or Dad, and then only on the Escadara."

"No. No." William repeated, still shaking his head. "You stop this or I will."

"I can't."

"You can't or you won't? I heard you curse that black pistol. I did. Have you forgotten?"

"No, I haven't forgotten. But I can't do anything about

this. I asked Pop to do this."

A hollow pistol report echoed off into the canyon.

"You asked him to give my son that damn black gun!" William screamed.

"I asked him to do something special for Will." Katharane tried to explain. "This is as special as he can think of."

"Special!" William stood up, wild with anger. "Special!"

Little Katty sat wide eyed, the wooden spoon in her hand, watching her parents. "No, Daddy, no," The child pleaded, still holding the spoon still in front of her lips.

"Shut up! Katharane Can...." William stopped.

"Canada. Katharane Canada Harrell!" Katharane snarled. She swept Little Katty into her arms, the child still clutching the spoon, and marched from the house with her.

With each evenings practice Will became more and more proficient with the pistol under the gunman's steady tutelage, and the bitterness within William for the gunman festered. Katharane saw it and so did Reid Stuart. The confrontation between the two men was coming, and soon.

"William is pushing him." Reid Stuart said to his daughter. They stood together on the veranda and watched William insist that Will practice with the rifle and not the pistol. The gunman stood, silent, his hands on his hips.

"He wants Will to learn to shoot with the rifle, too." Katharane said, softly. "He's pushing him, I know. But it is not an unpleasant task for Will. He enjoys shooting."

"I am not speaking of Will, Katharane." Reid Stuart said sternly. "He is pushing it with Canada. And, daughter, that is very, very dangerous."

Katharane drew in a deep breath. But she did not reply. Together, they watched Will take aim with his rifle, squeeze the trigger and the bottle explode.

"Too much whiskey courage and William challenges him." Reid Stuart dropped his head and shook it slowly. "I just don't know what to do, Katharane. I just don't."

Katharane gripped her father's arm. "It will be all-right, Dad. Just give it time." She said. But she, too, worried what time held for them.

It came as sudden and as unprovoked as a late June thunderstorm. Will had left the horse corrals to race to the house and retrieve his pistol for the evening's practice. But before he could begin his dash his father had interceded and told him. "Not today. No pistol shooting." The boy's shoulders slumped forward and, disappointed, he drug his feet across the hard pan to the veranda and into the house.

"'little practice won't hurt nothin'." The gunman said quietly.

Reid Stuart came up behind and close to the gunman as William wheeled on him. "You telling me how to rear my son, now?" William demanded, fury filling his voice.

The ferocity of his challenge caught the gunman off balance. "Well...Ah...No." The gunman uncharacteristically stammered. "Just...."

William cut him off. "It is none of your damn concern. My family is none of your concern. I do not need nor do I desire your concern. And I goddamn certain do not wish your advice as to what is best for my son." He spat the words at the confused gunman. And then without warning he punched the gunman in the face.

Without hesitation, closer to the gunman than any man could be but for the gunman's innate trust in him, Reid Stuart lifted the hammer guard and withdrew the black pistol from its holster. He took a step back and prayed this could settle things between his son-in-law and his partner without irreparable damage or bloodshed.

The gunman had never feared any man. He had never known that breath robbing tightness in his chest, that dryness of the mouth, that paralysis of muscles that such fear could bring. He did not fear William because he still had the black pistol to blast any such fear away. Instinctively his left hand went to his empty holster, went for the black revolver that had never failed him. It was not there!

William drove his right fist underneath the gunman's ribcage. The gunman dropped to his knees. He groped furiously at the empty holster. He looked at Reid Stuart. At first Reid Stuart saw confusion in the old gunfighter's eyes. Then it was there. What had never been there before, fear. Reid Stuart had seen it in other men's eyes, almost always in those who had faced the gunman. He had seen it in good men's eyes, brave men's eyes, even Pat Garrett's eyes, but never had he seen it in his partner's eyes, never in those gray eyes. Reid Stuart swallowed, tears came to his eyes. He wanted to toss the black revolver that now seemed so heavy in his hand to his downed partner. He did not. He watched.

William hit the gunman above his right eye. The old gunfighter sprawled backwards, penning his boots beneath him. He rolled onto his side and pushed himself up to his knees. William drove him to the ground again.

"That's enough." Reid Stuart said and he stepped between the gunman and William. "He's had enough and so have you."

"The hell I have! I've been waiting for more than eleven years for this." William snorted through his nose, his eyes fixed on the gunfighter who struggled to rise from his knees.

"And he's been waiting more than eleven years to have his go at you. Do you want me to hand him his pistol and let him have it?" Reid Stuart demanded.

William glared at Reid Stuart. He turned to walk away, but he stopped. Katharane stood ten steps from them. For a moment William and Katharane's eyes dueled for dominance, then William cursed again and stomped passed his wife and to the house.

Katharane watched her father raise the old gunman to his feet. The gunman leaned heavily against Reid Stuart. He sucked for his breath, coughed and began to sag back down to his knees. Reid Stuart gripped his right wrist and held his partner's arm securely draped around his neck and supported the gunman's weight upon his bony shoulders.

"You brought me to this, Stu'. You brought me to this." The gunman mumbled through his swelling lips.

Katharane stared at her father's terribly sad eyes. "I know I did, my friend. I know I did." Reid Stuart said quietly. "Come on now. I'll get you cleaned up."

Reid Stuart cleaned the gunman's battered face as best he could. But cleaning could not wipe away the hard damage William's fists had wrought, the gaping burst bottom lip and the swollen elongated black eye.

"What happened to your face, Mr. Canada?" Little Katty asked at the dinner table.

"My horse threw me." The gunman answered. He chewed the dark crisp thin slice of meat very slowly. His bruised and swollen face hurt each time he bit into the dark meat.

"It looks more like he got you down and stomped on you." Little Katty remarked thoughtfully.

The old gunfighter chuckled and tried to smile. "Yes. I suppose it does."

Little Katty laughed at his contorted smile.

"There is nothing funny about this!" Katharane snapped. "Pop's hurt. How dare you laugh at that."

"'not laughin' at Mr. Canada's hurt, Mama." Little Katty whined.

"That's enough Katharane!" William protested bitterly.

"It's all-right, Katharane. They're doing him no harm." Reid Stuart tried to intercede between the quickly escalating confrontation between his daughter and his son-in-law.

Katharane glared at her husband and her father.

"What did you do with the horse, Mr. Canada?" Little Katty asked, more shyly now.

The gunman winked at Will and said. "You're eatin' him."

"Huh-uh!" Little Katty said. "Me not eatin' no horse." She stared at the half-eaten piece of meat on her plate.

Even Katharane laughed at this. "Pop. You should be ashamed. Telling her something like that." Katharane scolded the old gunfighter.

As Katharane cleared the evening meal's dishes, Reid Stuart spoke to the gunman. "I've been planning to take the wagon into Tascosa for supplies."

"'send the Mex's." The gunman suggested.

"No." Reid Stuart said. "You and I are going into Tascosa with the wagon. Get your bedroll and your slicker."

"Tonight!" Katharane exclaimed.

"Yes, tonight." Reid Stuart said firmly.

The gunman struggled up from the table and limped to the front door. "I'll have the Mex's harness the mules to the wagon." He said as he went out the door.

William glared at Katharane and walked to the break front and pulled his whiskey bottle from it and disappeared into the house's great room. Will and Little Katty fled to their shared bed room.

Katharane turned upon her father. "He's hurting. He's in no condition to ride twenty odd miles on that damn rough wagon, Dad."

"And he's in no condition to face off with William, again, tonight." Reid Stuart said harshly. "And if you and William quarrel, which you may as William is already drinking, that could well happen."

"Not without his gun, he's not." Katharane shot back. "Would you take his gun away, again? Is that really a fair fight?"

"Would you have had me not to? He would have killed William, Katharane. Would that have been fairer?"

"No!" Katharane exclaimed. "But if he wanted to kill William, William would be dead. And you know that, Dad. But he did not do that."

"This is not finished between them. And unless we can find a way to finish it." He stopped. Then he said. "I do not believe he can continue to live under this roof, in our home."

"This is Pop's home, too, Dad!" Katharane cried.

"I cannot send William from you and from his children. But I can send my partner away." Reid Stuart swallowed and wiped at the tears on his cheeks. "And for you, Katharane, he will go." He said thickly.

Katharane stared at her father, at the terrifying truth of what he said, both as to William and the gunman being incapable of living together without violence and as to the sacrifice the gunman would make if Reid Stuart asked him to make it for her. "Then take Pop to Tascosa. Be slow in getting there and back. Let me have this time with William. Let me try to set this right. But you promise me that Pop is coming back. You must promise me that."

Reid Stuart shook his head. "William's already drinking. You cannot reason with him drunk."

"I know. That's why I want you to take your time. Give me a couple of days." Katharane pleaded. "Please, Dad. Don't we owe Pop at least that?"

"God, child! We owe him so much more than that." Reid Stuart said quietly. "So much more than that."

"Please, Dad."

Reid Stuart sighed and said resignedly. "All-right, Katharane." He lifted the old Sharps from its pegs beside the door and left.

William raised the bottle and swilled the whiskey down his throat. He had set the glass aside half a bottle ago. Katharane took a deep breath. She would rather have done this when he was sober. But she had only this night before her father and the gunman would return. She straightened, her cotton gown clung to her still shapely figure, she plunged forward. "You should not have fought with Pop."

William glared at her across the tilted bottle at his lips.

"Please. Put that down."

He tilted the bottle higher and the liquid inside the dark glass churned and bubbled as he struggled to keep his esophagus open longer with each swallow.

"You're almost twice his size and half his age."

"Would you rather I used a gun?" William slurred the question at Katharane. "Then he could have killed me."

"No!" Katharane exclaimed.

William took another drink. "Man has a right to defend his home, my home."

"And his! Damn you! And his!" Katharane cried. "This is Pop's home, too. Why can't you accept that?"

"Because it's more his home than mine, Katharane." William lifted the bottle and drank. "You see to that." His eyes tracked down the front of her gown. He licked at the few drops of liquor still on his lips and left his tongue exposed between his lips. "And maybe your more his than mine." He held the bottle in his right hand. He grabbed for her gown with his left. Katharane slashed his hand away. He laughed. "Not interested, huh?"

"Not with a drunk, I'm not."

"'didn't care I was drunk when we made his Little Katty for him." William stepped towards her.

Katharane backed against the bed. "That's right. I wanted my babies desperately, enough even to have them with you." Katharane snarled.

"You bitch!" William took another drink. "You never did it just for me!" He took another drink. "Well by God! This time you will." He punched her viciously in the stomach.

Katharane folded, her knees began to buckle, she sucked for breath, found it, straightened and stood up, defiance glistening in her eyes. William grasped the neck of her gown and ripped it open, his strength fueled by drunken desire and the fury of denial. He slugged her in the ribs. She staggered but refused to fall on the bed. William cursed her wildly. She shook her hair from her face, heard their bedroom door open and gasped. Will stood in the doorway. He held his pistol in his right hand. He pointed it at his father.

William stepped back, lifted his bottle and drank it dangerously close to empty. Will stepped in front of his father, still pointing the black pistol at him, his back to his mother. Katharane and William's eyes met and Katharane saw the intent in William's eyes. Will did not. Katharane flung her arms around her son to lift him and turn him away from the whiskey bottle which flashed towards his face. She was too slow and too weak. The bottle blasted into Will's face, burst into cutting, ripping shards, gashed his tender left cheek and almost severed his left eyebrow free of its tight mooring above his eye. Blood, blue, black and hot, shot out. Katharane, still clutching Will, collapsed backwards onto the bed, her gown trapped beneath her back. Blood cascaded from Will's open facial wounds across Katharane's naked right breast and down the concave of her stomach. And for an instant, just an instant, the shimmering white nakedness of her, stained by his son's rich red blood, made William hesitate, made him watch as it slid towards the darkness between her thighs.

Katharane heard the gunfighter's voice whisper to her. "Always there is one moment, a single instant when they hesitate. Whether it's fear or anger, need or needing, it does not matter. That is the moment in which you can kill them, the only moment, Katty. Kill them! Kill them!" She raised her knees high up against her son's armpits and drove her feet into William's groin. He clutched his angry testicles and dropped to his knees. Katharane rolled herself and Will across the bed and onto the floor on the other side. She freed the pistol from Will's clenched grip upon it. She stood up, leaving Will cradling his face in his hands on the floor, cocked the pistol and pointed it William.

William raised his head. "Even you wouldn't kill your children's father in their home, you tight-assed bitch." William slurred his curse through the hot decay of his dying drunkenness. He sat on his knees, leaning against their bed.

"No. Even I would not do that." Katharane said. She stared down into William's swimming eyes. "But he would. And not even his love for Little Kat will spare you from his gun when he sees what you have done to Will and to me." William went pale. Katharane's words sobered him. "Run fast and run far, William. For if my Pop catches you nothing on this earth can save you from his gun." Katharane's voice was strong and clear. "Never ever return. Never ever seek to take my children from me. For if you have ever believed me, believe me now. Come tomorrow I will set his black gun forever against you."

THE LAST BATTLE

Consuela gasped and crossed herself.

"Stop that!" Katharane demanded. "Help me." She struggled to hold Will's hands away from his flopping eyebrow.

Consuela sucked in a deep breath, prayed silently, grabbed the boy's right wrist, slammed his arm across his chest and nodded for Katharane to do the same with his other arm. "Sit on his arms, Senora. Pen them to his chest." Consuela said in her pidgin English.

Katharane penned Will's arms beneath her shins and used her knees to force his shoulders back down onto the kitchen table. Consuela stood behind Will and grabbed his ears and straightened his head. "Slide your knees forward and hold his face between them, Senora." Katharane did so.

Will cried. "Mama. Mama."

Katharane bent her face to his and kissed him passionately on the lips. "Yes, my beautiful boy, my love."

"No more, Mama. No more." He whimpered.

"Sshsh, my love, sshsh, soon it will be better." She whispered into his one open eye as she watched Consuela thread one of the long strands of hair from the black filly's tail through the sewing needle. Again she whispered. "Sshsh." And she kissed her son's lips with her lips apart, wet and warm and wonderful, and the boy murmured at her touch, unaccustomed to such invitation. Consuela approached from the top of Will's head. She bent over him, tilted the open whiskey bottle and flooded the dried blood from the gaping wound above his shut left eye. Will cried out with surprise and pain. But Consuela poured the disinfectant with purpose and volume into the wound. She set the bottle on the floor, bent again over Will and with all the strength in her small work worn fingers grasped the first layer of flesh beneath the top of the eyebrow and began to stitch it to the first layer of the torn flap. Now Will screeched with pain and with fury at the tearing hurt which once again beset his face.

Katharane bore her weight down upon his shoulders, clutched each of his ears and whispered over and over again. "Yes, my love. Yes, my love."

For one hour and one half hour more Consuela sewed at the gashes in Will's face. Until, mercifully, she had sewn all she could sew back together. Will lay spent and trembling from his futile fury on the hard wooden table. Katharane raised herself from him and stood on the floor.

"Senora." Consuela said softly.

Katharane slowly released her son from her gaze and looked at the Mexican woman.

"Senora. You must bathe the wounds each hour with the liquor." She handed the bottle to Katharane. "I will keep the little senora with my children and I will bring fresh cold water from the spring each time it is necessary and we will bathe his face and fight the swelling about his eye." Consuela paused. "And each time we will light a candle and pray that our beautiful Will will see again."

"He will." Katharane hissed. "With or without your God, my Will will see and he will be beautiful again."

"No, Senora. My skills are poor. We will remember his beauty but not the mirror. But with God's mercy he will see from that eye." She looked at the terrible purple bulbous glob that was the right side of Will's face and repeated. "With God's mercy, Senora." She pulled a short half burnt candle from her waistband, lit it and set it on the kitchen window's ledge.

It was not the gunman who Katharane struggled to restrain upon his and her father's return; nor was it for her injuries that Reid Stuart sought swift redress. At the sight of his grandson's destroyed face Katharane watched the cold darkness she had seen before in the gunman's eyes come slowly, but surely into her father's soft eyes. "Have the mules saddled. Pick the four best horses we have and put two each on string behind a mule. We ride day and night for Harrold. He'll be on the train." He commanded the gunman. And it was not Katharane's remonstrations which stopped his intended swift destruction of William, but Will standing in the doorway, his pistol cocked and gripped in his left hand.

"When it is time I will go." Will said softly, each movement of his mouth shooting hot pain across his face. Reid Stuart started for the boy. He stopped when Will raised the pistol and repeated. "I will go when it is time. No one else."

"Dad, please." Katharane gripped her father's arm. "Don't do this now. Please."

Reid Stuart stood staring at the butchered face. He looked at the gunman. He noticed the loop had been slipped away from the hammer of his black pistol. He looked again at his grandson, turned and retreated, defeated, into the kitchen.

As the gunman slid the loop back over the hammer of his pistol, he said. "Some things are better done now, Stuart, and not left to time or chance."

Reid Stuart shook his head, collapsed into his chair at the table and said. "No." It was not to be done.

For two weeks Will seldom left the house. Then one evening as Reid Stuart and the gunman walked from the horse corrals he met them. He carried his pistol and a box of cartridges. "Let me wear your belt." He said to the gunman and pointed at the gunman's worn black gun belt.

The gunman studied the boy. His left eye had not begun to open, though the swelling had begun to retreat from upon it. But the boy's right eye was clear and in it the gunman saw meaning and purpose, with that right eye he could shoot a pistol with his left hand and shoot it accurately. He nodded, untied his gun belt, pulled his pistol from its scabbard, handed the belt to Will and took Will's pistol as Will laced the tongue of the gun belt around his waist. The gunman shoved Will's pistol into the left handed scabbard and grunted. The cut away scabbard offered swift access to the pistol's walnut grip. The gunman guided the boy's unsure left hand to the pistol. But the grip had been, upon the gunman's insistence, designed for the boy's right hand. The gunman took Will's pistol from the scabbard and slid his black pistol into the scabbard. Will looked down at the dark hard grip and then at the gunman's face. No one had ever shot this pistol but the gunman.

407

The gunman nodded and said. "Go to it, boy." Will nodded and went to it. That evening and every evening he shot up ammunition by the box full, until he was more proficient with the gunman's black pistol and his left hand than he had been with his pistol and his right hand.

Two months passed before Will approached the horse corral. When he did he had one of Juan Romero's grandsons saddle a green bronc for him. Katharane saw the horse the boy had caught for Will and stood defiantly between her son and the bronc. "No." She repeated over and over, until her father and the gunman had arrived. It was the gunman who mediated between Will's determination and his mother's protestations. "Tomorrow, we begin again. You and me, boy." The gunman said. "And this time I will teach you to ride and shoot from a horse like a Comanche." To this Will acceded. The next morning and three month's of mornings thereafter he and the gunman worked in the horse corral. Will riding, first the gunman's old black filly, then his grandfather's gentle buckskin and finally the bronc which his mother had refused to allow him to ride. And at the end of each riding lesson and after the last pistol report died away into the darkness ascending from the canyon Reid Stuart embraced the boy, held him gently to him, always careful not to touch his face. And Will allowed this. And Katharane watched, hopefully, fearfully, and wondered. 'Was her son healing? Or was he learning to die?'

The cold brutal plains' winter hardly interrupted the daily riding and shooting for Will. He ignored the bitter cold which bit at the skin on the backs of his hands, as he was now shooting with both hands, his left eye having opened and his sight therein seemingly undiminished, or stung his face as he practiced changing the horse's gait with a shift of his weight, drawing and pointing two perfectly matched black pistols the gunman had somehow procured from the master gunsmith in Taos. One pistol fit his right hand and the other pistol fit his left hand, as if they were a pair of the fine doeskin gloves old Juan Romero crafted for him each Christmas. The gunman refused him live ammunition while he was riding.

"When will I be ready to shoot from horseback?" The boy asked.

"When you're ready." The gunman said.

"When will that be?" The boy demanded.

"When I say you are." The gunman snorted.

How Will's face was healing was not discussed. Katharane forbade any mention of the rippling purple scar above his left eye and across his left cheek. The Escadara retired within itself, and no outsider came because word had gone out that they would not be welcomed. Within the Escadara Will, still a boy, grew, gained skills in shooting and riding few could match, and was revered by his mother and his sister. Little Katty clung to his hand as long as he allowed her to do so, and she met him each time he entered the house with a smile, clapping her hands and reaching for his. And his grandfather found every opportunity to put his arm around the boy's shoulders, to pat him on the chest and to ruffle his hair. All but the gunman obligated themselves to Will's recovery. And yet, it was to the gunman Will turned more and more as spring came to the Escadara.

A late April morning Katharane blocked Will's and the gunman's exit from the kitchen table after breakfast. "Saddle the sorrels for Little Katharane and me." She told her father.

"What for?" The gunman asked.

"We are all riding to the JA's." Katharane answered.

"What the hell for?" The gunman cursed.

"To buy that stallion Tom Hawkins and Bose spoke of yesterday." Katharane said.

"Goodnight will ask a strong price for that animal." Reid Stuart warned. "And we haven't done that much breeding here on the Escadara."

"Whether or not he is used for breeding will be up to Will." Katharane said quietly.

"That's too much horse for Will!" Reid Stuart began. Then he stopped. He looked at his grandson. So much of Will's boyhood had been stolen by the brutality he had experienced. He would take no more of it, not for the cost of any horse. If Katharane wished for Will to have the stallion and Will wanted it, then Will would have it.

Will stared at his mother. He had listened eagerly to Tom Hawkins and Bose describe the great stallion Charles Goodnight had bred at his JA headquarters. The description of the stallion had been an effective ice breaker between Will and the two Goodnight cowboys. Will had talked a long while with them, until he reached up with his hand to brush a loose hair from his face and his fingers bumped across the scar on his cheek and the shock of it caused him to fall sullen and silent. Katharane had rescued him from the strained kindness of Tom Hawkins and Bose Ikard, and quickly the two cowboys had said there farewells and left Will and Katharane standing on the front veranda. She had not seemed to have been aware of his fascination with the stallion the two cowboys had described to him. Now he held her gaze for several seconds, trying to understand how she had understood, how she always understood. He could not. He touched his cheek carefully with his fingers as if he thought maybe, just maybe, the scars had vanished. They had not. He dropped his eyes. "But they'll see my face, mama." He said very softly.

"Yes. They will." Katharane said. She walked to her son and took his face in her hands and lifted his face to her's and kissed him on the mouth. He shuffled his feet, uncomfortable with this in front of his grandfather and the gunman. "They will see my lovely Will." She kissed his mouth again. "It is time, time for all of us to go out from the Escadara again. She has shielded and protected us while we have healed. Now we must take the strength she has given us the time to build and face the world."

Will trembled visibly. He tried to drop his eyes, again. But Katharane held his face and looked deep into his eyes. "Pop. You and Dad saddle the horses. Little Kat, put on your riding britches."

"Yea!" Little Katty cried and raced from the kitchen to do so.

"And Dad." Katharane said. "Ask Consuela Romero to see to the house while we are gone. Juan's boys will take care of the stock."

Will and the gunman stood by their horses as Katharane and Reid Stuart climbed the steps to Mary and Charles Goodnight's front porch. After each had greeted the other Mary Goodnight descended the same steps and walked to Will. He dropped his eyes and pushed his cheek close to his horse's face.

But Mary Goodnight, much as his mother had done, took his face in her hands and turned his damaged cheek so she could inspect it closely. She held Will's chin in her left hand and with the fingers of her right hand she first traced the scar on his cheek and then the one above his eyebrow. She breathed heavily, angrily, and she turned upon her husband, Reid Stuart, and Bose Ikard and Tom Hawkins who now also stood on her porch. "Only a man could do this to his son." She hissed. "A woman could never damage her child so." Her look challenged any to dispute her words. All were silent. She turned back to Will and kissed his cheek and the scar. He blushed as he withdrew a step.

"They didn't come all this way just so you could tell them how damnable mankind is, Mary." Charles Goodnight said to his wife. "They came to buy a horse."

"My Katharane's Will shall have any horse here he wishes to have." Mary Goodnight said as she turned to face her husband. "And you will not insult me by asking a price for it."

"Now, dammit, Mary!" Charles Goodnight began.

But Mary Goodnight cut him off. "And you will not insult me by cursing in my presence." She said pointedly to her husband. Then, and before he could protest, she sent for the stallion. "Mr. Ikard, will you and Tom be so kind as to bring the horse Will has come to see."

"Maybe best, Missus, if Will looks at that stallion in the round pen." Bose Ikard said quietly. "That stallion is still real raw."

"Very well." Mary Goodnight said. She laced her right arm through Will's left and extended her left arm to the gunman, who moved around Will's horse and let her slide it through the crook of his right arm. "Gentlemen." She said firmly. "Will you escort me to the horse corrals?"

"Yes Mam." The gunman said quickly.

Will did not answer, but he brought his step into rhythm with her's and the gunman's. The others followed them to where the stallion stood. He was gray into blue, and the muscles across his rump and through his shoulders seemed to recoil like highly tuned piano strings each time he took a step. Large dark wild, but not unkind, eyes stared down his long nose at the gathering outside of the round pen, where Bose and Tom were trying to train him to move at different gaits by means of a long woven horse haired riata which was attached to a soft doe skin halter which they had managed to slide over his ears and underneath his chin. Each movement spoke of strength and confidence. Each shake of his head flung his long dark mane into waves of defiance and challenge. Within his chest his heart pounded with more courage than most two horses possessed.

Bose Ikard put his right hand on Reid Stuart's shoulder and said. "Awful lot of horse for such a young horseman."

Reid Stuart nodded as he stared at the great animal. He sighed. "Maybe too much horse for my young man. You think, Mr. Ikard?"

Now Bose nodded and said kindly. "For any young man of Will's age, Mr. Reid."

Before his grandfather could answer, Will slipped between the heavy poles of the round pen and walked towards the stallion. The horse raised his head as high as he could and blew his warning at the small man-child that approached him so boldly. But Will kept to his slow approach and he, too, raised his head as high as his still short body could facilitate, dug his top teeth into the front left of his bottom lip and slowly, so slowly, raised his left hand and touched the stallion's nose.

The other's stood transfixed, powerless to aid Will if the stallion struck at him with his front feet and unsure even if they should. The stallion turned his nose slightly away from Will's touch, and as he did his frightened eyes seemed to focus on the horrible scar above the boy's eyebrow. The stallion breathed slowly out through his nose. He reached his nose to the boy's damaged eye and pushed at the scar. Will let him push his fear away, and the boy said the words to the horse that his mother had said to him to ease his fear during that time of great pain. "Yes, my lovely. Yes." Will pushed his face and his scars against the horse's nose and said. "I am not as beautiful as you. But with you, maybe I can become so."

Mary Goodnight stifled a cry as she and the other's listened to Will speak to the horse.

"Yes, my lovely, yes. Maybe, maybe." Will repeated his mother's words as he kept his face pressed to the horse's nose and rubbed the taut muscles along the stallion's neck. "Maybe when I am on you I will be beautiful, too." Will slid his left hand underneath the horse's neck and up into his great mane.

They all saw Will move his hand purposefully into the horse's mane, but it was Bose Ikard who realized what Will intended to do. "Get to the horses." He commanded Tom Hawkins. The two cowboys ran for their saddled horses that stood before Mary Goodnight's porch. But before Bose and Tom could mount and turn their horses back to the corral, Will grasped the horse's mane tightly with both hands and catapulted himself up and astride his massive sinewy back.

"Will!" Katharane cried.

"Dammit, boy, that beast will kill you!" Charles Good-night cursed, and he and Reid Stuart started into the round pen.

"No." It was the cold slow voice of the gunman. "Let him be. He knows this horse as the Comanch' would know him. Leave him to do this." He blocked their way into the round pen.

Bose and Tom sat transfixed by the sight of Will atop the never before mounted great stallion. When the gunman slid the restraining slats free of their guides to release Will and the stallion from their entrapment, they moved their horses forward to support Charles Goodnight's command. "Close that damn opening now!" Before they could do so, the stallion burst from the pen and streaked away. "He'll kill that boy, damn you!" Charles Goodnight roared at the gunman.

"No he won't, old man." The gunman said confidently. "No horse will ever kill that boy."

Will rode with an assured balance gained from hours of practice before the gunman's watchful eyes. He moved fluid like and easy to the great horse's sensibilities of the unaccustomed friction between the hide of his back and the boy's buckskin leggings. The stallion ran unrestrained for almost half a mile, then according to his own measure of what pleased him, he slowed to an ambling walk, and then he stopped and stood and waited. Will sat upon the horse's back and rubbed his neck and spoke to him over and over and over again. The horse accepted the boy being on his back and relaxed his poised muscles and sighed, and Will continued to speak in an ever softer voice to the horse. He pulled slowly against his mane, and the horse turned about and faced the corrals from which he had so shortly ago escaped. "Now, now, my love." Will said to the horse. "Make me beautiful to them again." And he pushed his hands firmly against the awesome muscles of the great horse's neck and the stallion responded by leaping forward into a ground eating gallop. This time he ran to the corrals.

Bose and Tom moved their horses in front of Katharane and Mary Goodnight to be able to block the stallion should he try to run them down. But the great horse raced back into the round pen and around and around it as they watched his head move up and down in cadence with his strides and Will's rhythmic rise and fall upon his back, horse and boy moving as one.

"What are we watching here?" Tom Hawkins asked softly.

"Young Alexander atop his Bucephalous." Bose Ikard replied.

Reid Stuart looked at the black cowboy. "You have studied the ancient Greeks?"

"Some." Bose stared at Will and the galloping stallion. "Some." He repeated.

Charles Goodnight slid the retraining poles back into place to make the round pen secure again. The stallion slowed, stopped, took a deep breath, blew it out. Then he breathed quietly, easily. Will slid from his back and stroked the sweat his friction had left there away with the palm of his right hand. The gunman withdrew a small canvas pouch from within his shirt. On it were stenciled the letters; "U. S." He untied the draw string which closed it and began to pour untarnished gold coins into his hand. "How much, old man?" He asked Charles Goodnight.

Goodnight shook his head. "No. Not for that horse and not for that boy. The horse is his." He pointed at the canvas bag in the gunman's hand. "Besides, I would always wonder by what means you came by that gold."

The gunman shrugged, dropped the coins back into the bag, retied the draw string and slid the bag back beneath his buckskin shirt.

Will and his stallion were inseparable. Day after day, week after week, month after month together they challenged even the gunman's horsemanship. Such riding by such a young man so marked upon such an animal as the stallion brought talk among a society of horsemen. From the Escadara and across the plains, even into the badlands of New Mexico, word traveled of beautiful Katharane Stuart's scarred son and the wondrous stallion he rode. Word found jealousy and coveting among good and bad and among an old and bitter nemesis who had once challenged the Escadara and there missed his opportunity for the lovely girl child who then lived upon the great ranch. Now he planned to have the woman that girl child had become and the stallion.

"Where is Tom?" Charles Goodnight demanded.

Bose Ikard took his time in answering. Until he knew his employer would not be avoided as to Tom Hawkins whereabouts. "With Miss Katharane and the little missy." Bose said quietly.

Charles Goodnight turned in his saddle and stared at the black cowboy. "Does Reid Stuart know he's there?"

"Mr. Reid would not say if he did or not. Now would he, Mr. Charles?"

"No. He would not." Charles Goodnight looked out across the milling cattle in the big canyon that formed the top most part of his range. He could see Reid Stuart and the boy on the stallion, and farther out he saw the gunman. "But if that damn gunman knew. He would not be here." He turned back to Bose. "And if he rides there, are you certain of Tom Hawkins' safety?"

Bose Ikard shook his head. "No. But Mr. Charles, Tom loves Katharane. 'has for a long time now."

"I cannot blame him for that, Bose. But it may be to his interest that we ride with Reid Stuart, Will and that gunman for the Escadara. These cattle can be left to the cowboys." Charles Goodnight said thoughtfully.

"Mr. Reid is leaving the round-up today?" Bose asked.

Charles Goodnight nodded. "Mid morning. He told me last night." Charles Goodnight sighed. "Coincidence or fate, Mr. Ikard?"

415

"Bad luck, Mr. Charles. Just bad luck for our Tom."

Katharane watched Tom Hawkins strong back shift as the sorrel horse shifted and picked its way through the thick cedars at the top of the Ceta. Kat followed behind him on her small pony and as she turned around and passed each stand of cedars she looked back and smiled at Katharane. A picnic, Tom Hawkins had skipped a day with the round up to ride fifteen miles to invite her and her daughter to picnic with him near the mouth of the big canyon. She smiled. To do this took more courage for him than to mount a young bronc. He looked back at her and he grinned. As she drew in her breath to call ahead to him the first gunshots rang from above them, from the corrals of the Escadara. She cried out and stared wide eyed at Tom Hawkins. They stopped and listened. More gunshots, some, most were muffled.

"The Romero's have forted up. They're firing from inside. Hear it?" Tom Hawkins asked.

"Yes. Yes!" Katharane gritted her teeth. They had made it inside from the corrals. At least some of them had, and now they were returning a determined fire upon their attackers. "They are safe inside."

"Until they try to burn them out." Tom Hawkins cautioned.

"Rock walls and a sod roof will not burn. Pop and Dad thought of that."

Tom nodded. "They would. They've been under siege. They know the weaknesses." Then he stopped and listened and understood. He had been long enough in these canyons to recognize the sound of hoof beats.

Katharane heard them, too. She lifted Little Kat from her pony and set her in front of her. "They're trailing us."

Tom nodded, again. "You and Little Kat ride for the big canyon and the round-up." He pulled his saddle gun from its scabbard. "I'll hold 'em here as long as I can."

Katharane stared at him. She had known that Tom Hawkins was in love with her. Now she knew he loved her as well. "Tom." She hesitated. She kissed her daughter's hair.

"It's the only way, Katharane." He nodded at Little Kat. "It's her best chance."

Katharane swallowed, stared into his quiet eyes, then she turned her horse and rode for the big canyon.

The stallion and the black filly raced south along the western rim of the high mesa. Reid Stuart, Charles Goodnight and Bose Ikard chased after them. At the junction of the mesa's western and southern rims Charles Goodnight and Bose Ikard bore east, searching for a grade their horses could descend safely. Reid Stuart reined in and dismounted. The gunman and Will plunged off an almost vertical drop of two hundred feet of loose reddish dirt studded with black volcanic boulders twice the size of their horses rising out of the red dirt like a forest of dark cacti.

"Look!" Bose Ikard pointed across his shoulder.

Charles Goodnight turned in his saddle to see the filly and the stallion fly off of the rim of the mesa and Reid Stuart adjusting the rear sight of his great Sharps rifle which stretched before him from where he sat cross-legged near the rim of the mesa. Its long barrel rested on the steel rod which Reid Stuart had driven into the hard surface of the mesa.

The gunman spurred the black filly, driving her forward off of her haunches which she tried to sit back on against the loose sliding slick giving dirt of the wall of the mesa. Instead of sitting back in the saddle to protect their balance like most experienced riders would have done, the gunman and Will sat forward against the front cantle of their saddles and gave their horses the bit and urged them on.

"They'll never make it, Mr. Charles!" Bose cried.

"They'll make it." Charles Goodnight assured him. "They're the finest light horsemen these canyons have known since the Comanche."

The filly and the stallion seemed to fly past the black volcanic bastions, always to find their feet just prior to crashing into one and sure enough to cut safely to the left or right of it. The two horses shot out onto the prairie.

"Katty! Ride to me!" The old gunman's voice rose like the high wail of the wolf, echoing through the light conducive air of the great Palo Duro, higher and higher, bouncing out across the prairie, filled with the old and aching and weary feelings of love and hope and despair and anger and courage and fear.

Katharane recognized the distant voice. She saw the gunman and Will riding toward her at full gallop. She swung her head and saw Charles Goodnight and Bose Ikard far away to the east. Then she looked over her shoulder and saw the Comanchero. He was gaining quickly on her blown horse. She put her hand against the side of the desperate horse's neck and eased it in the direction of the gunman and Will.

The Comanchero heard the gunman's cry, too. He drew his rifle from the saddle scabbard, bolted a shell into the chamber, raised the rifle and waited for his horse's stride to lift all four of its feet from the ground simultaneously.

On the mesa Reid Stuart set the firing trigger of his old Sharps, raised its sights and sighted through them and saw the Comanchero raise his rifle. Reid Stuart knew he could not risk the one in a million shot that might find the Comanchero and kill him. Instead he found the galloping horse's front shoulder, sighted upon it, lifted the Sharps from its prop on the iron stake and slowly swung the long barrel in front of the horse and, still easing the barrel ahead of the horse, squeezed the trigger.

A heartbeat before the Sharps roared the Comanchero fired his rifle. He blasted the sorrel's left hind leg from beneath the horse. Katharane felt the bullet strike the sorrel, felt the horse struggle valiantly to gather its torn leg back beneath it and knew it could not do so. She kicked her feet free of the stirrups, wrapped her arms around Little Katty, lifted the child free of the saddle, and as the sorrel collapsed beneath them, Katharane rolled to the right, the child clutched in her arms, and careened down into the grass of the canyon.

The Comanchero had but a moment of satisfaction before the air around him exploded with the concussion of the heavy fifty caliber slug's impact into his horse's shoulder. The horse nose dived toward the canyon floor. The Comanchero had no chance to save his rifle. He opened his hands and it flashed away. He put both of his hands upon the front cantle of his saddle and pushed up, kicking furiously to free his boots from the now deadly Spanish tapederos which covered the fronts of his stirrups, then he tucked his right shoulder and rolled free of the falling horse.

The impact with the ground ripped Little Katty from Katharane's arms. Katharane continued to roll. Her breath was knocked from her. She rolled for what seemed minutes but was but parts of a second, until the fall's momentum dissipated and she lay on her back and sucked for breath.

The Comanchero cart wheeled twice, then stopped himself with his hands, and sat on his knees and looked around. Little Katty stood a few yards from him. The child was confused. She turned her head from side to side, but she did not seem to see either the Comanchero or her mother, who had managed to sit up. The Comanchero stood up and walked to the child. He could hear the stallion's and the filly's hooves pounding toward him. He glanced over his shoulder and stared for a second at the great Goodnight stallion and thought. 'You and I. Together we could have taken whatever and whoever we wished and rode faster and farther than any who would chase us. But it's not to be.' He sighed, turned back to the child and slowly began to draw one of his pistols from its holster.

Little Katty stared, her eyes opened wide and willing, transfixed by the evil which glistened in the Comanchero's eyes, innocence into pure carnality. She opened her hands, which she held in front of her, and closed them, rhythmically.

Katharane realized the Comanchero's intent. She struggled to her feet but she was still too far from her daughter to save her. "No!" She screamed with fury and fright, pleading and damning, praying and cursing.

The gunman reached for his pistol. The stallion was three lengths ahead of his filly, closer to the Comanchero, closer to Little Katty, closer to Katty, closer... "Take the shot, Will! Take the shot!" The gunman beseeched the boy on the stallion which raced before him.

Will lifted his pistol from its holster, stood high in his stirrups, took a long, clean breath of air, held it in his lungs, tried to stop his heart from beating, waited for the stallion to gather all four of its feet beneath them, pointed the pistol and fired.

From the mesa Reid Stuart saw the Comanchero point his pistol at Little Katty, saw Katharane stand up, saw the gunman railing the black filly with his spurs, desperately, futilely trying to fly across the unforgiving distance between life and death, and saw his grandson, his wonderful damaged grandson, rise from his saddle and shoot. Reid Stuart saw the one in a million shot tear into the Comanchero's elbow, blasting bone from it, freeing the pistol from the Comanchero's grip before he could fire it. He saw the pistol falling to the ground. Then he swung himself astride the buckskin, still clutching his rifle, and rode for the far end of the mesa where Charles Goodnight and Bose Ikard had descended from it to the canyon floor.

The Comanchero squealed with pain and surprise, and grabbed his shattered elbow. "Madre de Criste!" He swore as he took a step toward Little Katty. He held another pistol in his right hand. He still intended to kill the child. He ravaged her with his wild eyes. Then he stopped. It was at first low and deep, more a rumble than a cry, but it rose in pitch and intensity until it whistled through the air. Little Katty watched the Comanchero's sun tarnished face go pale and ashen as he recognized the old Comanche death cry. He turned, but he turned too late. The stallion did not hesitate, did not flinch, he slammed into the Comanchero and sent him crashing to the ground on his back. The Comanchero rolled onto his stomach as the great horse surged across him. He struggled to his feet. With his right hand he still clung to his last pistol. His shattered left arm hung at his side useless. He stared into the bore of the gunman's black revolver.

Little Katty sat not three feet from the pistols. Katharane scrambled to her and pushed her away from the two combatants. When Katharane looked again, Will stood beside the gunman.

The Comanchero studied the gunman's grey eyes. They did not blink. The black revolver was still pointed straight at his heart. He looked at Katharane. But he stared into the angry and unforgiving eyes of an embattled mother. He turned to Will. "Por favor, el nino." He pleaded. His eyes opened wide with surprise as he saw Will shove his pistol back into its holster. He glanced at the gunman. His pistol, too, sat in its holster. 'You choose to die, a pistolero, rather than let me live, eh?' He thought to himself and smiled as he cocked his pistol.

The gunman and Will stood side by side, unblinking and quiet, almost as if they were about to draw against each other rather than the Comanchero.

"Vaya con diablo, pistoleros!" The Comanchero screamed as he jerked his pistol upward. He did not get it above his hip. Will's right hand and the gunman's left hand moved without motion, their pistols seeming as but a part of their hands. Will's bullet crashed into the Comanchero's right shoulder. The Comanchero screamed again and dropped his pistol. The gunman's pistol, still cocked, was pointed at his face.

Charles Goodnight and Bose Ikard had witnessed the gun-fight as their winded horses staggered the last few yards to Katharane and Little Katty. The Comanchero treated with the old man. "Mercy, senor. Mercy." He begged of Charles Goodnight. He looked back into Will's and the gunman's eyes and cried out. "No! Madre! Por favor! Por favor!"

"Vaya con diablo." Will softly mimicked the Comanchero as he pushed his pistol at the Comanchero's right eye. The gunman shoved his pistol close to the Comanchero's left eye.

"No! Goddammit! No!" Charles Goodnight roared.

Katharane turned Little Katty's face against her stomach. She knew that Charles Goodnight's commands were in vain as to the gunman for even she could not silence his gun once it was drawn. But Will's? Could Charles Goodnight quiet her son's gun?

Will's pistol raged in chorus with the gunman's. Their black revolvers belched smoke from the heavy loads they used and the hack sawed bullets ripped out the entire back of the Comanchero's head.

"Damn you!" Charles Goodnight cursed the gunman.

The gunman glared at the old plainsman. "You can go with him, old man. No man's ever looked into the bore of my pistol and lived to tell about it and none ever will as long as I draw breath. I put him down and I'd put a thousand down like him." He turned to Will. "You know this, boy. You draw on a man. You kill him. Live by it or you will die by it."

Will nodded and watched the gunman pull his knife from its sheath and step to the body of the Comanchero. With four swift strokes he etched the drooped E deep into the corpse's forehead.

421

"You bloody savage!" Charles Goodnight swore at the gunman again.

Reid Stuart dismounted and stepped to the gunman who now menaced Charles Goodnight. "Out ride, out shoot and out savage any of them." The gunman said to Reid Stuart.

"You've done that." Reid Stuart agreed. "And out loved them, too."

The gunman stared at his partner. Reid Stuart's words either confused or enraged the gunman for a terrible darkness came upon his face as he spoke. "You made good use of it all."

Reid Stuart nodded and said. "That I did. We all did."

"Miss Katharane." Bose said. Katharane turned to him. "Tom?" He asked.

"Oh! My God!" Katharane exclaimed. "Tom stayed in our canyon to try to stop them. There were shots, Bose." She stopped as she saw a great sadness welling into the black cowboy's gentle eyes.

"That explains why this butcher was alone." The gunman said. "Just too bad that damn cowboy wasn't good enough to get him, too."

"Good! Good!" Bose Ikard moved at the gunman and only Katharane stepping between them and grasping his forearms prevented more bloodshed.

"Tom, Bose. Tom." Katharane repeated. "We must get to him as fast as we can."

"Can't." The gunman snorted. "These horses are blown." He glanced at his filly, who stood spread legged with her head down, Bose Ikard's horse, whose chest still heaved with its heavy breathing, even Charles Goodnight's good grey trembled with fatigue. Only Will's stallion and Reid Stuart's buckskin stood with their heads erect, their ears alert, without any sign of fatigue or duress.

Will walked to the stallion and picked up his reins. "I'll go." He said quietly. Before he could swing himself up and into the saddle, Little Katty ran to him. She burrowed her face into her brother's chest. He had passed from being her brother. He had become something more for her, her protector, yes, but something more still, something indefinable, godlike. Now she knew no harm could approach her while she was in his presence. He lifted her chin and winked at her. "You'll be okay. Mom will see to that." He said to her.

She shook her little head. "No, Will. Only you, Will." She looked deep into her brother's eyes, into his brave heart and his good soul, and she smiled and this made Will smile back at her. She stepped back and Will jumped, stabbed the stirrup with his left foot and swung astride the stallion.

"Not alone!" Katharane cried.

"Get your saddle off of the black." Reid Stuart commanded the gunman as he pulled his saddle off of his buckskin. "This buckskin is the only horse we have with enough bottom left to run with that stallion." He helped the gunman swing his saddle across the buckskin. "We will be behind you, but too far and too slow to support you." He grunted as he jerked the cinch tight against the buckskin's belly. "Don't start thinking now. Shoot straight and shoot first." He jerked the cinch one more time and laced the cinch through itself.

The gunman swung up into the saddle. Reid Stuart rested his right hand on the gunman's left leg. The gunman reached down with his left hand and clasped Reid Stuart's forearm. "Straight and fast." He said. "Will and I will be waiting for you at the Escadara." Then two good horses and two brave men charged away.

Katharane, Reid Stuart, Charles Goodnight, Bose Ikard and Little Katty, who Bose now held in his arms, watched their straight backs diminish as the great distance of the big canyon made each rider appear of the same stature, until that distance finally swallowed the riders and they could see only the outlines of the two horses, far away, going fast, going forward, going unafraid into the darkness of the unknown.

Reid Stuart's long stirrups dangled beneath the black filly. They almost touched the ground as the tired little horse plodded after Bose Ikard's horse. Little Katty now rode on Bose Ikard's lap. Ahead of Bose and Little Katty, Katharane rode behind Charles Goodnight. The small procession moved slowly into the Ceta Canyon. Reid Stuart spurred the filly until she finally trotted passed Bose Ikard, his granddaughter, his daughter and Charles Goodnight. He cocked the hammer on his Sharps rifle. Ahead, somewhere in the Ceta he knew Tom Hawkins had waged a desperate fight to give Katharane enough time to save Little Katty. He knew that Tom Hawkins lay dead or dying and the vermin that had brought this upon Tom Hawkins might be perched close by like vultures if his partner and his grandson had somehow passed by them unknowingly. It was not for Charles Goodnight and his daughter to go first into this place of battle. It was for him to do this, and he did.

Before him Consuelo Romero straightened from where she bent over the prone figure of a man, Tom Hawkins. Now Bose Ikard and Charles Goodnight trotted passed Reid Stuart. Bose handed Little Katty down to Consuelo. She took the child and stood her on the ground behind her. Bose swung down and kneeled beside Tom Hawkins. He looked hard at the cowboy for several moments. Then he looked up at the Mexican woman. "He's alive?" He spoke the question.

Consuelo nodded. "But so little of his life is left within." She said sadly.

Bose looked at the small bunch of scrub cedars three yards passed where Tom Hawkins lay. Blood matted the grass, stained most of the lowest limbs of the cedar and tinted the ground beneath where Tom Hawkins strong heart had pumped it through the neat slice in his side beneath his left rib cage. "Bowie knife." Bose said softly to the bloody battle site.

"Butcher's knife." Consuelo said. She looked at Reid Stuart who stood beside Charles Goodnight and one of her son's, who held a Winchester in his hands and stared horror eyed at the blood. Katharane sat on her knees beside Tom Hawkins as, inexplicably, Little Katty moved passed her, sat herself above Tom Hawkins' silent face, lifted his head and slid her small lap beneath it. The cowboy groaned. The child stroked his face. All stared at the child, mesmerized by her instinctive kindness and her gentle courage. Consuelo broke the silence. "I have done what I know for your friend." She glanced shyly at Bose Ikard. He nodded his thanks. "Now, El Senor Reid." She said to Reid Stuart. "I have a son and a son-in-law bleeding in my bed, needing my care. I am here because that man." She pointed at the gunman, who with Will approached on their horses from the trail up to the tinajas. "With his black gun forced me to be here. I go now to my blood, El Senor." She pounded her chest with her closed fist. "And if he wishes to stop me, he will do so only if he shoots me with his pistola de negra." She stomped angrily passed the gunman and Will. Her son followed her up the trail.

Reid Stuart looked at the gunman and shook his head.

"What?" The gunman asked. "Hell! It was Will's idea. I just encouraged her a little."

Again, Reid Stuart shook his head.

"Cowboy got two of 'em before that Comanchero closed with him." The gunman said flatly. "Comanchero must have been in a hell of a hurry. Strange he didn't bother to finish gutting him." He looked at Tom Hawkins, then at Katharane and finally his cold grey eyes set on Reid Stuart. "He meant to have Katharane. He would have, had it not been for Will's shot." He squeezed Will's shoulder, approvingly.

"And." Reid Stuart said firmly. "If Tom Hawkins had not stood his ground and fought it out with them."

"Like I said," the gunman said, "the cowboy got two of them. He should have gotten all three."

Reid Stuart started for the gunman's horse. The gunman straightened in his saddle. Will moved the stallion in front of the gunman's horse.

"Dad! Pop! Enough." Katharane commanded from where she sat beside Tom Hawkins. "Tom Hawkins stood his ground for us. Will fired his shot for us. For us!" She stressed the last two words. "Now let us do for Tom Hawkins all we can."

Reid Stuart stopped and stared angrily at the gunman.

"Mama." Little Katty said softly.

"Yes, darling." Katharane looked into her daughter's deep brown eyes, then she saw the silver band the child held in the palm of her hand.

"It was in his shirt pocket, Mama." The child explained. "What is it?"

Katharane looked up at Bose Ikard. Bose pulled a piece of rawhide cord from his saddle bag and walked to Katharane, Tom Hawkins and Little Katty. He lifted the ring from the child's open palm, slid the cord through it, tied the ends of the cord together and gently draped it over the child's head and lifted her curly hair over the cord. "You keep it for him, Little Missy." Bose said. "Until he wake's up."

Little Katty smiled and fingered the ring.

"Why would Tom have a ring, Bose?" Katharane asked.

"Can't say." Bose answered.

"You can't or you won't?" Katharane asked.

"Maybe." Bose said very slowly. "Maybe Tom will say. Just maybe he will." The black cowboy said, almost prayerfully.

THE SHIELD BEARER

Tom Hawkins died that night. Katharane sought as she had done with the gunfighter to force Tom to will himself to live for her. But Tom Hawkins was just a cowboy. And as such he did not possess that arrogance of conceit such as the gunfighter possessed which would let him presume a love so strong that it could incite life could be a love meant for him. So, late in the night in Katharane's arms with Bose Ikard and Charles Goodnight attending Tom Hawkins died and Reid Stuart began to die.

Katharane found it on her father's back just above his left shoulder blade when she was washing away the dusty blood which had dripped from his left ear which a recoiling cedar branch had torn as he had galloped after an escaping calf in the Ceta, a black mole with spiders' legs springing out from it. For months the spider grew and as it grew Reid Stuart weakened. Then the spider's body, the mole, burst. It oozed a noxious drip of decaying tissue. Each night for weeks Katharane bathed and salved the spider's bleeding belly. Often she cleansed moss or mud, and once dung, from the seeping mole which the gunman had caked onto it, trying to alleviate Reid Stuart's suffering as Reid Stuart struggled to continue to ride and to work each day. The Escadara demanded long hard hours of work everyday from everyone who lived upon her passed the age of eight years. Of the men each day she required them to stay horseback from first light until early dark to maintain her and her stock. She demanded it even of dying men.

Reid Stuart and Katharane stood on the veranda and watched the old gunfighter limp to the corral, open the gate, walk through and close the gate behind him. Katharane worked her fingers, the way she had when she was a child, interlocking them, flexing them, then folding them across the knuckles of her other hand. Reid Stuart glanced at his daughter's hands. They were good strong hands. He was proud of them. He was proud of Katharane.

"Why is Pop angry so often now, Dad?"

Reid Stuart coughed into his fist. He coughed more each day now. And the quiet sure strength that had always been there was quickly slipping away from him. "You, Katharane, he's angry with you." Reid Stuart's eyes filled with tears.

"With me!" Katharane cried. "But Pop and I have always been so close, Dad. I love him."

"Yes." Reid Stuart nodded his head. "Yes. You do love him. But not as a woman loves a man."

"Pop cannot want that of me, Dad!"

Reid Stuart choked off another cough. He put his long bony arm around his daughter's waist. "You're my child, Katharane. You will always be my child. But you are a woman, also. One of the most beautiful and desirable women I have ever seen."

Katharane blushed.

"And Canada's never wanted a woman, never sought any relief from the feelings that haunt men there. Except for the two women he's loved." Reid Stuart pulled his daughter against his side and held her there as they watched the gunman saddle the black filly. "Oh Katty girl!" Reid Stuart whispered. "Can't you see? He came here so long ago because he couldn't have someone he loved. And if he couldn't have her he wouldn't have anyone. I don't doubt his sincerity in doing it, nor should you. He's lived by it. He's spent better'n thirty years making love to a saddle instead of a woman because of it. Now he sees you everyday, alone, here with him, yet so very far away. And try not to as he may he wants you and he cannot have you."

"He's spent thirty years making love to a dream, Dad, a dream. Isn't it time he stopped dreaming?" Katharane asked. "Even about me?"

"And do what?" Reid Stuart put his rough hard chin on top of his daughter's head. "I don't know what to do for him, Katharane. I love him. But God help me I have thought about shooting him."

"Oh Dad." Katharane laughed. "You're getting as bad as

he is about solving problems by shooting someone." When she looked up into her father's eyes her laughter left. Reid Stuart was tired and scared and sick. Katharane forced herself to smile into those old eyes and then she kissed his cheek. "Don't worry, Dad. We'll work through his. I promise. I'll speak with him. It will be better between us. You will see."

Reid Stuart nodded his chin against the top of Katharane's head. "Good. Good. You do that." He said. But the dark shadow of sickness and doubt did not leave his eyes nor his heart.

"What do you mean he ain't comin'?" The gunfighter stood in the kitchen doorway. "It's dawn. 'time to saddle up and be at it."

"You have the Romeros and Will. That should be enough help for today." Katharane said.

"That ain't the point." The gunfighter said angrily. "It's his damn ranch. Tell him to get up off his lazy ass and get to the corrals." He demanded."

Katharane reached and took the gunman's hands in hers. "I don't believe he can, Pop."

"It's not a matter of can or can't. He has to." The gunfighter pulled his hands free from Katharane's. He pushed passed her and walked into the bedroom where Reid Stuart lay upon the bed. He stopped next to the bed. "Get up, damn you Stuart." He swore, but his voice broke. He stared at Reid Stuart's disease racked body. A dark liquid drained from the open sore on his left shoulder. His body rattled with each breath he took.

Katharane watched the gunfighter. His hands trembled and he swayed, unsteady on his feet.

"Get up, damn you. Get up." He pleaded with Reid Stuart.

Reid Stuart opened his sunken eyes. "Is it time to saddle up?" He asked, his voice raspy and dry.

Katharane waited. She knew her father could not rise. She waited to see if the gunfighter would ask it of him.

"No, Reid. No. It's not time to saddle up. Go on back to sleep." The gunfighter's voice broke. He whispered. "Go to sleep. Just go to sleep."

Katharane caught the gunfighter's arm as he retreated from Reid Stuart's sickroom. She had never heard the gunman call her father by his given name alone. The gunman did not look at her. She released his arm and let him walk away. She watched him through the open kitchen door as he reached the corrals, lifted his saddle off of the cedar rail and moved to the black filly.

"Canada." Reid Stuart called from his bed.

Katharane pulled her gaze away from the corrals and went to her father. She rubbed his cheek.

"He was here." Reid Stuart's voice was weak.

"Yes. He was here." Katharane agreed.

"Where is he now?" Reid Stuart tried to raise his head.

Katharane laid the back of her hand on his forehead. "Pop's riding now, Dad."

"Send him to me, Katharane. When he comes in, send him to me." Reid Stuart coughed.

"I will, Dad. I will."

Katharane watched the gunfighter lead the black filly into the corral. The gunman limped now, more than ever before. His wounds ached, especially at the end of a long day's ride. But he rode almost every day. It was as though he believed he could ride away Reid Stuart's sickness. He could not. The black Buddha that grew ever larger on Reid Stuart's back and the putrid sore on his arm that would not heal were only the signs of the sickness that was settling inside of Reid Stuart's body and consuming it.

Katharane gripped her sides and wondered what terrible dreams she had brought to the gunman in the night. She was a woman now and better perceived the yearnings of men towards her. She felt a need to go to him. She walked to the corral. He laid his saddle across the top cedar rail of the horse corral which he and Reid Stuart had rebuilt after the Comanchero's first raid. The Romero boy, Miguel, led the black filly to her stall in the new barn. The gunman slid between the second and third rails of the corral. She caught him as he straightened, sliding her arms between his and locking her fingers together behind his back. She kissed him on his cheek and said. "You look tired, Pop."

"'gettin' old."

Katharane smiled at him and kissed his cheek, again. "You and Dad."

The grey eyes locked into Katharane's devastatingly brown eyes. "Is he better?"

She rubbed her cheek against the gunman's and said. "No, Pop. No."

"He's dying."

Katharane released him.

"He's dying." The gunman repeated. He chewed the inside of his cheek. "I've seen too many men die not to know." He sighed. "'caused some of 'em to die myself."

"Yes. You have." Katharane said. She crossed her arms across her stomach. "The twentieth century has begun and you are still wearing a sidearm, Pop."

"'reckon I'll wear it 'till I die."

"Yes. I imagine you will." Katharane sighed. "Let's hope it's not what causes you to die."

"'better that having it causes me to die, than not having it does."

"Do you believe that, Pop?"

"I have to, Katty. I've lived by it for all these years."

Their eyes met again. Each searched the other's for understanding, for acceptance, for love, unconditional and undefined. Love, each wanted it so desperately from the other and each felt compelled to withhold it from the other for neither knew what it was nor how to share it unconditionally, undefined. He dropped his eyes from her's and Katharane said quietly. "Dad wants you."

The gunfighter nodded and limped to the house. Katharane followed him to the house. She sat on the veranda and she could hear her father's voice weak and strained and unintelligible, interrupted only occasionally by the gunman's soft inaudible slur. Lulled by their familiarity she rocked and dozed until Will walked from within the house and touched her arm.

"Mom." Will said very gently.

Katharane sat up. "Yes. What's wrong?"

"Nothing's wrong, Mom. Granddad wants us to take Little Kat and all the Romeros into Tascosa and buy supplies."

"Now?" Katharane asked incredulously. "It will be dark before we reach Tascosa. And we will have to spend the night there before we can buy supplies."

"I know." Will said. "But Granddad says to do it now." The boy waited for his mother to speak. When she did not, he asked. "Granddad wants it. Should I get the Romeros to ready the wagons?"

Katharane swallowed. She surmised her father wished to spare Will and Little Kat the immediacy of his death, let them learn of it rather than observe it. And he desired none of the loud lamenting the Romero women would bestow upon his corpse. He wished for the stillness, the quiet that had first bred his love of the Escadara and the plains, in which to die.

"He wants you to go too, Mom."

She shook her head and said. "No, Will. I mustn't. I fear Dad would use that to leave us." She stopped, realizing what she said might make Will unwilling to leave, and she, too, wanted to spare her son this ordeal. "Besides, I cannot leave Pop alone. He might wander off."

Will chuckled. But there was only sadness in his eyes. Katharane kissed her son. "Go. Tell the Romeros." As he walked away she added. "Take care of your sister."

"Kat's mine." Will said. "I'll see to her."

Katharane smiled and thought. 'Yes, Will. Yes she is.'

As Will, riding the stallion, led the Romeros and Little Kat, who sat on one of the wagon seats between Juan Romero and Consuelo, away from the corrals the gunfighter came out onto the veranda and sat in the second rocker on the veranda beside Katharane and handed her one of the small snifters filled with brandy. Together they watched the small caravan depart.

"You and I have never drank before, Pop." Katharane said as she studied the liquor in the shaped glass.

"Tonight we will." The gunman answered, and with his eyes he urged her glass to her lips as he sipped from his.

Together they took small sips of the strong liquor. As it sedated her reluctance and restraint Katharane began to speak of what weighed now so heavy upon her mind. "Did you love her that much, Pop? So much you would never look for another woman? Could you really have loved her that much?"

"'dunno', maybe." The gunfighter swallowed another sip of the brandy, as unaccustomed to its effects as Katharane. "But whether I did or not doesn't seem to matter. Never did. I thought I loved her that much. I believed it everyday for almost twenty years. Until one morning I awoke and I loved you, Katty."

"Oh Pop! What's happened to us?"

"You've grown up. You're a woman. And women always change."

"No. It's not that I've changed, it's that you look at me as a woman." Katharane took a deep breath, and said, "And you want me as a woman."

"You just now figuring that out?"

Katharane's eyes began to swell. "No. I've known it for some time now. Dad told me. But I knew it even before that. I just didn't want to believe it."

"Reid Stuart told you that?"

"Yes."

"'guess he was a lot tougher than I ever gave him credit for being."

"He was tough enough not to begrudge you wanting his daughter."

The gunfighter felt the weight of the unfinished letter which he carried inside his shirt. "Maybe." He massaged his bottom lip with his tongue. "Maybe not."

"Damn you, Pop. Damn you for wanting me!" Katharane

said angrily.

"Why does that make you so angry with me? I wanted to love a woman that I knew better than I knew I would take my next breath loved me. Isn't that what a man's supposed to want from a woman?"

"Not you from me. Not you from me." Katharane whispered as she rose unsteadily from her rocker, moved to the gunman's and dropped into his lap, laying her face against his right shoulder, her hair catching the tears which scattered across his rough whisker stubbled face.

The plains' night came to Katharane and the gunfighter and held them in its dark hands, as it had so many times. They rested in its grip until the gunman sighed and said. "That woman I told you about when you asked about your mother. Do you remember?"

"Yes. I remember." Katharane said. It was one of their rides together that she often sought from her memory and let fill her mind just before she let sleep overtake her.

"She was married. That's why she couldn't love me anymore she said. So she just quit loving me. How can that be, Katty?"

"I don't know, Pop." Katharane lifted the brandy to her lips and sipped more of the dark liquid. She rubbed her head against the gunman's strong face, sipped more brandy and asked. "But you just didn't try again, Pop? You never looked for anyone else?"

"Can you look for your soul, Katty? Can you really find that like you would find a stray calf?" He gently rubbed his cheek against her hair. "No, my love. Love must find you if you are to be found at all." Emptiness, disillusionment rang in his voice. He had loved that woman. He loved Katharane. And yet he did not! He loved his idea of them. His soul was lost, lost in what he imagined them to be. He felt Katharane sipping the brandy. He rocked her, held her in his arms, until the narcotic effect of the alcohol, her deep weariness gained from too many hours during too many days at her father's sickbed and her emotional exhaustion drug her into a fitful but deep sleep. The gunman rose from the rocker, Katharane in his arms, her glass breaking as it struck the veranda's scarred floorboards, and carried her into the house, into her room, where he laid her on the sheets he had exposed earlier when he had turned the covers of her bed back and placed them so as to accept her wondrous form.

Katharane vaguely, intuitively sensed the familiar strength of the arms which lay her on the clean sheets and the unfamiliar taste of the lips which moved across her lips and she took those lips within her's and tried to hold them there until they were washed free by the salty wetness she tasted creeping into the corner's of her mouth as the strange lips pulled away from her's.

Katharane struggled to free herself from the tangled sheets and the hazy residue of sedated sleep. She straightened yesterday's dress which she had slept in and stumbled to her father's door. She listened. She heard nothing, not even his labored breathing, and panic plunged her through the door. And, nothing, the bed where her father had lain held only the smoothed blankets. The room which sickness had sucked the life from was indeed lifeless. No one was there. Katharane stood at the foot of the bed, confused. What had happened last night? She struggled to remember, but only the vague glimpses of the gunman carrying her to bed and of his back as he trudged away from her and out of her room came to her. What had happened? She looked about the room and on the small slatted table below the coal oil lamp beside the head of the bed she saw three sheets of large parchment paper, folded lengthwise, resting inside her father's Bible. The Bible rested atop a tanned leather valise which the gunman had crafted to hold Reid Stuart's incessant records of the stock of the Escadara.

Her hands trembled as she opened the Bible and lifted the parchment. Beneath it she noticed the eighty-eighth Psalm. Her eyes scanned the Psalm until they came to the last verse which she read aloud. "Lover and friend has thou put far from me, and mine acquaintance into darkness." She held the parchment against her chest and walked out onto the veranda and sat in the rocker in which the gunfighter had sat the night before and held her in his arms. She unfolded the parchment and read:

"Katharane Diane Stuart married to William Harrell. You have chosen to retain the name I christened you with. So be it. Katharane Diane Stuart, my daughter, on these few pages of yellow parchment I say farewell to you and I leave you some of the lessons I have learned. Lessons I wish you to know without the biting pain of experience. And to advise you as to paths you may find suitable to follow in dealing with the one gift, the only gift, Canada and I leave you—the Escadara.

By now you know that Canada is writing this for me. You could not mistake his script. It was by imitating his script that you learned your letters, to sign your name, to sing the Psalms and to help me keep the journals of the land and the stock of the Escadara. And it is well that I should be telling you this by means of his hand for that hand has long steadied me, has steadfastly supported any play I chose to make, and has unfailingly and unquestioningly placed itself between danger and death meant for me and you and the Escadara time and time again. But it is also that hand that makes it imperative that you abide by the course Canada and I follow. For without me to help guide it that hand poses certain danger and probable harm to you, to your's and to the Escadara.

Please! My daughter. Hear me out. Finish my pages to you before you judge me traitorous or fiendish or lacking in both compassion and fealty for you and to my partner.

Oh Katharane! How to say what the years have held silent within my mind. Katharane, your mother's name is written on one of the sealed documents encased within the leather valise which lay beneath this scroll. What good that name may do you now I cannot know. I only pray that it does you no harm. Read it if you wish. I never told you about your mother. It never seemed that the telling of it would mean anything to anyone, except possibly to the gossips which come to a place when more than those few who come to the place for the place find their way there. I took your mother from you, child. More truthfully, I took you from her. I will not justify this. I cannot. Other than to say I found reason to do so.

For her I gave you Canada. I think you were well served. Now I must take Canada from you. His love for you is strong, stronger than any I have ever known. But Canada has for too long known only one way in this world. And that is the way of his gun. His love and his gun, untethered by my judgment, would destroy him and you and the Escadara. So it is that Canada and I must leave the Escadara together.

But you! You must stay and preserve what is left of Reid Stuart and his partner, a man known to most only as a gunfighter. How you do this will rest mostly upon your own good judgment and your true heart. However you choose to do this, remember we built the Escadara for you and for your children and for their children. The documents signed by both myself and Canada, also to be found within the leather valise, say you are the sole and absolute owner of the Escadara and everything upon it. You alone, Katharane. You alone. Thus, whatever you choose to do with the following, if anything, it is your decision.

Guard every acre of the Escadara. Give up one acre and you surrender something that cannot be measured in length and width. You give up the integrity of the Escadara as one whole, one whole which is defended against all comers. The Escadara is a strong and sustaining spirit. But it is a spirit composed of each and every foot of the canyon and the Llano Estacado it encompasses. Lose any part of the Escadara and, just as the spirit of the Comanche fled the canyons of the Palo Duro after the Comanche fled the canyons in '74, so, too, would this spirit flee the Escadara. So you must guard against any encroachment. Protect each marker. Remember how much sacrifice and how many years went into placing them.

Constantly breed younger stock. Never let your base herd gain more than nine years. Either sell them, shoot them or drive them away before their tenth summer. Change bulls each fifth year. And bring in at least five bulls of a different variety. The canyon and the prairie of the Escadara will change but slowly, if at all. What grows upon her must change. Pay attention to what stock Goodnight runs. The old man is the master stockman of the plains.

Preserve and live in the home site. It has within its rock and mortar the goodness of your father and Canada and the Squaw Woman and, most of all, of you.

And Canada would have you know, and for the first time I am to know, what Escadara means. He says he learned it from Quanah Parker. He is not certain if it is a Comanche word or Spanish or a mixture of both, maybe Comanchero lingo.

But Kwanhah, chief of the Kwerhar-rehhuh-nuh Comanche's, told Canada that the brave that rode in front, alone, leading the other warriors was called the Escadara, the shield bearer. Under Comanche custom he was pledged to protect that shield and to die with it, and if he allowed it to be captured under any circumstances without his life going with it, he was banished from the tribe. Few braves ever took the pledge and the shield. The ones that did were believed to become immortal by the Comanche. That is the meaning of the name of our ranch and the sign that we carry as our brand. It is a sacred emblem and must by kept by you as such.

Mostly, be happy and live long. And remember, Katharane, given the chance almost any man will go into the belly of a woman. But only a few will care to know her soul. I love you. As does Canada. He would never tell you this. So I am telling you for him. It is something of him that you can keep.

At my time, which approaches relentlessly fast, Canada will take my body and do with it as I have asked of him. Katharane, Canada will never return to the Escadara. You must leave this be. You must! Forgive me, child! Forgive me, Canada! I used Katharane to gain access to your camp that first April third morning. Now I use her and your love for her to send you from the home more rightfully your's than our's. And yet you grin at me with that boyish twinkle in your eyes and nod and tell me it is no problem for you to leave the land you have stood as a sentinel over for some three decades plus, the land your very presence upon made known far and far across the prairie.

Thank you, my partner, my friend, my love.

Katharane, in this be strong, it is as it must be. Goodnight foresaw all those many years ago that it must by course be me that stops Canada. For only my hand or your's would he never draw against. Inevitably Canada and whomever you choose to love, and you must choose to love, Katharane, would face. Unless time should take such toll upon Canada as it has upon me, or unless his love for you should slow what no man yet has, Canada would surely kill your love. Either way what would be left to you? Hate for either that survived. Better that you should hate me than that. Canada well said that it was me that brought him to this. Thus, it is well that I take him from it. I feel vile and low. Maybe I am. But I have loved you both as truly as I have loved my home, the Escadara.

Much has transpired between yourself and your husband. More than I know, I am certain. And while it may be the greatest of my hypocrisies, I fashion in my last conscious endeavors to foretell in your future a reconciliation between you and William. Not of body or home, for I know you well enough to know that shall not be, but of spirit, of family. I intuit it to be better for you and your's than an unreconciled estrangement, which I fear Will may believe to be compelled to conciliate with his guns. In this Canada is in total disagreement and yet says he and I should have ended the matter with William, blood for blood, the hard headed inveterate old reprobate that he is, my partner. We have thought so single mindedly of Will in this. But what of Little Kat? Precious, loving, Little Kat; what is her father to her now? The father is not the son, Katharane. Remind Will of this, too.

My Colonel, William Harrell, Sr. is an honorable man. Honorable men do exist. I have known three. The large amount of money, both mine and my partner's, which I invested with Colonel Harrell has become a fortune I cannot feature. I have seen it enumerated on paper. But I do not understand such accumulations. I understand land acquired and cattle raised. But for you, for a woman alone, controlling a land as vast as the Escadara those accumulations inscribe in you, in your signature alone, power; and power you will need to hold the Escadara. Use it! Fight them, Katharane! Fight them that would take the Escadara from you! They will come. They will! Men lust for land almost as much as they do for that wetness between your thighs.

Katharane, if anyone should ask who you are, tell them you are a woman who as a child was cared for by a Comanche squaw woman who was the second niece of the great Comanche war chief, Quanah Parker, a woman who was loved and reared and fought for and kept safe by and taught to read and to laugh and to shoot and to ride and to raise cattle by her father, Reid Stuart, and a man known only as a gunfighter, a left-handed gunman from the Canadian River country, tell them you are the woman who owns the Escadara. And Canada says that if they should ask you a second time—shoot them.

Reid Stuart"

Katharane stood up, laid the parchment in the rocker, crossed her arms across her bosom and stared at the distant sky above the Tule canyon and she knew. She had never thought that the gunman would leave the Escadara. It was all he had. But it was not all he wanted. He wanted her and no one would ever want her with the ferocity he did again. She cried aloud. Her father had given her his love, his devotion, every day of his life, his land and his stock, but not even Reid Stuart could give her the common spirit she and the gunman shared. That was forever gone. She cried, deep and hard.

So very few understood, maybe Miss Mary and Bose, surely Charles Goodnight, it had been such a different time when Reid Stuart first brought her to the plains and the canyons of the Escadara. The plains and the canyons were different then, they demanded things of a man that were difficult to understand today and even harder to accept. It required then, men like the gunman to stand beside her father and Charles Goodnight until they could take hold of the plains and the canyons and reconcile that wild nature with humanity's, that different, gentler, more merciful men could survive here, lesser men than Reid Stuart, Charles Goodnight and the gunman, but men that community and peace required.

Katharane raised her head and began to chant the lyrics her mother, the Squaw Woman had taught her in her childhood, to pray to the wind and the long banished buffalo and the yearly Comanche rains of the spring and to the long flowing grass of the plains which sustained them all.

The gunfighter pulled the old coat close around him against the predawn chill of the plains. He truly enjoyed wearing it, partly because it was too large for him. He could move around inside of it. The coat hung almost to his knees. He had made it from an old bull buffalo's hide. He found it effective against all types of wind and with a slicker over it even weathered well against the snow. But hard rains could soak through it, making it too heavy to manage. He looked above him. Stars shone everywhere in the dark sky. There was no chance of rain. Katharane's bay horse moved gingerly through the scrub cedars which had now trespassed onto the flat prairie almost twenty yards before the canyon walls began. It was quicker this way and if he was to be pursued it would be by way of the Ceta out onto the big canyon's floor and around the dangerously steep walls at the mouth of the Tule. The short thick cedars, though dark shadows in the twilight, were easily enough avoided. And when the bay came too close to them they caused the gunman no discomfort because his worn chaps easily turned their heavy needles away and slid their branches passed his legs. The red mule on lead behind the bay slid passed the cedars without touching them. And Reid Stuart's buckskin flowed passed them like slow running water, barely jostling Reid Stuart's slumped shoulders and without endangering his precarious perch upon the saddle.

The gunman reached the edge of the canyon wall and dismounted. He looked down into the dark canyon. No light reflected from the narrow stream which navigated the Tule's floor more than one hundred and eighty feet below him. The lip of the canyon's other wall curved towards him quickly, until it seemed to merge with the lip on which he stood. Steep and narrow, these walls blocked the twilight's descent into the Tule, and his for now. With Reid Stuart barely able to balance himself on his saddle even on the flat true surface of the prairie, there was no chance he could stay mounted on a ride down a steep canyon wall.

He heard the rasp, turned, saw Reid Stuart sway on his saddle and begin to fall. He tried to run to catch his partner before he collapsed from his seat on the saddle, but the hip the breed had ripped with his knife caught and held him and forced him to stumble and hobble to where the body lay on its back on the prairie. He stared down at it. "You've been dead for an hour, Stu'. 'don't know why you just kept catchin' another breath." He put his hands on his hips. "At least you died in the saddle. The way you wanted." He looked at the bay, the mule and the buckskin. "'gotta' wrap you in something so I can tie you on the mule." He said aloud. He ran his hands down the front of his buffalo coat, nodded and removed the coat. He stretched it out on the prairie beside the body and rolled Reid Stuart's corpse onto it. He fastened the coat. But Reid Stuart had evaporated away on such a scale that he seemed in jeopardy of sliding free of it even though the prairie on which he lay was flat. The gunman walked to the buckskin, took out his knife and cut the leather tie downs from Reid Stuart's saddle. He walked to the body, kneeled beside it and tied the coat securely around his partner's body. He picked up the corpse, laid it across the mule's harness and used the last two strips of leather to tie it to the harness. He walked back to the bay, picked up his reins and swung painfully back into the saddle.

When the mid-morning sun bathed the canyon's walls in strong sunlight a horseman as skilled as the gunman stood a good likelihood of safely descending the steep canyon wall, but in the almost light of early morning it was not even odds that the best rider could make it. The gunman sat in his saddle. So much of his life had been the women he loved going away from him. Now he was going away, away from Katty. He stuck the bay with his spurs and the horse stepped off the canyon wall, jerking the mule after it and dragging the buckskin behind the mule. They slid for fifteen feet until the bay, the mule and the buckskin found their footing on the steep slope. The gunman helped the bay pick its way around the large boulders and the few cacti and cedars which had managed to cling to the shallow soil of the canyon's wall. Another fifty feet and the procession stumbled out onto a small plateau. The gunman rode to the end of the plateau. From here this wall of the canyon appeared to drop in a series of almost sheer vertical plunges, broken only by narrow ledges, to the still invisible canyon floor.

"No need killin' a good horse just to get to the bottom of a canyon an hour or so sooner. No need at all." The gunman said aloud.

He turned the bay and rode back into the plateau. He dismounted, dropped the reins and loosened the cinch to let the bay blow. He untied his bedroll and pulled it off the back of the saddle. He laid the bedroll on top of the heavy clusters of undisturbed blue stem grass which grew on the plateau. He draped the saddle bags over the bedroll. He pulled several clumps of the blue stem from the shallow soil and tossed some to the bay, some to the mule and he carried several to Reid Stuart's buckskin. He gathered five large round rocks and laid them in a circle where he had cleared the grass. In the center of the circle he placed a large flat rock. He gathered what limbs and branches he could find which the few small cedars which grew on the plateau had shed. He pulled his large knife from its buckskin sheath and shaved long curling strips from the cedar limb. He mounded the shavings on the flat rock in the center of the circle. He gathered dead grass, twigs and even some moss from beneath a rock and stacked them around the flat rock. With the remaining cedar limbs he built a tepee around and above the kindling stacked in the center of the fire ring. He kneeled on his left knee and pulled the small oblong tin box from his saddle bag. He held the box in his left hand and slid its cover back with his thumb. Inside the box eight sulphur tipped matches lay side by side. He took one match out. Then he snapped the lid closed and slid the box back into his saddle bag. He struck the match on the back of the heel of his boot, cupped his right hand around its flickering flame until it steadied itself into a constant burn, then he touched the match to the shavings. The shavings smoldered, then a flame grew up the side of the shavings. He withdrew the match and watched the tepee slowly catch fire. As the burning tepee collapsed onto the flat rock he pulled a small black coffee pot out of one end of his bedroll. He lifted the lid and withdrew a white handkerchief from the coffee pot. He loosened the rawhide string which gathered the four corners of the handkerchief together. Inside the handkerchief were dark burnt coffee grounds. He touched them with the end of his right index finger. He raised the handkerchief to his nose and inhaled the strong aroma which rose from the dark grounds.

"'coffee. 'ain't fresh coffee. But it's coffee." He said to no one.

He retied the handkerchief and dropped it back into the pot. He pulled the cork from his canteen and poured water into the coffee pot until it covered the handkerchief. He set the pot on the flat stone amidst the last of the flames from the cedar limbs. Sparks and cinders danced away. One ember landed on the back of his hand. Instead of shaking it free from its singeing perch he pinched it between his thumb and forefinger and dropped it back into the fire. He reached deeper into his bedroll and pulled out a battered tin cup. When the liquid in the coffee pot began to boil he slid his left hand into one of Reid Stuart's heavy leather officer's gloves. They were the only piece of Reid Stuart's equipment he had kept for himself. He had left the rest, including the Sharps rifle, for Katty. Reid Stuart had favored these gloves over all others, and he had faithfully conditioned them, first with buffalo tallow then after the buffalo had disappeared with lard from the cattle. With the glove to protect his hand the gunfighter grasped the handle of the coffee pot and lifted it from the fire. He poured a cupful of the steaming dark rich liquid into his tin cup. He returned the pot to its perch on the flat rock. He caught the ends of the two middle fingers of the glove between his lips, pulled his hand out of the glove, laid the glove on his bedroll, sat up on the toes of his boots, resting his buttocks on the backs of his boots, held the cup between his palms and sipped at the hot, strong, bitter coffee.

A pair of cat eyes watched him from a ledge across the canyon. The gunfighter stared into the glistening golden eyes and thought about his life, what he had done. He had no remorse nor regret, at least not as to anything he had done to another man. He felt no shame about his dealings with men. To him any dealing between two men was fair because either could see to the fairness of it. And if he did not, it was his choice, and, therefore, he felt no regret for what had taken place between himself and another man, even death. But with Katty, it was different. For her, he had many misgivings. He was not a man without passion. He had great passion. Passion had made him feared by most men, respected maybe by only a few, but not openly scorned by any. His passion had bound him to one other man, Reid Stuart, and from this passion had grown their unflinching partnership. But passion had also made him a sad and weary man that had known only one woman and had silently loved another for three decades. His passion was his greatest strength and his greatest weakness.

The eastern sky above the rim of the canyon began to glow. At first it was a deep rich blue black purple, a color almost without illumination, without light, like the first layers of paint on a canvas before the images begin to appear. The purple sky was only the slightest differentiation between the night sky and the line along the horizon marked by the rim of the canyon. As the gunfighter's coffee quickly cooled the purple sky gave way to a brighter blue, then quickly the blue was obliterated by bursts of white and silver and a cone of orange and yellow as the egg shaped top of the sun rose above the earth beyond the horizon.

The gunfighter poured the coffee from the pot on the ashes of the fire and stirred them with the tip of his right boot. He replaced his cup and the coffee pot into his bedroll, retied his saddle bags to his saddle and his bedroll atop them. He picked up the bay's reins and swung into his saddle. He rode again to the edge of the plateau. Now the canyon's stream was a visible thin dark line far below. He edged the bay off of the plateau. Many places along the canyon wall were still dark because the steep walls with its plateaus and ledges shaded parts. Above the rim, he knew, the sun was bathing the flat prairie with brilliant light. He smiled remembering telling Reid Stuart to always brake his camp on the plains before sunrise because in the early morning blindness could hide death riding in on him. It was out of a plains' sunset that Reid Stuart and Katty had first ridden into his camp. He drew in a deep breath. He missed Reid Stuart already. They had been each other's company for many, many years. He missed that good company and he longed for Katty.

The bay, the mule and the buckskin reached the canyon floor. They turned towards the Tule narrows and marched on. Clusters of bleached white bones littered the canyon's floor. A buffalo kill? No. It was too far from the rim of the canyon where, stampeded, they would have plunged to their deaths. And there was too few of them and the settlers had loaded even the ones which had dyed the grounds around the Walls white onto wagons and hauled them away to be ground into fertilizer. He reined the bay to a stop.

"'winter kill." He said to the bay horse. He patted the horse's neck. "You can tell a winter kill, son, when you've seen enough of it. It's the way the bones lie. 'course the coyotes and the vultures scatter the smaller bones. But those large bones." He pointed at a spinal column, ribcage and skull. "They stay pretty much in place. See the way the skull is almost facing the tail. She was standin' with her head down and turned to her side when she fell." He paused, thought for a moment, then he continued. "Cattle don't freeze to death. They suffocate from the ice coatin' their nostrils and it bein' so cold that their breath can't melt it." He chewed on the inside of his cheek. "Winter of '80 was like that. 'drove most of the small outfits off of the plains." He paused, then he said. "No. 'can't say the winter drove them out. 'most of them left after the first four weeks of blowin' snow and minus ten temperatures. Only a few hung on long enough to claim they were driven out by the winter." He patted the horse again. "By March fifteenth of '81, other than Bugbee, old man Goodnight, and a few others, Stu', Katty and I were the only ones left. 'wasn't bad bein' just us there again. 'wasn't bad at all."

The gunfighter touched the bay with his spurs. The bay stepped forth. The shallow draw which carried the stream was becoming deeper, and in places the soft short grass was displaced by a circle of solid rock which shone like a new silver dollar in morning sunlight. The bay was not a gentle pacer like his black filly. His quick gated walk jarred the gunman. He touched the bay

447

with his spurs again and the horse began to trot. The mule trotted after the bay and the buckskin easily kept pace. The gunman glanced over his shoulder to make certain Reid Stuart had not slipped from the mule's harness. He had not. The gunman spurred the bay once more. Obediently, the horse began to lope. The silver dollar patches of rock became elongated until they lost any semblance of the coin. The gunman gently reined the bay around the rock. The mule, wise from years of being on lead, watched the bay and faithfully followed each of his moves. The buckskin slid across the rock once before he, too, accepted the bay's lead. Thus, the procession snake danced its way along the canyon floor.

The gunfighter, relaxed by the accustomed swiftness of his ride, remembered other rides. He saw Reid Stuart and Katty, her green brown eyes and her auburn hair, and he heard her laugh. So he laughed. And the canyon mocked his lonely laughter. Jolted by the echo he jabbed the bay with his spurs. The horse jumped and lengthened his lope. The mule ran in earnest now. The buckskin surged easily along with long smooth strides.

The gunfighter stared at his hands and tried to clear his mind. He raised his head and saw the stream glistening as it flowed across the sheet of slick mossy rock just ahead of the bay and disappeared into a diagonal cut. He could only guess how far it was to the thick soft grass which covered the cut's bank on the far side. He stood up in his stirrups, took an extra dally around the saddle horn with the lead rope. He knew dallying the lead rope this tightly was dangerous, but he had no intention of leaving the mule behind. He lifted the bay's reins and the horse leaped. The mule leaped after the bay and the buckskin seemed to glide over the rock and the cut. They all landed safely on the other side.

He reined the bay around and stared into the cut's chasm. It was at least six feet across. The stream fell off the slick rock and vanished into the purple depths of the crevice. These depths were bottomless, cut into the blackness below by the stream and a thousand years. He wondered if the stream or the years had more to do with cutting the chasm through the rock. Years are powerful things. He turned the bay and rode deeper into the Tule, into its gorge which led to the sacred place of the Comanche and Katty's Squaw Woman. The gorge opened onto the high plateau above the far canyon where a blue haze shimmered. He rode to the blue haze and the edge of the far wide canyon which lay a hundred feet or more below the plateau. He turned the bay and rode up to the granite boulder passed the Squaw Woman's grave, dropped the bay's reins and dismounted.

He untied the old buffalo coat from the mule's harness, lifted it off of the mule and carried it to the base of the natural granite monument. Then he went back to the mule and retrieved a pick, a shovel, a mallet and a chisel and carried these to the monument. With the emptiness of the far canyon to his right, the black throat of the gorge far to his left, the stream falling off of the rock behind him, he raked the grass away from the base of the granite boulder and dug as deep a trench as he could with the pick and the shovel. He rolled Reid Stuart's corpse into the trench and shoveled the dirt and grass on top of it. He gathered large stones, as large as he could carry, and stacked them on top of this. With this done, he picked up the chisel and the mallet and began to work upon the granite boulder's smooth face. He struck the chisel with sure strong rhythmic blows. He worked without pause until his grip on the chisel slackened and a glancing blow from the chisel caused the knuckles on his right hand to slam against the boulder. "Dammit!" He cursed and flexed the fingers of his right hand. "'gettin' old, Stu'. I'm finally gettin' old." He began to work on the granite again. The steady report of the mallet against the butt of the chisel sang out into the canyon. Noon passed and early afternoon gave way to three then four o'clock. The mallet rang upon the chisel, chips of granite flew from beneath the bite of the chisel, and the canyon echoed the sounds. The chisel railed against the rock. He pounded the mallet against the butt of the chisel until it seemed as if the mallet could never stop. And with each blow Reid Stuart flashed before the gunman's eyes, until finally it was done.

He dropped the mallet and the chisel, stepped back from the granite boulder and read his inscription thereon aloud:

REID STUART

A MAN

WHO COULD LOOK IN HIS HEART

AND ALWAYS FIND THERE

THE RIGHT THING TO DO.

THEN DO IT.

The gunman stumbled across the rocks he had stacked on top of Reid Stuart's grave. He picked up the bay's reins and stuck his left boot in the stirrup. As he swung his right leg out, around and over the mule's lead rope and across the saddle, he saw the pools of the tinaja at the home site, he saw the snow and sleet and felt the fire which he and Reid Stuart had huddled around that first winter, he saw that first sunrise with Katty there and he saw Reid Stuart dead in the ground. He was tired, so tired. He wanted to be away. He ripped the bay's flanks with his spurs. Blood splattered across the rump of the startled horse. The bay reared. The gunman ripped his flanks again and again with his spurs. The horse charged forward, sparks flew from beneath his shod hooves as he raced across the outcropping of rock, dragging the mule and the buckskin after him.

The gunman had land, more land than he could ride across in days. He had cattle, thousands of them. He had money, lots of it, some of it in banks as far away as New York City. Banks he had never seen. What was it then that haunted his soul? Love? "Was my lovin' her so wrong, Stu'?"

The bay gathered itself as the edge of the far canyon's wall loomed in front of him. Love? Had he ever come close? Had he? A few yards before the edge the mule balked and he was jerked forward onto his knees for his resistance. The lead rope snapped. He heard the rope snap, he sensed the bay gathering himself to leap, but only vaguely as in a dream. He had everything and nothing, true, but he had Reid Stuart. He truly had that. Now he did not. "I tried Stu'. I really did." Beyond there was nothing, only empty space and the canyon's floor far below. Instinctively he sensed the futility of the bay's intent. But he was too late. The great horse courageously launched itself up and out into that emptiness above the canyon. His nerve held for a moment, then he panicked and screamed and pitched his head about. The gunman's hand flashed for his pistol. He drew it quickly, cocked the hammer and shoved the barrel between the flailing horse's ears and squeezed the trigger. Fire belched from the barrel, the bay's head jerked and fell forward. The gunman had always wondered what his last thoughts would be, would he have breath to know them. He raised himself in the stirrups to quit his saddle and cried out into the empty vastness. "Katty!"